The BARBAROSSA SECRET

CHRISTOPHER KERR

First published in Great Britain in 2022
Copyright © 2022 Christopher Kerr

The right of Christopher Kerr to be identified as the author
of this work has been asserted in accordance with the
Copyright, Design and Patents Act 1988.

All rights reserved. No part of this publication may be
reproduced, transmitted, or stored in a retrieval system, in any form or by any means,
without permission in writing from the publisher, nor be otherwise circulated in any form
of binding or cover other than that in which it is published and without a similar
condition being imposed on the subsequent purchaser.
This book is a work of fiction. All references to characters, businesses, places, events, and
incidents depicted in this book are the product of the author's imagination and are used in a
fictitious manner. Where actual public speeches have been used, these will be in the public
domain and have not been altered.

Where the book refers to actual persons, living or dead, their words or actions unless in the public
domain are entirely fictitious and any references to these do not in any way reflect or imply the
opinions of persons so mentioned. Whilst actual historical events may have been used to place
the story in context, the author does not accept any responsibility or liability whatsoever for
historical inaccuracies in this work of fiction.

Typeset in 11pt Adobe Garamond Pro

Printed on FSC accredited paper
British Library Cataloguing in Publication Data.
A catalogue record for this book is available from the British Library.

Dedication

To my beloved wife, Sheila, with whom I shared my idea for this book. She gave me the confidence and the encouragement to write this but sadly did not live to see publication

Forever in my thoughts

Preface

"Never forget that the rulers of present-day Russia are common bloodstained criminals; that they are the scum of humanity which, favoured by circumstances, overran a great state in a tragic hour, slaughtered out thousands of her leading intelligentsia in wild bloodlust, and now for almost ten years have been carrying on the most cruel and tyrannical regime of all time.

"Furthermore, do not forget that these rulers belong to a race which combines, in a rare mixture, bestial cruelty and an inconceivable gift for lying, and which today more than ever is conscious of a mission to impose its bloody oppression on the whole world. Do not forget that the international Jew who completely dominates Russia today regards Germany not as an ally, but as a state destined to the same fate.

"The danger to which Russia succumbed is always present for Germany... In Russian Bolshevism we must see the attempt undertaken by the Jews in the twentieth century to achieve world domination... It requires all the force of a young missionary idea to raise our people up again, to free them from the snares of this international serpent, and to stop the inner contamination of our blood."

Adolf Hitler – 1925
Extract from Mein Kampf

"It was in Britain's interest and in Europe's too, that Germany be encouraged to strike East and smash Communism forever... I thought the rest of us could be fence-sitters while the Nazis and the Reds slogged it out."

The Duke of Windsor – 13th December 1966
Article he wrote for the New York Daily News

Prologue

Saturday 15th February 2020, 3.00pm
Ludwig-Ganghofer-Strasse, Berchtesgaden,
Bavaria, Germany

The snow had fallen heavily and Gunther Roche wearily and warily faced the short walk from his customary visit to the Bier Haus, where he liked to join in with local gossip on his daily midday visit. Pulling his worn black leather greatcoat, with its large, military-style collar, tightly round him, he retrieved his Tirolerhut *(alpine hat), waved at his fellow companions as he opened the door to icy air, then trudged through the crisp fresh white covering that carpeted the landscape. Decidedly fit and spritely despite his ninety-seven years, he had retained remarkably good health, possessing a fierce determination of spirit fuelled by a lifetime of discipline. Gunther never accepted limitations and still drove his car regularly and attended a shooting club each week, where he had a reputation as a crack shot, often beating members in their youth. He refused to be bowed by age, although he was a little deaf and failed to hear the car moving slowly down the road from behind him.*

*His house was five hundred metres from the inn, and, as he opened the heavy wooden door, the warmth welcomed him in from the cold. He was glad his maid, Inga, had lit the open fire before she had left an hour before, after the first of her daily two-hour visits. Glancing upwards, he looked with pride at the red, black and white ribbon, hanging above the mantelpiece from which was suspended the black Iron Cross medal edged in silver, over which were crossed swords and oak leaves studded with diamonds. Then his eyes rested briefly on a black and white picture of a youthful, blonde woman who was dressed in a traditional Bavarian outfit, holding flowers in front of her. "Mein Gott, Karin, you were so beautiful," he muttered, dwelling briefly on the life he had shared with his wife for thirty-five years before cancer had taken her in 1978. "*Die besten Jahre *['The best years'],*" *he sighed as he sank into his armchair, ready for his customary afternoon nap.*

Three sharp knocks on the door interrupted his brief rest. Cursing, he rose slowly to his feet. *"Ich hoffe das ist wichtig [I hope this is important],"* he said loudly. He drew himself up, displaying the bearing of a much younger man, with a determination to avoid stooping and to stand up straight as had been drummed into him relentlessly, reminded that stance was a discipline reflecting dedication. Moving to the door, he looked instinctively towards the box where he still kept his Walther P38, always loaded, which had been his weapon of choice since 1937. He had been introduced to it during his time with the Hitler-Jugend (the Hitler Youth) at the age of fifteen, when he had proven to be an outstanding marksman. Gunther had excelled at everything then, fired with enthusiasm for the new Reich, taking fierce pride in his studies and passing out with an exemplary record. He was personally recommended for special training by no less than the Reichsjugendführer, GruppenFührer Baldur von Schirach, the head of the Hitler Youth, and was a proud recruit into the SS at the age of seventeen in November 1939.

He opened the door to two men, both with the look of officialdom he had come to recognise throughout his life. One was tall, with darkened glasses and carrying a briefcase, whilst the other was thickset, wearing a flat cap which Gunther thought looked a little out of place. The latter produced a card, upon which Gunther briefly glimpsed the words 'Bundesnachrichtendienst – BND' (the Federal Intelligence Service) together with a photo that he was not given the opportunity to verify before the wallet encasing the identity was snapped shut.

"Herr Roche, please may we come in; we are from Berlin and there are matters of national security we need to discuss with you." It was more a command than a request and Gunther stood to one side motioning them in.

The shorter man introduced himself brusquely: *"I am Major Wolf Dietrich, this is Oberleutnant Karl Schmidt and we are seeking information about your time with Leibstandarte SS Adolf Hitler from 1940 until 1945."* His voice was cold, expressionless and reminded Gunther of many he had served with who carried out their duties without thought or feeling but with a ruthless dedication to duty.

"Herr Roche, we are aware that you were in contact with British Intelligence during the war and we are seeking all documents relating to this and, specifically,

information we know you are aware of covered by the 'eins zu eins' ('one on one') protocol." He looked at Gunther directly and was met unnervingly by staring, ruthless, blue, unblinking eyes in response.

The old man sank into his chair with a deep sigh. "That was a lifetime ago and I have not thought about those days for so long," he said weakly, although within, he already felt the adrenalin pumping, an old instinct which always preceded moments of decisive action in danger.

"Please, Herr Roche, do not patronise me," Major Dietrich cut in sharply. "We know the leading role you have played and that, even after your retirement, you have still attended the annual rallies and reunions of the SS together with other Nazis. We are also aware that you travelled to, and were involved in, the Eagle's Lair in Argentina after the war. So, this is very simple: all we want are the documents relating to the talks with the British during the war. More importantly, you will tell us the whereabouts of the records relating to 'eins zu eins', which we know are in your possession. The dates we are most interested in are those around May to July 1941 and June to July 1944. If you give us the information we want, our orders are to leave you in peace but, if you do not, this may not be a good day for you."

The old man rose to his feet, his voice strong and authoritative, despite his years.

"Who the hell do you think you are demanding information? Do you think you frighten me? Mein Gott, I have fought the British in France, the Bolsheviks on the Russian Front and the Americans in the Ardennes, and I have faced tanks, machine guns and flame throwers. I have been wounded, blown up and engaged in street fighting with hand-to-hand combat. I have killed for what we believed in and what was right. You know why, because we had ideals, we had a Führer, we had greatness, and you know what, I would do it all again, even now. You are nothing, Major, coming here from Berlin with your petty demands and threats."

As the intelligence officer began to interject, Gunther Roche drew himself upright and saw his opposite was unnerved by his natural authority which, even now, at ninety-seven years old, he retained from a lifetime of discipline and dedication.

"I outrank you, Herr Major, as a former Standartenführer ['colonel'] and I have seen weasels like you before. You are ordertakers but will never understand the meaning of command. You make demands of me. Very well, I will show you the only evidence

I have kept from those years and then you will leave, but you will never, ever threaten me again. Most of it was destroyed in 1945 and we were given orders to do so which were carried out to the letter, as we did then, without question."

He moved towards the dark wooden box on the shelf by his writing desk; he carried on talking.

"We had discipline back then, with a national movement based on unswerving service to the Fatherland. We had pride, Major Dietrich, recognising that we Germans had a destiny to restore order because we were naturally superior as a race and were not frightened of saying so."

His hand found and tightened on the old, familiar grip. As he turned, his first shot caught the major totally by surprise, the second sending him sprawling to the floor. Gunther sensed but was belatedly aware of the gun in the hand of his other visitor, and before he could aim his own weapon, he heard the crack and felt a sharp pain to his chest as he collapsed. He looked his assailant in the eye as he instinctively felt his life rapidly ebbing away.

"Heil Hitler," he gasped, but was unable to raise his right arm, and then, with a last look of defiance: *"*Meine Ehre heist Treue *[SS motto – 'My honour is loyalty'],"* before his head dipped and there was nothing.

1

A Royal Seed

Sunday 9th October 1932, 11.30am
Balmoral Castle, Aberdeenshire, Scotland

"Your Majesty, His Highness the Duke of Saxe-Coburg and Gotha," announced the steward, giving the visitor the title he had formerly held and by which the sovereign had expressed the wish he should be addressed. The smartly attired Duke Charles Edward in a dark green tweed suit with plus fours entered and briefly bowed. He walked forward to shake hands with the bearded King George V, a large figure wearing a Balmoral grey, red and black tartan kilt, waistcoat, and long black jacket with two upper buttons fastened.

"Loyalties have divided this family during the Great War," began the King, "and you have lost much, dear cousin, in titles and property, I think. Goodness knows what our grandmother, Queen Victoria, would have made of all this."

This was the first time the two men had met since before the Great War had started in 1914 and now the British monarch had granted an audience to his German cousin who had written letters requesting this. The King motioned his guest to sit on one of the two elegant green upholstered gold gilt sofas forming a diagonal shape in front of an enormous fireplace in which flames crackled from huge logs, whilst he lowered himself slowly on the other.

"Or, indeed, our grandfather, Prince Albert. After all, we are both originally Saxe-Coburgs, are we not, with a proud German heritage?" Charles Edward countered, raising a wry smile, stroking his small, neat moustache as if to check it was as tidy as he had prepared. He was a meticulous man, and wanted to appear at his best.

The reply was cold and dominating, and the tone made it clear who was the senior in the room. "This Royal Family is the House of Windsor," the King boomed, "and we are English ruling the British Empire and her Dominions; I trust I make myself clear." It was a statement, not a question.

An awkward silence followed for a moment before Charles Edward replied in a more considered way, "Sir, I know you have done much to retain the honour of your family, and, of course, your position, which is respected throughout the world. Forgive my clumsiness, but so much has changed for me and my family since the war. I have been stripped of all my titles and vilified by the British press."

The King waved the moment away as if it were no longer important.

The Duke continued, "At least I wasn't pitted against the Tommys on the front, but I did end up fighting the Russians in 1915. Frightful lot; I regret to say I think we will both have problems from there in the future. Their Bolshevik regime is primitive, barbaric and brutal. Look what they did to the Czar and Czarina. I think often of poor cousin Nickie and his dear wife Alex; my God, and those beautiful children. They will stop at nothing in attempting to introduce the poison of revolution elsewhere. We have had our fair share of Communist vermin in Germany, but now, thank God, there is one up-and-coming leader in our midst who will stand up to them."

The King leaned forwards, suddenly interested, "Yes, this chap Hitler seems to be creating a bit of a stir, old boy. I believe he nearly won the presidential election in April, and I hear that in the July election, his Nazi Party won the largest number of seats in the Reichstag. Extraordinary, never heard of the chap until quite recently, but I'm informed he's a damned good speaker."

The large double doors opened and a silver tray was brought in by a liveried servant, upon which was a decanter and two glasses. The tray was left and the King surprisingly poured them both a Scotch, toasting his cousin: "Let past differences be past and let the future bring peace."

They raised their glasses to one another. As the King lit a cigarette, Charles Edward returned to the subject.

"This man Hitler is truly inspirational, Your Majesty. I have seen him address thousands with no notes, and his speeches just lift everyone; even those who may disagree are impressed with him. He promises to provide employment, housing, roads, order and a rebuilding of a new and proud Germany without lawlessness. The people cannot get enough of him and I have to say, having met him on a number of occasions, I have also become convinced that he is the right man to lead Germany. I have joined his movement."

The King rose and walked slowly to the large windows overlooking the gardens.

"I sometimes think it is a blessing that I am not free to join any movement or publicly express opinions. I sincerely hope you are right about your man, but I hear he talks of tearing up the Treaty of Versailles. Such unilateral actions or threats may create tensions and divisions which could be a catalyst for conflict. I think your Mr Hitler needs to moderate his tone, perhaps. My own two sons both fought in the war, and, I think all sides agreed, this had to be a war to end all wars after the slaughter of so many on the Western Front. I strongly suggest to you that it is important to all of us that treaties are respected which are designed to bring peace."

The King stood by the long windows staring out over the open Scottish countryside beyond and reflected on the staggering loss of life his country had suffered in the war, leaving a hole in an entire generation. He lit another cigarette. "Perhaps you should meet Bertie and David who are both here and explain to them how this man, Hitler, intends to create a new Germany. After all, it is the next generation who will inherit the results of decisions made today. We have an hour before lunch and then, perhaps, you may join us for the shooting. Incidentally, what does your man Hitler propose to do about the Russian problem?"

The Duke moved to the fireplace and turned, placing his hands behind his back, enjoying the warmth after a somewhat tiresome journey to reach the small station at Ballater from Aberdeen. He had been forced to rise early, catching the 8.05 train, which was an uncommonly early hour, in order to reach Balmoral for an audience scheduled, most inconveniently, to commence at 11.00am on a Sunday. Typical of his cousin, he had thought, demanding loyalty, lacking consideration, but expecting homage; however, he was on a mission with direct orders from his Führer.

"Sir, I have spoken with Hitler of the situation in depth. He says that Russia is ruled by a tyrannical, barbaric regime and that their ideas will contaminate the rest of Europe. They are a lower race with their leadership infiltrated by Jews with a desire to achieve world domination driven by an international Zionist conspiracy. Bolshevism has one aim which is to overthrow modern civilisation and our way of life by revolution. The Bolsheviks have murdered hundreds of thousands of their own people, annihilating anyone that they view as not one of them; that is why they killed the Romanovs. They threaten a bloody revolution to overthrow any regime in order to expand their perverse philosophy and every country in the world is threatened, unless we do something."

King George reached for a phone, speaking briefly before addressing his guest.

"Your leader-in-waiting – or Führer, as I believe he likes to be called – clearly has strong views, my dear Duke, and I regret that I do not share all of them. However, we must, of course, remain vigilant and ensure that the idea of a Bolshevik Russianbacked revolution does not take hold, the consequences of which are unthinkable. Furthermore, my dear cousin, I concur that they must not be allowed to dominate Europe."

The doors opened. "His Royal Highness, Edward, the Prince of Wales, Your Majesty, and His Royal Highness, George, the Duke of York." The two princes entered the room and warmly greeted the Duke with firm handshakes. The King excused himself, saying that that they would be called for lunch within the next forty-five minutes.

Two more glasses appeared, drinks were poured and the atmosphere became warmer as the charismatic Prince of Wales, clad in a smart, pinstriped, double-breasted suit, lightened the mood. "Could have bloody shot you a few years ago if we'd met in the trenches, you old traitor." He started with a disarming smile, which Charles Edward took in good humour.

The Duke of York, dressed like his father in a traditional kilt and smart waistcoat, merely added, "Whatever may confront us, we must avoid that ever happening again." As they sat down, Prince Edward energetically questioned Charles Edward, taking great interest in what was happening in Germany after hearing that his cousin was now involved in the Nazi Party.

"How on earth has this extraordinary chap, Hitler, managed to seize the moment? Many are saying he is a dangerous threat to peace just when we need to come together."

"I have come here," Charles Edward explained, "to rebuild bridges of understanding. I am working with Hitler on plans for the future and he has so many big ideas. One of which is to establish an Anglo-German Friendship Society to rekindle the
traditional ties between our countries and, of course, to avoid the possibility of war ever happening again." The two princes were engaged

by their visitor, who explained much about the envisaged new German order.

"Your father is concerned about the Treaty of Versailles, but the Führer has said it is a treaty which was ill conceived because it was overpunitive with levels of reparations that are ruining Germany. Surely, it is not unreasonable for us to question the justice of a settlement that will destroy our country and prevent reconstruction."

"This is what happens if you leave these things to bureaucrats with too many countries interfering in what is finally drafted," Prince Edward conceded. "I can see this chap Hitler's point, and I damn well agree in the Anglo-German thing – what about you, Bertie? We must never, ever suffer a war like that again, never."

The Duke of York nodded his agreement but added that he was concerned about some reports in the press of violence from the Nazis against their own people. Before breaking for lunch they accepted that the regime in Russia was a matter for international concern and that they should work towards ensuring that there was an awareness of the need to be vigilant of the Communist threat. Finally, as they were leaving the room to prepare for lunch, the Duke of York bade Charles Edward hesitate for a word. Lighting a cigarette, he sat on one of the chairs that were positioned on the outer edge of the room.

"I am deeply concerned that, that…" The Duke hesitated as he struggled then finally avoided his stammer to formulate the words into speech. "…That we may be introducing a Trojan horse into the League of Nations if Hitler becomes Chancellor of Germany with his talk of expansion. Charles, please tell me this man, this man has peace as a priority. My brother is easily persuaded but I, I am less so."

Monday 17th October 1932, 2.00pm
Office of the Deputy Director,
Colonel Stewart Graham Menzies,
SIS (Secret Intelligence Service – Forerunner of MI6),
54 Broadway, Westminster, London

A loud knock on the panelled door prompted the briefest 'yes' from the colonel. Greta Atkins entered and was waved to a plain wooden chair in front of a somewhat bland desk. She was a slim, imposing woman in her mid-thirties and always very smartly and expensively dressed, which got her noticed and opened doors for her. Today was no exception as she sported a wide-brimmed hat worn at a coquettish angle, a fur stole over a tailored jacket, beneath which a ruffled silk blouse added to the look, completed with a wide belt and pencil-fitted skirt which accentuated her figure. She had been called a femme fatale, which she quite liked with its hint of decadence. Her hair was a dark auburn, shoulder length, and her blue eyes sparkled, adding an edge of the alluring with a hint of the provocative.

Colonel Menzies looked up from his papers, his expression carrying a natural authority and a military bearing, his dark hair swept back with a full but neatly trimmed moustache. A sombre suit and tie so matched his office, Greta thought, which was lacking in any decoration, surrounded by frosted glass above dark wood-panelled walls. His keen eyes briefly glanced over her. "Never overdressed, Miss Atkins," he remarked, his eyebrows slightly raised in mock disapproval before looking more serious and opening a file. "I have a need to engage your legendary charm."

Greta crossed her legs slowly, but the colonel, as always, either did not notice or feigned to be unaware. She pulled out a long cigarette holder and waited until the colonel, at least, had the manners to offer her a light. She had worked for British Intelligence for ten years, gaining the colonel's admiration for her ability to extract information at the highest level through her considerable social connections. Growing up in a privileged landowning family had brought with it many advantages, which Greta was never slow to seize upon.

"Germany is a becoming a worry again with a resurgence in nationalism under this dreadful little man, Hitler." The colonel sheaved through papers on his desk, his eyebrows deeply furrowed. He then informed her of the subject of his interest, watching her exhale smoke deeply with a whistle as he told her that they needed to investigate: "His former Royal Highness, Charles Edward, the Duke of Saxe-Coburg and Gotha, the Duke of Albany, the Earl of Clarence and Baron Arklow." The colonel spoke the words slowly and precisely in his clipped, well-spoken manner. He went on to explain that Charles Edward was a known supporter and admirer of Hitler, with whom he regularly associated. He appeared to be engaged in arranging meetings with many of the who's who, and the colonel felt it was clearly no coincidence that he had sought an audience with the King at Balmoral over the previous weekend.

Reports had reached him that Charles Edward had been seen entering and leaving the German Embassy on at least four occasions since his arrival in England the week before.

"Oh, good Lord," interjected Greta. "With his titles he will be seen by some as combining the virtues of an English aristocrat with the rank of a German duke; and being related to the Royal Family will open many doors."

The deputy director of SIS leant forwards. "Miss Atkins, the former Duke fought against us in the Great War and now has close ties with this upstart Hitler and his cronies in Germany. I am concerned that Hitler is attempting to widen his influence in this country. On Wednesday, Charles Edward had lunch at the Ritz with Sir Oswald Mosley, the leader of the new British Union of Fascists, and he has had meetings with other influential people, including Viscount Rothermere, the owner of the *Daily Mail*, the *Mirror* and countless other newspapers who also holds Nazi sympathies. Since his arrival, he has lunched with Lord Londonderry, Sir Arnold Wilson and even Lloyd George. Heaven knows how many others he has been in contact with. I'm told he is to meet the young Douglas-Hamilton, the Marquess of Douglas and Clydesdale, tomorrow, and they are being joined by the Stockton MP, Harold Macmillan, who is a bit of a rebel within the Conservative Party."

Colonel Menzies was reading from papers in the file in front of him, which he shut with a sigh looking up at Greta with an expression of ruthless resolve, which she had seen before. "Are you getting the drift, Miss Atkins? He already has links with some of the most influential people in this country and is building more. We want to know with who and why."

Greta stubbed out her cigarette suddenly, sensing the gravitas of what was being said.

"We believe our friendly Duke intends to use his connections with the Royal Family to gather further support for the Fascists, linking them into a broader Anglo-German coalition movement. As you will no doubt be aware, Hitler has already very nearly gained power through his radical commitment to rebuild a greater Germany. He promises he will defend against Communism, rebuild military strength and restore German pride. He omits that he will achieve this if not by persuasion, then through intimidation. This man is a fanatic, Miss Atkins, who will, undoubtedly, become the leader of Germany; it is just a matter of time and his creed of total power gained at any cost must not spread to this country. Like Bolshevism and other forms of extremism, National Socialism is pervasive; an infection spreading amongst the disillusioned and the envious, and Lord knows we have enough of them in society.

"Once a number of more influential people are linked with this movement, it may become out of control, leading to civil unrest, anarchy, political instability or even revolution. I trust I need not spell this out further. We must be aware and forewarned of any potential trouble and where the support may come from. We think Charles Edward is here to begin a process of destabilising our establishment to make way for a Fascist revolution. Your job, Miss Atkins, is to get to know him and find out who, amongst the upper classes, is offering potential support or who may be wavering. We need to both identify them and then keep a close eye on them."

"My dear colonel, what are you suggesting I do?" asked Greta with mock disdain. "Surely, you could not wish me to mix with such a man no matter how well connected?"

The deputy director stood up, walking to the frosted glass window, drawing himself up as if seeking to emphasise what was to follow. "My dear Miss Atkins, we believe that there may be links being explored between the Nazi Party in Germany and those at the highest, and I mean the highest, levels of our society. If our suspicions are correct, this could destabilise the very foundations of our democracy. You need to find out more and, I regret, become involved, trusted and part of their inner circle. For that, you need flawless credentials. There is one who can help you into the inner circle; I think you know Diana Mitford?"

Greta feigned another look of shock. "Colonel, is there nothing you do not know about everyone? You are so nosey, but delightful too," she said with a mischievous giggle. "I taught Diana French in Paris in 1926 when she was sixteen, and what a darling beauty she turned out to be. Simply dazzling, but then she met and married that frightful Irish bore, Bryan Guinness. Last time I met them was at one of their debauched fancy-dress parties."

The deputy director leant on his desk, looking her straight in the eye. "You need to reacquaint yourself. She is the door for us because, my dear, this young Guinness bride has already taken a lover, none other than Sir Oswald Mosley." Greta let out a long, whistling breath.

The colonel continued, "Indeed, you may have met Unity, her sister – equally beautiful, I am given to understand. Both of them seem to be ensnared in this rather unseemly crowd of German sympathisers. Miss Atkins, this is so sensitive, you need to communicate directly only with me, not even the director of SIS or anyone in any other service, irrespective of rank. If you speak to anyone, I shall deny any knowledge of this. I cannot stress how carefully you must tread. I am afraid that the violence already employed by the Nazis in Germany will be used here. These people will stop at nothing, they are absolutely ruthless, and, as you know, I can and will authorise the issuing of a weapon to you, as previously. I am aware you omitted to return the one we obtained for you." He gave a rare smile, coughing as though covering up her misdemeanour.

When she left the dull, gloomy building that day, into an even gloomier late afternoon, Greta felt the weight of responsibility which was, she could not help but admit, tinged with just a hint of excitement.

2

Generalplan Reich

Saturday 22nd October 1932, 7.00am
Prinzregentenplatz 16, Second Floor, Munich

They waited nervously with some tension in the anteroom for his invitation to join him. The wide reception area was quite plain apart from a map of Europe on one wall and two classical-style paintings on the other of country scenes. A small crystal chandelier threw additional light over a simple wooden office desk, behind which a smartly dressed secretary in a dark suit sat at a typewriter, next to which was a tray of papers and a black telephone. Windows were at either side of what was a long, narrow space with a door behind, from which they had entered, and another large panelled door in front, by the side of which a uniformed guard stood. There was a palpable air that they were in the near presence of greatness and they were united in that but divided in much else. Five of them had been summoned and they all had unswerving allegiance to him, a total and incontrovertible loyalty, with a code of absolute discipline, not through deference to a superior, as may be learned in military service, but through instinct. All were long standing members of the Nationalsozialistische Deutsche Arbeiterpartei (NSDAP – Nazi Party).

On the left side of the large doorway was a simple couch, on which both Hermann Göring and Joseph Goebbels were sat, clothed in very different styles. Goebbels, a thin, short man, yet immaculate, was in a dark brown lounge suit with a fastened double-breasted jacket, beneath which he wore a white shirt and a simple neat matching tie on which, below the knot, was a silver eagle NSDAP pin. In contrast, Göring was more striking: taller, grandiose and larger in every way, his presence somehow filling the anteroom. He was smartly, if not flamboyantly, dressed in a Bavarian-style long dark grey jacket, patterned tie and a belt drawn over a portly figure with black trousers. On his left lapel was the small, circular maroon-edged NSDAP badge containing a black swastika in a white centre. They chatted animatedly in a low tone, both sensing the occasion.

By the long window, overlooking Prinzregentenplatz, stood the solitary figure of Reichsführer-SS Heinrich Himmler with his arms folded in a brown uniform jacket, jackboots, and black trousers. He checked through the net curtains furtively, then glanced at his watch. He did not like being kept waiting, although on this occasion, he would not show it. He briefly removed his wire-framed glasses, wiping them with a precise movement before turning, clenching his hands behind his back, his eyes looking upwards as if held in divine contemplation.

On the other side of the room, Martin Bormann and Rudolf Hess, both wearing brown uniforms with red armbands displaying the black swastika on a white circular background, could be heard discussing party finances.

The phone rang, and Rudolf Hess glanced towards the secretary, who smiled briefly and nodded. "*Danke*, Johanna," he acknowledged before walking to the centre of the room, placing his hands on his hips, his large eyebrows giving gravity to his words.

"*Meine Herren*, before we go in, as the Führer's adjutant, I am instructed to tell you that what we hear today must not be shared with anyone, not even by you to excite the masses, Herr Goebbels." The last remark drew a brief, quiet laugh, acknowledging the, by now, legendary communication skills exhibited by Goebbels in his role as Reich leader of NSDAP propaganda. "The Führer has decreed that anyone who attends this meeting is bound by a sacred bond of secrecy. You are his most trusted, but if you talk of this to anyone, you will suffer the consequences. No-one in any part of our movement knows what we are speaking of this day. irrespective of their rank or status. Please follow me."

As Hess approached the door, the armed guard stepped smartly to one side, clicking his heels before allowing them entry. Hess led the way, stopping just inside the door.

"Mein Führer, the President of the Reichstag, Hermann Göring, Gauleiter Joseph Goebbels, Reichsführer-SS Heinrich Himmler and Gauleiter Martin Bormann."

Hess stepped back to allow the others to enter. There, standing in front of a relatively simple double pedestal desk, stood the Führer, Adolf Hitler, striking an authoritative pose with his arms folded. Smiling briefly, he muttered the words, "*Willkommen, meine Herren*," as each one walked forward, raising their right arms smartly in salute, followed by a brief shake of the hand. Hitler acknowledged them by bending his right arm upwards from the elbow in his customary manner then waved them towards seats that were haphazardly positioned in front of his desk.

Hitler's uniform had become smarter of late, no longer merely being a brown shirt and tie. He was wearing a military-style tunic, still brown, with two breast pockets and four gold buttons down the centre over the traditional jodhpurs with fitted knee-high jackboots. A tanned thick belt was round his middle and a leather strap ran diagonally from his right shoulder to meet the belt on his left side. His Iron Cross decoration was worn beneath the left-hand breast pocket, below which was his black wound badge decoration (*Verwundetenabzeichen*) from the Great War. On his left sleeve was the red armband bearing the swastika whilst on his tie just below the knot was a golden pin depicting an eagle clutching the party emblem in a wreath.

"Providence has chosen our moment to act," he began quietly. "Now, our time is upon us and we shall seize this moment of destiny, creating the new Reich without spilling a single drop of German blood." His slightly guttural voice had utter conviction, and he looked at each of them deeply in turn with steely, unwavering blue eyes. His look was startling, intense, almost hypnotic, and every person in the room held on to each of the Führer's words as though they were addressed to them personally. "You have been chosen because of your loyalty to me, and your belief in my vision of the National Socialist Reich. This will be a greater Germany where our superiority will take over lands in which we can expand the German race, and that is our destiny. I feel myself to be the executor of the will of history. What people think of me at present is all of no consequence. Our great purpose must be to expand, not into the West, although we will avenge the sell-out of the so-called Treaty of Versailles." His voice rose as he raised his fist in the air and then pointed at each of them. "We shall rip up the treaty which was a betrayal of our race in the Jewish plan to weaken us for their gain. We shall begin by taking back what was taken from Germany, but that is just the start for us. Our destiny, *meine Herren*, lies in the East, where we shall free the world of Bolshevism and make room for a greater Reich."

The Führer seemed to grow in stature as he spoke, gripping everyone with his purpose and unflinching resolve. Even Göring had found that he had become utterly inspired by this man, despite once saying that whilst he admired Hitler, he would never become mesmerised like some 'simpletons' claimed to be after his speeches. Now, he recognised that he was following a great leader that would bring Germany deliverance. When he had heard about this former army corporal with his Charlie Chaplin-style moustache amazing and galvanising people with his oratory in beer halls, he had initially been cynical. But he went along to a meeting out of curiosity, a night that swept his doubts away and changed his life. That had been in 1922 and, in just ten years, this inspirational man had led their movement from nothing to the verge of total power in Germany, giving Göring the position of President of the Reichstag no less.

The Führer strode towards a large world map adorning one wall, then, shaking his finger at them, he exclaimed, "We will never be contained, never, but we shall grow and grow, taking land in a glorious mission of *Lebensraum*. We must first take back what is ours by right, secure our borders, and annex territories of value to the Reich, but then we shall expand eastwards to take over land currently populated by Slavs and Jews. Providence calls upon us as the superior Aryan race to purify by removing the lesser races who contaminate the land we need. This is the soil policy of our future. The Bolshevik filth must be eradicated, and in that, we have traditional allies in many other nations, including the British. They will become our partners in this great struggle because they want order and have no love for these people. In this glorious crusade we will even be supported by the Catholic church. They despise the Bolsheviks and the vile Communist ideals that threaten us all. Many will want to join our cause. I call this Germanisation and nothing will stop us from triumphing. We have the iron will, driven by our strength, and our great people will give us their blood rising to this momentous mission." His voice had reached a crescendo with the final words. His eyes displayed his complete dedication to purpose, and then he paused, staring at the map is if entranced by the moment.

No-one moved, or spoke, or even desired or dared to interrupt other than to follow and wonder at the audaciousness of their leader.

He placed his hand on his heart. "I feel this is the moment that is chosen for me as I become the Führer of all Germany. There is only one task: Lebensraum, not as a philosophy but as our sacred purpose, a glorious objective to which the German people will rise like a flood. This is the law of inevitable expansion creating living space where Germans prosper and the Reich can grow. There will be war, but a glorious war in which Germany will be victorious, without betrayal, because that is the destiny for this Reich. We shall seize Poland, then the Ukraine and execute Germanisation, introducing Germans and removing the natives. We must free the land for Aryan Germans to gain control of resources and ensure no food shortages for our people. We shall be like the British in India and treat the original inhabitants like Indians. I intend to stay this course with ice-cold determination, conquering for the German people, conquering for a new Germany, overcoming all obstacles, and no-one will stop the greater German Reich, noone." His arms flung out wide as he shouted, repeating the last word: "*Niemand.*"

At that moment Goebbels was unable to contain his absolute admiration further. He jumped to his feet, crying out, "*Heil Hitler!*", his arm outstretched proudly, as the others in the room followed his example, driven by the occasion and filled with it.

Hitler bade them sit. "*Meine Kameraden,* you have been chosen because you will sense this great purpose, this moment for Germany. Others within our movement have not the foresight, or the belief, or the will. What India was for England the territories of Russia will be for us. Whatever we do or say over coming years, Russia will be our ultimate prize and conquest. The German colonists will live on handsome, spacious farms, with Reich services lodged in marvellous buildings and the governors in palaces. The Germans must be a closed society uncontaminated with the Slavs or their Jewish masters. We will protect our great nation like a fortress. The least of our stable lads will be superior to any native." The Führer had begun to speak more quietly, but his purpose was unshakeable and those in the room loved him for it.

"Now I want us to relax and consider our moves carefully, and to assist us in this purpose, I think we should enjoy some tea." He picked the phone up, telling his secretary, Johanna Wolf, that his guests were ready. Shortly afterwards, tea was served with chocolate biscuits and scones by Johanna. The Führer thanked her, calling her 'Wölfin', using his pet name for her, before she put a hand over her mouth, curtsied and left, looking a little embarrassed. "You will note," he said, smiling at his guests, "that we are served using the finest Nymphenburg porcelain. Our great culture will be celebrated across the world when we rebuild Germany."

Hitler quietly explained to his guests that National Socialism must be the single party for Germany, within which, he pointed out, they could welcome people with diverse views but united behind the greater good for Germany. "*Ein volk, ein Reich, ein Führer*, for which the seeds have already been planted, and the roots for this transformation are spreading." He stated that his strategy for the coming years was already well advanced but careful preparation to realise the purpose was essential; he wanted each of them to perform a crucial role.

"We must never allow others to know about the master plan except what part they have to play when the time is right. If we provide a unifying aim in our crusade to others within the world we can bring a global unity behind our grand purpose. Whatever we do as we take power, whatever agreements we make, whatever assurances we give, shall all be with one eventual purpose, Lebensraum in the East.

"First, we must consolidate our power in Europe and be seen as invincible, which will give strength to our negotiation – or, as I prefer to call it, the dictating of our terms. Then, from our monumental territorial foundation, we shall attack Russia with millions of our invincible soldiers, backed by the British, with an unstoppable force.

"This will be known as the '*Generalplan Reich*', but it will not be written down, not by anyone, not even by you, *mein Reichsführer*, with your meticulous attention to detail."

Himmler immediately stood, clicking his heels, and extended his arm in salute with unquestioning acceptance. "*Jawohl, mein Führer.*"

Hitler looked at each of them in turn, with his penetrating blue eyes. "I will rely on only those who need to know. That way, only those that we permit will ever be party to this great enterprise – one on one ('*eins zu eins*')." The Führer rubbed his hands together in delight at the moment of revelation he was now sharing. He turned to Rudolf Hess before sitting at his desk. "I believe you have a briefing to give us?"

Hess stood up, raising his arm briefly. "*Mein Führer, kameraden*, we have an operative in England whom we call Agent Prinz, and his mission is to infiltrate the highest levels of their society. I can confirm that he has succeeded in meeting the King, the Prince of Wales, the Duke of York and some of the leading members of their ruling classes, including some senior politicians." There were audible expressions of surprise. "Agent Prinz believes there are many in the English establishment who can be relied upon to support us as we develop and put in place our plans. These are people of both political and military influence. When the time is right, we will need to strike with fury, with a combined AngloGerman momentum that becomes unstoppable. The anti-Russian seeds are being sown in England, but we also need to develop common aims on which we may eventually capitalise, nurturing a bond with many in their society who openly distrust the Jews. The British are obsessed with their royalty and their class system. It is our aim to build ties and involve these people in avoiding conflict and creating a collaboration network. Already, Agent Prinz tells me that the Prince of Wales is quite an admirer of the Führer."

"Ah, *The Man Who Would Be King*," quoted Hermann Göring with a broad smile. "A book worth a read by Rudyard Kipling," he added, noticing the questioning sneer on Himmler's face.

The Führer replied, "Perhaps when he is, he may be useful to us."

3

Goodnight Sweetheart

**Friday 28th October 1932, 7.30pm
Savoy Hotel, The Strand, Westminster, London**

They alighted from the cab in evening wear as the uniformed doorman in a top hat held open the door. The older of the two, Mona Maund, was somewhat outdressed by Greta Atkins, but that was OK. She knew her companion dressed to impress and that she loved being somewhat ostentatious. Mona had been with SIS for a year and relished the variety of roles she found herself in but felt ill fitted to this one, playing the escort and appointed chaperone to her glamorous colleague. Frankly, it was somewhat tiresome, but she looked forward to meeting, assessing and reporting on the variety of society guests to whom she may be introduced.

Greta had every inch dressed for the evening with a long, lowcut, white silk dress that showed off her body in a most alluring manner like a second skin, with a split revealing daringly exposed legs; a fur stole wrap, open at the neck, revealed a pearl necklace dipping to her cleavage; and silver high-heeled sandal shoes were complemented by a jewelled pattern. As if this was not enough, a shimmering tiara over her long wavy auburn hair added glamour, giving her the look of a princess. As she emerged, one of her evening glove-covered arms supported an elegant slim extended cigarette holder, which she drew on coquettishly whilst the other held a silk bag matching her dress. As she entered the hotel, Greta drew discreet, admiring glances and more direct notice from some who dared risk admonishment from their partners, all of which she was demurely aware but deigned not to acknowledge directly.

Mona had opted for a simple lime green evening gown, fastened with a bow to the neck and a matching belt, with plain but laced Oxford shoes. She carried a heavier mock Gladstone handbag. Her outfit was completed with a rather clumsy-looking trench coat. She was not used to this type of venue but the colonel had assured her that her role was as chaperone, observer and nothing more, for which she was grateful.

When they entered the foyer, a shriek of delight greeted them as Diana Mitford floated across in a red chiffon gown, so radiantly beautiful, Mona thought, with a slight pang of envy. *"Darling, mais comment allez vous Madame?"* Diana exclaimed with a ravishing, engaging smile to Greta, who gave a mock curtsy, responding with, *"Je vais très bien merci, Madame, puis je presente Mademoiselle Mona Maund?"* The two shook hands with a smile before Greta continued, "Diana, your French pronunciation is no better for my teaching. My goodness, how many years now since I taught you in Paris? Six, I think."

Diana guided Mona to the concierge to leave her coat before excitedly beckoning. "You must meet Sir Oswald – he is such a hoot, and simply divinely handsome with it; oh my goodness, and we have a real German prince dining with us too. He is a grandson of Queen Victoria." They walked towards the Lancaster Ballroom, from where, as they drew closer, they could hear the sounds of band music playing the current familiar hit 'Goodnight Sweetheart'. They were welcomed into the ballroom restaurant by the maitre d', who escorted them to a table not far from where the familiar and well-loved band leader Carroll Gibbons was alternately conducting then playing the piano with the Savoy Hotel Orpheans. At the table they were introduced to Diana's younger but equally beautiful sister, Unity Mitford – or Bobo, as Diana referred to her – dazzling in a silver gown, and then the somewhat plain-looking newspaper magnate, Viscount Rothermere.

Diana then executed a dramatic curtsy in front of a distinguished man, announcing him as, "His Highness, the Duke of Saxe-Coburg and Gotha."

He immediately stood, introducing himself with, "Please, do call me Charles Edward," then kissed the hands of the two ladies, bowing politely, his eyes widening as he looked at Greta, holding his gaze upon her for a moment.

Diana then guided them to the head of the table, where an imposing man stood in an immaculate dinner jacket, winged collar and white bowtie. He appeared tall, with wavy black hair and a trimmed moustache, standing erect as though in military pose. "Finally, I have the pleasure of introducing the man of the moment in this country, the leader of our new party, the British Union of Fascists, Sir Oswald Mosley." He bowed deeply before welcoming them to the table.

Diana bade Greta sit next to Charles Edward, and Mona with Viscount Rothermere, whilst she sat to the right of Sir Oswald, barely taking her eyes off him. Two places remained vacant and Sir Oswald informed them that they were awaiting very esteemed company before summoning the waiter ordering drinks, although he reassured his guests that Champagne would be served later. Turning to Greta, he opened with, "I understand you are an associate editor with *Vogue* magazine. Do you have a position regarding the new politics of today?" His voice was cultured, charming and very disarming.

"Sir, I leave those matters outside my work, but I admire strong leadership, which I believe has been lacking in this country. From what I gather, you bring a fresh way forward and if that brings unity under your leadership, then I can only admire such strength."

This drew an immediate, "Bravo," from Duke Charles Edward, clapping his hands, as Sir Oswald did likewise.

The Duke interjected, "We also have a leader-in-waiting in Germany, who will soon be in power. Do you think Adolf Hitler will be good for us?"

"I am impressed with what I have read about him," Greta responded. "Germany lost so much after the Great War and I think the victors demanded too much. There has been chaos, and this Hitler seems powerful, promising stability, a rebuilding, with order and a new start. That can only be good."

This time it was Unity Mitford who applauded eagerly just as the drinks were served.

The conversation flowed with enthusiasm for the potential of a fresh era of politics spreading across Europe. Charles Edward began discussing more closely his views of a new Germany in which Greta affected both keen interest and informed awareness. As he spoke passionately about his earnest admiration for Hitler, describing him in almost heroic terms, Unity Mitford joined in saying that she would adore meeting the Führer in person. The Duke said that he often met him and that he would be delighted to, perhaps, arrange such a visit for both sisters to accompany Sir Oswald, who, he confirmed, Hitler endorsed. Mona Maund, meanwhile, was discussing the current views of the newspapers, especially those of the *Daily Mail*, with Viscount Rothermere, the owner, appearing to keenly absorb all he was saying as, indeed, she was, preparing to report back later to Colonel Menzies.

The head waiter appeared, whispering in Sir Oswald's ear, who then stood, bowed and excused himself 'merely for a few moments', as he needed to greet his guests. The table waited expectantly, in some anticipation of who they were being joined by, as no-one had been informed. Shortly thereafter, there was a stir in the great room, with many guests rising as Sir Oswald re-entered, accompanied by Lord Louis Mountbatten, who waved to some and occasionally shook hands with others as they approached the table.

Sir Oswald stood back, introducing his guest. "May I present Lord Louis Mountbatten – although I'm told we may call him 'Dickie' – together with his companion, Madame Yola Letellier." Lord Louis smiled graciously, exuding charm, before kissing the hands of each lady in turn, expressing that he was 'delighted' to meet them.

He stopped by Charles Edward, smiling broadly. "My dear cousin, glad to see you back in the fold, as it were."

Yola was in her twenties, diminutive, very slim, with short wavy hair and dressed in a mid-calf maroon shimmering dress which was very much late 1920s in style but appeared extremely chic. Lord Louis wore a dinner jacket, a white wing-collared shirt and matching bowtie, black trousers with a silk stripe down each leg, and highly polished shoes, whilst a white top pocket handkerchief completed his outfit.

Discussion became animated as dinner was served over the current political climate. Lord Louis began quizzing Sir Oswald about the new British Union of Fascists, or BUF, raising questions about reports of violence surrounding public meetings which he felt were detracting from the message. "Essentially, many of us have sympathy with your movement, dear boy, and, indeed, the aims of this extraordinary chap, Hitler, but there are some pretty alarming stories coming out of Germany about people being attacked by uniformed Nazis. We are not a nation drawn easily towards violence or civil unrest. It smacks of revolution, which is completely alien to our way."

Sir Oswald quickly pointed out that such reports were often exaggerated by the press and put about by hostile elements, such as Jewish organisations and Communists. He stated he had met Mussolini, 'Il Ducie', of Italy and drawn more inspiration from his success rather than that of Hitler, although he had been impressed by what he had heard about him. Charles Edward pointed out
that Hitler was gaining a huge following and that, in his view, Germany, under the Führer's leadership, would be a bastion against Communist Russia, who were the real threat.

"My dear cousin," he said to Lord Louis, "if you met the Führer, I think you would be impressed. I have never met a man more inspired, more on fire with a desire to effect change for the good of Germany. He wishes to unite us and bring order and stability, and I do believe him to be one of the greatest men of our time."

Greta patted him on the arm, stating how impressed she was with his admiration. The Duke kissed her hand, making her giggle, and he was utterly smitten by her attention.

The band struck up 'Goodnight, Sweetheart' for a second time. Lord Louis immediately rose. "May I have the pleasure?" He bowed to Yola, taking her by the hand and guiding her to the dancefloor. Within a few seconds, other dancers stood back to admire the couple, who glided effortlessly across the polished floor and were utterly together in their steps, Lord Louis clearly enjoying the attention he was attracting.

"What a wonderfully talented, snazzy, handsome, cultured man," Diana Mitford quipped, prompting Sir Oswald to give her a mock hurt expression before inviting her for the next dance. As Lord Louis and Yola returned to the table to loud applause, the band leader, Carroll Gibbons, voiced his pleasure at being graced by a Royal presence. He then announced that the evening should now become slower and more intimate with 'The Pagan Love Song', a somewhat risqué and perhaps more decadent version of the fashionable Boston waltz.

Charles Edward seized his moment, standing and bowing to Greta. "My dear, I would be humbled if you would allow me this dance." She looked deliciously coy for a moment before letting him lead her to the floor. As they danced, the Duke told Greta how terribly wonderful he had found her company and how charming her lively interest in current affairs. His steps were less assured or fluid than Lord Louis', and executed with a degree of military stiffness, but he was, nevertheless, clearly versed in the latest dance style. Greta confessed she had been fascinated to find out he actually knew the Führer and showed great interest in how Hitler captivated crowds.

"Simply everyone is talking about him, darling; tell me, is he as frightfully entrancing as they say?" she asked. This was a subject Charles Edward felt relaxed to speak about, which was a relief to him as he was almost completely overwhelmed by Greta. Now, he was animated, giving more confidence to his dancing moves, telling her that he had been utterly spellbound by Hitler when they had first met in 1921. As they moved into the next dance, he recounted to her how the Führer could hold the attention of anyone with his gift for speaking and how he seemed possessed of endless inspiration with total conviction, simply captivating his audiences.

"It is as if he is inspired by Providence," he enthused, "and he talks unashamedly of making Germany proud and strong again, rebuilding with a future wherein the German people will triumph over every adversity." He took Greta into his confidence, asking her if he could trust her not to tell anyone what he was about to reveal. They stopped dancing for a moment, and he held her by the hands, his voice dropping in tone. "When Hitler was on the run from the authorities after attempting to start a revolution in 1923, it was I that hid him for the first days and sheltered his supporters for some months, which is unthinkable for someone in my position." He moved her back into the dance. "So you see, my dear, you are dancing with a criminal."

Greta laughed playfully. "I think you are definitely a touch mischievous, Your Highness," whereupon he told her to call him Charlie.

As the evening drew to a close, Diana stood and thanked them all for coming, proposing a toast to Sir Oswald for success with his new party. She concluded by saying how agreeable it had been and that they must do it all again sometime. Charles Edward, having had two large brandies on top of much Champagne and gin before dinner, was insistent that they should all come to Germany and have dinner with the Führer. He was adamant that he could make the necessary arrangements. Lord Louis diplomatically responded, stating that, as far as his position went, such a step would have to be sanctioned through the right channels. Unity Mitford was more enthusiastic, gripping Charles Edward's arm.

"Oh, please do make it happen, Your Highness. That man Hitler is so absolutely divine."

As they all bid farewell, Charles Edward escorted Mona Maund to a taxi, after she had diplomatically declined to remain behind for cocktails, leaving him free to retire with Greta to the American bar.

A pianist was playing rag-time music as they both entered with her arm linked loosely in his. "Charlie, I think we should have two *hanky pankys.*" She giggled at him, informing him that it was a special cocktail drink invented by a famous lady bartender who had served there some years before, made of gin, sweet vermouth and Fernet-Branca. After watching their drinks being made, they sat in a quiet alcove, where he took out a silver lighter, snapping it alight for her cigarette held ready in a holder, before lighting a large cigar. Greta knew this was her opportunity, and she intended to make the most of it.

Charlie was quite a handsome, imposing man but lacked the natural commanding authority of Dickie Mountbatten or other members of the royal circle she had met previously. His eyes were very much of the family, inheriting the look she recognised from paintings of Prince Albert, and yet he also exhibited features from his grandmother (and godmother), Queen Victoria. He was not tall, walking with a slight stoop, but carried an air about him which was unmistakeable as one used to privilege and respect. Although aged forty-eight, Greta thought Charles Edward appeared older but knew he suffered from chronic rheumatism, and this was a characteristic she had seen before in others who had served in the Great War.

They enjoyed some initial chit-chat about their respective schools and background, during which she learned of his strict upbringing and that he had been to Eton before attending a military academy in Germany. She informed him that she had attended Cheltenham Ladies' College, being the daughter of a wealthy landowning farmer from Norfolk, with a family history stretching back to the Norman conquest. As their second cocktail was served, and he was beginning to be less reserved in the manner with which he looked at her, she judged the moment was right.

"So this extraordinary man, Hitler, how well do you know him personally? I mean, does he actually trust you to share his thoughts and hopes with others here?" She looked at him, her eyes open wide with admiration, which Charles Edward found completely disarming. The pianist was playing 'The Charleston', adding to the lightness of the mood and the frivolity, despite the seriousness of her task.

"Greta, he trusts me completely, which is wonderful, and I have agreed to help him in any way I can because, put simply, I totally agree with and support his aims. He has entrusted me with important work, about which no-one knows except those closest to him."

She put his hand in hers. "Oh, Charlie, that sounds wonderful and all jolly exciting. If he is to make Germany strong again after that rather silly Versailles treaty, he needs strong people like you on whom he can rely." She squeezed his hand and he was melting, irresistibly drawn towards her with her beautiful blue eyes and exquisite form. She delved further. "Oh, do tell me more, it is just too thrilling."

Charles Edward leaned forward, looking at her earnestly. "The Führer believes that to protect us from Jewish domination or the threat from the Communists, we must prepare by learning to ally ourselves with others so that when the time comes, we are strong enough in the world to resist and overcome them. So, I am here covertly, as it were, to talk to as many people with influence as I can, and begin to build alliances, but all this is secret. I do not mind sharing this because I know you will understand and see how noble the cause is."

Greta was a willing, supportive, enthusiastic listener, and he began to tell her all about those he had spoken to as she listened, wide-eyed, admiring how he had managed to open so many doors. She disappeared to the cloakroom twice for no other reason than to scribble, frantically noting down the long list of people, before she forgot, whom he had been talking to, together with the reactions they had given. She was genuinely surprised that already the German embassy in London had been infiltrated with Hitler's supporters and that Charles Edward was sending messages almost daily back to Munich for the attention of the Führer. As she looked at the names, it was like a who's who of British society, many drawn by Charles Edward's position and status as a perceived member of the Royal Family.

Politely declining Charlie's invitation for further aperitifs which they may share more privately, she did give him her telephone number but promised she would call him at the Savoy, where he was staying, within the coming days. He told her that he was not due to return to Germany for another ten days and earnestly hoped they could spend more time together. As she left, he kissed her hand, but she threw her arms around him, saying, "Darling, it has all been so lovely, and I will call you, I promise," giving him her dazzling smile before he closed the cab door.

By 1.30am, she had given Colonel Menzies a short briefing by phone, arranging to meet at his office the following morning at 11.00am. Before she put the phone down, she could not resist a quip: "Oh, and Colonel, you will be pleased to know that my virtue and reputation remain untarnished," which exuded no response apart from a long sigh, before she heard the click of the receiver being replaced.

4

Eagles on Prey

Saturday 15th February 2020, 7.00pm
Maximilian Strasse, Berchtesgaden, Bavaria

The chime from Dr Walter Friedman's doorbell at his surgery and apartment not far from Gunther Roche's house, situated in a smart neighbourhood, was as unexpected as it was unwelcome. At 7.00pm he was about to settle down for the evening in front of the TV and catch up on the latest news on the spread of the coronavirus that was becoming a matter of grave medical concern. On opening the door, the cold, aloof face behind the shaded glasses was enough to tell him that this was official business, for which he had been called on many times before.

"Herr Doctor, I am Oberleutnant Schmidt of the BND and we need your assistance. May we speak in private, please?"

Walter took him through into his consulting room, sitting himself behind his desk.

"You have a patient by the name of Gunther Roche on Ludwig Ganghofer-Strasse," Schmidt said coldly. It was a statement, not a question. "There has been an accident and he has been shot. I regret he did not survive. I must stress, Herr Doctor, in the strongest terms, that this is a state matter and that no-one must be aware of the cause of death. Your patient died of natural causes."

As Walter listened, his heart sank; Gunther Roche had been a dear and valued friend, but he showed no emotion as the intelligence officer explained his requirements. There was no feeling in the face of the man sitting opposite him but an aloofness he had seen too many times before, especially from those for whom violence was employed as a means whenever necessary.

He was told to attend Gunther's house, which had already been cleaned, and issue a death certificate stating that he had died of a stroke. The stated reason for calling was because the old man had telephoned earlier complaining of feeling unwell with dizziness but that he had died before the doctor could reach him. He was informed that the body was to be removed by others and that he should ignore anything else he witnessed at the scene. Showing no emotion, Dr Friedman carefully noted down what was required of him. Schmidt asked if there were many who were close to Roche, or if he ever took the doctor into his confidence about the past, especially his service during the war. Walter stated that these matters were rarely spoken of anymore and that he knew very little of the old man's background. Schmidt abruptly stood up, gave Walter a card and asked that he be called if anyone was taking an interest in Gunther Roche in the aftermath of his passing. Finally, he was told tersely, "You will understand, Herr Doctor, that we have never met and that there will be consequences if you fail to keep this confidential." All that was missing, Walter thought ruefully after the BND man left, was a clicking of the heels and an outstretched right-armed salute.

"*Mein Gott*, does nothing ever change," he said to himself wearily before putting his coat on for the brief drive to his former companion's house. As he entered, there was no sign of anything being out of place except that there was a covered body lying on the floor. He knew, even before he took Gunther's pulse, it was pointless as he lifted the cover to see blood in the chest region. He also knew before he looked that there would be a gunshot wound and, sighing, he replaced the cover over his old friend before standing to say a farewell.

"You were loyal to him until the end, and I can only admire that in you despite our many differences over the years. Goodbye, Herr Reichsmarschall, your secret is safe with me, God bless."

He spoke the words out loud, wiping a tear from his eye as he went to the wall and removed the Iron Cross, pausing for a moment to admire it before slipping it into his pocket. He wrote out the death attendance note, then, shutting the door for the last time, he walked very wearily through the snow to his car. God, he felt so tired of so much. How he despised the corruption that he knew still gripped Germany, of which he had allowed himself to become a part.

Returning to his home, he completed the paperwork, adding his signature to the death certificate confirming his complicity in yet more gross state corruption. He had endured a lifetime of cooperation with people like Schmidt because, for the most part, he justified to himself, it had been for the better good. This was a country where in his younger days espionage and counterespionage had been rife, where loyalties to varying factions and political creeds were vying for credibility. Some believed passionately in the new West Germany; others allied themselves with the Communist ideas espoused in East Germany. There had also remained a loyal core who still looked back to the 'glorious' era of the Third Reich. Many in his neighbourhood were families of former Nazis, and Dr Friedman, whilst having no affiliation, had benefitted from their patronage and generosity.

As a young doctor, in the mid-1970s, he had battled with his conscience over corrupting influences but, ultimately, the pragmatic dictated the course he took and it was not unrewarding. However, once he had taken the Devil's purse, he recognised there could be no going back. From the start of his medical career, he had been called upon to do 'favours', which had meant adjusting documents, including death certificates, but this one was already very different.

There had been many deaths over the years in the local area that had been 'unexplained', initially involving those who had remained living there after the war. There were rivalries, old scores to settle and alleged traitors from the former regime of Adolf Hitler. Berchtesgaden was a favoured place from the late twenties onwards for those who had allegiance to the Nazi Party. This had become a close-knit community tied by their loyalty to the Führer, who spent much of his time in his beloved Alpine retreat there which he named 'The Berghof'. The area had become a select place to live by those close to the leadership of the Third Reich. In the thirties and forties, it had become something of a tourist attraction, when thousands of admirers would gather at the bottom of the drive by the entrance, hoping to meet Hitler in person. Sometimes, his parents had told him, Hitler would invite a random family from the crowds to join him for tea in his home overlooking the mountains but, alas, they were never chosen.

As a boy, Walter recalled his parents telling him how great the Führer had been and proudly boasting how they had taken his sister, Helga, up the road to the Berghof in the hope that they might see him. On one particular day, when Hitler had come out to meet the crowd, he had walked over and not only spoke to them but also picked Helga up. She was fourteen years older than Walter and he could recall her wallowing in the attention that this accolade gave her, elevating her to a status he could never achieve. She would talk excitedly of it as a young woman, saying it had been like a thrilling visit to Santa Claus. Yet, a few years later, she would not speak of it, nor ever did again. His parents had a photograph of Helga at five years of age being held by a smiling Hitler whilst his mother stood looking up at him with complete adulation. The photograph remained on display until the mid1960s, when Helga announced that she and the family she was starting would not visit unless they removed it.

The spectre of Hitler's influence remained throughout Walter's childhood, and both his parents never lost their admiration for him, proudly recounting to visitors their experiences of actually seeing or conversing with the Führer. Whilst Walter had no such loyalty or fascination for a person who had been in power before he was born, he would concede the undoubted influence of Hitler's leadership, diplomatically avoiding the friction flowing from any disagreement with his parents. Even when he was a young adult, they would still talk of the great days of the Reich and would never countenance any criticism of Hitler. They lived in a sizeable property not far from the Berghof known as 'Adleransicht' (Eagle View) on Scharitzkehlstrasse facing the mountains, enjoying privacy with gates and a private drive. His father had a doctor's practice in Berchtesgaden, and in the Nazi era, he had provided consultations to officers who were stationed at the Berghof and their families.

Walter Friedman was eleven when he had been introduced to Gunther Roche by his parents in December 1963, although he had seen him fleetingly on previous visits. Gunther had arrived one day with another man called Otto and his parents had told him they would be staying for some time. They said that it was a secret the two men were there and he must not speak of it to anyone else. The two guests began chatting to Walter, fascinating and captivating him with exciting stories from their time as soldiers in the war. He learned that they once had been fugitives hiding from the occupying forces of the Allies. They had regaled the young boy with thrilling tales of bravery as 'knights of the Reich', not least their daring escape from a prison camp with others dressed as American soldiers. They told him of their experiences parachuting together, ending up in great battles or having been engaged in missions rescuing others from the clutches of the enemy. Walter learned, many years later from Gunther, that the Otto he had met then as a boy had actually been Otto Skorzeny, one of the legendary military heroes of the Reich. The two of them had once been on a daring mission to liberate

Mussolini from captivity in the mountains, taking him without a shot being fired, before delivering him safely to Hitler two days later.

"We dropped without warning from the sky in gliders, like eagles on prey," Walter recalled Gunther saying. He was a giant figure to the young boy, standing tall with thick blond hair and smiling blue eyes, full of adventure. Walter never knew why they were there, but they said they had been on a secret mission which no-one could ever know, which fascinated him.

Otto left after a few months, but Gunther stayed on, spending much time with Walter when he wasn't engaged in his work, which he carried out in an office set up in one of the outbuildings. He had valued boyhood memories of the many long walks they shared, or of the times when Gunther took him climbing, where he exhibited a wonderful agility, teaching Walter new skills in ropes and how to abseil down sheer drops. He stayed nearly a year, leaving in late 1964, when he bid the family farewell, telling Walter he was going to join other loyal and brave followers of the Reich in Argentina. When he left, he said he wanted to give Walter something special from the war, presenting him with his SS fatigue cap, saying that he must always wear it with pride but, perhaps, only privately.

Gunther never stayed more than one night again, but occasionally he would pay a visit and hold 'business' discussions with Walter's father before sharing a meal with the family. He was always amiable and good-natured, often bringing Walter gifts from his travels abroad, spending a great deal of time in South America. The last time he had visited the family home was in the summer of 1972, when Walter was on vacation from studying at medical school. He recalled Gunther saying to him that great changes were happening in the world and that a new and exciting future lay ahead for Germany. Walter had debated civil liberties with the older man, who, he remembered, listened intently to his dreams of global changes and a more liberated society. Gunther had said to him that, in his view, strength came from discipline, but he respected the young student's views and his hopes for the future. At dinner, Gunther had spoken enthusiastically about Walter's sense of idealism, which he compared to his own many years before.

"If you can look back in the future and be proud of your ideology when you were young, and not hide from it when you are older, nor it from others, then you will have achieved something rare."

Gunther had left the house the following day and Walter heard nothing from him again until twelve years later. It was in September 1984, when his secretary had announced that there was a Gunther Roche in reception who, he had claimed, the doctor might remember. "He has asked me to check whether he can have his cap back," she said quizzically. He had entered the doctor's consulting room and embraced Walter like a long-lost relative. Smilingly, and with immense charm, he had asked if the doctor would take him as a patient as he had purchased a house locally and planned to retire there, a request which Walter readily agreed to. Gunther had been a kind of heroic icon whom he had never forgotten. He now had grey hair but retained his pencil moustache, which gave him a kind of film-star distinguished look.

He still recalled vividly the many times he had spent walking, talking and debating with this man who, he had felt, was both ruthless and genial, a contradiction that fascinated him as a young man. Gunther informed him that he would be visiting from time to time, but he would not yet be moving there permanently. He would only meet Walter one more time that year, an occasion about which he had been sworn to secrecy but which now had such relevance.

In the late 1980s, Gunther began spending more and more time at Berchtesgaden. They had refreshed their relationship and had struck up a renewed connection that turned to friendship, meeting regularly for a few beers and debating the politics of the day. Gunther never hid his allegiance to his past or to the beliefs he retained but respected Walter's ideas, even when they vehemently disagreed. As Gunther often said to his friend, "If we had no differences, we would have nothing to fight for, and I would fight to defend your right to debate with me, even though, my friend, right will always be on my side." Despite their friendship, there was always an edge to the older man's words that was both ruthless and uncompromising.

Walter sighed deeply. So many years had passed and now this. "They can do this to such an old man." Pouring himself a generous Schnapps, and then another, he sought out some records his parents had loved. Reaching for one that had been a favourite of his mother's, he placed it on the turntable. The slow, seductive timbre of Marlene Dietrich drowned the crackles of the 78rpm disc, as she sang the haunting words:

"Vor der Kaserne
Vor dem grossen Tor
Stand eine Laterne
Und steht sie noch davor
So woll'n wir uns da wieder seh'n
Bei der Laterne wollen wir steh'n
Wie einst Lili Marlene."

Before the song had finished, Walter had already decided that he had no choice but to act.

Sunday 16th February 2020, 6.00am
Alster Waterfront, Hamburg, North Germany

The telephone by his bed interrupted his sleep. Hans Schirach reached clumsily for his landline, which was rarely used these days, wondering who the hell it was. "Schirach, hallo."

The voice on the line was faltering, almost pleading. *"Bitte, ist das Hans Schirach? Aus* Der *Spiegel?"*

"Ja… Who is this?" Hans responded curtly.

"My name is Walter, please, I know your mother, but she does not know I'm calling. I knew who your father was too and I need to meet with you."

The past tense referring to his father jolted Hans wide awake and he sat up suddenly very aware. "Who are you, please? You claim to know my mother, please tell me who she is."

There was an audible sigh, before he heard, "Eva Schirach, but you never knew your father. She told you was it was a casual fling with a man whom she never stayed in touch with. In fact, she told you he never knew she was pregnant. Have I said enough?" The adrenalin was pumping now as he sat by his bed, reaching for his notebook.

"Please, I need to see you. I cannot say too much over the phone, it is too dangerous. Herr Schirach, I am party to a secret that involves your father and I need to tell you what I know." There was something in Walter's imploring voice that gave sincerity to his words.

"Where are you from and how do you know my mother?" Hans asked. "Is there no way you can email me? My account with *Der Spiegel* is secure, so you have nothing to fear. I work on the investigative team and we deal with matters of national security"

"Please, Herr Schirach," the unknown voice interrupted, sounding more desperate, "you do not understand, they are everywhere and infiltrate everything. I can only tell you one on one. *'Eins zu eins'*. Do not even repeat those last words to anyone. Hans, I must see you, but I cannot tell you who I am; not yet, but I will if you agree to see me. If we meet, I will give you a message for your mother and she will verify my identity, but, before that, you must not inform her of this conversation. I can also tell you, if for nothing else, this may be the greatest scoop of your career.

So will you agree?"

Hans was due to meet with his colleague from Berlin the following day for a briefing on the German covid-19 plan covering the controversial restrictions the government were considering on freedom of movement which were being denied. The plan was highly classified but, as usual, the personal indiscretions of one minister had given *Der Spiegel* the sensitive information for a story. However, something, just something drove him to change everything and make arrangements to meet his unknown caller. It was as much for professional curiosity as anything that he accepted Walter's request, or so he tried to convince himself.

Monday 17th February 2020, 6.00am
Salzburg Airport, WA Mozart, Austria

Walter Friedman sat in the business lounge with a nervous sense of anticipation tinged with relief. He had never in his life acted in a manner outside that which was expected of him or so boldly taken matters into his own hands, and he was shocked at his own temerity. Despite his nervousness, he knew this was the time to act, and for all the right reasons. He had allowed too many people to exercise control over his life for too long. When he was younger, he had held such lofty ideas of helping others through his medical studies. When his father, Friedrich, had first spoken to him about acting for the greater cause, referring to a new Reich, he had felt some unease but had accepted the need to prevent Germany sinking into the abyss. Friedrich had informed him, as he prepared to join his father's medical practice, that there were certain favours that may be required of him. "I have never flinched from my duty to Germany," his father had said to him, "and you need to understand that the movement continues. Whilst you may question it, as I did not, I hope you too will understand there is a greater need beyond our own selfish thoughts."

Both his parents used to talk about the glorious days of the Reich and he ceased debating the issue in his teens as he knew it was pointless. Their creed was entrenched like so many families with whom they mixed as he was growing up. Even some of the teachers at his school would take the pupils into their confidence and quietly speak, as if sharing a secret, about the old days and the pride of the German nation. Many people spoke of a resurgence and rumours often surfaced of former leading Nazis having been seen, including the Führer himself. There was sometimes nervous talk shared of a Fourth Reich being created with its base in South America, but such talk was supressed. As a young man, he had reluctantly allowed himself to continue executing the wishes of his father and of those around him which, he accepted, had assisted him in many ways. Loans were easily accessed, discounts on goods organised, and payments made to assist him with housing. Walter had been told that if ever there were any issues which needed attending to, a network called *Die Spinne* was there to help, quietly and without ever being referred to by name. All he needed to do was call a number, explain his issue or need, following which he would receive a call days later informing him that matters had been taken care of.

As Walter waited for the call to his 7.05 Lufthansa flight to Hamburg, he returned to the bar for a third large Schnapps, this time drinking a little more slowly. He rehearsed in his mind how he could break the news to a person he had not met before, not only about the death of the man's unknown father but also the extraordinary events surrounding Gunther's life. At least there was one final task he could perform for his old friend and fulfil a wish that he had sworn he would carry out. In this, he felt a sense of pride in what he was now doing that he had seldom known in his life.

5

The Congress of Victory

Sunday 3rd September 1933, 1.30pm
The Nuremberg Rally, Nuremberg, Germany

The Zeppelin field, where the National Socialist Rally was being held, was already a magnificent sight, with masses of huge flags visible all around the perimeter, as their large Mercedes approached with small red, white and black swastika pennants flying on the front of each wing. There were enormous crowds of people being directed by smartly uniformed men, many of whom raised their arms, clicking their heels as the car passed. Diana Mitford was almost beside herself with excitement, frequently grabbing the arm of Sir Oswald Mosley, sitting by the window in his BUF Blackshirt uniform, to point out something that caught her attention. Duke Charles Edward sat in the front next to the brown uniformed driver who was also acting as their bodyguard.

On the other side of Diana, her sister Unity was chatting animatedly to Greta Atkins. "Oh my goodness, Greta darling, do you think we will actually get close to him? I want him to see my new badge." Unity had been presented with the maroon, white and black circular Nazi Party swastika lapel badge by Charles Edward which she now wore proudly on the left side of her jacket.

"He knows you are here, ladies," said the Duke over his shoulder, "but I regret the Führer may not have the time to meet with you personally on this visit."

As they drew to a halt behind a small queue of cars by an opening in the ranks of uniformed men lining both sides of the approach, a smart young officer walked towards the car. The door was opened by a guard, who then snapped to attention, raising his right arm. They were greeted by the officer introducing himself as Gruppenführer Baldur Benedikt von Schirach. "The Führer has asked personally that I look after you and take you to your places, but I regret that Sir Oswald will then accompany me to be with guests on the podium. I am sure that the Duke of Saxe-Coburg and Gotha is more than capable of looking after you."

Von Schirach was an imposing man in his late twenties, slim yet having a full face, with an engaging smile, and impeccable in appearance. He had a military badge on each lapel of his tunic, a swastika armband with an unusual white stripe interrupting the normal continuous red (which Charles Edward informed them was the insignia of the Hitler Youth which von Schirach led) and immaculately parted chestnut wavy hair. His eyes were large, Greta noticed, as they met hers, and they were quite delightful if not striking. "Please allow me the honour of showing you to your places." Another plus, Greta noted, admiring his polished English; *he is obviously a man with good background and breeding.*

As they passed through the phalanx of guards, all snapped to attention as they saw von Schirach, their officers immediately stiffening before giving the Nazi salute with a pronounced *'Heil Hitler'*. Then a vast space opened to them; a huge amphitheatre which simply took their breath away. There were innumerable red flags bearing the *Hakenkreuz* ('swastika') set around an enormous arena in which there were ordered spaces separated by lines of guards, all in military uniform. Stepped sloping perimeters on which throngs of people were sitting surrounded the central open space. Down the centre, separating the thousands of people gathered, there was a wide cleared corridor area that stretched in a straight line from one end of the arena to the other. Three giant red banners with swastikas hung above and behind an impressive and imposing raised area a short distance from where they had entered, towards which von Schirach led them. At the front was a rostrum surrounded with Nazi insignia, on the top of which were microphones and, as they drew nearer, they could see various figures engaged there in earnest conversation.

"Oh, good Lord, Diana, look…" exclaimed Unity, unable to conceal her excitement. "That's Hermann Göring talking to Joseph Goebbels."

Von Schirach turned to her with a smile. "*Mein Fraulein*, I will ask them to wave to you in a few minutes."

Unity grasped Greta's hand, shaking it, almost dancing with delight. Von Schirach led them to an area cordoned off by ropes, with orderlies in white uniform there to greet them, before bowing to take his leave. *"Heil Hitler."* Unity could not resist, before he left, extending her right arm. He clicked his heels, smartly returning the salute and giving a sideways smile to Greta.

After he had departed with Sir Oswald, Unity giggled. "He's quite a dish. I think I need to bag myself a German." Greta playfully retorted that the young officer had been giving her the eye, which, she had to admit to herself, he had been, for which she was not a little flattered. That would certainly not be in her report to Colonel Menzies. Champagne was served by the orderlies and the air of expectation was electric.

Suddenly, a band began playing and line after line of troops marched smartly in perfect drill formation, passing their position, turning at the dais and creating differing formations for their march back down the central arena space. Some were in black, some brown and others in field grey. Many carried eagles on top of long standards like the insignia of Roman Legions. At the far end of the stadium was a stepped area, on top of which an enormous eagle dominated the scene, adding a stark sense of authoritarian order over the parade. One of the orderlies spoke to them, inviting that they look up immediately, pointing to the podium. Both Göring and Goebbels were stood looking down directly at them, then they waved, smiling, before raising their arms in salute, to which both Unity and Diana immediately responded in like manner, drawing a cheer from those around them. Greta had to admit to herself that the spectacle was incredibly impressive, if not almost hypnotic. A large military band took up position in the middle of the arena, before a guard formed up in front. They were armed and raised their rifles, firing three times. This brought a dramatic silence for a moment as the crowds were held in awe.

There was a roll of the drums, then a trumpet fanfare, before they began playing the 'Horst Wessel Song', which drew a deafening roar from the thousands gathered there. Then all began joining in the words, the brass and drums beating and leading the singing to a crescendo on the higher notes. As the band marched towards a side exit halfway down, there were shouts all around the arena from those commanding the uniformed troops, bringing them to rigid attention. The voice of Goebbels filled the air from loudspeakers echoing across the throng: "*Mein Kameraden*, loyal members of the *Nationalsozialistische Deutsche Arbeiterpartei*, the Führer, our Führer, Adolf Hitler."

An even louder roar than before went up and a sea of outstretched arms were raised in the Nazi salute as everybody, as one, rose to their feet. This time, the music changed to the national anthem. "*Deutschland, Deutschland über alles*," almost drowned by the rapturous crowd as, at the far end of the arena, beneath the giant eagle, a lone figure was marching in, behind whom there were three further figures, then columns of uniformed men marching in perfect goose-step.

"*Das ist der Führer.*" The orderly smiled at them before raising his right arm, as the entire crowd cheered their approval.

Charles Edward, dressed in the uniform of a Gruppenführer himself, explained the various events as they unfolded, the first of which covered the Führer pausing and saluting in front of a monument honouring of the dead (*Totenehrung*), followed by the Consecration of the Colours, which involved the touching of a bloodstained flag (*Blutfahne*) onto new flags. This had become an important, virtually sacred custom at such events, and the ceremony was almost religious in its execution. The Duke explained that the blood was that of a National Socialist martyr who had died at the failed 1923 revolution, or Munich Putsch, led by Hitler in the early days.

The Führer had then walked down the centre of the arena towards the raised area, drawing huge cheers from the adoring masses. Moments later he appeared on the podium, flanked by Rudolf Hess on one side and Hermann Göring on the other. Then there was the march past by a parade of the Hitler Youth and Greta found herself watching out for their host guide, Baldur von Schirach, and was not disappointed. He took the stand next to Hitler, both their arms outstretched, as proud lines of uniformed boys marched in perfect unison, turning to the podium and giving the Nazi salute as they passed.

Greta reflected that the organisation of so many to create this spectacle was extraordinary, remarking so to Charles Edward. "That is the discipline of this movement," he replied, "which is like no other in the world." Finally, a guard of black uniformed soldiers formed up to the front of the stand, goosestepping into position, in front of which marched an officer with a drawn sword. They jumped to attention on command just as Adolf Hitler strode back into view on the podium, his right arm extended stiffly, turning from the centre and then to each side of the arena. A wild cheer went up and the people were all on their feet.

The orderly leant across. "What we have been waiting for, the Führer's speech," he announced, breathless with anticipation.

Hitler took his position at the centre of the podium and did not speak immediately, taking control of the atmosphere as he soaked it up. He folded his arms, and as the crowd began to quieten, he placed his hands on his hips before speaking quietly in a measured tone, each word seeming to hold the entire arena in electrified awe. Then, he would pause, creating more drama, the timbre of his voice rising each time he continued, drawing and increasing the excitement of the crowd, which hung on to his every word. As he was reaching the first crescendo, he pointed, shook his fist and threw both arms wide to accentuate his language, drawing roar after roar from the crowd. Then there were spontaneous cries of, "*Zieg Heil*," shouted as he stood still, his chest thrust forwards, once again, his arms folded. The Führer awaited silence before speaking again. He had the entire stadium in his hands and Greta observed women close to their position with tears of emotion running down their faces in abject adulation of this man which was almost akin to worship. Turning, she observed Unity, equally overcome with emotion, dabbing her cheeks with her hanky.

All of those there could not fail to be impressed with the spectacle, although, in Greta's case, this was mixed with a profound unease and distaste for the National Socialists and all they stood for. She despised the militarism and could see the dangers it presented for the future. Like many others, she had an abhorrence for anything militarist, having lived through the horrific slaughter of the Great War. Her father had died at the Somme in 1916 and his body was never recovered, which she had not, nor could ever, come to terms with. Then his two younger brothers were lost the following year in the Battle of Passchendaele, wiping out an entire generation of her father's family. To add to her tragedy, her eldest brother was killed in the final conflict of the war in October 1918 at Amiens. He had been a guide in her life, always there for her when she was a child, making her feel safe. Her mother had been left completely devastated and had never recovered from the grief that blighted her life, destroying her ability to ever take pleasure in anything. This flagrant display of weaponry, military ceremony and posturing from Hitler did not impress her inwardly. In fact, she detested his triumphalist rhetoric combined with the arrogant contempt that he openly directed towards those he perceived as enemies, or blamed for Germany's decline or 'betrayal'. As she watched, feigning admiration, the words of the man on the platform added to and reinforced her complete dedication to her mission.

After the speech and further march pasts, they did not stay for later events, and at the appointed time, Baldur von Schirach appeared to lead them from the arena.

"Wasn't the Führer magnificent?" he exclaimed. "Now we can all rise to this great vision he has created for us." Turning to Greta, he said with an engaging smile, "Fraulein Atkins, I believe you are covering this for your magazine and I am informed you wish to feature leading players from our movement. I would be happy to grant you a personal interview and I will answer all questions candidly."

She knew his intentions, sensed them, and, despite herself, she was drawn to a situation which she also knew was dangerous. Greta was careful never to allow her personal feelings to override her duty. That had helped protect her over the years and enabled her to carry out her work without being compromised. "That would be an honour, Herr Gruppenführer," she found herself saying to this handsome, cultured officer.

"Then I will be equally honoured if you would join me for dinner afterwards," he responded, bowing to kiss her hand as she readily agreed. She knew she was kicking herself and yet buried her inner alarm with the justification of, *Why not? It can't do any harm.*

Charles Edward, who had extended the invitation to Sir Oswald Mosley to lead the BUF delegation to the rally, had been careful to insist that he also bring the 'delightful' Mitford ladies and 'that ravishing, Greta Atkins'. He knew that Diana Mitford was the mistress of Sir Oswald, but by inviting both sisters,
important appearances were being kept. Others there at the behest of Charles Edward as part of his drive to improve Anglo-German relations included MPs, ministers and those from the higher ranks of British society. Greta reflected ruefully on the irony that only fifteen years

before, many of those there had been on opposing sides and now they wanted to celebrate a remilitarisation of Germany.

As they were driven away, she turned to the Duke. "I hope you don't mind me dining with von Schirach, Charlie darling, but it will be such a scoop for us."

He waved the matter away as of no importance, telling her to give von Schirach 'a damned good grilling'. Charles Edward had developed a close friendship with Greta and was infatuated with her, but by carefully avoiding his advances, whilst always allowing a certain flirtatiousness in their times together, she was keeping him very interested. As Greta boasted to Colonel Menzies during one of her reports, "He sings like a canary if I just flutter my eyes; oh, the poor boy."

In that year, Hitler had become Chancellor and effectively wiped out any political opposition. Greta had gathered from the Duke that the Führer desired to develop an Anglo-German alliance against Russia on terms which, with the growing support that Charles Edward was building, were becoming a potential reality. A growing list of society names broadly supportive of Hitler had been compiled resulting from Greta's friendship with Charles Edward, and SIS began the process of infiltrating those under scrutiny, either through personal or official relationships.

Charles Edward's supremely secret role, he had told Greta, was to foster Royal sympathies towards the aims of the Nazis. However, the night before the rally, he had admitted something far more sinister after a dinner with much Champagne, grasping her hand as he revealed to her the Führer's masterplan. Hitler wanted the Duke to exploit his connections with powerful people in British society, establishing who might support the undermining of Parliamentary sovereignty with the aim of establishing a dictatorship following the German model but with Royal credentials.

"The Prince of Wales could assume a pivotal role, in the Führer's view, and restore respect to a more meaningful monarchy with real authority. After all, the people adore the man. This is pure genius, I think," the Duke had boasted to her.

Colonel Menzies was constantly pressing Greta for more information and had stated that the Munich Rally of that year was a perfect opportunity to capitalise on the trust she had gained. She had not yet had the opportunity to inform him of the latest alarming revelations. Whilst with the delegation in Nuremberg, it was impossible to communicate directly with London, but arrangements had been made for Greta to liaise with her 'old friend' Mona Maund, who was visiting Nuremberg University as part of her research work in Astrophysics. They had decided to meet and have tea in the late afternoon following the rally at the Hotel Deutsche Hof, which was where Hitler was staying, in a bold move in order not to draw suspicion.

They met on the corner of Frauentorgraben, making their way past crowds of brown-shirted men. The hotel was draped with numerous swastika flags hanging all the way round. On attempting to gain access, they were challenged by two guards. Greta showed the papers that Charles Edward had given her carrying his authority and they both clicked their heels smartly, giving the Nazi salute. Inside, they made their way into the tearoom adorned with photographs of the Führer and other notable visitors. They selected a corner table in a long room with large windows lining one side. Greta spoke openly about her extraordinary experience at the rally, for the benefit of anyone listening, their waiter smilingly remarking how wonderful it must have been. Then leaning forwards, she announced excitedly she was to interview Baldur von Schirach, head of the Hitler Youth, that evening, followed by dinner, causing Mona to gasp in surprise. As Greta spoke, she slid an envelope under the table into Mona's waiting hand, continuing to talk, as though nothing had taken place, in excited overtones about her experiences. They both openly agreed that this new Germany was such an exciting place to be with all the changes taking place.

After their tea, they hugged before parting, and Mona whispered to her, "Oh God, this is dreadfully dangerous, please be careful." They agreed to meet three days later for lunch in the hotel restaurant for Greta to pass on further briefings. As they left, a short man in a double-breasted trench coat rose from the table nearby, placing the notes he had taken into his pocket before following them out.

At 7.00pm precisely that evening, Greta watched the large Daimler car draw up outside the Hotel Victoria as arranged. Two men alighted in uniform, one standing by the vehicle and the other approaching the concierge, who in turn guided him to where she sat in the opulent reception lounge. The man clicked his heels. "Fraulein Atkins, *bitte*, I am Feldwebel Dieter Schneider, it is my duty to escort you to meet Gruppenführer von Schirach." Greta allowed herself to be escorted to the waiting vehicle, where the other man snapped to attention as he opened the door for her.

She had prepared for the interview by writing her core questions down, but, as customary, they were only a guide and she never necessarily stuck to script. She had dressed down, at least for her, as she felt was befitting for a first unescorted meeting. A black fitted Chanel suit, a knee-length skirt, cardigan-style jacket, trimmed and decorated with black embroidery and gold-coloured buttons seemed appropriate, together with a long set of pearl beads. The single-breasted jacket was fastened but her blouse allowed a hint of cleavage. Her outfit was completed with a half-white and half-black bag with matching shoes. As she climbed into the car she could not deny, despite an attempt at self-denial, a pang of excitement. It had been a long time since she had been wined and dined by someone she felt attracted to, and there was something about this man.

Within a few minutes they drew up at the very elegant exterior of the Grand Hotel on Bahnhofstrasse. Either side of the main entrance stood two armed guards in black uniforms whilst the red NSDAP banners hanging down the building added an irrevocable sense of confident authority and power. The door was opened, and the two guards stood to attention as she was escorted inside. As soon as she walked in, the manager of the hotel greeted her, bowing, before guiding her towards tall double doors at the end of a wide marble-floored corridor.

The manager knocked, then, on opening the door, he announced, "Herr Gruppenführer, it is my honour to present Fraulein Greta Atkins," at which point he stood to one side, allowing her entrance. The room was on a grand scale with pillars, a ceiling with a painted fresco and ornate velvet-covered furniture. Von Schirach, looking distinguished in a dapper double-breasted pinstriped suit, walked forwards, extending his arm, as she did likewise and he kissed her hand, bowing deeply.

"This is a great pleasure, Fraulein Atkins; perhaps we might dispel all the titles and use our real names. I am Benedikt; may I please call you Greta?"

He is quite charming and delightful, thought Greta, feeling disarmed within the first few seconds. He bade her sit on the crimson-covered chaise longue whilst he sat in a Chippendale chair opposite which placed him higher than her, which she sensed was, perhaps, to place her at a disadvantage.

"Herr GruppenFührer – sorry, Benedikt, may I commence by asking you a little of your background?"

"But of course," he responded, "that is why you are here, is it not?" The latter statement ended in a question which was slightly stressed and she sensed an element of flirtation. "Greta, once I have answered all, doubtless I shall have surrendered my life story, then the moment will have arrived when we can enjoy dinner. I trust that perhaps I might then get my revenge and ask a little of you?"

Greta was surprised to hear that he was of Sorbian origin from a Slavic region of Germany quite closely related to the Polish. He confessed that he may not be considered the typical Aryan that National Socialism embraced. He said he was of noble birth, however, which she had guessed, but that his mother was American and English had been his first language as a boy.

"In fact, Greta, I believe my American credentials are inalienable as two of my ancestors were signatories of the United States Declaration of Independence."

Greta was genuinely intrigued to find out what had drawn him to National Socialism, finding that her questions were as interesting to her personally as in her professional capacity as a journalist. Benedikt had been drawn to military service, like his father, and when his brother had committed suicide in the aftermath of the Great War, he became drawn to this movement which spoke out against the Treaty of Versailles and Germany's betrayal.

"I was an idealist at eighteen and wanted to achieve great things. By the time I was twenty-two, I was already running the Party Student's League, then I became leader of the Youth, then the Hitler Youth in 1933. It was so quick, but I felt I was making a difference for my country."

After an hour of giving very candid answers to her questions, Greta felt a genuine warmth towards Benedikt, sensing his in return. Impressed by his sincerity, she also found herself drawn to his charismatic nature, which she could not deny was rather delightful and very appealing.

6

Revelations

Monday 17th February 2020, 8.30am
Flughafen Hamburg (Hamburg Airport Helmut Schmidt)

As the flight touched down, Walter's sense of unease became heightened, making him agitated. All the words he had rehearsed over and over in the night and on the flight no longer flowed. He had made copious notes editing and adding more on the journey as he strived to remember dates, names and details. Leaving the aircraft, he suddenly felt very cold, pulling his fur-collared coat closely around him. His mind was full of jumbled facts; he wondered whether he might forget important details and appear completely incoherent and unreliable. The adrenalin from the shock of the murder he had been exposed to was far worse than any previous experience over his long career. In reality, he knew he was actually suffering from shock, shaking from time to time, and somehow, despite his nerves, he was relieved he could speak to someone. In the concourse he searched for the Radisson Blu Hotel, finding an exit sign that took him over a foot bridge from the terminal to the reception area. He texted Hans and waited anxiously for a response, looking back from where he had come as if expecting to be followed.

His mobile buzzed and the message said simply, "Please join me in the Circle Bar. How shall I recognise you?"

He responded he was carrying a zip file under his arm and was wearing a shirt and tie with a long black coat. Walter walked towards the bar, and as he entered, a tall man with slightly unfashionably long blondish hair rose from a corner seat in jeans, a grey anorak and black round-necked sweater.

Walter was first to speak. "Hans Schirach?" The other nodded. "*Wie geht es ihnen?* ['How are you?'] I am Walter – *mein Gott*, you look like your father," he exclaimed awkwardly, then apologised for his clumsy outburst.

Walter asked the younger man if there was somewhere they could go more privately, but Hans said he would like more information first, which he trusted Walter might understand. They sat in a quiet corner of the large modern bar.

Hans ordered two coffees and looked Walter straight in the eye. "Forgive my directness, but why have you contacted me?"

Walter unzipped the folder he was carrying, retrieving an old black and white photograph which he passed to Hans, showing a man in his forties smiling with his arm around a boy with mountains behind them. On the back of the photo was written, "*Dearest Gunther with Walter – December 1963.*" There was something in the photograph that made Hans tremble, anticipating what he knew was to follow. "This man is Gunther Roche; he is your father and that is me next to him as a boy."

Hans looked again at the tall, smiling man with the neat moustache, dressed in traditional Bavarian clothes, and there was no doubt of the likeness to himself. His heart was thumping as he was facing, for the first time, an image of a person that he had sought to know more of all his life.

"I think you need to tell me more; much, much more," he said curtly.

Walter nodded understandingly. "Of course, this will be a shock to you. I know that your birthday is 3rd November 1984 and that your place of birth is shown on your birth certificate as being Salzburg, Austria. I think you will agree that is correct?"

Hans was trying to maintain a calmness despite feeling completely thrown off balance and unprepared for this.

"Forgive me, let me introduce myself properly. I am Dr Walter Friedman, and I have a medical practice in Berchtesgaden. I can now tell you that I am the doctor who delivered you at birth when your father was present. Now, please may we go somewhere private?"

Hans briefly nodded and, after speaking to a receptionist, more coffee appeared, which was brought by a waiter who showed them into a meeting room, in the centre of which was a table surrounded by six chairs. A flip chart and a white board were at one end of the room; a single picture on the wall showed a view across the Norderelbe River in the centre of Hamburg with a boat framed against the Gustav Adolf Church Tower. They both sat opposite one another and the process of pouring the coffee seemed somewhat surreal in the moment. Walter unzipped his folder again, extracting his notes before reaching for another photograph.

"Here is another of your father on the right with my father taken during the war."

This time there were two men, and Hans took in the black SS dress uniform the man he now recognised as his father was wearing. The other man was in a lighter-coloured uniform which he knew was the field grey of the Wehrmacht.

"They are outside a fortification on the drive leading to the Berghof."

Hans was a journalist and he knew well that this was the mountain retreat of Adolf Hitler. Walter added, "You may begin to understand a little of why I have come to see you privately, but there is so much more."

Walter sighed deeply, wondering whether he should continue but knowing he must. He began relating to Hans the life he had known as a child living in the shadow of the Third Reich. He watched Hans's growing interest and astonishment as he spoke about the happy times he had spent with Gunther Roche and how, for a brief time, he had become like a heroic father figure to him, taking him climbing, sharing exciting stories and talking with enthusiasm about the glory days of the Reich. Walter told him that he recalled Gunther saying to him on many occasions that he knew the Führer personally and that he was a figure he revered. He felt a pang of sorrow for Hans, hearing both good and bad about his father in equal measure, mixed with guilt that Hans would never have the opportunity to know the warmth of this man that Walter had come to admire as a boy.

Despite Walter's initial admiration, he made clear to Hans that as he grew up, he became disillusioned with Gunther's unshakeable beliefs in a system which Walter viewed with distaste and horror. He recounted how they often held lively debates as he became more politically aware in his teens but stressed to Hans that his father never disparaged him for his views. "Your father and I became good friends despite our many differences, and I can tell you he was a good man even though you may despise his uniform and all it stood for."

Walter paused for a moment, dreading what he next had to say. "Hans, I am afraid I also have to tell you your father has passed away."

Hans sat back in his chair and gave out a long sigh even though he had been expecting as much. All his life he had nurtured the hope he would meet his father and share with him his hopes and beliefs, learning what it was like to truly belong. He had become hardened since learning his craft in investigative journalism, a position in which he excelled, but suddenly he was a real person like many of those whose lives he probed into, and he felt disorientated.

"Herr Doctor, I am truly sorry if I have been abrupt with you, but you will appreciate there is much to absorb."

They shook hands and Walter got up to look out of the window. "I hardly know where to start with this, but I can tell you that your mother knows everything and has tried to protect you all your life. She knows too that upon your father's death, I would be telling you what I am about to say. Your father wished that I reveal everything to you, some of which you will not wish to hear, but I promised I would do so."

Walter returned to the table and selected another photograph from his file, which he stated he had been given by Gunther ten years before. At first glance, there was nothing strange about the image except that the quality was better and it was much larger than the others. Clearly professionally taken, it showed Gunther Roche in a black SS uniform, wearing the Iron Cross, with just the hint of a smile but projecting a steely look in his eyes. His body was angled away slightly, so that his head was turned to stare at the camera in an authoritative manner.

"Perhaps, as you look at this, you may think nothing remarkable, but then there are two things you should notice; the first is that your father is wearing the uniform of an SS Oberstgruppenführer. That is one rank below Reichsführer-SS, a title which was held uniquely by the supreme commander, Heinrich Himmler, until 1945. Now, please turn over the photograph to see the second noticeable feature."

As he slowly turned the picture over, Hans's eyes widened before letting out the expletive, *"Lieber Gott in Himmel."* On the reverse was stamped 'Reichskonferenz – July 1954 – Buenos Aires', beneath which was an eagle clutching a swastika.

"I have no knowledge of your father's movements at this time except that he visited us occasionally, although I never saw him from 1972 until 1984."

The younger man whistled his shock, shaking his head as if unable to comprehend it.

"It is a lot to take in, Hans, I know." Walter patted him on the shoulder before returning to his seat. "But I regret there is much more." Walter extracted another image, this time in colour, of another man in a brown Nazi uniform, with his arm extended, standing next to Hitler, in front of which there were marching youths. "Do you recognise this person?" he asked.

Hans looked carefully, as there was something familiar about this rather imposing figure. He had seen countless images of Nazi leaders from that period but only recognised some of the major players. It was not an area he had covered except in his early days of journalism when he had tried to expose some war criminals who were still at large. However, he had been told then not to probe further as it was too sensitive and warned that he should consider his career.

"This man is Baldur Benedikt von Schirach, who headed up the Hitler Youth before the war, and he was in the inner circle of the Führer. I can also confirm, Hans, that he is your great-grandfather."

Hans placed his head in his hands, then, shaking himself, he looked at Walter. "Jesus Christ, do you fancy a drink?"

Within minutes, a bottle of Schnapps was on the table and they downed two large measures.

"I presume you have proof of all this?" Hans asked, to which Walter responded he could check with his mother. Walter told him that von Schirach had had an affair with a British secret agent in 1933, and they had a son, Siegfried.

"He was brought up by nominated foster parents like many thousands under the Nazi Lebensborn programme which they set up to produce perfect Aryan children sired by nominated fathers. Siegfried had been placed with foster parents because neither parent could risk being part of the potential scandal. He was fortunate to be looked after by decent people, enjoying a good education, and ended up working in local government. He married your grandmother, Hanna, in 1954, and they had a daughter in 1955. She is Eva, your mother. Sadly, Siegfried died of cancer ten years later. In 1974, von Schirach died, and, at that time, his former British lover wrote to Hanna telling her of the identity of her husband's father."

Walter paused, pouring more drinks, and they both touched their glasses together as if toasting the moment. "Hanna naturally shared her daughter's heritage with Eva. Your mother was young and was initially fascinated by her family connection and began attending the covert National Socialist conventions taking place at that time, becoming quite involved. It was at such an event that she met your father in February 1984 and that is when you were conceived.

"The night of your birth, I was called by your father, who asked if he could come to my surgery, saying he had an emergency. When he arrived, he ushered in a woman who was in labour. She was your mother and I delivered you within an hour. I was sworn to secrecy and told that it was imperative no-one learned who was the father. Your birth was registered just over the border in Austria to avoid being traced back to Gunther. This was arranged through *Die Spinne* network which helps ex-Nazis who served the Third Reich. Eva was a wonderful mother to you and I know this because she and I have remained in touch at the behest of your father. This allowed him to support your upbringing financially, which he arranged through me. He always wanted to learn about your progress, in which he took great interest."

Hans interrupted, "What happened to my father?"

It was an inevitable question and Walter paused, hardly wishing to add to the revelations he had already given. "Your father and I became very close as I performed my role of go-between, and especially so in recent years. I knew the work he was involved with was highly secret, but I never probed, respecting our friendship. I always thought he was on the verge of telling me something, but then he would hold back. Hans, there is information I have to give you which is very important. Your Father said there was an expression that protected a secret he had sworn to keep until death, but it was haunting him. He called it '*eins zu eins*' and that hundreds of thousands of lives had been lost because of it. He also told me that I should never repeat the expression to anyone but you, or my life would be at risk. He did say that he held the key to this secret which, if revealed, was so great that it could destabilise the entire structure of the Western democracies, undermine political institutions and potentially lead to conflict, whilst having the potential to destroy the EU in one stroke. I have come to give you this key.

"In his final days, your father was in exceptionally good health for his age, possessing the fitness of a much younger man, even still shooting as a hobby. He was strong, unrepentant for his life, and I respected that, as he respected my views. I was with him only days ago, and there was nothing wrong with him. There never was anything wrong with him, but I have terrible news for you. They killed him." The doctor faltered in his words. "I signed his death certificate, but I can tell you, despite what it says, he did not die of a stroke. I am very sorry."

Hans looked directly at Walter, shaking his head as if not comprehending what had been said. "Please, Herr Doktor, who killed him? Tell me what happened to him."

Pausing for a moment, Walter sighed, knowing this was the time. "He was shot, and I can also tell you that the Bundesnachrichtendienst are involved. My God, Hans, I have dealt with their kind all my life and you have no idea what they are capable of. Nazi Germany has not been defeated; it is here right now, but in a very different form. They no longer goose-step the streets or hold great rallies. They do not need to because, as your father told me, there is already a New World Order that overrides democracy and nation states. I know they are ruthless because I have lived with them, benefitted from them, and lied for them." Walter looked at the young man before him whom he had brought into the world and suddenly wondered whether he had done the right thing meeting him.

"When I was at your father's house one day, he asked me to fetch a large folder he had placed in the side attic inside his bedroom. He showed me photographs of what he called 'the great days', and that was a subject that we used to have banter over. However, on this one occasion, he said that he had left a trail for you because the Reich had been betrayed in 1944 and, like the Führer after the Great War in 1918, he wanted that to be avenged. He said there was one document that would be the final key that you need to unlock what he described as the

'Barbarossa Secret'. Your father entrusted me with a copy of that document to give to you after his death and he stressed that you should know there are only two other copies, but he did not tell me where. He hoped you might use it to expose the betrayal, but his greatest wish was that you use it to protect yourself."

Walter retrieved a large thick brown envelope from his document holder which was sealed with round red wax on the flap, into which a swastika was imprinted. "This has never been opened and I have no idea of its contents. Finally, Hans, he said that he was tortured by the fact he never met you nor told you he loved you, which was the biggest regret of his life. This all represents the final wish from your father: that you know the truth. Please keep this folder and the photographs. I want you to realise the danger we are all in, and part of me never wanted to contact you, but I gave my word to your father."

Walter stopped and pulled a plastic card from his inside pocket, giving it to Hans.

"I have much on my conscience, and in order to assuage this, I decided, some years ago, to make contact with an organisation which collates information on the Nazis and their kind. They provide complete anonymity, confidentiality and advice, even offering to protect my life. They know of me by name and if you are in trouble, just call this number. Ask for Rubin Horowitz, who will give you any help you need."

Walter took up a notepad, scribbling the name down before passing it to Hans, who looked at the card. It was printed with a plain dark blue top and bottom split by a white centre, on which was a curious but faintly familiar blue star logo with what appeared to be a flame emanating from the top left point. In the centre was a telephone number with '24 hours' written after in brackets. There was nothing else on the card, which Hans slipped into his wallet.

Walter felt a wave of relief flow through him as though a huge weight had been lifted, but suddenly, he felt exhausted and emotionally drained. He slumped in his chair, finally breaking down, both at the grief he felt and a life he had allowed to be usurped by others. This time it was Hans who offered the comfort, thanking Walter for his honesty and for fulfilling his father's wishes.

Walter shook his hand solemnly. "I have one last item for you and I can tell you your father was very proud of it." He pulled the Iron Cross from his pocket, suspending it from its ribbon before giving it to Hans. "This is the Knight's Cross of the Iron Cross with Oak Leaves, Swords and Diamonds. This was given to your father by Adolf Hitler personally. I know that he was a deserving recipient as a very brave man, whatever you may think of his motives. There were only ever twenty-eight recipients of this." Hans took the medal, carefully folding the ribbon with an almost reverent respect for his father, despite the utter revulsion he had felt for the Nazi regime all his adult life.

Before they parted, Walter insisted that they left separately and that Hans should leave first by a staff exit from the hotel. It all seemed a little surreal, but Walter was insistent, repeating again that the various factions in Germany were utterly ruthless in the pursuit of their aims. No-one took any notice of a solitary figure clutching a document holder, leaving from a side exit door a short time later just as Walter appeared at the bar, ordering two drinks before returning to the meeting room. Thirty minutes later, a tall, bulky man in a black leather jacket rose as Dr Friedman exited the hotel, heading back into the airport whilst others outside watched for anyone else leaving the reception exit, noting the numbers of departing vehicles.

7

Triumph of the Will

Tuesday 28th January 1936, 4.00pm
St George's Chapel, Windsor, England

For Charles Edward, it had already been an exhausting day, attired in the heavy full-dress uniform of a Stormtrooper (SA) general of the German army, complete with a *Pickelhaube* traditional spiked helmet. His dress had already drawn much bemused attention by members of the Royal Family as they had gathered to begin the procession through the streets of London behind the Union Jack-draped coffin of the late King George V atop a gun carriage. However, Charles Edward felt proud, not only to be included as part of the procession but in fully displaying his loyalty to Germany and the Reich. The Führer had made it clear that this was the time to evaluate loyalties, apply the right pressures and ensure the foundations were put in in place for his great strategy. Now, as they left St George's Chapel, mindful of his mission, he felt the hand of destiny upon him. He did not have to wait long for the opportunity to present itself.

"Charlie, dear boy, how the devil are you?" were the surprisingly cheerful words of the former Prince of Wales, now King Edward VIII, slapping him on the back as they entered the private apartments. "Listen here, old chap, I'd rather like to arrange a brief chit chat if you are free before dinner, which is going to be a pretty tedious affair. The ghastly thing is we are going to have to stay in our uniforms, but I actually quite like yours, damnably much smarter than ours."

Charles Edward turned to the King, solemnly expressing his sympathy at the loss of his father, a great monarch who was respected throughout the world.

"Yes, too dreadful," the King replied, "but he had been ill for some time and now he's left the whole beastly business of ruling the country to me. Somehow, I'm thinking all the fun in life might have to be extinguished."

They agreed to meet in the Prince's private rooms, which he still occupied, politely excusing themselves to other guests.

Half an hour later, Charles Edward was escorted down a series of corridors to a modest study by a liveried member of the Royal Household and asked to await 'His Majesty'. He sat in a high-backed leather armchair, staring at the paintings of former princes arranged around the room, quickly rising and bowing as the new King entered, his accession having been proclaimed on 21st January 1936, the day after King George V's death.

"Let's forget the protocol, Charlie. Please just call me David when we are in private." He smiled at Charles Edward warmly, and the two shook hands in the manner of a friendly greeting. "I have someone I'd like you to meet," he announced, "but don't tell anyone or I'll probably get locked up in the Tower."

He left the room and then the sounds of a raised female voice and giggling could be heard. Re-entering, the King announced, "May I present the future Queen of England, Wallis, currently a Simpson, but let's not mention that. Darling, this is our frightful German relative, the Duke of Saxe-Coburg and Gotha, but we call him Charlie. He's a chum of Adolf Hitler and a member of the Reichstag."

Of course, Charles Edward had been fully briefed about the relationship between Edward and Wallis, but the meeting came as a shock. He bowed to her, kissing her extended hand.

"Oh, I am so very disappointed, Charlie," she said, giving him a dazzling smile. "I was hoping you would do one of those wonderful Nazi salutes." Her American drawl added to the friendly informality.

The King bade them both sit, pouring drinks from a tall crystal decanter, then sat by Wallis on a Chesterfield settee. "Wallis may stay, Charlie – I want her to hear this. I am informed by friends that just over a year ago, your chap von Ribbentrop, the Commissioner for Disarmament, met with a number of people here, many of whom I know very well. Moreover, you too seem to be cultivating many friendships here with those, shall we say, of note. I have it on good account that you believe there will be a time when there will be the need for an Anglo-German pact or alliance against Communist Russia. Furthermore, a little bird informs me that you also think British democracy would be well served by more power being concentrated at the top. My problem, dear Charlie, is that I do not know where all that would leave me, and please understand we are talking hypothetically and in the strictest confidence."

He opened a silver box, offering it first to Wallis, who took a cigarette, sliding it into a holder, and taking one for himself after Charles Edward declined.

"Your Majesty," Charles Edward stumbled for a moment, struggling to address the King more informally, "the Führer has made it very clear to me that it is a matter of the highest priority that we stand united against Communism. Their aggression would put paid to all the good work we have put in to build peace. Herr Ribbentrop has assumed ambassadorial duties across the Reich and I understand he is building connections with those who have sympathy with our aims. On the key area upon which you have touched, I can categorically assure you, sir, that it is because Hitler believes in powerful leadership that he concludes your rank and status is uniquely suited to the development of Britain in the future, a view shared by so many of your loyal subjects."

The new monarch took a long draw on his cigarette then put his head back in thought as he exhaled, gazing upwards towards the panelled ceiling, "Then, my dear chap, you should accompany us to Sandringham, as I think we have much to discuss. Right now, however, we must rejoin our guests and try to enjoy this frightful business as we dine in St George's Hall. A cosy late lunch with three hundred others, what a bore!"

Thursday 30th January 1936, 1.00pm
HQ SIS, 54 Broadway, Westminster,
London Office of the Deputy Director

Colonel Menzies stood up as Greta entered and, unusually for him, walked around his desk to greet her with a firm handshake before gesturing to her to sit. "Sorry you've been so poorly – dreadful nuisance, this TB. How was the healthcare in Germany?"

She looked more drawn than he had seen on previous occasions but was still striking in a somewhat overstated outfit which, as usual, would undoubtedly draw attention. She wore long, baggy white trousers, a figure-hugging dark blue top teasingly cut above the bust, with a large jewelled pendant, over which a black tailored pinstripe jacket with a white top pocket hanky completed the look. A beret was perched at a jaunty angle over her long curly hair swept back revealing earrings matching her pendant.

"It was awful, Colonel, but they looked after me well, assisted greatly by the influence of Charlie."

"And of von Schirach?" he asked quizzically, peering over his glasses. She felt his eyes boring into her. Her pulse quickened but, despite the enquiring direct look from the colonel, she did not flinch, calmly replying, "Oh, he was marvellous, initially arranging the best healthcare for me, but

I have hardly seen or heard from him since my illness. I never could get much from him and I think he found my relationship with Charlie rather tiresome and lost interest. The man had only been married just over a year when I met him, so he should learn to damn well behave. You men can be simply impossible, you know," she said with a coquettish look that always made the colonel sigh.

This was the first meeting she had attended at the colonel's office for nearly two years, although she had continued to feed intelligence information gleaned during her stay in Germany. In February 1934, Greta had informed the colonel that she was going to meet Hitler, having been invited by von Schirach to visit the Berghof, accompanied by Charles Edward. However, on her return to Germany, she had fallen ill and was unable to go. After her illness, she had offered to remain in Germany for a period, fostering relationships within the Nazi leadership, who enjoyed entertaining her as a member of British society who could be trusted. Mona Maund would visit her and she would pass messages and reports to her and receive instructions from the colonel via the same route. The Gestapo had started to watch Mona after the Nuremberg Rally of 1933, reporting their suspicions that she may be a spy to Heinrich Himmler. However, because Greta was under the protection of Baldur von Schirach and Charles Edward, Himmler had decided not to take action until it suited him, recognising that when the time was right, compromising others in the Party could assist in furthering his own ends.

In answer to the colonel's questions over her treatment and healthcare, she briefly spoke about the months spent in the sanatorium and the slow road to recovery, dismissing it in her customary stoic way. "It was all rather disagreeable really, and very inconvenient."

The colonel paused as though he was about to say something, but then reached for a thick file and took out a sheaf of papers held by a clip. He stated that this was a list of highly influential people who were now not only openly supportive of Hitler but who were suspected of being sympathetic to the idea of changes to British democracy.

"This is, in effect, treason. However, if they were involved in a plot against the monarchy, it would be high treason. The nightmare would be, would it not, if the monarchy were part of this. Your friend the Duke of Saxe-Coburg and Gotha has been invited to Sandringham this weekend by no less than the King. I think it would be good for your health to attend, as it were, and I'm sure the King would welcome your company, if not only to keep his damned floozy Wallis Simpson happy. Rumour has it that the King is not exclusive amongst her admirers and, perhaps, lovers. You might pursue that line of enquiry as well as seeing what the good Duke is up to. It is common knowledge that a number of guests from the funeral are going to Sandringham, so it will be very easy for you to ask Charles Edward if you can be invited. He is staying at the Ritz so you may wish to call him now." He gestured to the telephone.

It was more of an order than a request, but Greta was used to his ways, often telling him how impossible he was. She was put through to Charles Edward's room and they arranged to meet for cocktails within the hour. Colonel Menzies concluded the meeting by checking she felt well enough to carry out her mission, which was a nicety as he expected her sense of duty to overcome any other issue. Her retort that her delicate state of health would shield her virtue merely resulted in another customary sigh before she left. As the door closed, he chuckled to himself, shaking his head.

Two hours later, Greta emerged from the Ritz into the early evening darkness feeling very pleased with herself, having secured her invitation to join the royal party and feeling warmed by three cocktails. Charles Edward escorted her to the taxi, looking forward to their rendezvous for dinner later at Claridge's, one of his favourite haunts.

Arriving at her apartment in Portman Square, she looked up to see the curtains closed on what was her lounge, which she knew was not how her maid would have left the room. The front door was closed, but her instinct told her something was very wrong and she decided to go to the lower rear entrance round the side of the building. Slipping the key in the door at the bottom of the steps quietly, she entered the old scullery, listening for a moment before creeping in. Whilst she thought she might call the police, she had been in tough situations previously and this was no different, except it was in her own home. Slowly she edged her way up the back stairs, hoping she had left the door open at the top. She listened again, but there was total silence. Finally, she reached the door, which was ajar, and she opened it inch by inch, straining to hear any sounds. As she peered around the edge, she felt, rather than saw, the cold metal of a gun being pressed against her temple.

"Move! Upstairs, now," the voice commanded in a pronounced German accent. Greta's heart was pounding hard, the adrenalin making her breathless, almost disorientated. He was just behind her, the weapon now against her neck. Her thoughts were in turmoil as she tried to evaluate survival strategies, but much would depend on whether he was alone. However, on entering her sitting room, another man in a dark double-breasted suit was waiting. He was thickset, with swept-back dark hair, and she recognised the heavy gangster type often used by security services for certain more physical aspects of their work. She glanced around the room; drawers were open with the contents strewn across the floor and it was obvious that her apartment had been searched.

"You will reply to each question we ask," the man behind her snapped. "If you do not, you will not leave here alive. It matters not to me one way or the other. Do you speak German?"

She nodded; her mind was racing, but she appeared calm as she was told to sit in an armchair whilst the man holding the gun pulled up a long stool which he placed opposite to her.

He told the other man to watch over them whilst 'we talk', which meant that his companion now took control of the gun. "I will not give my name, but I work for the Dienststelle Ribbentrop and we are not official, so understand we are not bound by the normal rules. So, you will now answer my questions. Who is Mona Maund?" Greta's thoughts were to put him more at ease by answering whatever she could truthfully or inserting elements that interrogators would know to be true. This was part of the training she had undergone when she had joined SIS. "She is a friend of mine from university."

The man opposite her had short cropped hair, which was greyed at the edges, and was dressed in a long black coat, beneath which he wore a tie not quite pulled to the neck. His eyes were hard, with no emotion, and his whole bearing appeared utterly ruthless.

"When did you last see her in Germany?" His voice was harsh.

Greta thought for a moment, then: "We met a number of times because she was studying there. We saw each other in 1933 when I was in Nuremberg for the rally and she visited me in 1934 when I was recovering from my recent illness, but I have not seen her since my return."

The man looked at her, his eyes narrowing. "How long has she been working for the British Government?"

She looked back at him directly, sensing his slight unease with her confidence. "She works in academia as far as I am aware, doing research into astrophysics. I was not aware she was with any Government department."

"I will ask you more directly." The man sighed impatiently. "How long have you known she works for the Intelligence Service?"

Greta knew she had to give them something. "I think she was doing something on the quiet when we were at university, but she called it hush-hush and we kind of didn't talk about it much, although I did push her a little on it when I started in journalism."

She began coughing repeatedly, explaining, as she gasped, that she was still recovering from the effects of TB. She said she needed her handkerchief and reached for her handbag, asking, between breathless spluttering, for a glass of water. He curtly ordered the man holding the gun to go, taking the weapon from him. She was struggling for breath and her coughs became more pronounced in between trying to speak.

He snapped towards the door. "Dieter, for Christ's sake, get the goddamned water quickly." Then it was his turn to face the barrel of a gun as he turned back to her.

She stood back quickly with the words: "I am a marksman and I never miss." She fired at an ornament close to him, which shattered. "Gun on floor now," she shouted. The German complied immediately, placing his hands on his head. His colleague ran into the room, her next shot hitting him in the arm. He collapsed, writhing and moaning.

"Now I will talk and you two bastards will listen. *Verstehen!* ['Understand!']" she shouted in an almost military tone. "I am under the protection of Gruppenführer Charles Edward Gotha, who is here in London and reports directly to the Führer. I am a friend of Reichsjugendführer and Gruppenführer Baldur von Schirach. I am also a friend of Unity Mitford, who is currently staying with the Führer as his personal guest. One call from me and you will both be shot if I do not do this myself. You pigs come in here claiming you work for Ribbentrop's outfit. You better have a good explanation when I inform Hitler himself about who has raided my home."

"Please, Fraulein," her former interrogator pleaded, "we are just obeying orders." The other man looked up at her, saying weakly that he needed a doctor.

She picked the phone up and dialled a special police number, keeping them both covered with her gun. "I grew up with guns and was trained by soldiers. This is my favourite, a Baby Browning, and I am deadly with it" Greta hissed at them. "If you ever come to this apartment or anywhere near me again, I will kill you without hesitation."

They knew she meant it and, at that moment, she really did.

Two hours later, they were both in police custody, pending interrogation and diplomatic exchanges, whilst Greta was arriving at Claridge's in a dazzling silver dress, gathering all eyes upon her as she was greeted by Charles Edward. She told him that her flat had been raided by German Intelligence but that the police had intervened, not giving further details other than to say it was because she had a friend whom they suspected worked for the British Government. She insisted that it was better the matter was left there, as she knew already of competing factions of the Nazi Party and did not want his position compromised. The Duke agreed, deciding he would say nothing unless approached on the matter when he returned to Germany.

Saturday 1st February 1936
Sandringham Castle Estate, Norfolk, England

They had travelled by train from St Pancras, via King's Lynn, to the tiny station of Wolferton at 10.00 am. There, a royal guard lining the platform awaited the disembarking guests. Outside, Duke Charles Edward and Greta were invited to climb into a large Rolls-Royce for the journey to Sandringham, only ten minutes away. On arrival at the estate, they turned through huge double intricate iron gates into a winding drive before entering a straight majestic boulevard approach to the front of the house. A grand archway entrance faced them, flanked by three-storey-high windows topped by gothic-style arched roofs over an impressive redbrick building. To the left were additional buildings forming a half courtyard, into which the Rolls swept, turning to bring them close by the entrance, where liveried staff were lined up in black uniforms with red waistcoats.

They were approached by a footman, who bowed, asking them to follow him. They traversed a large long room which their guide informed them was the saloon, with three huge arches dominating the space, above which a wooden gallery added to the grandeur, all watched over by portraits of Queen Victoria and Prince Albert. They were then led down a long corridor with walls covered in a mixture of paintings of country scenes and various personages in dress ranging from the Tudor period to the nineteenth century. The footman took them up some stairs to a drawing room overlooking the garden, inviting them to sit. Within minutes, the King entered, accompanied by Wallis Simpson.

"Your Majesty," began Charles Edward, "might I introduce a very good friend of mine, Miss Greta Atkins, whose people hail from Norfolk."

Edward VIII bowed deeply then gave Greta a dazzling smile. "You must call me David, my dear Greta, when we are in private. I can't bear all this stuff and nonsense all the time. Where have you been hiding her, Charlie? She is simply ravishing."

The King introduced Greta to Wallis Simpson, and Greta curtsied, thinking it was the right thing to do. Wallis giggled, telling her she was a little premature as, "I'm just a commoner. I can't think why David allows me to sit in the same room."

They all laughed as Greta confessed she had no 'title' or rank either.

"David, at last I have found another common woman; I'm sure this one will not bore me like some of your other friends," Wallis remarked, her relaxed way putting Greta instantly at ease.

The doors opened and the same footman entered who had greeted them, this time with a silver tray on which drinks were served. The King offered round cigarettes from a marble box before lighting one himself, addressing Charles Edward: "I wanted to spend a little time with you, old chap, to touch on what we spoke of after the funeral. Need to do it this morning, as I will not be staying tonight. Can't bear it here. The only reason I've come to this stuffy old place is because there are still some wretched guests who need to be attended to after the funeral. I find it all so damned suffocating. It reminds me of the staggeringly tedious times I spent here with my father. A car will take Wallis and I away after dinner to a house not far away, where we are staying with friends. My brother, Bertie, will look after you both tomorrow. There is a shoot if you wish, and the ladies will all congregate, led by my sister-in-law, Elizabeth. Plenty to do and see if you like that sort of thing."

They drank their pink gins together, after which Wallis invited Greta to join her in a private apartment where they could talk.

The King walked to the window, looking out over the gardens and countryside beyond. Lighting another cigarette, he turned to Charles Edward. "A direct question. Exactly what does your Führer want to see happen here? I will not allow my country to be torn apart by strife, nor could I countenance violence on the streets." His look was resolute, focussed and unwavering.

Charles Edward sensed the unease behind the question and knew his response was key to the success or otherwise of his latest mission which, only days before, had been given to him by Hitler.

"Sir, neither the Führer nor myself would wish any change to be achieved where civil unrest might result. In Germany, we have transformed our government with the endorsement of the people. The Führer wants to see a strong ally in Britain and believes that the Royal institution is suited to greater authority than your government permits. The late King, your father, intervened in parliamentary sovereignty, using his considerable powers to force the government's hand on the Irish question in both 1914 and 1924. These actions showed that those in your parliament still hold the monarchy in great esteem. Political power is changing across Europe, sir. Our concern is that democracy may not deliver the strong leadership we need to stand up to Communism and Socialism, with their anarchist agendas. The imperative is that we jointly face the threat from Russia."

The King sighed deeply. "My dear Charlie, I am part of a constitutional monarchy and it must not be perceived that I might wish to change this, no matter how frustrating this can be from time to time. I cannot help but feel I am like a bird with its wings clipped and, perhaps, envy the powers now assumed by your leader. However, one must question. Are there not dangers of power excesses? I am concerned about

Hitler's rebuilding of the German military and talk of expansion. I cannot imagine anything worse than another conflict with the carnage caused by modern weaponry and the horrors we experienced in the Great War. For that reason, I must make it clear that I would not sanction war nor use my position to influence others to support such an aim."

Charles Edward recognised he now needed to push the point to gauge the King's reaction. "Sir, many of the most influential in society in this country are concerned about the threat from Russia and from left-wing elements here who could become part of an insurgency. Surely, it is better that we, at least, appear to have a united front prepared to stand against Bolshevism represented by strong powers such as Italy, Germany and Great Britain. To that aim, the Führer believes that Germany may need to expand eastwards to secure within its borders those who are more naturally German, but that does not need to precipitate war. A greater Germany will provide a buffer against Russia. So much is changing in Europe; in Spain, the military have made it clear they may not put up with a left-wing government if one is re-elected this month. We must be strong and resolute in our defence of decent standards and order."

The King walked across to Charles Edward, pulling a chair directly opposite the man who was first cousin to his late father and a grandson of Queen Victoria and Prince Albert, sensing the kinship. "Charlie, please tell your friend Mr Hitler that we broadly share his concerns but not, perhaps, his expansionism. I am happy to permit, without being seen to, your continued discussions with those holding sympathetic views. However…" the King paused, pointing his finger at Charles Edward, "if I sense one jot of treason, or a lack of patriotism, I will equally use all my influence to resist and, I can assure you, to crush any such move."

When Greta and Charles Edward left on the Sunday afternoon, after a morning's shooting followed by a lunch served in an estate lodge, they both felt a sense of fulfilment. Wallis Simpson had welcomed Greta as a fellow 'commoner' and had given an insight into the future direction she thought David would adopt towards the policies being advanced by

Hitler. She had told Greta that the King thought Hitler was a somewhat ridiculous figure, but he admired his strength. He had informed Wallis that he wanted the monarchy to flourish under his direction and assume more vitality. Further, he was not averse to considering the use of the Royal Prerogative, despite this not having been formally exercised for over two hundred years. Wallis had also confided in her that she enjoyed 'playful flirtations', justifying them with: "I simply adore the attention of charming men." She had leant towards Greta, as if sharing a naughty secret, before saying in a low voice, "I've got quite a crush on that German ambassador chap, Joachim von Ribbentrop; he just looks so irresistible in uniform. Got to have a little fun before being Queen, don't you think?" There was much to report to the colonel.

The Duke, albeit not obtaining the tacit approval of the monarch for German expansion, had established some royal empathy towards the Führer's position and consent to progress his mission to build alliances within influential society. He was looking forward to his return to Berlin and making his report in person to Hitler.

8

The Shock of History

Monday 17th February 2020, 6.30pm
Offices of Der Spiegel, Ericusspitze 1, 20457 Hamburg

The security officer on the gate hardly raised an eyebrow as he drove up to the barrier. "Hans Schirach, political department," and he was through into the underground car park.

He had left the Radisson Blu Hotel at Hamburg Airport over two hours before but had diverted to Planten un Blomen, a park about three miles from his office. Clutching the document holder in his arms, he had walked aimlessly, turning over and over the events of the day. All his life, he had wondered about his father, even what it was like to have a father, and the thought that he had been alive only days before haunted him. *I could have met him,* mein Gott, *after all this time.* He sat on a rock at the small lake facing the pagoda by the Japanese gardens. It was cold and the light was fading, but it was somehow tranquil. Pulling the photographs out, he looked at each in turn, particularly liking the one of his father in the more relaxed pose with Dr Friedman as a boy. *That could have been me,* he thought fleetingly but very sadly. It was as though he was seeing the man rather than the soldier, unlike the other photos. Although he had to admire the appearance of Gunther Roche in the uniform of an SS Oberst-Gruppenführer, the image awed and horrified him in equal proportion, projecting such a powerful if not daunting look. As the light failed, he decided to go to his office; home did not seem the right place to settle his thoughts into a practical plan.

At his desk, having closed the door, he prised out a large brown envelope from the document holder Dr Friedman had given him. Placing it on the desk, he looked at the crimson seal with the National Socialist Reichsadler emblem of an eagle holding the swastika, hardly daring to reveal the contents. He tore the flap of the envelope around the seal in order not to disturb it, although reflected that it was not of acceptable historic value in today's world, where such items had become unwanted reminders of the past. He carefully slid out the contents, comprising a smaller thick envelope with his name on it scrawled in long right slanting handwriting; what appeared to be a legal document printed on two folded pieces of thick cream paper, which, from its discolouration at the edges, showed it to be many years old; and a further folded sheet of A4 paper. His natural curiosity as a journalist took him to the older yellowing document first. It was not well worn and had obviously rarely been opened. He slowly and carefully unfolded it, revealing paragraphs of typed text, but it was the signatures that immediately drew his attention, his eyes widening in disbelief and incredulity at what he was seeing. His heart was thumping as he began to realise the ramifications of what was being revealed.

On the bottom left side was a signature he had seen before, that of Adolf Hitler, next to a circular stamp of the eagle around which were the words 'Der Führer und Reichskanzler'. The date was handwritten underneath, 16th July 1944. Beneath this was another signature which was simply one word, 'Rommel', under which was typed 'Feldmarschall Erwin Rommel, Commander Army Group B'. However, it was what he saw on the right side of the document that astounded him, making him shake his head in disbelief. *"Du lieber Gott,"* he breathed out loud.

Towards the base of the document was the signature 'Dwight D Eisenhower' above the title 'Supreme Allied Commander – Allied Expeditionary Forces' with a handwritten date of 17th July 1944. Beneath this was an easily legible handwritten 'B.L. Montgomery – General', with the title 'Bernard L Montgomery, General Commanding 21st Army Group' also on 17th July 1944.

The words within the document were written in English, which Hans spoke fluently, and his surprise turned to total shock as he read:

TOP SECRET
OPERATIONAL ORDERS
Applying to
ALL GERMAN ARMED FORCES IN EUROPE
AND ELSEWHERE
And
ALL ALLIED ARMED FORCES (EXCLUDING THE USSR)
IN EUROPE AND ELSEWHERE

1. The German Government and Governments of those Countries represented by the Allied Forces (excluding the USSR) have indicated a desire to reach a peace settlement which may be imminently concluded.

2. In the event this settlement is concluded the Führer and Chancellor of Germany has ordered that, upon the command being given under clause 7 herein, the German High Command will immediately surrender all German Armed Forces to the command of the Allied Forces but the command structures and ranks of existing German personnel shall not be changed unless for essential operational reasons.

3. These Operational Orders commit the Armed Forces in the land, sea and air of both the German and the Allied Armed Forces to combine under the Command of the Supreme Allied Commander and to jointly resist in the event of any threats of aggression or attacks by the Red Army of the Soviet Union against Allied or German Forces.

4. The overall authority of the Führer over German forces shall remain and all German ranks are bound by their oath of loyalty to the Führer.

5. The territorial integrity of Germany, Austria and the Rhineland shall be guaranteed and any attempts by the Red Army to invade any territory currently governed by or allied to Germany shall be resisted by whatever military means are necessary.

6. Germany shall immediately commence withdrawal of all forces from France without hinderance by the Allies and surrender the means of government to the Free French under the command of General Charles de Gaulle, hereinafter known as the Provisional Government of the French Republic.

7. Confirmation of these orders becoming immediately operational shall be the password 'Barbarossa' which will be jointly given by the Führer of Germany and the Supreme Allied Commander, at which point all hostilities must cease forthwith between the armed forces of the Allies and Germany.

8. Once the password is given, the German High Command and all ranks of the German Forces will obey and execute all orders given by the Supreme Allied Commander without argument or comment.

9. The decision of the Supreme Allied Commander will be final if any dispute arises on the interpretation of this agreement or on any operational matters.

10. Disobedience of any orders in relation to the execution of these Operational Orders will be considered a serious matter and dealt with under the laws and jurisdiction of the country in which the perpetrator resides.

> *Signed separately at the Reich Chancellery Berlin by the*
> *Führer and Reich Chancellor*
>   *and by the Supreme Allied Commander*
>   *and by Field Military Commanders*
>   *of Allied and German Forces at Colombelles, Normandy*

The place of signing and the date of the signatures of Eisenhower Rommel and Montgomery were handwritten. Hans placed the document back on his desk, trying to take in all he had seen. The day had already been overwhelming and he hardly dared examine either of the two remaining items. He decided on a quick and strong coffee from his personal office machine before taking a deep breath and unfolding the next piece of paper. He was no longer surprised to see the eagle and swastika which was top centre of what appeared to be a letter. The date was 14th September 1983, with an address in a place he had never heard of in Ascensión, Argentina. It was written in Deutsch gothic script, headed top centre with the words: 'Reichsparteitag ["Reich Party Convention"], 32nd Congress of the NSDAP' and titled beneath, 'The Power of the Fourth Reich'.

This was an announcement of the event and the venue which was confirmed as being at Buenos Aires-Sheraton Hotel scheduled for three days commencing on Thursday 2nd February 1984, with a grand dinner to be held following the congress on the Saturday. He was puzzled why he should have been given this, then the realisation hit him. Could this be the Nazi event which his mother, Eva, had attended and where he was conceived? His eyes were about to leave the paper when he looked at the bottom and his shock was palpable; just above the round eagle and swastika stamp were the words 'by order of Reichsmarschall Gunther Roche'.

After a further moment of disorientation, he reached for his mobile phone. "Mother, are you free for me to call? I need to see you urgently." When she enquired why, he found it hard to speak the words. "It is about my father; I know who he is."

There was a delay before he heard the sob of emotion. "I knew this day was coming, we do need to talk."

Within minutes, he was speeding towards the outskirts of Hamburg, already sensing danger but still feeling unreal as he kept checking his mirror to see if he was being followed. Pulling into the quiet street where his mother lived, he had a sense of inquisitive unease already knowing this was, as Dr Friedman had said, 'the greatest scoop', but, for once, that was not his motivation for needing to know more.

Monday 17th February 2020, 7.30pm
Headquarters of Bundesnachrichtendienst
(BND – Federal Intelligence), Chaussees Strasse, Berlin

"How the hell am I meant to explain your complete and utter *Vermasseln* ['screw-up'] to the Chancellor?" The Director of Internal Affairs at the BND was furious. "You were sent to find information, and we end up with two dead and nothing else apart from a few wartime photographs, not even any leads. She is going to want blood for this; this could be the end of both our careers. Our boss does not suffer fools, as we all know. Christ, you know her ruthless reputation. They say even Putin is wary of her, and now I have to tell her we have nothing!"

Schmidt had barely rested since his return from Berchtesgaden and was nearing exhaustion but knew that rest was not an option for more reasons than he would tell the director. "Herr Director, we may have something. I had our tame doctor followed because we established he was a friend of Roche. He met someone in Hamburg today at an airport hotel. Regrettably, we do not know who, as yet, because the man he was with gave us the slip, but we have a description of him. There was no reason for the good doctor to go to Hamburg and, having met this person, he flew straight back, which makes me suspicious. Perhaps, a consultation with the doctor? I am sure he will agree to talk." Schmidt was careful not to mention the document holder that Dr Friedman had been carrying.

"My orders, Herr Schmidt, are clear. There are documents that we know Roche had in his possession which we have to obtain that relate to Roche's wartime service and his activities afterwards with the Nazis. We are to use any means to locate these, but we also must not attract attention. Anything you find, you will not study but give to me personally and I will present it to the Chancellor. You will not read the contents, or if you do, you will forget what you have seen. This is of such national importance that if you talk of this or communicate with anyone about this, the consequences for you will be dire. Do I make myself clear? Nothing must leak out. When this mission is over, you will deny it ever took place to anybody who speaks of it, including me. I can tell you now that the Chancellor herself will never admit to knowing anything about it. Finally, Herr Schmidt, failure is not an option. You will use every means you already have a reputation for, if necessary."

The director told Schmidt that whilst he could use local agents, they should be briefed that information was needed for an investigation into the Nazi era tracking down the elusive *Raubgold* (missing gold stolen hidden by the Nazis at the end of the war) of a staggering value, much of which had never been recovered.

Schmidt was booked on the earliest flight back to Berchtesgaden before the meeting had concluded. He hated being criticised by the director, whom he regarded as an imbecile. Equally, he had no time for fools like his former superior, killed by Roche, who had no idea of the higher purpose in which Schmidt was engaged. He had lacked the ruthlessness, dedication and discipline to achieve results that would be restored to internal security in the future. Schmidt's allegiance was to another who would give the orders and to whom he would give a more complete briefing.

Monday 17th February 2020, 8.00pm
Strandtreppe, Treppenviertel Blankenese, Hamburg, Germany

Eva sat on a large sofa with tears of emotion rolling visibly down her cheeks. The news of the death of Gunther had hit her very hard despite the years. The revelation that her son now knew the identity of his father which she had promised to keep secret added to the depth of her feelings. Hans stood with his back to her looking out of the large picture window at the lights reflected in the River Elbe, which stretched in a long silvery line below. He felt angry at his mother yet was trying to understand the trauma she said she had felt hiding so much from him.

"Hans, your father was wonderful to us. We lacked for nothing and you had the best. This beautiful house, and all we have is because of him. Dr Friedman used to deal with everything on his behalf. I never met your father again; we parted shortly after you were born in 1984, but he kept in touch, always asking how you were, through the doctor. I sent pictures, school reports, but letters were forbidden as they were too personal. I also never spoke with Gunther again after the end of '84, which we both agreed was for the best. Hans, whatever you read or think now, he was a good man in many ways despite his belief in a dreadful ideology. History may judge us harshly and often rightly so, but he stood for what he believed in, however misguided. I wanted you to meet him and suggested it, but Dr Friedman said he would never agree to it."

Her son turned angrily. "My great-grandfather was a friend of Hitler; my father was a Nazi leader. Oh, God, Mother, you were part of that too, and you probably still are. How could you, after what they did to this country, to the world, to the Jews, the camps and the genocide? Now I have to face I am a descendant of monsters."

"How dare you speak to me in that way?" Eva's voice now rose in anger. "I was misguided and left the Party years ago and hate what the Nazis did to Germany. In the 1970s and 1980s there was political confusion and anarchy. We had the Baader Meinhof gang, or the so-called Red Army Faction, kidnapping and shooting people in the streets, Arab terrorists, murder at the Munich Olympics, aircraft hijackings, civil disorder and riots. I just wanted order in Germany." Her voice shook, becoming emotional. "I have protected you all these years from all this because both your father and I knew it would be difficult. Your great-grandfather, von Schirach, may have been a huge figure in Hitler's entourage, but your great-grandmother, Greta, was an English spy. Should we admire her more because she was fighting our forefathers? There are no answers, Hans. Both of them served their countries, no matter how we may judge them today; we were not there to understand their motives. Both fought for their ideals; she as a spy and he as a soldier. At the time they met, Greta did not believe that Baldur von Schirach did anything wrong other than, perhaps, indoctrinating the youth of the day into National Socialism through the Hitler Youth. I never met my grandmother, Greta, but I know she was an MI6 agent in the 1930s and that during the war, she worked closely with Winston Churchill. She wrote about her role in a letter she sent to your mother with some diaries in 1974, after von Schirach died, having kept matters secret all her life. I have the letter hidden somewhere, which I will show you one day. It seems she was quite an extraordinary person who was involved in espionage at the highest level, but she asked my mother not to reveal what she had done. I think back then it was classified and probably still is. I have never told anyone as Mother said it could potentially still be very dangerous if any of it got out.

"My mother, your grandmother, died too young in 2007, but I can remember her dancing with joy when the Berlin Wall came down in 1989. The world was so different then. The official NSDAP was dissolved in 1985 because they had successfully infiltrated government, business and financial institutions, and were embedded in other countries. Nazism was embracing democracy, gaining power through stealth and influencing regimes, but I became disillusioned after you were born loathing everything about the Nazis when I learned the truth of what they had done. At least there was some optimism in the late 1980s that the world was changing, with Reagan, Gorbachev and Thatcher breaking down barriers between East and West, ending the Cold War; it seemed a new and better order was emerging."

Hans was struggling with the enormity of the day and collapsed in a chair, asking his mother if he could stay. He listened as she explained how she had become drawn towards National Socialism. "There was rioting in the streets, murders of prominent people, shootings and kidnappings, and order seemed to be breaking down. When Mother told me in 1974 who my real grandfather was, I was fascinated. I was nineteen, studying at university, and suddenly I found my family had once been important. I looked at everything to do with National Socialism and they seemed to provide a buffer against anything Communist or anarchist. Soon I had met other students who were part of it. I went to meetings and then began to become involved. Most of us had no time for the anti-Jewish thing, but we kind of ignored all that. It seemed as though this secret Party meant law and order with a pride in Germany that we had lost." She sighed. "It somehow had a real appeal after the violence of the seventies."

Eva told her son that she had become a secretary of the local Party and then was promoted to area leader as a result of which she was invited to the congress of 1984. "I knew the Reichsmarschall by name but had never met him. This was a title given to him because they abandoned using the term 'Führer' after the death of Hitler, which we were told was in 1962. Yes, we were informed he did escape from the bunker in 1945, and that seemed an exciting secret, although the rumours were always there.

"*Mein Gott*, when I saw your father at the rally, he was amazingly dressed in this beautiful uniform, so proud, self-assured, handsome and strong. It was irresistible to me and I'm afraid I fell in love before I even said, 'Hello.' I watched him speak but heard nothing, and just knew I had to meet him. It was not hard as he loved to mingle, shaking hands and wanting to know who everyone was. When we were introduced, I curtsied, which was a little ridiculous, but I was overawed. He smiled and said, 'Fraulein, I am not royalty, and it should be me that bows to you.' He then did so, after which he raised my hand and kissed it. It was so delightfully old-fashioned. I nearly swooned on the spot. He asked me to join the top table for cocktails after the dinner, which I could not resist. Then he invited me to his suite to discuss the political organisation of the movement after disbandment of the Party, and that, my son, is all you are getting on that night, except to say I have always loved him from afar." She looked down, her face held within a moment of grief.

"I'm sorry, Mother, I really haven't had time to take all this in. I have no right to condemn. Forgive me." Hans went and sat next to her, and they hugged.

"I'm sorry too, Hans, but what I did was because I always wanted to protect you."

Eva went to her study, returning minutes later with a small box. "There are not very many, but these are some photos from those times." They shared a bottle of Chablis and toasted his father as they looked through the images. There were a few snaps of him with her around Berchtesgaden, where, apparently, they had gone climbing together even quite late in her pregnancy. Then there were some more formal ones of him in uniform and Hans had to agree he looked very imposing and exuded authority. Unlike those of many former leaders of the Nazi Party, they noted that he appeared to have a wry smile in many of the pictures. Hans reflected that maybe he did not want to be a figure of fear like Hitler but then realised he was simply trying to excuse who his father was.

When he retired to bed that night after warmly embracing his mother, he said out loud, "My Father, this day is not in vain. I will follow the trail and will not let this matter rest. God bless you." He felt he had already made peace with the father, who had denied him, yet he could not reconcile his feelings with the contradiction of his father's allegiance to Nazism. *Tomorrow is just the start*, he told himself as he drifted into an exhausted sleep.

9

The Berlin Olympics

XI Olympiad

"Ich rufe die Jugend der Welt!" (I call the youth of the world!)
Adolf Hitler

Wednesday 5th August 1936, 2.00pm
Reichssportfeld, Berlin

The VIP spectator stands were set around the Führerloge in which Hitler himself was sitting surrounded by his entourage but noticeably with Deputy Führer Rudolf Hess in a brown uniform to one side and Reichsmarschall Hermann Göring in a light suit with a matching trilby hat on the other. As the Führer had entered, there was a roar from the crowd, whilst a band struck up the favourite Nazi anthem, 'The Horst Wessel Song'. Across one half of the Olympiastadion, the crowd of spectators began displaying an enormous message with black squares held aloft to make a dramatic display, '*Wir gehoeren Dir* ["We belong to you")', a gesture repeated at intervals. Hitler would occasionally stand, smiling, then draw himself to attention, extending his right arm stiffly drawing huge cheers. Each time he entered the stadium, the crowd was beside itself with excitement, displaying their adulation and national pride.

The lunch for VIPs had been nothing short of spectacular, served with Champagne by white-clad stewards, and an extraordinary choice of dishes. The Führer had mingled with guests and visited various tables, shaking hands or raising his right hand to return a salute. He was accompanied by Joseph Goebbels, who would whisper in his ear before approaching certain guests, ensuring he knew their identity. Greta watched him, fascinated by the brief smiles combined with the stern look of authority marking himself as the power in the room, as he unmistakably was.

As he approached their table, his face lit up and his piercing eyes took each of them in before he accepted Unity's hand, kissing it and briefly bowing, then speaking in German: "The Mitford family, I know, and we are honoured to have both mother and daughters. *Ach*, and, of course, the Duke of Saxe-Coburg, I trust you are well, Herr Gruppenführer." He looked directly at Greta. "This lady, I believe, has sampled our healthcare. Mein Fraulein, I am delighted to meet you. You are well recovered, I trust?"

Greta replied in fluent German that the care had been excellent and that she was grateful to both Baldur von Schirach and the Duke for their help. Hitler replied that the Party would always look after their own. He turned and kissed Unity on both cheeks, clicked his heels and moved on.

Greta had been made aware that Unity had become close to Hitler the previous year through her briefing with Colonel Menzies, which was further confirmed when she had received an invitation to visit the Berghof from Unity in the autumn of 1935. She had declined, saying she was still recuperating from TB. By the time of the Olympics, it had become common knowledge that the Führer and Unity had a very close friendship, although no-one in Germany guessed or spoke of more, or dared to. Greta was pleased, however, to accept the invitation to join the Mitfords in their private box, which had been arranged by Hitler for

Unity. Colonel Menzies wanted to establish how the German infiltration of society was progressing, who the influential British guests were, and what they were saying. Once again, she was reliant on Mona Maund for communication with London despite Greta's experience earlier in the year with German Intelligence. Colonel Menzies felt that Mona would be treated with less suspicion because she had returned with a position as science attaché to the British Embassy in Berlin.

Their box was next to the British VIP guests' area and each day Greta would recognise many faces she knew. Former Prime Minister Lloyd George was there that afternoon, sitting with Sir Anthony Eden, the Foreign Secretary, Lord Wellington, Lord Rothermere, Sir Arnold Wilson MP, Thomas Moore MP and a young MP she had a faint recollection of but could not place.

"Oh, darling," Diana Mitford told her. "That is Lord Clydesdale, Douglas Douglas-Hamilton, not only an MP but a future Duke no less. Pretty dishy, I would say, and an RAF officer to boot. He's quite dashing, and apparently, he's the first to have flown a plane over Everest."

Greta made a mental note to meet this young man and learn more. She wasn't a great fan of sport, but that afternoon they watched the black American athlete, Jesse Owens, running the two hundred metres, urged on by huge roars from the crowd as he romped home to victory. There was great excitement as it was announced he had broken the world record, winning his second gold medal of the Olympics. She watched Hitler raise his arm in smiling acknowledgment to the athlete's bow but knew that the Führer would not have been pleased. His avowed aim was that German Aryans should dominate the Games and triumph.

Wednesday 5th August 1936, 8.30pm
Savoy Hotel, Fasanenstrasse, Berlin

Joachim von Ribbentrop, the German ambassador to St James, greeted each guest as they were announced by the Master of Ceremonies personally. He was dressed in a black dinner jacket, white winged collar and bowtie, with a chain across the right side of his chest bearing two eagles and the *Hakenkreuz* (swastika). He was hosting the dinner to which Charles Edward, Greta, Diana Mitford and Sir Oswald Mosley had been invited, although Unity was dining with the Führer elsewhere. This was an event organised by *Deutsch-Englische Gesellschaft* (the German English Society) to promote closer ties between the two countries. They were taken to the long top table which faced a series of smaller tables spaced around the magnificent room hung with chandeliers, and ornate red and gold-trimmed velvet curtains over baroque-style windows. They were joined on the table by Lord Rothermere, the Duke of Wellington, Lord Mount Temple, Archibald Ramsey MP and the secretary of the Anglo-German Fellowship, Ernest Tennant. Greta was making careful mental notes as she was introduced to those present and who accompanied them.

Her attention was diverted by the entrance of the 'dashing' Lord Clydesdale, immaculate in a dress uniform of the RAF, accompanied by a petite blonde-haired woman in a long black shimmering dress announced as the pioneering aviator Hanna Reitsch. Various guests joined their table, including a polite young German academic who introduced himself to her as Albrecht Haushofer, saying that he had heard of her illness, asking about her recovery. In their conversation, he mentioned he was a member of the Geographical Society in Berlin and, like her, he was writing for a periodical. He said he knew the Deputy Führer well as they had studied at university together and he now worked for him assisting with foreign affairs.

The Master of Ceremonies requested silence for the 'surprise' guests of honour, announcing first: "*Meine Damen und Herren*, a founder of our Party, a standard bearer in the Putsch, a fellow prisoner sacrificing freedom together with our Führer for his country, the Deputy Führer, Rudolf Hess, accompanied by his wife Ilse." At once all stood, most raising their arms in the Nazi Party salute as he entered in a black uniform, with silver laurel insignia on his lapels, his wife on his arm in a light blue dress with chiffon trim.

The booming voice announced the next guest: "Fighter pilot ace, hero of the Putsch, President of the Reichstag, Supreme Commander of the Luftwaffe and Reichsmarschall, Hermann Göring." He strode in alone, smiling to right and left, to loud applause, his white dress Luftwaffe uniform looking imposing with gold braid, medals on the right side of his chest, and the 'Blue Max', or *Pour le Mérite* medal, at his neck.

Greta was sitting only two places away from the Reichsmarschall, who sat next to Douglas Douglas-Hamilton and Hanna Reitsch. Göring was introduced to Greta and he was, she thought, full of charm with impeccable manners. He spoke excellent English, complimenting her on her beautiful outfit, which put his uniform to shame. She looked coy and asked if she might swap her pendant for his wonderful blue medal, to which he roared with laughter, saying, "Like all you English, you leave us with nothing!" He struck up an earnest conversation with Douglas-Hamilton and Hanna about flying, which was a passion he shared with both of them. She was developing her skills as a test pilot and had gained a reputation for daring in the air whilst holding world records in gliding. Douglas-Hamilton, she learned, was a squadron leader who professed he was fascinated by the new aircraft he had heard were being developed in Germany. Göring proudly announced, "We will have the greatest modern air force as we rebuild our new Germany. We must work together to defend against the aggression from the Communists in the East which may, one day, require us to unite in a great crusade. We need to create space, change borders and remove the threat of Communist tyranny."

Greta then listened as Hanna Reitsch poured out her enthusiasm for the Führer's aims of a strong bond between their two countries, saying that his vision was extraordinary. She declared that in her view he was the most enlightened leader of modern times, drawing applause from the Reichsmarschall. Greta decided to push the conversation and test the reaction. "Please, Herr Reichsmarschall, forgive me for interrupting, but do you think the English might stand firm on maintaining the terms of the Versailles Treaty which may risk war?"

Göring looked at her confidently. "I have many friends in England and they are telling me that we must resist the threat from the East. Charlie," he looked at Charles Edward, "you spend so much time in England with people who matter; tell us what you believe?" The Duke stated that there was admiration for what was happening in Germany and people wanted to see similar changes and stronger leadership in Britain. "Even those at the pinnacle of British society are pledging themselves towards an alliance with Germany against Russia." As Charles Edward stated this, he put his finger to his mouth, indicating a secret, before asking Douglas Hamilton for his view.

The squadron leader's tone was measured. "I have to say to you all that many in positions of authority in my country are concerned about Russia, but the scars of the Great War worry them too. Yes, many openly admire the Führer, but whether they favour a crusade against Russia is open to question. I think we need to build on our relationship and bring our two nations closer, trying to find common causes that we can unite behind. My belief is that if threatened by the evil of Communism, the need to unite with Germany may be an inescapable, unstoppable necessity."

"Then let us drink to that," exclaimed Göring. "Tomorrow, Squadron Leader, I would like you to accept a personal invitation to join with me and inspect a Luftwaffe unit and its aircraft; you, my dear Hanna, must be there too."

Greta noted the squadron leader's ready acceptance, wondering whether he too was being controlled by Colonel Menzies or if he was genuinely interested in the aircraft development taking place in Germany. Much discussion took place during dinner over the future shape of Europe. As views were expressed, or names mentioned, Greta would carefully take mental note, and when she escaped to the bathroom, she frantically scribbled a summary of recollections for her report to the colonel. There was no doubt in her mind that Germany had an expansionist policy and that seeds were being sown for eventual action against the Soviet Union. Perhaps Albrecht, Hess's foreign affairs man, might be the next stop for a little inside information. As the dinner finished, there was a smoking break before the speeches. She took her opportunity, excused herself, and went to where Albrecht Haushofer was sitting.

"Forgive me, but I was fascinated to hear of your connections with the Deputy Führer. As I write for *Vogue*, I wondered whether I could just ask your opinion on a couple of matters?"

Albrecht stood up and smiled, motioning her to some seats away from the table, offering her a cigarette, which she took, allowing him to light it. Greta went straight to the point, asking him if he thought there would be an alliance between Britain and Germany against Russia. His reaction surprised her, as he told her there were factions for and against any aggression, but there were those who considered expansion in the East to be a sacred quest, annexing territory, with a resettlement of peoples or even entire countries. He indicated that there were people who wanted to resist and dared not, talking in the third person in order, she recognised, that he was not indicating his support or otherwise for any views.

"You may not quote me because I have done no more than tell you what I have observed. I will deny all I say now, but I believe we are heading for war and that an effort is being made to make any effective resistance in England impossible by making sure opinion will not permit it. A form of subversion of democracy by stealth is underway, ensuring that those that matter are on our side. I am informed, Greta, that your King has already expressed some sympathy with the ideas being put forward, and he is more powerful than most realise. There is in place a strategy to seduce your beloved Royal institution for the greater good of the Reich and Lebensraum or colonisation."

Albrecht paused, summoning a waiter carrying a tray of Cognac glasses, taking one, which he downed immediately before reaching for two more, passing one to Greta then glancing around as though concerned he was not overheard. He leaned forward earnestly. "Yours may be a constitutional monarchy, but one word, one gesture from your King, and so many in power will fall dutifully in line and refuse to resist Germany's aims. I have not said this, but for the sake of peace, your monarch needs protecting, possibly from himself."

Greta's heart thumped as she took in the implications of his words. She looked at the smartly dressed man and sensed an earnest need to put out a message by any means yet seek not to be the source. He was quite handsome, she observed, guessing they were of similar age, with a square face and neatly trimmed moustache. He wore a dinner jacket with a somewhat flamboyant white bowtie, giving the impression of a slightly eccentric individuality.

"So, Greta," he said loudly, "I will finish by saying to your paper that the Olympics have been magnificent so far and that I have told you on good authority that we will win the most medals. You may quote me on saying that it has been wonderful for the youth of every country to take part and that we learn from this to live in peace."

As the Master of Ceremonies called people to order, Greta shook the hand of someone she felt was utterly genuine, sincere and, like her, extremely concerned. She had the feeling their paths would cross again.

Before he retired to bed, Greta kissed Charles Edward on both cheeks, thanking him, as always, for a wonderful time. They had danced and, having had rather too much to drink, he had been a little over enthusiastic as they waltzed, holding her too closely, during which she became aware of his obvious ardour.

"Charlie, we must stop immediately," she had reprimanded him. "We are in public and I do not wish to be embarrassed."

The Duke had stepped back, appearing bashful, yet this did not prevent him from declaring to her that he loved her as they ascended the stairs. Greta tapped him on the nose, teasingly, chastising him further, then waved him to his room. *Poor dear man*, she thought to herself, as she descended rapidly to the cocktail bar, nodding at those she recognised and joining a young man, who smiled as though he knew her well, although he had never met her.

"Dearest Greta, how lovely to see you," he declared, ordering two Mary Pickfords, watching the bartender mix the rum, pineapple juice and grenadine, which he already knew she loved. He escorted her to a red velvet-covered chaise longue, allowing her the high back end, smiling as he introduced himself in a low voice. "Guy Burgess, old girl, good to see you. I believe you have something for Mona." As she shook her stole from her shoulders, he gallantly took it from her, draping it across an adjacent seat as he slipped the envelope in his jacket pocket. "What the blazes are we all really doing here?" he asked. "I'm producing a programme for the BBC on the Olympics. Not been given much else to do yet in terms of digging around other than keeping my ear to the ground. What are you up to? Don't worry, Mum's the word." He was handsome, cultured, confident and very poised, making her feel quite at ease. Clearly well educated, he looked every inch the English gentleman.

"Not a lot, really," she responded. "Actually pretty tedious, as I'm not into sport and they were all talking Olympics over dinner. Very little to report to anyone." The words tripped off her tongue as she made a mental note to mention this conversation to the colonel. She had, in effect, given Burgess a security-sealed envelope containing the most explosive information of her career. *My God*, she thought to herself with a suppressed giggle, *they might put me in the Tower of London*.

10

The Barbarossa Secret

Tuesday 18th February 2020, 6.00pm
Alster Waterfront, Hamburg

With his mind still in some turmoil, it was not until he returned home after work the following day that Hans remembered the envelope with his name on. He still had a sense of adrenalin within, as though he was in danger, and it had been hard to concentrate. He had kept the document holder with him, even taking it with him into the televised press conference with Angela Merkel. A dozen cases of coronavirus had been reported in Bavaria and he was feeding his colleague in Berlin over the phone with questions for the Chancellor. He knew what had been discussed at the highest level about restricting citizens and wanted a story from the official denial that a lockdown had been considered amongst other measures being hidden from the people. He had indirectly, through his colleague, been talking to the Chancellor of Germany, posing questions that now seemed insignificant when compared with what he was aware of. He was in possession of information that was dynamite politically, which, whether she was aware of it or not, she would have to deny; however, despite the temptation to catch her off guard, he knew the time was not yet right.

Walking to the surprisingly traditional wooden drinks cabinet that his mother had given to him, he pulled down the flap, placing a glass on the polished covering, into which he poured a Schnapps. A second followed, then he went to sit in an armchair, for once ignoring the TV news channels. He undid the zip and pulled out the large cream envelope on which his name was handwritten. Was that his father's writing? A shiver went through him. He opened the envelope with a paperknife, full of nervous trepidation. The paper was high quality, with several A4 sheets folded and typewritten, although the opening greeting was handwritten:

Berchtesgaden Montag, 26th April 2010

Lieber Hans,

When you read this, it will be because I am no longer alive and I so wish we could have met but it was not to be. I did hold you as a baby and shared the joy of your birth with your wonderful mother. I knew she would look after you well, which she did, always keeping me informed of your progress. I am proud of what you have achieved in life without the pressures of terrible decisions I have been faced with in my own. Whatever you may think of me in the modern world, please understand that I did what I did because I believed it was right. My good friend of many years, Dr Walter Friedman, the 'go-between' passing communication between your mother and I, chastises me and we argue, but I still adhere to what I stood for, although with many regrets.

I am your father, but I will not preach to you. Much will be written about me and I will leave it up to you to judge. There are so many different ways of representing 'the truth'. I do not wish to make any excuses but will tell you a little of what shaped my life and let you be the judge. I will also give you some facts which may be the greatest secret ever known and one which could have the capacity to bring down governments and even lead to conflict. This could be the greatest gift I can give which may help you protect yourself and, perhaps, give you 'a story', and that makes me smile.

I was born in Dresden in 1922 to wonderful parents who cared for me and my younger sister, Ilse, in a home where we were happy as children. My father, Manfred, was an army officer in the XII (1st Royal Saxon) Corps, who survived the Great War and was proud of his country. My mother, Hildegard, did some administrative work for the Saxony government until we were born. After 1918, Papa joined the Freikorps, then he was given the opportunity to join the army of the Free State of Saxony. They were both killed in the terrible air raids on Dresden in February 1945, together with my dear sister whom I was very close to.

In 1932, I joined the Deutsches Jungvolk, a new youth group which taught outdoor pursuits, discipline and fitness. Then, at thirteen, in 1935, I was enrolled in the HitlerJugend, which was a great experience where I learned about German patriotism with a new pride. There were wonderful pursuits, including camping, survival, shooting, comradeship, hunting, mountaineering, even flying instruction, and a rigid, unswerving obedience to a code of behaviour. We were constantly training in fitness, and were taught about military tactics, famous battles and weaponry. In 1936, I was selected to be in a parade at the Berlin Olympics, where I received my marksman award as the region's best shot from no less that ReichsjugendFührer Baldur von Schirach himself. I was so proud and totally dedicated to the national cause under the Führer.

In 1938, I was handpicked by the SS and offered officer training. During this time, I was seconded to a Luftwaffe base and learned to fly many aircraft, a skill in which I excelled. When I passed out in 1940, I was given the honour of being enrolled in the elite Leibstandarte SS Adolf Hitler unit. I saw combat in France, Holland and Yugoslavia. It was at that time I won my first Iron Cross. In April 1941, I was recalled and ordered to commence intense low-level flight training in a captured British aircraft, a Westland Lysander. It was a brilliant aeroplane, and I learned to land it and take off again in a space of less than one hundred metres. My training was carried out at the Messerschmitt airfield at AugsburgHaunstetten. I got to know Deputy Führer Rudolf Hess at that time, who took an interest in my training; we were both keen flyers. He told me that he would be working with me, but it was all secret at that point and he could say no more.

In May 1941, I was astonished when I heard the Deputy Führer had flown to England, but then, a few days later, I was even more incredulous when I was ordered to fly to England on a mission I could mention to no-one. The orders were given directly to me by Reichsmarschall Hermann Göring in person, so you might imagine my shock. I was summoned to his office in Berlin, where I was informed of the reason for my training. He confided in me that all this was part of a policy the Führer called 'Generalplan Reich'. This was the planned expansion of Germany in the East and the conquest of Russia. An invasion of Russia was imminent in what became known as 'Unternehmen Barbarossa'. He informed me that Hess was involved in peace talks with the British to secure support for the invasion.

There were many in Britain who, before the war, had openly declared they would support Germany in seeking the overthrow of Communist Russia. The Führer had wanted to avoid war with Britain and secret communication was taking place with leading members of the British ruling class with the aim of potentially toppling Churchill and even replacing the King. The information was strictly shared on a one-to-one basis, and never written down. It was guarded by a code of secrecy called 'eins zu eins', and Göring made it clear that if anyone betrayed this, they would be immediately shot. I was in no doubt that this included me. No-one knew what took place at this time at the secret talks apart from a select few entrusted with the Führer's purpose.

The more Hans read, the more open-mouthed he became, uttering brief exclamations of surprise at each twist and turn described in his father's letter.

My first mission to England was on 20th May 1941. I took off in the Westland Lysander from Dortmund to save fuel as the aircraft range was 1,600 kilometres, with an auxiliary tank, and the round trip, allowing for winds and diversions, left little room for error. I flew to a country house called Ditchley, in Oxfordshire, where I landed on a lawn. I took a briefcase with papers in it, which Göring checked himself before waving me off warning me, with a smile, to keep my eye out for 'aircraft of the

Hun'. The Lysander was marked as a British aircraft, so I felt safer over England than over Germany.

This was the first of many such flights that May and June before our invasion of Russia on 22nd June 1941. On one occasion, as I was landing, I saw the Deputy Führer standing on a terrace at Ditchley with Winston Churchill. You can imagine the shock. My guns were loaded and I could have annihilated the British Prime Minister there and then! Hess often used to come and greet me, wanting to discuss what was happening back home, and we developed a kind of friendship. He was particularly upset by the press reports in Germany made which him sound a traitor, but it was all a cover for the greatest mission of the war and of his life: that of cooperating with the Allies on the overthrow of Soviet Russia. He said it was the proudest moment of his life to have been selected and entrusted by the Führer with such an historic task. The strategy we adopted in our talks with the British later became known as the 'Barbarossa Secret'. I made trips to England throughout 1941 and on one occasion actually landed at their fighter airfield at Biggin Hill. Then, in early 1942, it all stopped and there was nothing for two more years.

I was posted back to my SS unit, serving in Russia in the summer of 1942. There was intense fighting as the Russians were counter-attacking along a number of fronts. We had lost some of the ground taken during the previous winter. I led a section which was to take two strategic bridges at a place called Rostov-on-Don. We seized our objective, enabling the town to be retaken, and that meant we could advance again on a broad front. At the end of 1942, after a number of successes, our unit was under-strength for the next assault. We were pulled back to France for regrouping. I was summoned to Berlin and told I was to meet the Führer. He personally presented me with the Knight's Cross with Oak Leaves. Hitler said I was a true Knight of the Reich and it was one of the high points of my life. I was promoted by him to the rank of Hauptsturmführer (Captain) and invited to join the elite protection unit in Berlin.

From that point, I was often asked to partake in special missions, and the Führer himself used to invite me to his office occasionally to get an 'impartial' view of strategy from an active serving officer. I think he had issues with some of his generals. I felt honoured to be so trusted. In July 1943, I was asked to join a special mission with my friend, Otto Skorzeny, to rescue the Italian leader Mussolini, who was being held *prisoner in a mountaintop hotel. We flew in by glider, liberating him without a shot being fired, and delivered him to the Führer. For that, I was promoted again to the rank of Sturmbannführer (Major) and presented with the Knight's Cross with Oak Leaves and Swords by Hermann Göring. My military career was thriving, but for me, it was service to the Fatherland that mattered.*

During 1943, I spent time between Berlin and the Berghof in Obersalzberg, and was sometimes even invited to join the Führer and Eva Braun for tea. We used to sit on the balcony overlooking the mountains and it was only here that the Führer seemed to relax. It was in the spring of 1943 I met Karin, a beautiful friend of Eva Braun, and we were married at the Berghof that summer. Our wedding was wonderful and was attended by the Führer, Albert Speer and Joseph Goebbels. She could never do enough for me and became the most loyal companion of my life, never questioning my long periods away but accepting them as necessary. Sadly, she could not bear children, but she was wonderful with them. In a way, it was a blessing because I would have been an absentee father. I missed her terribly when she passed away in 1978, after which I never wanted to marry again.

In January 1944, I was summoned to a meeting with the Führer at the Reich Chancellery. There were six others there, including Reich Minister of Armaments Albert Speer, Hermann Göring, Heinrich Himmler, Martin Bormann, Joseph Goebbels and the geography academic Karl Haushofer. The tone was very sombre. Hitler announced that we would lose the war unless we prevented another front opening. For that purpose, he had assigned Rommel to ensure that our Atlantic Wall was reinforced in France to repel the expected Allied invasion. He told us that the primary purpose remained the annihilation of Russia and that Germany needed to renegotiate a peace treaty with the Allies, similar to that put forward to Britain in 1941 by Hess.

The Führer informed us of the full details of the Barbarossa Secret, which, at that time, was only fully known to Hess, Göring, Himmler and Goebbels. Hitler told us that the war should have been over because Hess had agreed a peace treaty with the British in 1941 conditional upon us penetrating within thirty kilometres of Moscow. Further, the USA had committed to join Britain in backing our Russian offensive if Moscow fell. By January 1942, our main forces had reached twenty-eight kilometres of central Moscow, with Panzer units under twenty kilometres from the Kremlin!

Imagine this: German officers in forward positions reported being able to see the domes of the capital through their binoculars. However, we were betrayed after the Japanese attack on Pearl Harbor in December 1941. The USA declared war on Germany and Churchill changed his position on peace negotiations. The only concession we were left with was that if we took Moscow, the USA would cease military operations against us and, with Britain, they were prepared to guarantee most German European borders. This had been in exchange for guarantees by Germany of the absolute sovereignty of the British Empire and an abandonment of our treaty with Japan.

At the 1944 meeting, the Führer laid out a number of scenarios with incredible foresight. He stated that if an Allied invasion of France succeeded, we would lose the war because Germany would be facing an attack on too many fronts. His plan was that we should then sue for peace and propose a joint German Allied offensive against Russia. However, if this failed, he stated we could still win the peace and laid out a strategy for a post-war Europe in which Germany could triumph politically and commercially. He foresaw that a military alliance would eventually still be needed to provide a bastion against expansionist Russia. He had made contingency plans to leave Germany for an 'Eagle's Lair' in Argentina, from where he would remain Führer influencing or directing Germany's future. He was upbeat, saying that wielding political power with stealth instead of stormtroopers may be the way forward and that nothing would prevent our eventual triumph. He also announced we had developed new weapons technology giving us bargaining power, which, I can confirm, included the atomic bomb.

During 1944, my flights to England resumed, but the destination was changed to the Prime Minister's house at Chequers, which was much more accessible with fewer trees, making it easier to land. At least now I was in the know and could more easily discuss directly with Hess the tone of his meetings with Churchill and report these to the Führer. In July 1944, I flew from Berlin directly to a field close to Allied HQ in France, taking with me three documents called 'Operational Orders' signed by the Führer, one for Germany and the other two for the Allies. I delivered these documents directly to Rommel personally and no-one else, as ordered by the Führer. Rommel then held a secret meeting which had been arranged with the Allies.

Everything began to go very badly after that. Rommel suffered serious injuries in an air attack on his way back from the meeting and was hospitalised. We were suffering treachery from within, including a failed attempt on the Führer's life a few days later in a bomb plot. After this, Hitler no longer had faith in his generals and abandoned his final attempt at a military execution of 'Generalplan Reich'. In October '44 I met with Feldmarschall Rommel, who had allegedly been involved in the bomb plot against the Führer, which he denied. In advance of his subsequent 'suicide', I retrieved his copy of the Operational Orders. This was part of a pact forced upon him whereby it was also agreed he could avoid a show trial, have his honour protected and his family looked after, if he took his own life. I have to say how composed he was that day, despite what he faced, when I arrived with those tasked with ensuring his demise. I saluted him before I departed and genuinely felt that Germany had lost a patriot. Hess said that if Rommel had not been seriously injured after his meeting with Montgomery, and there had been no bomb plot against the Führer a few days later, a combined Allied and German offensive would have been launched against Russia. Imagine that: no nuclear threat, no Communists, no cold war, no divided Germany and no fear of Russian aggression. It was ours for the taking.

 I left Berlin for a period as my unit was assigned to the Ardennes offensive in November 1944 known as Unternehmen Wacht am Rhein, or Battle of the Bulge. After the first few days, we were making incredible progress and I was in the thick of it. It was like the glorious days again, advancing fast with our armour, but the Americans fought back fiercely. I was recalled at the end of December 1944 and began more flights to and from Britain.

 In January 1945, Hess was negotiating with Churchill directly for the Führer's safe passage from Germany to Argentina. Once again, I saw him with Churchill at Chequers. I was even presented with a box of Romeo y Julieta Cuban Cigars by Churchill to thank me for my many missions. He joked that I might even be considered for a British gallantry medal. Hitler's escape to the Eagle's Lair in Argentina was tied in with Germany's agreement to release our nuclear research together with rocket and other weapon technology and hand over our scientists to the USA and Britain. Our ultimate guarantee of safety for the Führer, and other senior Party members, lay within an agreement to effectively bury the Barbarossa Secret, whilst also maintaining strict secrecy regarding the negotiations. However, there was another matter that gave us a final guarantee of safe passage.

In March 1945, things had become pretty desperate and I helped plan the Führer's flight from Berlin with Eva Braun. It was highly risky as he insisted on remaining in his bunker until the end. He personally awarded me the Knight's Cross with Swords and Diamonds in the Führerbunker on his fiftysixth birthday on 20th April 1945. He made me the youngest colonel in the Reich, giving me the rank so that my position would be respected and my orders followed without question. He charged me with the task of liaising with the Allies on the Barbarossa Secret and matters regarding his security after he left Germany. The Führer married Eva Braun on 29th April and it was decided they would be flown out the following day. Hans Baur, Hitler's personal pilot, flew some of us out of Berlin after the wedding ceremony. Goebbels said he would remain in the bunker to the end and give his life for Führer and Fatherland. Hitler ordered him to leave for the sake of his wife Magda and the children, but he refused, saying it was the first time he had ever disobeyed an order from Hitler. When the Führer heard he and Magda had poisoned his children a few days later, he was stricken with grief, pacing for hours. The amazing fearless pilot, Hanna Reitsch, who remained so cheerful in these final days in the bunker, flew Hitler and Eva out on 30th April 1945, taking off from Hermann-Göringstrasse, now Ebertstrasse. There is so much more to tell, but I have given you some pieces of the jigsaw and know, with your investigative zeal, you will unearth the rest. It would be too dangerous for you if I was seen to be the source of what you now reveal. Your mother can give you some details, together with my old friend Dr Friedman.

I can tell you that when the Führer was in Argentina, we built a nuclear facility, and that was one of the ongoing insurance policies we needed to protect us, together with the fear of the Barbarossa Secret being made public.

Now I will turn to the part of the Barbarossa Secret that we called our Royal protection. There were papers in which we recorded the Führer's plans to avoid war, and subsequently seek peace with England, in which members of the British Royal Family and senior politicians were involved. The Führer hatched plans for a coup in England, and a number of very prominent and influential English people were prepared to support this, including those right at the top of their society. There was a German relative of the British Royal Family who was pretty instrumental in the 1930s and '40s in organising this. He was Charles Edward, Duke of Saxe-Coburg and

Gotha, and a grandson to Queen Victoria. He was very influential, even flying to America in 1940 to meet President Roosevelt, where he was welcomed at the White House. His mission there was to broker an early commitment from the USA to join a crusade against Russia, but he was not part of 'eins zu eins'. Like most of us in the Party, he kept meticulous notes and records which included discussions held with the Duke of Windsor regarding a return to the throne. There were many other papers recording covert plans involving the Royal Family, including a strategy where George VI would dismiss Churchill and sue for peace. These were hidden in 1945, but as part of the agreement for the Führer's safety, we agreed to give them to the Allies and they became known as the Marburg files. We saved the reputations of many, including Royalty, by working with the Americans and British to clean the files after the war. There are very many in positions of power who would not wish details of this information coming out. As I am one of the last remaining alive to have this knowledge, you may understand that I am inevitably quite a target.

During the negotiations for the Führer's safety, it was agreed that a list of those bound by 'eins zu eins' should be shared. The Americans and the British were terrified of the Barbarossa Secret getting out, and the list of all those party to this provided mutual survival insurance. All of the original on that list have now died apart from myself. However, although it was agreed that the information would die with them, certain members on the list could pass it on to one named person which was limited to the Führer's successor and the heads of state of Britain and the USA. In the case of Britain, that included both the monarch and the Prime Minister.

In November 1960, I was appointed Reichsmarschall by the Führer, a title which had not been used since the last holder, Hermann Göring. I was only thirty-eight years old. In effect, I was Deputy Führer, but I let the title of Führer go in 1962 when Hitler died. By then, we were no longer marching in uniforms, but we had successfully infiltrated former members of the Party into positions of power in Germany and in the USA. We were becoming the dominant force here and elsewhere. By 1984, it was decided that the NSDAP should be disbanded as we were already achieving many of our key aims with a plan to consolidate our power through the emerging EU. We had people within the regime of East Germany before unification and we were so powerful that Gorbachev in Russia dared not do anything when we organised the fall of the

Berlin Wall. Many of the former Communist GDR are now in top government posts in the BRD (German Federal Republic). I retired from taking an active role in our movement in 2001, which by then had become more like a secretive pressure group but with a significant influence on power. There were some who wanted us to be more open, galvanising a right-wing political movement, even to rebrand a new party, but as I handed power over to my successor, I cautioned against this. I felt we could achieve much more by stealth working within the establishment.

I met your mother at our final rally in 1984 and she made an incredible impression on me. She was outspoken, vivacious, quick-witted and efficient yet also disarming. I had read her area reports with interest and had asked to be introduced. When I heard she was the granddaughter of the legendary youth leader Baldur von Schirach, I was stunned, and it almost seemed like fate had drawn us together. It was at this event that I wore my uniform for the last time and watched the flags with the swastika being lowered also for the final time as the band played the Horst Wessel song. Many of us were unashamedly openly emotional and I recall shedding a tear. We had a huge picture of the Führer at the head of the park where we held our rally near Buenos Aires and marching columns of men in brown, field grey and black uniforms just like the great rallies of the glorious days in the 1930s. After the dinner and ball, your mother and I melted away and spoke for hours and hours. I had never felt so close to anyone so quickly or with such spontaneity in my life. She was and remains such a beautiful spirit, and I admire her very much.

Do not judge her by your standards today, where liberal ideas are so quick to condemn. She was talented, intuitive and a formidable organiser. We had a wonderful time together but sadly far too short. We both knew, after you were born, that for your safety and hers, it was impossible. The children of Nazis were discriminated against, vilified and have suffered greatly. She wanted to protect you, and for all these years, she has always put you first, even denying me access when the temptation to see you was too great. She has been a dedicated mother to you, and who could wish for more? You must also understand she left the Party as soon as you were born and never became involved again, a decision I was happy she took as it allowed her to concentrate on your welfare.

I have had so many challenges in life that I never would want you to face and seen things that even haunt me to this day, but, my son, I remain proud of my service to the Fatherland and my Führer. Forgive what you may not understand, but please believe me when I say, I loved you from afar.

Alles Liebe,
Für immer
Dein Vater

He had signed the letter in ink.

Hans rose from his chair, walking slowly to his cabinet, where he poured another generous Schnapps. He was on an emotional roller coaster and, despite his revulsion at the past, he could not help feeling some pride in the man he had never known as his father. He had so many questions, not least who the doctor had done work for and who were his contacts? Was there an inner circle of people his father still mixed with? Who had taken over the Party after his retirement? The extraordinary, momentous discovery he had just made in reading his father's letter was almost too much to absorb and he paced the room trying to make sense of it all. Despite the shock of all he had experienced, the emotion of hearing about his father's death, and the connection he felt in reading his letter, there was another side of him that recognised he was on to an incredible story. However, he also realised that to go further would be to travel a dangerous road and that he needed to protect what he had uncovered and not least his own life. He could feel the adrenalin of danger, but there was also an undeniable, irresistible excitement within him. *Where to start?* Suddenly, on impulse, he reached in his wallet, retrieving the blue card with the star logo that Dr Friedman had given him, and dialled the number.

11

Ordnung Muss Sein

('There Must Be Order')

Tuesday 18th February 2020, 5.00pm
Maximilian Strasse, Berchtesgaden, Bavaria

Dr Friedman was tired. The last three days had been exhausting emotionally and physically. All his life he had spent compromising so much for outcomes that he did not seek for purposes that he was not party to. For once, he felt some satisfaction that he had refused to be totally complicit in the cover-up of the murder of his friend. At last, he had struck back by sharing his guilt and revealing the secret that he had kept for thirty-five years since he had brought Hans into the world on that November night in 1984.

The chime on his bell brought him back to the present. Sighing deeply, he opened the door to an expressionless face that he recognised as the man who had instructed him to visit Gunther's home days before and issue a death certificate. He was in a black coat with the collar drawn up around him and was followed by a short, thickset man with a goatee beard in an anorak and flat cap.

"May we come in, please? You will remember I am Karl Schmidt and this is my local colleague, Dieter Kranz." The request was icy cold and Walter stood to one side as they entered.

They were shown into the consulting room, where the doctor was told, "Please sit. We have some questions." The shorter man began going through papers on the desk in front of where they were sitting. Walter started to object, but Schmidt silenced him curtly. "Please, Herr Doktor, this a matter of national security. You will answer questions or suffer the consequences." The look in the intelligence officer's face left Walter with no illusions. This man had the ruthlessness that he had seen in so many over the years, and he sensed he was in mortal danger. "Yesterday, you travelled to Hamburg. What was the purpose?"

Walter responded nervously that he wanted to visit friends he had not seen for some time, as his heart thumped and he tried to suppress a shake in his hands. He was about to continue when he saw the gun in Schmidt's hand.

"I will ask you one more time only. The purpose of your visit?"

Walter recalled a conversation he had once had with Gunther about undergoing an interrogation where, in the SS, they had been instructed to give vital elements of truth to cloak the lies which may be necessary to ensure survival.

He began nervously. "I called *Der Spiegel* on Sunday to tell them that Roche had died because I knew he had once been an important Nazi. I have sold them stories before."

The blow when it came was as unexpected as it was painful. Schmidt had used the back of his hand with a callous viciousness. Walter fell to the floor, where he was kicked in the abdomen, causing him to lose his breath. The smaller of the two men then lifted him bodily back into his seat. Blood from a cut on his upper cheek seeped over his lips. Schmidt looked him straight in the eyes, pulling his face forwards then forcing Walter's head backwards. "Who did you see, Herr Doktor? I have little time and you mean nothing to me. Tell me what I ask or, as I have said, suffer the consequences. Who was it?"

Despite his predicament, Walter began to feel a growing sense of anger replacing the sickening fear. It was as if the instinct of selfpreservation was starting to raise a desire for aggression which he tried to suppress. He found himself feigning a trembling and weakened voice. "Please, I do not know, but I was told only his Christian name of Gerhard." He told his assailants that he had agreed to meet this journalist at the hotel by the airport and give him information about this man he knew had once led the National Socialists.

Suddenly the chair was tipped over and, once again, he felt a harsh pain as Kranz kicked him in the chest before raising the chair in the air. "*Nein*," barked Schmidt. "Only if he does not answer."

Walter saw the snarling aggression in the shorter man's face, his eyes full of hunger for violence. Schmidt put his gun against Walter's head. "You carried a case into the hotel but left without it. Please tell me what was in it?" The somewhat strange politeness in the question only added to the ruthless, icy-cold menace.

Walter's anger was bubbling inside like a volcano at these bastards who had haunted every moment of his life, blighting every ideal, eating into his conscience like an invasive cancer corrupting his very being, but he fought to restrain his impulse. "There were photos of me as a child with him, and some of him in uniform when he was at the Berghof with Hitler. I gave him the file and said they could publish whatever they wanted."

This time there was no assault, merely a silence as Schmidt sat back for a moment, drawing a deep breath. "Then, Herr Doktor, as we both know, journalists for *Der Spiegel* always leave a card, a code or a contact number. Where is this?"

Walter protested that no such information had been given to him, at which point Kranz pushed over a glass-fronted cabinet containing antique medical equipment with an explosive crash. The next second he felt the weight of Schmidt's closed fist smash into his face. For a brief moment he blacked out, then he was vaguely aware of being straightened in his chair, blood pouring from his nose. His fear had been replaced with a furious desire to retaliate like a caged animal, his conscious thoughts being taken over by a primeval instinct for survival.

Barely able to hold back his urge, he began coughing as he spied the heavy marble inkstand within a metre of his face. His movement when it came was sudden, violent and utterly unexpected, catching his assailants completely off guard. From his limp, slumped position, his hands shot forward, swinging the inkstand against Schmidt's shocked face, catching him in the temple, causing him to scream in agony and fall backwards. Walter's eyes were wild, gripped with his desire for blood, stamping on Schmidt's face and grabbing the gun from his fingers. The two men grappled, both blindly struggling to fight off the other, until there were two gunshots: one from the weapon being fought over, causing Schmidt to cry out; the second discharged from Kranz's handgun into Walter Friedman's neck. Falling limply to the floor, Walter turned and, in his last breath, looking defiantly at his attacker, he gasped the words, "*Eins zu eins,*" before smiling for the final time.

Schmidt rolled backwards, gasping for breath, his arm held tightly against his side, from where blood was beginning to flow. "Get the dressing box from the car," he commanded. "I need to talk to Berlin. Do it now!" he snapped at his hesitating subordinate. "Then find the keys to this *scheisse's* car."

Tuesday 18th February 2020, 9.00pm
BND Headquarters, Chaussees Strasse, Berlin

The Director of Internal Affairs paced his office, breathing heavily. He was a tall, thin, imposing man with parted grey hair and iron-rimmed glasses with a military bearing. Heinrich Hoffman was renowned for his single-mindedness and thoroughness. He was not easily ruffled, but he knew the seriousness of the mission, although, frustratingly, not all the detail he would normally like to possess. It had only been five days since he had been entrusted with security for the former British Prime Minister, who was coming for an 'informal' meeting with the Chancellor. He had sensed it was, perhaps, not as informal as he had been briefed. This, he was told by the Chancellor's senior advisor, was a highly secret visit and was being held for reasons of ensuring *'Ordnung Muss Sein'* ('there must be order'). That, he knew, was indicative of a meeting of importance. It was an expression he well recalled from his military days to justify some of the more violent tactics employed which were sometimes deemed necessary and often denied afterwards.

He had personally overseen the escort of his VIP charge, who had arrived in a private jet to Berlin Tegel Airport. Motorcycle outriders had surrounded a bullet-proof, blacked-out limousine for the hour-long trip to the Chancellor's retreat at Schloss Meseberg, north of Berlin, with traffic held back to ensure the journey was unimpeded. That part was normal for a VIP visit, but such transport and arrangements were not normally laid on for unofficial visits by former political leaders. Equally surprising was that no officials accompanied the former Prime Minister and, upon her arrival at the Baroque Palace, she was met at the entrance to the imposing white building by the Chancellor herself, standing alone.

Heinrich had been asked to make himself available for the meeting in case sensitive issues may need special scrutiny. This was a role he had long been used to, having served in the security forces since his time as a young officer in the Stasi, the former East German secret police, which he had joined in 1985. He was a practical but ruthless achiever of his objectives, gaining no satisfaction in unification with West Germany, which he regarded as having a corrupting, degenerate influence. Nevertheless, he was nothing if not pragmatic and had relished the opportunities of proving himself in a new regime where he was admired for his efficiency. Despite his normal reserve, he found it hard to hide his surprise with what he was to be told that day.

Summoned into a large ornate office with a huge chandelier, he was invited to sit at the end of a short, polished table, at which the Chancellor sat, facing her former opposite number from Britain. A teapot and cups were on a silver tray and he was asked if he would like a drink which he politely declined. He was then fixed with the steady gaze of his boss as he was made to understand very directly that he must never share with anyone what he was about to hear. "During the War," the Chancellor started, "Hitler made some secret agreements with the British and the Americans which the world would find unbelievable and impossible to accept, especially as this has been covered up for generations. These accords covered a joint Allied/German offensive against the Russians in 1944. There are only three originals of these documents and no copies. After successive leaders in the United States and Britain passed the information on to their successors, it was decided by the former US President and the British Prime Minister that the time had come to consign this dreadful episode to a history that was best kept secret for all time. This is why my help is being sought. Both the current Prime Minister of Britain and the President of the United States have not been made aware of this and even I am not party to the detail of these secret agreements, which are now to be destroyed.

"However, as you know, Gunther Roche, the former leader of the so-called Fourth Reich, resides here in Germany. He has copies of these agreements which, if made public, could cause a terrible breakdown in order with catastrophic consequences. You might imagine what Putin would do with such information, using it to justify marching into the Ukraine and taking back the former Soviet states. The threat would be massive to Poland, Slovakia, Romania, the Baltic States, with the potential of reigniting conflicts over Bosnia, Croatia and Serbia. Social unrest would explode with riots in London, Paris and here in Germany. I can assure you, Herr Director, governments would fall with the resulting anarchy. Such information would potentially destroy NATO and then think what a free reign that would give to President Putin. Our old threat from the East will be there once again. *Mein Gott*, I dare not even imagine the consequences."

The Chancellor sighed, looking down at the papers in front of her, shaking her head. Then, as if seized with renewed resolve, she fixed a piercing look directly into Hoffman's eyes. "This may be the single most important mission I ever entrust to you. You will visit this man, Herr Director, and find these agreements or any documents relating to them. Roche lives in Berchtesgaden; we must execute a forensic search of his home, ensuring every possible place is examined and that every one of his contacts is interviewed. We must also interrogate him, but this operation must only involve a minimum number of persons. There is a secret protocol that you may use to describe what you are seeking which is covered by the words, '*eins zu eins*'. This is like a password and will inform anyone in the know that you are one of the very few who are aware of the secret agreement. Your operatives should not be briefed on what they are seeking except to say we are investigating the activities of former Nazis in order to assist finding the looted gold the Nazis hid at the end of the war, the *Raubgold*, most of which has never been recovered."

The Chancellor stood up, making it obvious the meeting was over. "One last thing, Herr Hoffman: you will report to me, and only to me. Any documents recovered will not be read but surrendered directly to me. You will understand our old term; this is to make sure '*ordnung muss sein*'. The agreement and any documents relating to it pose a massive threat to public order and political global stability." The director snapped to attention, then bowed to the former British Prime Minister, who smiled briefly in acknowledgment, before executing a smart about-turn and marching from the room.

That was only the previous Thursday; now he had another death to report and knew that he was in for a customary dressing down. In his former days, he knew how he would have dealt with the incompetence of minions like Karl Schmidt, by making an example of them, but today was different with so-called democratic rights. Still, he had one ace up his sleeve to report to the Chancellor privately: a phone call that had been received at Dr Friedman's house whilst clearing-up operations were taking place.

Tuesday 18th February 2020, 10.30pm
Alster Waterfront, Hamburg

Hans watched the motorcycle courier leave with a roar, feeling some relief to have relinquished the documents, tinged with an enormous sense of apprehension at what he now faced because he knew he could not just let this go. Returning to his apartment, he determined to find out more, not least from those his father knew but also from those who may still be alive. Dr Friedman and his mother were the only links he knew to his father, but he possessed an inquisitive journalistic drive and, if he was honest, it was not just about his father he sought answers. The documents he had seen and the explosive information contained in his father's letter threw up so many questions.

He found the number and dialled; the answer was swift: "Hello. *Guten abend.*"

Hans was so preoccupied with his thoughts he hardly noticed the voice was different. "Walter, it is Hans, I have so many questions; *mein Gott*, you will not believe all I have uncovered. Can we talk?"

The voice at the other end was slight and impersonal. "Ah, Hans, but which Hans? I know many. Your surname, *bitte?*" The words did not fit and Hans was momentarily disorientated.

"Walter, are you OK?"

There was silence for a moment and then Hans abruptly ended the call, his heartbeat quickening. Then, searching through his personal contacts, he found the name Bernhard Meyer from *Berchtesgadener Anzeiger* (a local newspaper in Berchtesgaden). Bernhard and Hans had been fellow students at the Humboldt University of Berlin and they had remained in loose touch ever since, occasionally meeting. He was now deputy editor of the local paper and had a reputation for forensic investigative reporting where he would gather intricate details to enlarge or improve a story, which he then syndicated to national papers. *Der Spiegel* had occasionally published his work, prompted by some help from Hans, which had given Bernhard increased status in journalistic circles.

His friend answered immediately, asking how he was, but Hans interrupted. "Bernhard, please listen carefully, I am on a story so great, so unbelievable, it is hard even for me to grasp, but I need your help urgently. I also need you to check on someone I know." His voice had a nervous edge and he was aware that everything was beginning to assume dramatic proportions as though he was living in a fantasy, yet it was so real and almost suffocating. He knew he was genuinely nervous yet also excited despite wanting to express grief over the loss of his father.

"Christ, Hans, what is the matter? Are you giving me a scoop? Because we could do with one down here." Bernhard tried to inject some lightness into his words to balance the drama he sensed in Hans.

"Bernhard, do you know of a Dr Walter Friedman? He lives on Maximilian Strasse, in Berchtesgaden." There was a pause and Hans was already anticipating the response he dreaded.

"*Verdammit*, Hans, are you a clairvoyant? Of course, I know him, or knew him. We just had the police story that he was killed in a road accident an hour ago on Saltzburgstrasse near the Berghof. There is speculation it was suicide because he drove straight into trees; no other vehicle involved. Apparently, there was a big fire. Hans, are you there? Hans!"

Bernhard then heard the half sob of his old friend before he heard his shaking voice. "*Scheisse*, then they got him and the swine will come for me. Bernhard, my life is in danger. Can I come over, perhaps stay a couple of days? But please, you must not tell anyone I am coming. I will drive because it is safer. There is a story here that is beyond incredible and, if I live, then we will make Bernstein and Woodward seem like amateurs." He forced his laughter as he referred to the famous journalists who had exposed the Watergate scandal in the 1970s, bringing down the US presidency of Richard Nixon. His friend immediately agreed he could stay for as long as he needed.

"But Hans, please, what is going on?" Bernhard pleaded, to which the reply came: "It is '*eins zu eins*'. I will be there tomorrow. Tell no-one."

12

Operation Willi

Friday 11th December 1936, 10.01pm
The Drawing Room, Windsor Castle

The radio broadcast of *The Comic Opera* was sharply cut short. "We interrupt this programme for an important announcement." Then, after a few seconds: "Ladies and gentlemen, this is Sir John Reith of the BBC. May I present His Royal Highness, Prince Edward."

The broadcast crackled for a moment as the former King and Emperor took his place before the ironically castle-shaped microphone, banging his leg as he did so, sending an ominous knock live to his audience across the Empire and to the listening world:

> *"At long last I am able to say a few words of my own. I have never wanted to withhold anything, but until now it has not been constitutionally possible for me to speak.*
>
> *"A few hours ago, I discharged my last duty as King and Emperor, and now that I have been succeeded by my brother, the Duke of York, my first words must be to declare my allegiance to him. This I do with all my heart.*

"You all know the reasons which have impelled me to renounce the throne. But I want you to understand that in making up my mind I did not forget the country or the Empire, which, as Prince of Wales and lately as King, I have for twenty-five years tried to serve.

"But you must believe me when I tell you that I have found it impossible to carry the heavy burden of responsibility and to discharge my duties as King as I would wish to do without the help and support of the woman I love...

"I now quit altogether public affairs and I lay down my burden. It may be some time before I return to my native land, but I shall always follow the fortunes of the British race and Empire with profound interest, and if at any time in the future I can be found of service to His Majesty in a private station, I shall not fail.

"And now, we all have a new King. I wish him and you, his people, happiness and prosperity with all my heart. God bless you all! God save the King!"

At 11.30pm the phone rang again as Greta Atkins was about to retire to bed, having spent time talking to friends over her telephone about the abdication. She had already taken a call from Unity Mitford, who had stated that the Führer was greatly disappointed. She was excited, saying that Hitler was to offer the former King and Wallis Simpson a personal invitation to visit Germany. "You simply must come if David accepts and we can catch up." She added at the end of her call, "Such a pity, all this, and I jolly well think he should have been King. Darling David was such a dish."

Greta now answered the telephone, half expecting who it was, and smiling to herself that she was correct, having long become used to the fact he was no respecter of time.

"Menzies here." The familiar voice was sharpened by the phone line. He never used his Christian name because, she had reflected before, he demanded respect, an attitude that she wickedly teased. "Dreadful business this, tonight, but it may have removed a greater part of the problem we have had with this growing support for Hitler. Look here,

Miss Atkins, there's to be some kind of party at Cliveden, Lady Astor's place in Buckinghamshire. Loads of people apparently being invited from the who's who, including your friend Charles Edward Duke of Saxe-Coburg, the new German ambassador von Ribbentrop, plus the chap tipped to be next US ambassador, Joseph Kennedy. If you can get Charles Edward to come over that will guarantee you an invite. Nancy Astor is promoting the 'Cliveden Set', a ghastly circle of people that you may have heard of sharing similar views on firm government, anti-Semitism and the fostering of stronger ties with Germany. The Mitfords are involved, Lord Rothermere, Sir Oswald Mosley, of course, Douglas-Hamilton, a few MPs, plus some mainly young people, but my concern is that this growing 'set' are becoming quite fixated on the Nazis. Tonight's announcement was a bombshell, but then, twenty minutes ago, I took a call from Dickie Mountbatten. They are intent on inviting the former King and Wallis Simpson. The party is scheduled at the end of the second week of January, so you have time to prepare."

Greta was able to inform Colonel Menzies that an invitation to visit Germany was to be extended by Hitler to Edward and Wallis Simpson. The head of SIS drew in his breath audibly. "These cads are attempting to destroy this country's institutions, Miss Atkins, and if they succeed in getting the infernal Prince Edward into their camp, heaven knows what they will try next. I need you to find out if the rumours are true of an affair between Simpson and Ribbentrop. God knows what influence that slippery German chap has already exerted on her. Try and spend some time with that damned floozy and see what we may be able to use as an appropriate lever to prevent this ridiculous liaison progressing to marriage. May be worth you getting in touch with Mountbatten. He feeds me tit-bits and loves to feel involved in intelligence issues. I think it's time we took him into our confidence and get him firmly onside. As always, my dear, you will report directly to me or through your old friend, Mona Maund, who is now principal secretary to Sir Oswald Mosley and accompanies him everywhere. I presume you still have possession of your gun, which I will renew your authority to use but only if you must. Last time, you left quite a mess for me to clear up."

Greta was quick in her response, drawing a customary sigh from the deputy director. "Dreadfully sorry, I shall be more considerate next time, my dear Colonel, and, perhaps, merely leave bodies to remove; far less inconvenient. Well, now I shall look forward to a very entertaining and informative party. You do give me the nicest assignments. Goodnight, Colonel."

The following day, Greta placed a call through to Brook House, the Park Lane penthouse home of Lord Louis Mountbatten. After a few brief words with Lady Edwina Mountbatten (rarely home amidst rumours of numerous affairs during her constant travelling), with whom Greta had a passing relationship, she heard the familiar warm, clipped voice greeting her: "How frightfully nice to hear from you, old girl, especially at this somewhat turbulent time."

He was always so utterly charming, and Greta had long been an admirer of this dashing naval officer, who was ebullient, poised, with an extraordinary charisma that lit up a room as he entered. "Dickie, I need to see you as a matter of pressing importance on a private level, but it is one of national importance too."

The earnestness of her tone immediately impacted on Lord Louis. "I confess I am intrigued, but of course, my dear, when had you in mind? I have to attend a meeting today with Bertie, our new King, before a meeting of the Privy Council, but then I will be free. Shall we meet at the Dorchester for an early dinner, say, 7.00pm?"

She arrived just after 7.00pm, sweeping down Park Lane in the chauffeur-driven Rolls-Royce that Lord Louis had sent to pick her up. As customary, her outfit drew more than a few admiring glances: a figure-hugging, floor-length, off-the-shoulders, vampish silver dress with a generous split, revealing teasing views of her long legs, as well as matching high heels, a fur stole and glittering hanging diamond earrings. Her long cigarette holder was held coquettishly as she alighted from the car; a liveried doorman in a top hat was holding the door open and standing to attention. She swept in to be greeted by Lord Louis in a dress Naval uniform dazzling with gold decoration and rope braid hung across his chest from his shoulder whilst medal ribbons added to this man of stature. "Utterly delighted to see you, and looking ravishing, if I may be so bold." He bowed before kissing her hand.

"Dickie, you are a complete show-off." She smiled broadly at him.

She accepted his arm as he led her to the Dorchester Bar, where they were welcomed by Harry Craddock, the renowned bartender from whom Lord Louis ordered two Manhattans, for which Craddock was famed. "Devastating, all this dreadful abdication business," he began, as they sat sipping their cocktails at the bar, occasionally waving to other guests, who nodded to him. "Poor David, we tried right up to the end to stop all this, but, you know, there is part of me that thinks Bertie is absolutely made for this moment and that he is the right chap. Today, I helped persuade the Privy Council that we should give David the title Duke of Windsor. Two reasons: one, it satisfies the need to keep him onside with a title. He will still be referred to as His Royal Highness, and two, because it prevents him taking up political office or speaking on political issues, which could be frightfully embarrassing. They dug their heels in about giving Wallis any title, which, I must say, I was a tad pleased about. She isn't really made of the right stuff, you see. They conceded allowing her to be referred to as the Duchess, but no full title in the way she is addressed."

Greta looked directly at him. "That is partly the reason I wanted to see you. I have something I need to tell you and for which I will need to seek your help," Greta ventured. "Dickie, I have not been entirely open with you about my work and what I actually do."

Lord Louis sought her hand, kissing it once more. "My dear Greta, I am, perhaps, a tad more well informed that you might believe. Colonel Menzies and I have been sharing a little about you, for which I trust you will forgive us both. He has sketched in brief details and I will, therefore, save you the embarrassment of telling me you are working for British Intelligence; but Mum's the word, eh?! I have not, however, been fully briefed on your mission or the circumstances surrounding it. Come, tell all, but shhh." He smiled broadly, putting his finger to his lips before escorting her to the elaborately decorated Promenade Restaurant with its imposing Corinthian marble columns, exquisite chandeliers and lanterns, with exotic ferns, giving it a sense of decadent palatial opulence. A table had been prepared at the end of the long room and a screen separated it from other guests, who were seated some distance away. A piano played and a young American singer by the name of Danny Kaye was presenting songs of the time which he introduced with a relaxing subtlety mixed with a sharp, friendly wit.

The head waiter greeted them before the sommelier came to take their order for wine. Another Manhattan was served because, as Lord Louis wryly put it, "These are hard times which we need to smile our way through."

Greta related the story of the increasing German attempts to infiltrate the establishment and, more importantly, those of influence within British society. Lord Louis was openly astonished as she reeled through the names of many involved, no more so than when he heard of the discussion between Charles Edward and the former King the previous year at Balmoral. She looked at him earnestly. "We believe that this is the nearest thing to a coup being organised in the event that the British government stands in the way of German aspirations for territorial gains in the East."

They paused as the salmon course was cleared in preparedness for a T-bone steak that Lord Louis had promised would be the best she had ever tasted. A waiter approached the table, removing the cork from a bottle of Dom Perignon Vintage Champagne, offering Lord Louis a taste, who waved acceptance for the pouring of two glasses into beautiful crystal flutes. The waiter bowed to Greta, and more formally to Lord Louis, before backing away from the table.

Greta continued, "Your cousin, Charles Edward, Duke of Saxe-Coburg and Gotha, is a member of the Reichstag and serves Hitler with a passion. He believes that there should be an alliance with Britain in the conquest of Russia, possibly even joint military action. Regrettably, it is my belief, Dickie, that David, our former King, has been seduced into this way of thinking. The result would be too horrifying to contemplate of a German dominated Europe under the ruthless dictatorship of Adolf Hitler. There would be no balance of power, and our government may be forced to acquiesce because of pressures from within. At worst, we must consider that there are many who would support the return of Edward VIII to the throne with Wallis as Queen, even if it required military intervention." Greta looked imploringly at her friend, a man she had truly grown to respect but whose loyalty she knew she had to test. "Dickie, will you help us? First, at very least, by speaking to David and strongly warning him away from taking a path that could lead to anarchy, even civil war and the threat to democracy itself? Second, by putting pressure on those who are being seduced by appeasement, or worse, giving support to Hitler in the belief that the avoidance of conflict overrides other considerations? Whilst we know there are many, like Mosley, who are persuaded by the simplistic, deluded view that totalitarianism will triumph over adversity, we need to target those whose views we may divert. I am, I suppose, entreating you, my dear Dickie."

Lord Louis sighed deeply, suddenly looking as if he was carrying a huge and wearisome responsibility. "My dearest Greta, I have no time for these odious, distasteful megalomaniacs who appoint themselves as posturing dictators and, I confess, even less time for the thoughtless people or minions who sycophantically pander to their autocratic excesses. Sad to say, however, it appears that no matter how atrociously these dictators behave with whatever powers they appoint to themselves, people idolise them in the most extraordinary fashion. Remarkable, really, and even more so when my dear family is involved; otherwise, I would attribute it to lack of breeding. This damn fool little corporal from Germany with the silly moustache never impressed me other than with his desire to reintroduce order to his country. However, his appalling record of violence, his treatment of the Jews, arrests without trial, imprisonment of opponents and a ruthless abolition of free speech tell me what we are dealing with. I agree with Mr Churchill, and his son Randolph, who are both warning of the dark clouds of war once again descending on Europe. Hitler and his distasteful gang are odious thugs, but the danger is that out of disorder, they have seduced many of the social elite to back them." Lord Louis took Greta's hand and, for the third time that evening, kissed it in the most gallant fashion. He grinned boyishly at her with a twinkle in his eye. "You see, my dear, breeding will always out, and I can assure you, despite you checking out my credentials – a touch clumsily, perhaps – that my loyalties are absolute to my King and to my country and that my resolute sense of duty will never falter, not now, not ever." He spoke the last words with a severity of commanding seriousness, then, more lightly: "But I will forgive the utter hurt you have caused me by doing what I would have done to you."

They both laughed with the release of tension between them and the relief of sharing a trusted confidence.

Saturday 12th December 1936, 2.00pm
Offices of the Reich Chancellery (Reichskanzlei),
Wilhelmstrasse, Berlin

The afternoon was cold and windswept as the line of large Mercedes cars swept up Wilhelmstrasse one after another. Despite the bitter temperature, four armed guards in black uniforms stood outside, spaced ten metres apart with two either side of the tall entrance to the Chancellery. As the vehicles entered the courtyard at the front of the old Baroque palace, a dedicated officer to each snapped to attention, raising an arm in salute before greeting their assigned occupant. One after another, the trusted elite of the German government were driven to the meeting to which they had been summoned by the Führer at 7.00am that morning. Reichsführer Himmler was already there, having customarily arrived exactly forty-five minutes before the prescribed meeting time, immaculately dressed in his black SS uniform. He was met by Karl Haushofer in an untidy suit, who failed to return Himmler's brisk, right-armed '*Heil Hitler*', which the Reichsführer found intensely irritating. Haushofer, he knew, was an academic advising the Führer on geographic issues relating to Germany's sacred right for eastern expansion. Reichsmarschall Hermann Göring arrived in full dress uniform at 1.45pm, a little perturbed that he had missed his planned luncheon party at Carinhall, his country residence north-east of Berlin. Reich Minister Goebbels appeared a little dishevelled, despite wearing his customary brown uniform, which Himmler noted as he watched each arrival through the ground-floor ante-room. He felt a sense of Spartan Teutonic superiority over them, seeing a decadence in their living styles. Others followed in quick succession: the architect Albert Speer in a trilby and double-breasted suit; Martin Bormann in a brown uniform, whom Himmler dismissed as something of a thug; and, finally, Deputy Führer Rudolf Hess, who, like Himmler, was dressed in a black uniform with silver epaulettes.

As the new arrivals joined Himmler, each briefly greeted the other with the shortened right-arm salute, bent at the elbow which had been adopted as a more informal version of the stiffly outstretched *Heil Hitler*. The echoing of female shoes on the marble floor announced the arrival of Emilie Schroeder, the young, cheerful and outgoing member of Hitler's private secretarial team.

"*Guten tag liebe Herren.*" She beamed at them. "The Führer will see you now." Then, lifting her finger to her mouth in a mock secret gesture, she added, "He is in a very good mood, you might even get cakes with your tea," drawing a loud guffaw from Göring.

"Dearest Christa [her familiar name]," Göring slapped her on the back, "you always light up every occasion. Perhaps, you should work for me. I share wine with my staff whenever we can make up a good reason."

Christa laughed in response, and no-one noticed Himmler raising his eyes to the ceiling and grimacing at this disgraceful lack of formality. Christa led them down the corridor up the white stone stairs to a short hallway, in front of which were the tall double doors that led to the Führer's study, where she bade them wait outside. She went to a colleague, who placed a brief call, and then Christa gestured to the door, announcing, "You are permitted to enter the Reich Chancellor's office." A guard on one side of the entrance jumped to attention, then clicked his heels before opening the doors.

Hitler was standing in front of the French windows that opened onto a balcony he had asked Speer to create three years before in order to be more visible to the crowds. He was attired in a single-breasted brown uniform jacket with the golden Party badge on the left side of his chest, the Iron Cross and the black decoration for the wounded below, with a thick chocolate-coloured belt. He motioned they sit in the armchairs spread before his desk. They could feel his iron will, his authority and power, which were overwhelming. Goebbels felt waves of emotion and admiration for his leader that he could never understand but which directed his unswerving loyalty.

Hitler began, "Today is a propitious day for Germany if we grasp what Providence has given to us. As you know, the British King has abdicated, who was and remains sympathetic with our great mission. Our operative, agent Prinz, has confirmed that the former King commands great loyalty from many of those in positions of power, with an equally loyal following from the workers. He understands our need to expand eastwards and annihilate the scum that rules the bestial races that make up Russia. Now is the time to put our great plans into effect. We will liberate the world from these mongrels who contaminate the blood of Europe. We are the superior race, and this great task, this mission, falls upon us, and we will not fail but triumph with our iron will." The Führer's voice had risen to a crescendo with his last words, which he completed by thumping his clenched fist down on the table. All stood in unison, raising their arms stiffly in salute at this inspiration, this god amongst men.

The Führer raised his arm as if talking to a massed rally, then, waving his finger to the right and to the left, he declared, "We will never be cowed as the superior race, never. We will not be dominated by Jews, or Slavs, or Poles or the Ottomans nor ever the Bolshevik scum. Germany shall be the invincible power that, at last, dares to speak the truth about superior nationhood, the destiny of our people and the purity of our race." His voice dropped, adding contrast and more depth to his words. His piercing blue eyes sought each of those present in turn. "We shall seek allies in our mission and Britain must never be our natural enemy. As your Führer, I am inviting the former King and his future bride to come to Germany. Imagine the message that will send to the world as they see your Führer with the former King of England standing together. Imagine the legitimacy that will lend to our cause." The phone rang on his desk twice and stopped. Hitler folded his arms and a triumphant look came into his face with a broad and rare smile. "I have a plan that will assuredly bring Britain to our side in our momentous struggle, remove all opposition to our aims and give us the greatest alliance the world has ever known." The Führer returned to his desk, asking that their guest join them and that tea and cakes should be served.

The door swung open and a tall, smart, imposing man in naval uniform marched in with thick, swept-back silver hair and an Iron Cross at his neck. As he entered, he halted, stood to attention, giving a naval salute before approaching the smiling Führer. The two men shook hands warmly before both raised their right arm in mutual recognition and respect. The Führer turned to the room. "*Meine Herren,* Rear Admiral Canaris, our Head of the Abwehr ['German Intelligence']. He will present our plan."

The admiral smiled broadly then, once again, extended his arm, to which the others stood and responded.

He began, "This morning, the Führer and I discussed the constitutional crisis in England and believe this represents our great opportunity. The Britishers are in awe of their monarchy and hang on to this anachronism because they always look backwards as a nation, *ja?*" There was a murmur of acknowledgment with a suppressed chuckle from Goebbels and Göring. The admiral continued, "We replaced our Kaiser 'Willi', and the weak democracy which followed, with more effective and decisive leadership. Leadership with an iron will and a driven purpose expressed through the Führer. Well, we must, as Napoleon said, understand the mind of our enemies, and in so doing, we must consider Britain. However, the British Empire need not be an enemy but could be our greatest friend. Our plan is simple: we use their monarchy to lead them in our direction and abandon democracy. They now have a disenchanted former King whose future wife's honour has been insulted and his own called into question. As our agent Prinz tells us, he has many powerful friends and he is broadly sympathetic with our aims. We are embarking on a plan for him to retake his throne, as rightful heir, with greater powers, supported by those we already know are loyal to him, and those who recognise the need to annihilate Communism. Naturally, we would endorse him and, if necessary, intervene militarily to back him. The aim? Simple: we establish strong, authoritarian leadership in England, as we have here in Germany, using the legitimate monarch to achieve this. We have called this '*Operation Willi*'.

"I have arranged for our ambassador, von Ribbentrop, to attend as many social events as possible in England where he can influence and gather sympathy with our cause whilst encouraging support for the restoration of the rightful King. There are many in positions of influence in Britain who would endorse a more powerful monarchy, including, we believe, the former King himself. Subtlety is the key to success here and a coup would be executed with stealth. First, the customary Royal Assent to Laws would no longer be guaranteed. Moving on from that, the Royal Prerogative would be used as a means of power broking until the King assumes total authority. Then, it is a short step to following the path set so brilliantly by our Führer. As insurance, we will, at the same time, arrange for contact with the new King George VI, through trusted intermediaries, with a similar agenda, but he is nothing like his brother and can hardly speak coherently." He raised his hands as if in mock despair, drawing laughter from Hitler, which was quickly echoed by others in the room.

"We believe this is the time to put in place plans for the restoration of Edward to the throne that is rightfully his and form an invincible alliance as the former King admires our Führer. We know both Royal brothers are anxious to avoid war at all costs, and political democracy may be an obstacle to peace, as we are already seeing views expressed against appeasement by people like Mr Churchill. We are fortunate, I think, that we have the weak Mr Chamberlain and not Mr Churchill as Prime Minister. We see current events as an extraordinary opportunity to begin Operation Willi, restoring power and respect for the British monarchy. I think history adds legitimacy to our aims. Herr Haushofer?"

Karl Haushofer stood up. "*Mein Führer*, with your permission. Throughout history, superior nations have emerged to create the culture which follows. Europe has become contaminated and the purity of our Germanic race is under threat. It is imperative that we cleanse central Europe and geographic history teaches us that this is our right. We are naturally the *herrenvolk* ['master race'], with our pure Aryan blood. Civilisations only triumph where strength is asserted and land occupied by superior races who can then absorb the territory into their own. That must be our destiny, just as the Romans created their empire, instilling their will and their ways upon lands from which they prospered. Germany is the greatest nation in the world, as we proved at the Olympics, taking more medals than any other. Britain is our natural ally, sharing many of our ways, and their Royal Family is descended from German blood; but the country suffers from weak democratic government. We can restore their national pride with strong leadership and an alliance with Germany."

The Führer had risen from his chair and was rubbing his hands together, then he marched to the phone. "Where are the cakes and tea? My guests are waiting," drawing laughter from all present.

As he put the phone down, Hitler walked to the map on the wall, sweeping his hands across Europe. "This operation will be part of our grand design to bring civilisation and an order to the world that has never before been known, overseen by the invincible strength of the new Germany."

13

'Better the Child Should Cry'...

"It is better the child should cry than the father."
Old German proverb

Thursday 20th February 2020, 11.00am
Franziskanerkirche and the Old Cemetery, Baumgartenallee,
Berchtesgaden, Bavaria

The black Mercedes hearse moved slowly towards the Franziskanerkirche [Franciscan Church] in the centre of the town, where a surprising number of mourners had gathered. From 9.00am, people dressed in black had been arriving; many of them were elderly and some were being helped to chairs which the priest had been instructed to organise outside. Others were in wheelchairs, but almost all the elderly men present had medals proudly worn evidencing their service to the Fatherland. There were younger men in attendance in black uniforms with silver epaulettes but no discerning additional decoration. As the hearse had arrived at the church, almost all those outside, that by now numbered over two hundred, either stood to attention or stiffened in their wheelchairs and gave the Nazi salute. The young men at the rear unfurled two flags: one was red with a white circle and black swastika in the centre; the other showed the older German national symbol of the cross in black in the centre of an outer white cross. As they held the flags on their long poles at an angle, the attending police watched impassively and did not intervene despite the illegal display of such insignia.

A number of men in leather jackets watched from the edge, taking photographs and occasionally briefly speaking quietly into lapel radio microphones. As the hearse was unloaded for the ceremony, two black-uniformed men stepped forward, clicked their heels and placed a red, black and white ribbon down the length of the coffin, before turning as one, raising their right arms and marching away. No-one knew who had paid for the funeral, as instructions had been given by telephone followed by transfers of money into the accounts of the funeral directors from an unknown source. Directions had been precise both in terms of times and the manner of the service. Veterans and their guests were to be given absolute priority for access and seating. There was even a private medical ambulance on hand, staffed by a complete paramedic team. There had been some scuffles at the edge of the crowd as a number of men dressed in dark overcoats had begun photographing those in leather jackets who had earlier been taking photographs of the attendees. Once again, the police appeared not to notice and were barely visible for a period.

Hans was watching the entire event from a first-floor room of the Hotel Alpina, overlooking the rear access where the mourners were gathering, which Bernhard Meyer had organised the night before through his contacts in local business. They had agreed to split up and, as Bernhard would raise no suspicion as a journalist, he had mingled amongst those attending, stopping to address and interview the veterans, asking about their wartime service.

They had stayed up late the night before after Hans had made the long drive from Hamburg, arriving at 6.00pm, having set off from his apartment at 4.00am. He had taken a number of unnecessary turns off his route and parked to see whether he was being followed, waiting five minutes, before continuing his journey.

After initial greetings, despite being tired, Hans had poured out his story as an astonished Bernhard struggled to grasp the enormity of what he was being told. The local journalist began taking notes, as he had done from his earliest training, creating headings in order that he could revisit and create a credible and well-edited story later.

"*Lieber Gott*, Hans, this is all incredible, beyond belief, and if it was not you speaking to me, I would not believe it."

They had parked Hans's car in the garage, which Bernhard never used at the house, and both agreed it was critical that no-one knew he was there. When Bernhard informed him that his father's funeral was to take place the following day, it was Hans's turn to be incredulous yet strangely uplifted by the fact he was there.

"Bernhard, my father was murdered and I know it was by those bastards in the BND. I need to know why and how this whole thing fits together." After planning their strategy for the following day, they finally retired to bed at 1.00am, although neither were tired as they both felt an adrenalin-fuelled sense of excitement and anticipation.

In the morning, Bernhard drove them to the outskirts of the town, and they made their separate ways to the location of the funeral. Hans took the keys from reception to an upper floor room, from where he had a clear view of those attending. He began taking photographs through telephoto lens of those he perceived to be working for the BND. They stood out with their utter disdain at the solemnity of the occasion but had obvious interest in those attending. *What kind of country have we become?* he mused, thinking that these men were reminiscent of the Gestapo from the days of National Socialism and, like then, it appeared that life was expendable in the interests of the state. As the coffin arrived, he experienced an overwhelming wave of emotion as this was the closest he had ever consciously been to his father. For a moment, he found it hard to suppress the tears that filled his eyes, but then he forced himself to continue observing those attending, taking photographs.

At the last moment, just before the doors of the church closed, a long grey limousine with darkened glass windows drove up to the gate, from which four men alighted, one holding open a rear door. Two further matching vehicles followed, pulling up behind the first, and the doors opened but no-one came out. A tall, imposing man in dark glasses stepped out of the leading limousine in a black three-piece suit and was escorted up the pathway by those who had been in the car dressed in long black coats. The camera shutter repeated, taking a number of images of the man entering the church, shadowed by those who were obviously there to protect him.

Suddenly, he could not resist the desire just to be there and, leaving his room, he descended the back stairs and exited through a fire escape door. He cut across the grass onto a small road, walking away from the church, then cut across onto a track which led to an intersection, where he doubled back down into Franziskanerplace, pausing outside a medical centre as he surveyed access to the church. Two police officers were leaning on their car at the front, seemingly non-attentive and impervious to passersby. A small group of BND agents were gathered near the front entrance but did not appear to be watching the street. He walked past the entrance on the other side of the road, passing a shopping complex, then crossed over, walking back up the street but taking a left turn into a narrow lane bordering the church wall in which was an arched doorway with a round iron ring which he was able to turn and open. Inside, he could hear the echoing voice of the priest offering prayers. He was in a narrow corridor which had an opening to the right in front of which was a large wooden screen. Peering around it he could see the congregation about ten metres away. He noticed some empty benches next to the screen and he edged around it and slid quietly onto the first bench, where he watched the unfolding ceremony, very aware that this was the funeral of his father.

There were readings and more prayers, and then the priest announced that there was to be a eulogy. The man who had been whisked to the funeral in the limousine stood up, removed his dark glasses and walked towards the altar, in front of which the coffin was situated draped with the wide red, white and black-striped ribbon. As he approached the coffin, he bowed before turning to the assembled. Two young men in black uniforms who were standing either side of the main aisle clicked their heels and stood to attention briefly, before smartly reverting to an at ease position.

"*Meine Herren*," he started, his words echoing around the church, "some here, of course, know me, others will not recognise me, but some may think, s*omething about him is familiar.*" The voice was soft, cultured and yet commanding, seeming to electrify those watching. "You should know my rank and position: one which has not been used publicly for some time. I am revealing today that I am the Reichsmarschall of our great movement."

The men in uniform, once again, snapped to attention, this time extending their right arms. There were gasps around the congregation, then a number of men stood, also raising their arms in salute. At the back of the church, two men in leather jackets exited, one already speaking into his radio.

"Today, we remember the previous holder of this great office, bestowed upon him by the Führer himself in 1960. There should be an Iron Cross upon the casket of this heroic man. Not an ordinary Iron Cross, but one with a diamond cluster, oak leaves and swords which was personally awarded to him in April 1945 by Adolf Hitler in the Führerbunker. Sadly, we have been unable to trace his decoration, which we know he used to proudly display in his home." Hans's heart leapt a beat as he thought of the medal, given to him by Dr Friedman, that he had decided to cherish in honour of his father.

"There were only twenty-eight of these ever awarded, but in my view, this man deserves the greatest award ever given in the history of the

Fatherland, the legendary Knight's Cross of the Iron Cross with diamond cluster, golden oak leaves and swords." A murmur of assent was heard around the church.

"There was only ever one recipient, the great Hans-Ulrich Rudel, who once had the temerity to land his squadron of Stukas and Focke-Wulfs on a US air base before inspecting their troops, who were on parade."

There was laughter from the congregation.

The tall man continued, "Today, there will be a second recipient: our former leader, Reichsmarschall Gunther Roche."

Applause came from the congregation interspersed with shouts of '*zieg heil*'.

"Our leader not only served Germany with gallantry throughout the war; he helped our Führer escape…" He paused, looking quizzically at his audience, who were captivated by his words.

"But *nein*, that is impossible. Didn't he die in the bunker? That's what I was told."

More laughter, and a few handclaps.

"Apparently, this is proven because they found his teeth and hid them in Russia. But wait, the extraordinary thing is that he had changed sex! Ach, well, it was before this became fashionable, because the teeth were eventually identified as those of a woman. Then, recently, more teeth were found by the Russians, which they announce are Hitler's. Never use a Russian dentist! Then, after they are given a cursory inspection, they hide them again. Perhaps, even the Führer's teeth frighten them!"

He raised his hands as if in despair, to the delight of those present.

"Gunther was an extraordinary man, excelling from his earliest days in the service of our great cause. A marksman in the Hitler-Jugend, a Luftwaffe-trained pilot, an SS officer eventually joining the Leibstandarte SS Adolf Hitler unit. He served with honour in France, Holland and Yugoslavia, and excelled in our Russian campaign. He joined the operation to liberate Mussolini from captivity in the audacious mountaintop raid by glider with the great Otto Skorzeny. They escaped from captivity together after the war by borrowing American uniforms and walking out through their prison gates. I am informed they both regretted dressing so scruffily."

There was more laughter.

"They lived together for a while here in Berchtesgaden right under the noses of the Allies. After the war, Gunther joined Hitler in Argentina and helped shape the new Germany, steering us to economic triumphs, which was the vision of our beloved Führer. We even sold arms to the Jews! I can't imagine who could make up such nonsense, but this all helped us become the country we are today, dominating the EU. We should call it Grosse Deutschland because, as other countries make a greater mess of their economies, we impose our rules. We no longer need marching soldiers and blitzkrieg, but German strength has reasserted itself with stealth under our leader, our Reichsmarschall. Gunther retired from his role in 2001, having helped us reunify our nation, cleanse the country of Communists and destroy the left-wing terrorism of the 1970s. We no longer hold power, but we exert it, and we will seize back what was ours, as we did in the 1930s. Gunther Roche laid the foundations of our new Reich, our Fatherland, rebuilding our strength with economic weapons, from which we are rising again and with which we will triumph through our iron will." His voice had risen to a crescendo as he banged his fist into his other hand, emphasising the moment.

Hans was suddenly aware that one of the men who had accompanied the speaker as a bodyguard was observing him, and then he watched as he alerted another, who turned to look across at him. He rose from his seat and slipped behind the screen as the voice of the speaker continued to echo round the church. Once in the corridor, he ran out of the building, following the track into some trees near the Old Cemetery, emerging onto Sonnenpromenade. Pausing briefly to check behind him, he crossed quickly onto some grass, heading into more trees, then turned round again, breathless. He could see no-one other than two tourists poring over a map and pointing to the Franziskanerkirche. He walked slowly towards the Hotel Alpina, smiling at reception, as he walked past and upstairs to his room, where he collapsed on the bed, his breaths coming in short gasps. He was unaware that outside one of the tourists was talking into a radio.

Returning to the window, he watched the man whom he now knew as Reichsmarschall exiting the funeral first and then being driven away, with one of the other cars following. The second vehicle had moved to the edge of the cemetery, awaiting the slow march of the pall-bearers carrying the coffin to its final resting place.

Hans collected his thoughts together and texted Bernhard that there may be nothing in it, but the limousine security detail seemed to be taking notice of him. The reply was short: *"Christ, were you there? It was like a Nazi rally. I have something. Be there soon."*

Hans ordered a snack meal of schnitzel with buttered vegetables and a bottle of Grauburgunder [Pinot Gris] from room service. He gulped the first glass of wine, trying to steady his frayed nerves and take in all he had seen. It was, as Bernhard had said, more like a rally than a funeral, and it was obvious the speaker was known and admired by many in the congregation, but as Reichsmarschall! His mind was struggling to absorb what he had witnessed. He had the pieces of the jigsaw but was trying to fit them into place. Why was his father killed, and was this all linked to the Barbarossa Secret? There was no autopsy report on the death of Dr Friedman, but he knew already it would be covered up, just as the murder of his father had been.

Exhausted after the events of the last two days, he slumped into an armchair in the corner of the room and had drifted into a fitful sleep when he became aware of an urgent knocking on the door. Peering through the peephole, he was relieved to see Bernhard and was shocked, on opening the door, to find he was accompanied by an elderly man wearing a Bavarian hat in a wheelchair being pushed by a silver-haired woman, both dressed in black.

"Hans, this is Wolfgang Richter formerly a Feldwebel ['Sergeant'] with the Leibstandarte SS Adolf Hitler. He was assigned to Berlin in 1944. I have explained you work for *Der Spiegel* and that you are investigating the death of Gunther Roche as you believe he has been murdered. Herr Richter worked directly for Gunther up to the end of the war and afterwards. This is his wife, Rosa, who is a former member of the Party after the war."

Hans bowed and shook hands with them both, thanking them for agreeing to meet with him, giving Bernhard a brief but astonished smile. The older man loosened his scarf, undoing his coat top button to reveal an Iron Cross as if to add to his credentials. He had a thin pencil moustache, and, despite being in a wheelchair, had an unmistakeable military bearing.

"I believe you seek information about Reichsmarschall Roche and the secret role he played in the final days. How much do you know?" The elderly man looked directly at him. He was clearly sharp, very sharp, and Hans sensed that they may have struck gold. He decided to try using something that would resonate, if this man had been really close to the centre.

"Herr Richter, I have uncovered information that suggests to me that the Reichsmarschall was murdered because of *'eins zu eins'*."

The reaction was instant. "*Gott in Himmel!* How do you know this? No-one ever speaks of it – not then, not now." Wolfgang sat upright, looking at him very directly. Hans reassured him that it was because he had known the Reichsmarschall personally through a mutual friend, Dr Walter Friedman, and that he had shared a little of his past from the days of the Third Reich. He told Wolfgang that he understood this related to matters that were of the utmost secret to those entrusted by the Führer.

"Herr Richter, all I require are a few answers so that I can complete the jigsaw of information. I am seeking a motive for what I believe was a state-sponsored assassination of Gunther Roche. I have to tell you that his friend Dr Friedman has also been killed and I know the two deaths are related. I need your help."

The old man reached behind him, gripping his wife's hand. "Rosa has always wanted to forget my role in all of this. You know, those were great days when Germany was strong in its beliefs and true to principles. It is all gone now, with all this so-called diversity. We are being contaminated by immigrants, a lack of political will and, once again, we are becoming weaker. Once, we commanded respect because we were powerful." He closed his eyes, remembering.

"I served under Sturmbannführer Roche in Berlin from mid1944 until the last days of the Reich. He was an inspirational leader and totally loyal to the Führer. I knew he was involved in intelligence work, but he could not share much of this with me as it was so secret. He explained to me that he was bound by a code of '*eins zu eins*' which meant most of what he knew was known only to those he had had direct contact with. I was also told, very directly, that any information so classified with that term would carry the penalty of death if it were shared with anyone but himself.

"In 1945, in the last days, I was entrusted with ensuring that certain orders were executed and one of these carried the '*eins zu eins*' protocol. He told me that he needed to arrange for papers to be safely secured from discovery in case Berlin fell. A number of files were given to me, all labelled '*Operation Willi*'. He told me that these related to the involvement of the British Royal Family in an alignment with Germany and what their role might be if Germany invaded Britain. This was being coordinated via the Duke of Saxe-Coburg and Gotha, whom I had seen many times. I remember meeting him in the Führerbunker in April 1945 and found myself bowing to him. I knew he was royalty and that somehow still meant something."

Wolfgang Richter sighed deeply, his eyes narrowing as if the memories were painful to recollect.

"I took the files and undertook not to read the contents, but, of course, I did have a brief glimpse. I was staggered to see records of meetings held between the Duke and various British leading figures, including the former King Edward VIII and George VI. What surprised me more was that there were documents not only predating the war, but there were others dated from 1940 onwards relating to ongoing discussions not only just with the Royal Family but also involving the British Prime Minister, Winston Churchill. I also saw reports to the Führer signed by Rudolf Hess after 1941 when he had been denounced as a traitor. You may imagine my surprise, but I was glad, as I had always believed that Hess was a loyal member of the Party. Despite the extraordinary contents of the files, I did not read anything in detail as I was a mere sergeant aged twenty and I felt guilty for just looking. I have never shared this information with anyone. I journeyed from Berlin to a place called Marburg, where I gave the files to an intelligence officer we knew we could trust, Karl von Loesch. The papers were described to me as 'insurance' by Gunther Roche, hence the reason they were not to be destroyed. I believe von Loesch buried the files in a forest. Subsequently, in May 1945, I was given an order by Roche to authorise von Loesch to reveal the location of these files to the Allies.

"The only other information you might wish to know, which I was informed was *'eins zu eins'*, was that I acted as a go-between after the Führer escaped Berlin. Radio communication was considered too dangerous, but at that point, Hitler was still in Spanish territory. Roche flew me to and from various locations, where I would deliver or pick up papers, or even briefcases of documents. We were operating openly with the co-operation of British and the Americans. It was crazy, as though we had never been at war at all. I was informed that our safe movement was guaranteed because of a greater *secret*, but I was never told what it was and few of us even knew of its existence.

"On one occasion, in late May 1945, Gunther confided in me that we needed to eliminate potential sources of any leaks of the Secret covered by '*eins zu eins*'. I was with Gunther when we delivered orders to British Intelligence authorising the death of Heinrich Himmler, who had gone behind the Führer's back in attempting to broker peace discussions with the Allies. The story put out was that he had committed suicide, but he was killed by British Intelligence not least because he may betray the Secret. I oversaw the poisoning of Karl Haushofer in 1946 because he was a traitor and had started talking to British Intelligence. His son had been shot the year before because he was involved in the bomb plot attempt on the Führer's life. We also organised smuggling cyanide to the prison where Göring was being held during the Nuremberg trials in 1946. On that occasion, Göring had stated he would rather take his own life than face hanging, but we assisted in the process. We were told he was making too many high-level friends and offering information in return for protection and benefits for his family. Gunther told me that an orderly had administered the cyanide. The Americans put a statement out that he committed suicide the day before his execution and helped cover up what really happened.

"After the war, I remained in service to the Party and saw the Führer on a number of occasions in Argentina and Chile. He was never the same again and always had a melancholy sadness about him, but he still carried greatness on his shoulders. We remained absolutely loyal until his death in 1962. I continued to work for the Party, admiring the brilliance of Reichsmarschall Roche in achieving the restoration of Germany, until the final conference in 1984, after which I retired, although I still assisted the Party occasionally.

"I have one last matter I can share, which happened in the 1980s. I was aware we made an arrangement with British Intelligence to despatch two people which would ensure the final protection of the Secret. The first was Albert Speer, Hitler's former close associate, architect and Minister for Armaments whom we poisoned in a London hotel in 1981. Speer was beginning to talk too much, even offering an exclusive on a story he had to tell to the British press. We sought permission from MI6 to have him 'taken out'. The second was Rudolf Hess, the former Deputy Führer, who was being held in Spandau Prison, Berlin. In 1987 he was killed, ironically by the British, despite him being held in Germany. I was told that he was part of the Secret and that Russian Premier, Gorbachev, wanted him released. All I knew was that the information he possessed was so sensitive that the British could never risk it ever becoming known and it was subject to *'eins zu eins'*. Our contacts in MI6 informed us that British Prime Minister, Margaret Thatcher, had stated Hess could not be released whilst he was still alive and a request was made, to which we acceded. They released a story that he had hung himself; quite an achievement for a ninety-three-year-old!

"The only other information I have is that Gunther once informed me the Secret guaranteed the safety of the Führer, our community and the survival of many others. This Secret was known by twenty-one people in 1945. By 1985, he informed me only five remained alive, including Hess. When I last saw him five years ago, Gunther said he was the last person alive from that time possessing the information, which only three others in the world knew of. He never divulged to me what this Secret was but did say he shared it with the British Prime Minister, the President of the United States and Queen Elizabeth II."

Bernhard whistled in astonishment at this revelation.

A loud knock on the door broke the dramatic pause that followed. Then, as Hans looked at Bernhard, there was another knock, followed by, "Bundespolizei, you will let us in now!" Hans nodded to Bernhard, who opened the door to reveal two men in black coats and dark glasses. Both had drawn guns, which they lifted as they entered as though not to threaten.

"Hans Schirach, you will come with us, please," the first man stated. "The rest of you will not speak of this to anyone. If you do not, Mr Schirach will return safely and then, Mr Meyer, you may even get your story. If you go to the police, this will not end pleasantly."

The second man went to the window, holding his weapon back against his chest as he peered out. He nodded to the other, who went to the door, checked the corridor and then led Hans from the room, snatching his camera up from where it had been left on the windowsill.

14

'TheAstorgruppe'

Saturday 16th January 1937, 7.00pm
Cliveden House, Buckinghamshire

A procession of large cars swept down the long drive to the Victorian Palladian style-mansion, floodlit to the front, showing off its arcaded terrace and colonnaded entrance. Cliveden often held such society parties or weekend events, but this one was different. The former King, Edward – or David, as many there would refer to him – was to attend in his last British social event before departing for Austria, where he had chosen to settle in the short term after his abdication. He was the draw of society, and despite the negative view of the event by George VI, he had not put pressure on those with whom he closely associated not to attend, out of a final courtesy to his brother before his departure.

The guest list had been closely studied by Colonel Menzies, who had summoned Greta the preceding week for a briefing.

"Ah, do come in, delighted, as always. Your sense of fashion does you credit, Miss Atkins," he remarked with a sigh.

Greta never ventured anywhere without paying careful attention to her appearance, which had, in no small way, assisted her career. She also took an impish delight in dressing up a tad more lavishly when visiting the colonel. This day, she wore a tightly fitted black skirt, a wide white belt, with a Gucci black and white bag complemented by matching high heels. A coquettishly worn Garbo slouch hat completed the outfit, with black netting draped teasingly over the eyes.

"Are you flirting with me, Colonel?" she teased, breathing the words to him, as she extended her cigarette, waiting for him to light it.

Colonel Menzies had long ago learned to put up with Greta's rather tiresome habit of taunting him with her 'womanly wiles', as he dismissed them, but despite his reticence and show of disdain, he could not help but enjoy the banter. On this occasion, he raised his eyes to the ceiling, as if seeking inspiration from above, before reaching for a file, from which he extracted a typed list. "Miss Atkins, I have the entire guest list for this dinner party, and we need a strategy of attack. This 'Cliveden Set' is becoming the fashionable group to be amongst and they appear to represent quite a cross-section of society. They openly discuss and debate the direction political power should take and, I am informed, there is a growing number expressing sympathy and support for Nazi Germany. We have recently received intelligence from Berlin that their Foreign Minister, von Ribbentrop, has been boasting he can lever power through these people and thereby prevent resistance to Hitler's flouting of the Versailles Treaty. That treaty, put in place at the end of the Great War in 1919 to prevent another war, is increasingly becoming seen as an irrelevance by the Germans, which threatens the peace of Europe. Hitler claims the reparations and terms of the treaty are inequitable and that his country has been saddled with impossible demands and many in this country agree. Ribbentrop claims that such is the power of this 'Cliveden Set', which he refers to as the 'Astorgruppe', that their sympathy gives Germany confidence in the freedom to re-arm."

The colonel rose from his seat, wandering to a brown photograph on a side table of a group of soldiers, which he showed to Greta. "These were my fellow regimental officers at the start of the Great War in 1914.

I was in Flanders, Miss Atkins, in the trenches, and I witnessed the most unspeakable horrors." He sighed deeply, then, after placing the photograph back, he added, speaking slowly, "Out of that gathering of sixty-five officers, four of us survived the carnage. It is because of those damnable memories that Ribbentrop and his cronies are able to gather sympathy for their cause of supposedly trying to maintain peace by giving to Hitler what he wants. Do you see? Despite my abhorrence of war, I regret that I have to agree with Mr Winston Churchill that we cannot simply sit back and allow Hitler to go unchecked. Last March he marched into the Rhineland and we stood by and did nothing. In July, he sent troops into Spain to side with Franco's Nationalists or fellow Fascists. Both of these actions are in breach of the Treaty of Versailles, but no-one appears to have the appetite to stand up to Nazi Germany. This 'Astorgruppe' must be watched and, more importantly, we need to know where our former King stands on these issues. He is shortly leaving to take up residence in Austria on Germany's doorstep where I'm sure there will be even more attempts to influence him.

"Your primary aim will be to ascertain how much real power there is, or the ability to influence power, amongst those attending the dinner who exhibit sympathy towards Germany; and how much of an endorsement our former King appears to be giving. If you get a chance, steer Charles Edward into conversation with the Duke of Windsor and the German ambassador. Von Ribbentrop is quite aggressive and outspoken, a ghastly upstart of a man by all accounts, but we might gather the Duke's reactions to one of Ribbentrop's customary tirades on German foreign policy. He's frustrated because he hasn't succeeded in getting an Anglo-German treaty that will let them take over half of Europe and seize the former German colonies in Africa. As they are now showing more of their true colours, these Nazis are seeking to ensure Britain does not stand in their way. It will be interesting to see how those in our establishment are reacting. Oh, and a tip, my dear: the son of the outspoken Mr Winston Churchill is going. Randolph is quite a handful after a drink, and like Ribbentrop, he has a reputation for blunt outbursts. These rather brash chaps could be a useful weapon or catalyst for you."

The colonel picked up his phone, ordered tea, seeking a cursory nod from Greta that it was for two. He then reached for his pipe, which he lit slowly, puffing large clouds of smoke as he patted the top of the glowing bowl with his fingers rhythmically. "We need to establish the date for the forthcoming trip by the Duke to Germany and whether they propose making it some kind of state visit. If you can use your influence on Charles Edward, you might warn him that if the Duke intends to go in any official capacity, Parliament may block it, causing yet more scandal. I am hoping you can get Lord Louis Mountbatten to have some deep conversations with the Duke, as this may be his last chance before he and Wallis leave the country for their so-called exile. Oh, and watch the interaction between Wallis Simpson and Ribbentrop; I'm sure you can spot the sort of damn fool nonsense you females get up to."

Greta stubbed out her cigarette with a dramatic display of surprise. "My dear colonel, I am shocked at your outrageous slur on the fairer sex, denigrating our honour in such an uncalled-for manner. I have a good mind to defect to the Bolsheviks. When you have finished ruining my former unquestionable admiration for you, can you give me a quick resume of some of those attending?"

The colonel indicated that he had placed a red mark against those of interest and handed the list to her. "You will need to do your homework and evaluate where the sympathies of those attending lie. Lady Nancy Astor is a rather fierce, prickly type, so I should be a little wary of her. We don't want to risk you losing favour with the hostess. First woman to take her seat in the House of Commons, so brooks little argument from those who disagree with her. She has something of a reputation for being abrasive and she has anti-Semitic tendencies. Extraordinary thing is, she appears to be anti-Catholic as well, so something of an enigma. This 'Cliveden Set' seems to be growing in number and influence, so we need to be on top of them. You will be interested to know that our old friend

Albrecht Haushofer will be there, whom you may recall is a friend of the Deputy Führer, Rudolf Hess. He seems to know a great deal from what he told you when you met him at that dinner during your time at the Olympics and so may be worth having a quiet word or two. I shall be available all night if you get a chance to pass info, which saves you having to remember too much. Just pop for a walk with your old friend Mona Maund and she'll do the rest. Oh, and I'm also sending Guy Burgess over, whom you've met, to sneak about the place and pick up any little extras, but only you have the connections to give us the real inside story."

On her return to her apartment, Greta studied the list, taking mental note of those of interest. The Marquess of Douglas and Clydesdale, Douglas-Hamilton was escorting the German aviator Hanna Reitsch, whom he had been with at the German English Society dinner she had attended five months before. Other names marked in red, apart from the Duke of Windsor, included Sir Oswald Mosley, Lord Rothermere, Sir Arnold Wilson MP and the Italian ambassador Dino Grandi, who was known as something of a womaniser. The future US ambassador, Joseph Kennedy, had been highlighted with the words 'anti-Semite?'. Albrecht Haushofer was asterisked and she recalled him as a decent sort with whom she had established some respect and rapport. There were other names she knew, including Diana Mosley (formerly Mitford) and her sister Unity, who by now had become a favourite in Adolf Hitler's inner social circle. As she perused the list, many of whom were leading members of society, she realised she needed to prioritise her connections.

That had been a week before, and now she was in a RollsRoyce with Charles Edward, Unity Mitford and Guy Burgess, whom Greta had cleverly proposed to Unity could be her 'safe' chaperone for the evening as someone she knew well and could vouch for. Greta was wearing a simple silk cream long-fitted dress with a cowl neckline which hugged her body, although the bottom half flared from the thigh. Unity was in a layered white chiffon dress, off the shoulder on one side, with triangular edges adding definition to the layers. Both Charles Edward and Guy

Burgess lavished praise on them as they had emerged in their outfits to join them for the hour's drive to Cliveden.

As they approached the house, Unity spoke excitedly about the evening. "I can hardly believe we are sharing a table with the former King and Mrs Simpson. Oh, darling Charles Edward, was all this your doing? You are so wonderful."

The Duke denied that he could take credit, as such matters had not been influenced by him. Greta secretly smiled to herself, having arranged the seating through Dickie Mountbatten. They were not only to be seated with the Duke of Windsor, but Lord Louis had organised the entire plan with the Astors. On their table would be Lord Halifax, a close associate of and advisor to Foreign Secretary Anthony Eden; von Ribbentrop; Dino Grandi; Sir Oswald Mosley with his new wife, Diana; Joseph Kennedy; Albrecht Haushofer; Randolph Churchill; Douglas-Hamilton and Hanna Reitsch. Lady Astor had agreed with Lord Louis or insisted that she simply had to be seated with this exciting group, which effectively made it the top table.

They swept through the enormous iron gates and down the long, gravelled drive towards the frontage of the mansion with its extended entrance and impressive Georgian facing above. An arcaded terrace stretched to right and left of the building, which was floodlit, imposing itself on the wide approach. The drive gave way to a large open area with building wings to either side of the house, creating a square where uniformed footmen were directing the vehicles under the scrutiny of a tall man in a long dark coat with a three-cornered hat. As they stopped, the door was held open by a liveried servant in a long, red, gold-buttoned coat, white shirt and matching bowtie, who took their invitations. He bowed, stepping back, and gestured them to follow him through the entrance, where he handed the invitations to another red-frocked footman who was wearing a white wig with ponytail.

As they entered, they were announced in a loud, lofty voice: "His Highness, the Duke of Saxe-Coburg and Gotha, accompanied by Miss

Greta Atkins, together with Lady Unity Mitford and her escort, Mr Guy Burgess."

The vast hall was filling with guests, many of whom were instantly recognisable society figures and included some from the showbusiness community. They were offered Champagne and were immediately approached by Lord Louis Mountbatten, looking magnificent in full white naval dress uniform with blue sash. *A showman as always*, Greta thought. He bowed graciously, reintroducing them to his diminutive, petite yet pretty companion, Yola Letellier. She curtsied, bowing her head, around which she wore a floral band over short, curly chestnut hair and a threequarter length, silk light blue dress. "*Enchantée*," she whispered, stepping back behind Lord Louis.

"Absolutely delighted to see you all, and Charles, dear boy, I'm surprised you have time to be here now you are a fully-fledged member of the Reichstag and, I hear, President of the German Red Cross too. Unity, good Lord, looking as ravishing as ever and, I'm told, quite a hit with this funny old chap, Mr Hitler."

Lord Louis could not help but notice, with a touch of delight, the slight wince by his cousin at the somewhat mocking way he had referred to Germany's leader; Führer was the term of respect expected if not demanded at home. Unity hardly noticed because Hitler had told her that, in private, she could address him directly as Adolf. However, she had changed this to '*Mein liebster Adolf*', which would gain a playful reprimand from him for being too forward. She knew it infuriated his admirer Eva Braun, who had, rather tiresomely, become a member of the inner circle. Unity was sworn to secrecy about her intimacy with him because, he had told her, it would weaken the national perception of his single-minded dedication to Germany on his historic mission that Providence had chosen for him.

There were chairs all around the great entrance hall, some positioned at small tables, allowing guests to socialise in groups. Lord Louis directed them to an area under an enormous portrait of their hostess, Nancy Lady

Astor, with her hands held daintily behind her back in a flowing white robe. This was to the left of a huge sixteenth-century stone fireplace, which was a massive welcoming centrepiece to the grand open space in which large logs crackled with welcoming flames. The walls were panelled and the room surrounded with suits of armour and tapestries, adding an historic flavour of grandeur. Already seated was a young man with swept-back brown hair talking animatedly with a rather flamboyant dark-haired bearded man, whom Greta already knew as the Italian ambassador Dino Grandi. He had previously given her a card at a dinner dance, asking her to call him, informing her that he could arrange a special tour of Italy with a wink and smile that had left her in no doubt as to his dishonourable intentions. As Dickie introduced Dino, he dramatically raised the right arm of each lady in turn, kissing their hands with a flourish, before Lord Louis announced that the younger man was Randolph Churchill.

"This is the son of Winston who is causing you two chaps a little discomfort, I think, with his speeches warning us of cataclysmic disaster if Hitler and Mussolini get their way."

Dino immediately lifted his hands in alarm, straightening his dinner jacket with an exaggerated gesture. "*Dio Mio, Eccellenza*, I keep telling you, Il Duce wants peace and has stated this again and again. Mussolini wants order not war."

"My father is warning us of the truth," interrupted Randolph, "which is plain enough that Germany is intent on expansion, and unless we prepare, we shall be too weak to prevent it."

"With the greatest respect, young man," Charles Edward countered, "I think the Führer has made it clear that he is concerned about the threat in the East, from the Bolshevik Communists."

His voice was agitated and Greta was poised for what she already knew was going to be a quite entertaining, lively occasion.

Randolph stood up, a glass of brandy in his hand, despite the fact it was early evening. "I believe, sir, you were introduced incorrectly. As a result of you being defeated in the last shindig, when you forsook your grandmother by fighting for Germany against England, my understanding is that you now have no titles at all."

There were gasps at Randolph's brazen outburst, and Charles Edward's face reddened as he shook with anger, despite Greta squeezing his arm.

"By God, sir, you insult me openly. We have no time for your father, this upstart, Mr Winston Churchill, who holds no office, and I am damned if I will accept this from you. You will apologise." His voice had risen and others began to look at the developing scene.

"Enough!" The commanding voice of Lord Louis cut in with a ruthless tone which brooked no dissension. "I am here as a representative of the Royal Family. You will both cease this now, especially in front of the ladies. My dears, please accept the apologies of both these men. Waiter, more Champagne."

At that moment, the small chamber orchestra in the corner of the great hall began to play and another man joined them, which assisted in diffusing the moment. He did not wait to be introduced but approached with his hand held out, saying in a confidant drawl, "Well, hello, my name is Joseph Kennedy, and I am delighted to make your acquaintance. Guess I'm going to be ambassador here and I'm told I am sitting with you guys."

He shook hands with Lord Louis, without bowing, who introduced everyone, and to Greta's amusement, he bowed to each of the ladies with his hand held stiffly behind him.

"I haven't been briefed on what I call the Duke," Kennedy stated loudly yet hesitantly. "Can you assist me, sir? I don't want to end up in your Tower of London."

His warm humour changed and lightened the mood just as Lady Astor mounted some steps to a dais at one end of the hall, waving her arms, bringing silence to the room. To her left, a Master of Ceremonies dressed in a red jacket and white bowtie announced, "Distinguished guests, Members of Parliament, my lords, ladies and gentlemen, pray be upstanding to welcome your former King, the Duke of Windsor, accompanied by Mrs Wallis Simpson."

The orchestra struck up the national anthem as they entered, and as the music faded, there was an initial ripple of applause, which grew until it became tumultuous. The former King was dressed in a black dinner jacket with a large white Victorian bow around his neck which accentuated the style of his appearance, although he initially appeared slightly shy. Then, his face broke into a smile as he nodded courteously, acknowledging the unexpected welcome. Wallis Simpson was attired in a long, black, shaped sequinned dress, showing off her figure, whilst a jewelled tiara completed her outfit. She smiled broadly, waving and blowing kisses to the guests.

Lady Astor nodded to the orchestra, who broke into the tune, 'For He's a Jolly Good Fellow', which drew laughter, and the Duke immediately saw the funny side before waving his hands in a mock subduing of the music.

The Master of Ceremonies now asked the invited guests to move to the French dining room to take their seats. He then approached Lord Louis, requesting that both he and Charles Edward, together with their respective guests, wait behind whilst others were seated. The great hall began to empty and Lord Louis led them to where Lady Astor was standing sharing Champagne and talking animatedly to the Duke of Windsor and Wallis Simpson. The former King graciously stepped forward, bowing to Unity and Greta, who curtsied, before he took each of their right hands, kissing them in turn. "Delighted you both could come, I think you know, Wallis."

He turned to shake the hands of Lord Louis and Charles Edward. Wallis smiled at the two ladies, who curtsied again.

"Oh, goodness gracious, do not let anyone see you doing that." She laughed, then, coquettishly: "They've refused me any right of royal recognition; but, don't tell anyone, when I marry David, I will be a duchess. We have agreed that in our home I will be called Your Royal Highness. I guess that may be treason, right? Or is it sedition?"

This time, the entire party laughed, which lifted the inevitable tension that resulted from this being the Duke of Windsor's first engagement since the abdication.

15

An Extraordinary Meeting

Thursday 20th February 2020, 3.30pm
Hotel Alpina Ros Demming, Berchtesgaden, Bavaria

They descended the back stairs slowly, one of the men wearing dark glasses in front of Hans, the other behind, both with their weapons drawn. For some reason, although alarmed at his predicament, Hans did not feel unduly threatened by them but very apprehensive as to his fate. As they reached the rear door, the man at the front turned. "Herr Schirach, my name is Stefan. We wish you no harm and if you do as we ask, you will be returned here later. You will switch off your phone now please. You will not speak to anyone or attempt to escape. Please understand, we are ordered to protect you, but only if you obey orders."

He opened the door, looking furtively beyond the frame before summoning Hans to follow. As they crossed the grass into the trees both men were turning constantly, watching as though wary they were being watched themselves. They cleared the trees to Sonnenpromenade where a large grey limousine was waiting, which Hans presumed was one of those he had seen earlier arriving at the funeral. This was surrounded by four further men, with guns in their hands, who were also continually looking around and dressed similarly to those who had taken him. There were three rows of seats in the car and Hans was bundled into the rear seat before the others climbed in.

The limousine sped off, turning right onto Maximilianstrasse, passing the Franziskanerkirche where the funeral had taken place which already seemed a long time before. There were eight in the limousine apart from Hans. Two in the front next to a grey-haired driver, three in the row behind and one either side of Hans in the rear seat. Suddenly the vehicle turned sharply and Hans saw two police officers on the street diving out of the way.

"*Scheize*, the bastards are on to us," the driver grunted, seizing a radio microphone. "This is Oberst ['Colonel'] Hoffman, we have trouble with the police which means the BND will be involved. Additional security measures needed. Activate aerial cover." The vehicle increased its speed.

"Roadblock ahead," one of the men in the front shouted.

Hans could see a police car across the road with a group of officers standing either side. The limousine still seemed to be increasing speed. Stefan, sitting to his right, turned to him. "The car is bullet-proof and bomb-poof, Herr Schirach, please do not worry."

Suddenly, the Mercedes swerved to the left then right, shrieking around the police car barrier as shots were fired, and there were metallic bangs with some craze marks appearing on the windscreen. One of the men in the front seat pulled out an automatic weapon, lowering his window and firing a long burst backwards. As he leant back in, he looked back with a grim smile and in a loud voice, heightened with tension, announced his shots had been over their heads to warn them.

Hans could feel his heart thumping as adrenalin ached within his body; sweat began pouring down his face and his hands shook. Stefan spoke again, rapidly but reassuringly. "We all have military training. There is nothing to fear. You are in safe hands."

Hans did not feel reassured, his eyes darting around him.

The radio crackled into life and a voice announced, "Aerial cover will be in place within minutes."

They shot out of the main built-up area of Berchtesgaden onto Obersalzbergstrasse leading towards the wooded area and the Alpine backdrop beyond. Having picked up speed, suddenly the car gave a sickening jolt and slowed; Hans could see why. Ahead of them were three blue and yellow police vehicles parked across the carriageway, blocking the road entirely, with their lights flashing. In front of the roadblock and facing them was a military light infantry vehicle (LIV) with a heavy calibre-weapon mounted on top. Either side of the LIV were a number of uniformed personnel in helmets. Two further cars were parked either side of the road and standing next to them were men dressed in the leather jackets Hans had seen at the church that morning. The driver of the limousine leant forward, pressing a button, and spoke using the hands-free.

"BND ahead, five hundred metres; roadblock with armed Serval [military vehicle]. Confirm aerial surveillance."

They crawled slowly forward, each of the armed men in the car cocking their automatic weapons with a loud rasping noise. Stefan told Hans to get his head down. "They may be using armour piercing, and we could be compromised."

As if on cue, there were a number of loud bangs as the limousine was hit by a short burst of fire, but nothing penetrated. There was a crackle from the vehicle speaker then a voice: "Aerial now deployed; you have two Tikads ['drones'] fully armed above you complete with grenades. We have you on visual – on your orders, Herr Oberst."

The grey-haired driver turned towards them. "No-one will use their weapons until I say, unless I am neutralised. Your duty is to protect Herr Schirach, and those orders come directly from the Reichsmarschall."

All those in the vehicle stiffened with a rapid, "*Jawohl.*"

The limousine came to a halt fifty metres from the roadblock. There was an eerie, tense silence, which to Hans seemed never-ending. The colonel behind the wheel spoke again: "They cannot see how many there are of us with our darkened glass. On my command, all will exit except Stefan, who will protect Herr Schirach. Stand behind the doors with your weapons trained on the helmeted soldiers. They pose the greatest risk."

There was a loud squeal of loudspeaker feedback outside and then an emotionless staccato voice echoed down the road: "We are Bundesnachrichtendienst ['BND']. You are in an impossible situation. You will leave the vehicle. Open the doors, drop your weapons to the floor, and exit one person at a time with your hands on your head. If you do not obey these orders within one minute, you will be eliminated."

The colonel turned again with a grin. "I think it is time we turned the tables and took control." He reached for a microphone attached to the dashboard, flicking a switch marked PA.

"*Guten tag meine heren.* I am Oberst Klaus Hoffman, formerly of the KSK ['Kommando Spezialkräfte – Special Forces']," his voice boomed out back at the roadblock. "That'll unsettle the bastards," he muttered before lifting the microphone and continuing, "We have overwhelming superiority and we have you covered. Please place your weapons on the floor and move the vehicles. You will dismount from the LIV leaving the machine gun pointed skywards."

There was another silence, but Hans could clearly make out some of the soldiers laughing. The LIV began to move slowly towards them with men walking behind taking cover, some holding their guns to their shoulders, aiming at the stationary limousine.

Colonel Hoffman spoke towards the hands-free. "Feldwebbel, take out the police vehicle directly ahead of us to our right side."

The response was immediate: "My pleasure is your command."

The colonel muttered, "Now the show starts."

Suddenly there was a sound like a thunderous rolling drum followed by huge crashes. In front of them there were flashes as glass shattered and pieces of metal flew off the police car which began smoking and then collapsed as the tyres were hit. The blue lights on the top disintegrated, and one door swung open then hung off the body at a crazy angle. The LIV stopped, then reversed, and stopped again.

"Grenade in the trees to our right, Feldwebbel." The colonel spoke icily and with total command. Within seconds there was a vivid flash and a deafening explosion in the forest adjoining their position; all the men in front of them threw themselves to the floor as splinters and branches from the trees scattered the scene. Thick smoke drifted across the road, joining with that already coming from the wrecked police car.

The colonel lifted his microphone again, his voice carrying absolute authority. "You will obey my orders now. Remain on the floor, push your weapons away from you and place your hands on your head. Drivers of the remaining vehicles will move them to the side of the road immediately. You will then leave the vehicles and lie back on the floor You will drive the LIV towards the trees to your right, raising the machine gun to a vertical position. Then dismount and lie on the ground – now!"

There was a pause and some excited shouts could be heard. The colonel leaned forward. "A burst of fire to the left of them, please."

There were loud, repeating rhythmic cracks and the ground to the left of the roadblock erupted as clods of earth were thrown into the air. Hans could see the men lying on the ground burying their heads in their arms; many of them had already pushed their weapons away from them. The LIV turned and moved into the trees as the police cars were hurriedly moved to the side of the road, after which the drivers dropped to the ground.

Colonel Hoffman's terms rang out: "Your commanding officer and the senior BND person present will now stand; you will walk slowly towards the limousine with your hands on your head. If you fail to comply, my next command will be to open fire on you. We have armed Tikad drones airborne and we can observe your every move. You will do this now! *Schnell!*"

A few seconds later, a tall man stood up in the black uniform of the BPOL Bundespolizei – ['German State Police'] with helmet, body armour and balaclava. From the right, another man appeared in a black coat and dark glasses. Both men placed their hands behind their heads and, as they approached, Hoffman's voice rang out again: "If we see any back-up forces within one mile of this position, we will open fire and you will all die without warning. Remember, you are under aerial surveillance."

He turned. "Exit now with weapons ready. Doors for cover and fire if anyone moves ahead." The doors immediately swung open, and within a moment, six men were standing outside the limousine, their guns held into their shoulders and trained on the men on the ground fifty metres away. The colonel exited from the front left door, shouting, "Halt," as the two men came nearer. He saluted. "I am Oberst Hoffman, *guten tag*, you will introduce yourselves, please."

It was not a request and the two men sensed his military command.

"Polizeihauptkommissar ['Chief Inspector'] Ernst Raedar of the Bundespolizei," said the first, automatically saluting the colonel facing him.

"Remove your eye goggles," the colonel commanded, before turning to the other rather swarthy man in the long black coat, who muttered sullenly, "My name is Karl Schmidt of the BND."

Hoffman walked to them. "Your rank?" he snapped at Schmidt.

"Oberleutnant, Herr Oberst," came the reply quickly and instinctively to the command.

The next order replaced Schmidt's insolent demeanour with utter fear: "You will kneel on the floor now."

Colonel Hoffman slipped his hand inside his coat, pulling out a Luger pistol, which he placed against the temple of Schmidt's head. "This is an old but favourite weapon of mine." The colonel spoke icily. "I hope it is still reliable because I have my finger on the trigger, and if the mechanism fails, I will blow your brains out. You will tell me now what you are seeking and why you are here. You have seconds to tell me or I will kill you right now."

Schmidt began to shake, "Herr Oberst, please, I am just obeying orders. I was sent to retrieve papers relating to Roche's war service and anything I could find about those around him. His doctor took documents and handed them to someone in Hamburg, and my mission is to retrieve them. We traced the journalist whom he gave them to and his number plate was picked up on cameras travelling here. We watched for him and he was spotted at Gunther Roche's funeral."

The next question filled Schmidt with an increasing sickening terror. "How was former Reichsmarschall Roche killed?"

Schmidt looked up at the colonel, seeing his ruthless stare, and his words tumbled out almost incoherently, "It was not meant to happen, but he pulled a gun and killed my colleague and I had to stop him. Please, my God, please, it was not my fault." He was thinking desperately, panicking, knowing his life was dangling by a thread, letting the words tumble out, his voice shaking: "It is *'eins zu eins'*."

The colonel hesitated then turned to the state police officer who was standing behind the kneeling Schmidt, looking terrified at what he was witnessing. "Hauptkommissar, I should have this pig shot, but I will spare him for now. We are leaving. Tikads will continue to monitor your movements and if you attempt to follow us, your men will die. Do you understand?"

"*Jawohl Herr Oberst,*" came the quick reply.

Colonel Hoffman addressed him directly: "I will give you a message for your director. You must speak only to him. You will say there must be no attempt to take action or trace us after we leave here nor any publicity. You will use three words which he will need to report to the Chancellor who will authorise what I have demanded; these are '*eins zu eins*'.

"You will confirm with the director that there must be no report made of this incident by you or any of your men, *verstehst du*?"

Hauptkommissar Ernst Raedar confirmed his understanding, respecting the military authority of a fellow officer despite him being an adversary.

"You will now return to your men, taking this *scheisse* with you, and order them to remain on the floor until we have left. I have no quarrel with you, Hauptkommissar, but if you do not follow my orders, many lives will be lost. *Auf wiedersehen.*"

The colonel snapped to attention, giving a salute, and walked back to the car. The police chief inspector barked orders as he walked slowly back, Schmidt following in a slouching, defeated manner.

Seconds later, the limousine began moving, the middle windows open and automatic weapons poking through held at the ready. They drove towards the gap where the roadblock had been, smoke still billowing from the wrecked police car. None of the prone figures moved and soon they swept past more police holding traffic back, but no attempt was made to stop them. As they climbed up the alpine road, the pangs of fear that had gripped Hans began to relax a little, although he remained apprehensive despite not feeling threatened by his abductors. Only moments before, he had been yards away from the man who had killed his father. He had wanted the colonel's Luger to fire in a primeval desire for revenge, despite having been a lifelong pacifist. He had felt hate in that moment but now began to feel quite numb. They passed a sign for the Berghof, and Hans ruefully reflected on the irony that so much of his life now was affected by what had taken place there and in that era. Minutes later, they swept onto a narrower road and an entrance next to which a sign announced Kempinski Hotel.

The trees surrounding the drive were golden in the failing light as the late winter sun bathed the dramatic alpine scene; mountain peaks beyond added magnificence to the view. They drove up the short incline past a vast, semi-circular building and then turned, approaching the entrance, which was down a broad approach driveway dissecting two curved buildings. A further concave structure in the centre contained the entranceway flanked by men smartly dressed in black coats, some wearing dark glasses, whom he presumed were guards.

As the car stopped, Stefan turned to him. "It has been a pleasure travelling with you. I hope you found the journey comfortable." He shook Hans by the hand before departing, which provided some reassurance.

The colonel then spoke. "Please follow me and do not speak to anyone until we are in private. This will guarantee your safety."

Seconds later, he was ushered through double glass doors into a large, modern reception area with huge windows giving views to the majestic scenery surrounding the hotel. He was led across the polished wood floor down a corridor to double doors outside which two further guards stood who raised a hand to the colonel as he approached. He knocked at the door and motioned Hans to enter. A further corridor beyond opened to a vast seating area overlooking the descending view into a wooded valley beyond which the mountains towered majestically over, providing a breath-taking backdrop.

There were easy chairs and a meeting table set to one side, whilst a bar took up a corner on the other. However, it was the person who rose from the table who immediately took Hans's attention, for it was he who had given the eulogy at his father's funeral. He was a jovial-looking figure in his mid-forties, Hans guessed, slightly overweight, but tall with swept-back black hair and startling blue eyes. There seemed something familiar about him, but Hans could not place how and where he may have seen him. Still dressed in his three-piece suit, he walked across with his arm outstretched.

"Please, my name is Manfred and I am grateful you could come." He smiled benevolently without acknowledging Hans had been taken by force, as he shook hands with a firm grip. "Herr Schirach, it is a great honour to meet with you. I knew your father well and I can tell you, he was a great man. Please, be seated." He gestured to two traditional armchairs in front of the window. "Perhaps you would care to join me in a brandy?"

He walked to the bar, pouring two large Cognacs, placing them on a round pine table in front of the armchairs. "Colonel, thank you for bringing our guest and congratulations on a magnificent outcome this afternoon."

The colonel stiffened to attention giving a right-armed salute that Hans had only ever seen before this day in old newsreel footage from the Nazi era.

"I have already received a call from Berlin that *ordnung muss sein* ['order must be restored'] and it seems there will be no more problems from our friends in the BND, at least for now. Perhaps you will please give me some time with Herr Schirach alone."

As the door closed, Manfred sat in the armchair gazing out over the dramatic alpine scenery, seeming for a moment to be lost in thought. He took a generous slug of his drink. "Herr Schirach, or perhaps I may call you Hans?" He continued without waiting for an answer, "First, you will want to understand how I know Gunther Roche was your father. That much is simple: it is because he made no secret of it to me. He knew I treated every word with confidence, almost as if it was *'eins zu eins'*, eh?" He smiled engagingly as he saw Hans react to the words.

"I was introduced to your father in 1984 after I attended the first and last official uniformed rally of the Party with my mother as a teenager. I remember there were so many legendary figures there including a former leader of the Leibstandarte, SS Adolf Hitler, General Wilhelm Mohnke; the Luftwaffe fighter pilot ace, Hans Rudel; the legendary commando, Harald Otto Mors; together with two of Hitler's pilots, Hanna Reitch and Hans Baur. My mother also introduced me to Himmler's daughter, Gudrun, whom she regarded as one of her great friends. Your father promised that he would always ensure we were looked after by the Party which paid for my studies at Munich University from where I graduated in Law. Afterwards, I was offered a job working for the Party on my graduation and worked very closely with your father. He was a visionary reformer and a brilliant organiser developing our sphere of influence, helping us achieve positions of prominence both here and in the USA."

Manfred took the glass from Hans and walked to the bar, refilling their drinks. Moving to the huge window, he beckoned Hans to join him, then he pointed, asking Hans to look at the edge of the hotel grounds, where a small grassy hill led into some trees beyond. "That was once called Göringhügl Hill because it was a raised area on which guests used to sit and relax admiring the view in the grounds of Hermann Göring's house here. It was called Landhaus Göring and he would walk over this hill, the one we are on now, to the Berghof, which, as you will know, was the residence of Adolf Hitler."

He paused, sipping his drink, looking away to the mountain peaks, then sighed and turned decisively. "Do you see something familiar in my appearance?"

Hans returned to his earlier thoughts and felt intrigued. "Well, I did think there was something familiar about you. Have we met before?"

Manfred laughed at his response. "I think we may have done in a previous life, perhaps. Allow me to introduce myself properly." He waited for a second then spoke slowly. "My name is Manfred Hermann Albert Göring."

The shock as Hans heard the words was consuming and he was utterly taken aback, whispering, "*Du lieber Gott*," walking back and slumping in the armchair.

The man standing opposite was now instantly recognisable, having the features of the Hermann Göring he had often seen in books about the war or in the media. Manfred carried the same distinguished air, with an engaging, even disarming smile. His dark wavy hair, prominent cheekbones and even his frame leant an almost uncanny feel to the moment, as though he was in the presence of the man himself.

"I think we might need yet another Cognac, and then I think I should fill in some gaps for you." Manfred walked purposefully to the bar, where he picked up a phone, giving some orders in a voice with a ruthless air of authority. He returned, handing a glass to Hans, who took a large, sip feeling a warm, welcome glow calming his racing adrenalin as he tried to formulate his thoughts into words.

"I am like you, with my pedigree," Manfred continued. "I bear a striking resemblance to the Reichsmarschall, *ja*? Well, he was my grandfather. I was born in 1967 to my mother, who is none other than Edda Göring, his beloved daughter. She had an affair with a leading German politician, an ambitious young man in his late thirties whose political career was taking off. He would eventually achieve high office but this would not have been so, had she ever revealed his identity as her lover and father of her child. Like you, I share the privilege or curse of our forebears, and many did suffer terribly as *Hitler Kinder*, including my mother, whose only sin was to be the daughter of a prominent Nazi."

Göring sat down, looking directly at Hans. "I am the holder of my grandfather's office given to me by none other than your father who, in turn, received his position directly from Adolf Hitler. After I attended the last rally in 1984, I was captivated by the wonderful sense of order and authority I could see the Party represented. Your father was the catalyst and inspiration behind me joining the movement. Please understand that I do not hold the fanatical views of those who were anti-Jewish. This was an obsession of a former era where many countries had anti-Semites, including the father of the revered US President, JFK. It was a common philosophy but plays no part in today's world."

Hans abruptly cut in as he had heard apologists before whitewashing history and he felt a flush of anger. "The Nazis were responsible for more than just anti-Semitic philosophy. That does not excuse or explain the camps, the persecution, the slave labour under your grandfather, nor the slaughter of millions of innocent people, including anyone who opposed Hitler. Herr Reichsmarschall, if that is what you now are, your movement was responsible for genocide."

To his surprise, Göring smiled in response, sighing. "Herr Schirach, those were terrible actions taken by people who went too far, but they had to take difficult decisions in order to cleanse Europe of contamination. Look what is happening now in Germany: uncontrolled immigration under a Chancellor who craves the adulation of the masses by seizing on a situation, claiming it will enrich our culture. There is rising crime as a result, a housing crisis, strains on our economy and no-go areas in many cities where Germans fear to walk the streets. What was our crime? That of securing Germany and needing land to expand our superior race."

Hans knew it was pointless debating with a man whose entrenched values had deep roots built up throughout his adult life. A pragmatic approach was necessary, as he felt his life was still in danger, countering with, "I may not agree with you, but in a democracy, we have the right to disagree and that is what I would defend."

The response was unexpected from Göring: "Bravo, then we are in agreement that our way of life should be protected but also, perhaps, respected."

The latter point was made with a ruthless edge and with the voice of a man, Hans recognised, who wielded absolute power. He now needed to establish where the ground lay. "How did you find me and what is the purpose of me being your, er, guest?"

Göring looked up earnestly. "As you are now aware, there were discussions between Britain and Germany in 1941 in order to achieve peace, and secure both British and American support for our attack on Russia. This was known as the Barbarossa Secret and guarding this has been our insurance for the last seventy-five years."

He stopped for a moment, looking at Hans directly, as if assessing his reaction, before continuing, "We have had, in effect, a mutual deterrent which has protected our movement, and which has also safeguarded the political establishment of other countries, particularly Great Britain and the United States. If the Secret ever got out, the implications would be cataclysmic, causing massive uncertainties and civil unrest. The institutions of which we are now a part would be threatened together with our powerbase. That is why you are here, because we now want to close the file on this forever. Finding out about you was easy because we knew your mother attended the 1984 conference and, as you know, my kind always keep meticulous records. Your father told me you were the great-grandson of Baldur von Chirac and your mother had the good grace to give you that surname. We knew that you were a journalist working for *Der Spiegel*, and that you had met the unfortunate Dr Friedman. I alerted my men that you may attend your father's funeral and they were issued with pictures of you. One other little matter which also assisted was that we have agents inside the BND who told us that they were also seeking you because they believe you may be in possession of something they want, and we want, Herr Schirach. Perhaps, we might now agree on something. Shall we drink to peace?"

He raised his glass and, despite himself, Hans raised his in return, feeling anything but relaxed.

16

The King Pretender's List

Saturday 16th January 1937, 10.00pm
Cliveden House, Buckinghamshire

The dinner was over and cigars had been lit after the formalities, which had included a gracious speech given by Lady Astor, from the centre of the table, thanking those attending. She had said the house was greatly honoured by the presence of the Duke of Windsor, who was, and who would remain, in her words, 'more than a Duke', to a storm of applause. The former King, sat to her right, had stood, bowing, to acknowledge his support. Joachim von Ribbentrop had enjoyed the evening and was holding court about the need for the return of African colonies to Germany. Lord Halifax was responding that this would directly contravene the Treaty of Versailles, which Ribbentrop dismissed as a historical irrelevance to the new Reich. The Champagne had flowed generously and the conversation had been lively, mainly fixated on the politics of right and left and the stability of peace in Europe. Ribbentrop was seated next to Wallis Simpson, who, Greta noted, seemed to be taking considerable interest in the German ambassador. The Duke of

Windsor did not seem to notice, as he was in earnest conversation with Charles Edward and Joseph Kennedy. The former King was flanked on his other side by Yola Letellier and Lord Louis Mountbatten, so dashing in his white naval uniform. Opposite Greta were the beautiful German pilot Hanna Reitch and her companion Squadron Leader Douglas Douglas-Hamilton. Further down the table, Unity Mitford sat with Guy Burgess, next to her sister Diana and her husband Sir Oswald Mosley. Seated opposite their host, Lady Astor, were Dino Grande, the Italian ambassador; Lord Halifax; Albrecht Haushofer; and Randolph Churchill. Greta decided to make a contribution, which she hoped would have the desired effect. She was not disappointed.

"Your Excellency," she said, addressing von Ribbentrop loudly enough to be heard around the table, "you make much of Germany's rights for the return of African colonies, and the regaining of territory in Europe, but does not this bring a threat to peace? Is that not what Mr Winston Churchill is warning us about? Surely, we could not countenance the prospect of war?" She noticed Albrecht Haushofer giving just the slightest nod of his head approvingly.

Von Ribbentrop looked at her with undisguised contempt. "Madam, these are complex matters of state, perhaps best left to those of us who understand the issues, but, of course, Germany does not want war."

Randolph Churchill, red-faced, interjected somewhat brashly, "Then why does your leader irritatingly talk about taking back what belongs to Germany? Seems to me, old boy, that your Führer is, indeed, seeking war and my father is waking us all up to what stares us in the face. Hitler needs stopping. The sooner the better." He slammed the base of his hands together with a flourish before taking a large gulp of his drink.

Lord Halifax mitigated. "There are so many views, but I think the overriding consideration must be peace at all costs, and for that, we need to negotiate with this chap Hitler."

Charles Edward entered the fray. "I am, perhaps, unique here in that I am a member of the German government serving as a representative in the Reichstag. Our Führer is, I think, a great man, the like of which we have rarely seen. He possesses vision, clarity, purpose and embraces order, which is what he seeks; a return to order, but not without principle. Germany did not sign the armistice to be humiliated but in order to end hostilities. We have suffered the imposition of impossible reparations and sacrifices yet, despite this, our Führer is rebuilding Germany, restoring pride to its people."

The Duke of Windsor cut in with precise, immaculately spoken English: "Then, perhaps, I am even more unique, for I am a former head of state of the United Kingdom, the British Empire and Her Dominions."

The entire table hushed and talk appeared to die away around the room.

"I was King and I remain dutiful to my country, continuing to serve whenever I may be called upon. I have watched Germany reassert itself under this man, Adolf Hitler, and he appears to offer them admirable leadership. We must never return to war, and I can assure you here and now that I will devote myself to the cause of avoiding conflict. There are many who have pledged their allegiance to me, which I am grateful for and humbled by. I too, pledge that I will not fail their support and I shall do all that remains in my power to secure peace in Europe. I can tell you all that I have received an invitation from the Führer of Germany to meet with him, which I have accepted, although nothing has yet been agreed."

There were gasps around the room, followed by applause.

The Duke continued, "I believe this may herald an opportunity for our two countries to re-establish ties and work tirelessly for peace. I would hasten to add that I shall not be visiting Germany until after I have made an honest woman of the lady by my side, who has, for some extraordinary reason, agreed to be my wife during a wedding which shall take place on June 3rd this year." There was a ripple of laughter, followed by delighted cries and more applause.

Lord Louis Mountbatten then stood. "I believe that in this wonderful moment, the toast must be to His Royal Highness, the Duke of Windsor, and his future bride, Wallis."

As one, the room rose, lifting their glasses in the direction of the former King, who smiled, raising his glass in response. At that moment, von Ribbentrop clicked his heels, raising his right arm stiffly in a salute, which, to others there, appeared somewhat vulgar. Sir Oswald Mosley was a second behind, and then Charles Edward followed suit, but the momentary embarrassment this unseemly exhibition caused was soon forgotten as conversations resumed.

"Charles, I really think there is a time and place for these frightful displays of yours," Greta whispered in his ear. His response was to cough as if covering up a rude riposte. Von Ribbentrop had consumed a large quantity of Champagne and exchanges between Randolph Churchill and himself were becoming more animated. *Exactly as planned*, Greta noted with some satisfaction, thankful for Dickie Mountbatten's complicity and influence over the table plan.

Suddenly, as if on cue, von Ribbentrop slammed his fist down on the table, pointing his finger at Randolph Churchill. *"Du bist verdammt*, you and your father insult the Reich again and again. Who do you think you are? Under the guidance of our Führer, we will rise up and triumph over our oppressors. You British think you can push us around; well, we will show you when we retake what is ours, and if you do not agree, then we will be at war, yes, because of your intransigence. We will take back our colonies; we will expand because that is our destiny, to cleanse Europe of contamination, securing our rightful space, and no-one will stop us. Lebensraum: remember this word because that will be the Germany of the future. Your Royal Highness, forgive me, I am drunk, but this man is a *Dumkopf*, and so I will not share a table with him. Goodnight."

Von Ribbentrop stood up, clicking his heels, then gave yet another right-armed salute before walking out. Charles Edward followed, excusing himself from the table, assuring Greta he would return shortly.

Sir Oswald Mosley did likewise but bowed before leaving, asking to be excused.

"A somewhat uncouth little man, clearly lacking breeding. He should have gone to Eton," a smiling Randolph Churchill announced, raising his glass to onlookers with a grin. Once again, the hum of conversation resumed. The sound of music began drifting through and guests would leave and return to their tables, dancing in the main hall, where the American dance band leader, Benny Carter, had taken up station. This had been arranged by Joseph Kennedy as a gift from the US government to the occasion. Greta had noted the reactions of those around the table, particularly of the Deputy Führer's friend Albrecht Haushofer. He had not given the Nazi salute, nor, indeed, had he followed von Ribbentrop from the room. He was now in conversation with Douglas Douglas-Hamilton, the future Duke, and they appeared to be striking up a friendship. Dino Grandi, the Italian ambassador, had also, surprisingly, not shown support for von Ribbentrop, yet Italy was the closest ally to Germany. In fact, he had raised his arms in despair at von Ribbentrop's outburst. The Duke of Windsor had merely said, "That was a little unfortunate, but these sorts of scenes can be quite jolly, really. Adds a little spice, don't you know."

Greta was interrupted in her thoughts by the polite, clipped English of Albrecht Haushofer: "Please, you may recall me, Albrecht Haushofer, we met in Berlin last year at the Olympics. May I have the pleasure of this dance?"

"My dear Albrecht," she beamed at him, genuinely pleased to be asked, "how frightfully gallant of you; of course I remember you. I would be delighted."

He guided her to the dancefloor. He was quite a dapper man: tall, fairly slim, his dark hair sleeked down with a precise parting to one side. He had a long face with a prominent nose, but his moustache detracted from this, adding to a distinguished look, almost giving him a movie-star appearance. He had a gentle expression and Greta found him utterly charming. As they waltzed around the dancefloor Albrecht talked animatedly about the changes taking place in his country, then suddenly added earnestly, "All this is coming at a terrible cost; there are many of us who are uneasy about the Führer and wish to avoid war. Fraulein Atkins, my friends believe you have connections with British Intelligence. I do not expect you to confirm or deny this, but if you wish, I have some information which you may find useful. If you have no interest, please, we can resume our talk about Germany's achievements."

Greta had an instinct for character assessment and somehow knew he could be trusted. "I too have many friends," she replied, as they continued dancing, neither denying nor admitting to his presumption. "Perhaps we could meet in the drawing room in half an hour, if you know where that is?"

They returned to the table and Greta decided to attempt further provocative conversation to establish the former King's position on Germany. She prompted Charles Edward: "Oh, Charlie, you must tell David about the Führer's plans to reunify Germans who have been alienated through history." She turned to the Duke of Windsor. "Sir, just as blood ties are important to your family, so Charles says they are to the German people."

The former King looked at Greta, his face breaking into the most disarming smile. "My dear Greta, you do seem to always have such a grasp of what is happening. Perhaps you should follow the example of our host, Lady Astor, and enter the House of Commons. A somewhat vulgar place, I fear, because they have directed much of what has befallen upon me."

Wallis joined in remonstrating in response: "Dearest David, darling, they have not succeeded because we are together and, my goodness, we have all these wonderful friends."

The Duke lit up a cigarette and then said reflectively, "Indeed, we have, Wallis, and we might need to test their loyalty one day." Greta made a mental note to pass that back to Colonel Menzies.

Charles Edward cut in. "Sir, my lovely companion was referring to Germany's demands to be allowed to reunify with those of our race across Europe. We call these people *Volksdeutsche*, and by accident of history or design, their rights to be German have been lost. This is particularly so in Austria, where our Führer was born, in the Sudetenland of Czechoslovakia, and in the Danzig area of Poland. We believe the Treaty of Versailles to have been an unjust imposition which not only crippled us but discriminated against us. This is why we have had to be strong in reunifying the country of Germany itself which suffered internal divisions. That has been the achievement of a strong centre of power under the direction of one Führer." Greta was delighted; it was a tirade she had often heard from her admirer in private conversation, attuning himself to Hitler's more recent pressing demands for territory.

The Duke of Windsor looked earnestly at Charles Edward. "Charles, your chap Hitler has achieved much, but, I believe, perhaps, at a price to which I am not sure our Anglo-Saxon temperament is well suited. Whilst I may not be a happy advocate of democracy right now, it has served us well for quite a while. I am not sure, either, that we are ready to return to a feudal system, although had it not been for Parliament, I feel sure that the recent crisis of which, regrettably, I have been at the centre, might have been avoided. I will, of course, support any moves to prevent war, and it seems to me that if your leader has a just cause, then we should endorse it. Mr Ambassador-in-waiting, perhaps you might acquaint us with your thoughts or those of your country?"

The Duke turned to Joseph Kennedy, who bowed before speaking. "Your Royal Highness, my position and that of the United States is, I believe, a unified one. I will speak straight, sir, because in Massachusetts that is our way. In my life, I have achieved much through decisive action. I believe in strong leadership, and whilst minorities may be affected, the greater purpose justifies the outcome. There appears to be a growing Jewish refugee problem in Germany, which is regrettable, as is their treatment, but the outcome will be better, I believe, than what went before. Perhaps there is some truth in the claim that many Jews suffer from the history they created for themselves. Whatever we believe, maybe the world does need a new order. My son John is an admirer of Adolf Hitler and intends to travel throughout Germany this summer. This is a time for change, Your Royal Highness, and America will not stand in its way, nor will we countenance a return to war."

Greta excused herself, saying she wanted to talk with some acquaintances, feeling she had already achieved much in the mission set for her by Colonel Menzies. She entered the drawing room with its oak-panelled walls covered with portraits of people from long ago. A white marble fireplace flickered with the flames of logs that crackled, evidencing that it was well tendered. The room was ostentatious and quite breath-taking. Although she had been shown it on a previous visit, she had never really taken it all in. Another fireplace at the opposite end to the former was in medieval stone, whilst tapestries complemented the many paintings under a decorative ceiling replete with carved ornate woodwork.

"Fraulein Atkins." Her thoughts were interrupted by Albrecht as he walked towards her, his arm outstretched. She shook his hand, the formality seeming obtuse but strangely conducive to the real purpose of their meeting.

"We have little time," he began earnestly, speaking in a low voice. "This house is crawling with Gestapo, who are checking everything. I thought all this National Socialism was good at first, but now…" He paused, as if gathering his thoughts, then lowered his voice even more. "Now no-one trusts anyone anymore; it is as if we are being governed by a regime of suspicion. Two years ago, purges began and they never cease. Everyone is watching everyone and no-one asks questions, or dare say anything when someone disappears. Children are informing on their parents, and neighbour on neighbour. They are setting up camps in Germany where people are taken without trial. Some of us are trying to organise some resistance, but at the moment, it is impossible. Even my father is with them, welcomed by them as a respected geography academic. They like to have legitimacy, and his theories about the need for German territorial expansion have been seized upon. These are strange and dangerous times. My university friend, Rudolf Hess, is both a fanatical supporter of Hitler and the Deputy Führer, but he has confided in me that he is concerned about peace. They want peace with Britain, but what they plan is a different peace which does not threaten or compromise their aims of military conquest. They desire the overthrow of your government and having this replaced by a puppet regime of their own with King Edward back on the throne." The door opened, and a man entered who, upon seeing them, apologised and withdrew as though he had interrupted something.

They moved to the white fireplace, then Greta took his hand.

"Albrecht, I want to trust you, but it is all so confusing right now. Loyalties are split and we do not know who we can trust or quite what to believe."

He took her other hand in his, kissing both of them in a chivalric gesture. "Greta, I have a list that Charles Edward and von Ribbentrop have compiled of those holding positions of influence in Britain that can be relied upon for full cooperation, if not collaboration, with Germany's aims for a coup. This has already been presented to the Führer and I know it to be genuine because it was shared with my father. You must do what you can, please, I worry for my country, for your country, and the world. Hitler is obsessed with his 'guiding hand of Providence' and he will lead us all into a catastrophe."

He pulled an envelope from his pocket, which she took, stuffing it deftly into her evening bag. Then, he kissed her hand again. "*Auf wiedersehen*, I wish we had met in kinder times." He looked at her with warmth, but also with sadness, and walked away. After he had left the room, she overheard, for a second, a muffled but urgent whisper from outside the door. Moving quickly to another door further down the room, she exited and walked rapidly back to where the dance was continuing to a rag-time song.

Walking into the dining room, she moved towards where Unity Mitford was seated, holding court with excited admirers about her friendship with Adolf Hitler. She caught Guy Burgess's eye, who gave an imperceptible nod before leaving the room. Greta rejoined the party, where conversation had switched to lighter matters regarding the forthcoming social scene, including Royal Ascot, the Derby, Wimbledon, Henley Regatta, Cowes and where horse trials were taking place. Suddenly, Greta felt very far removed from this world and filled with a desperate need to wake everyone up. The utter futility of that society facing the ruthlessness of a Nazi German threat made her shudder. Within minutes, Guy Burgess was back on the scene and he gave a brief smile, which was the signal. Greta begged leave of the table, saying she was taking some air and that she would return shortly. She left the dining room, requesting her coat and stole from an obliging servant, then she was through the great hall to a corridor with a door to the right, which she opened. A plain stone staircase descended in dim light to an arched entrance at the bottom with glass insets.

The air outside was bitingly cold, but she scarcely noticed as she walked across the gravel to a clump of tall shrubs. Mona Maund greeted her old friend warmly, throwing her arms around her. They moved to the other side of the shrubs, avoiding the light coming from the house and external lights on the towering terraces. The band music was loud from above them, even in the garden. "Oh my goodness, Mona, we have struck gold tonight. I have a list of powerful British people whom the Germans believe can be relied upon in supporting some kind of coup. They even believe they can replace the new King and restore the Duke of Windsor to the throne." She reached for the envelope Albrecht had given her and was handing it to Mona just as a torch shone directly at them.

"You will give that to me, please." The German-accented voice spoke in a hiss that made it clear this was not a polite request. Both women took a step backwards, as they had been trained to do, giving them space. However, their attacker moved with them and they could now see a gun pointed at them. His face was not clear in the dim light, but his menacing words caused clouds of condensation in the cold night air. "I will stretch out my left hand; you will place the envelope in it immediately."

Greta needed to play for time as her hand attempted to open her evening bag without this being noticed. "Can you tell us who you are first, please?" She knew as she spoke the words that they sounded utterly ridiculous.

"That is irrelevant," came the swift reply. "Give me that paper, bitch, or I will shoot one of you immediately. There will be no warning." Mona had begun to pass the envelope over when the shot came. They heard a grunt from their attacker as he fell, lifeless, to the ground.

"You had better both get back inside," came the cheerful voice of Guy Burgess. "You'll catch your death of cold."

17

A 'Private' Royal Visit

**Tuesday 5th October 1937, 2.00pm
HQ SIS, 54 Broadway, Westminster, London.
Office of the Deputy Director**

Colonel Menzies was pacing his office and had been doing so for over an hour. Normally a calm man, seldom raised to anger and described as poised and easy-going by colleagues, he now felt anything but calm. He was furious that the Home Secretary, Samuel Hoare, normally a person upon whom he could depend, had denied his request to embed intelligence staff with the Duke of Windsor, purportedly as attending government officials, on the planned visit to Germany. He had worked with Hoare in intelligence in his early days with SIS and had respected his work which had resulted in a successful spy network being established in Russia. He had also assisted him in the coup of recruiting Mussolini in Italy to feedback intelligence information in the 1920s. That morning, he had attended what was meant to be a relatively routine meeting at the Home Office in King Charles Street in order to finalise plans for the Duke's forthcoming trip which was exceedingly tiresome and, in his view, utterly misguided. Despite the intervention of Lord Louis Mountbatten with an attempt to persuade the former King to suspend or cancel the visit, the Duke had refused to change his mind.

For weeks, the colonel had been working to exert pressure on the Duke of Windsor not to continue with the planned visit through trusted connections with whom he had influence. The King himself had written a private note to the Head of SIS asking that 'every possible means should be used to discourage and prevent his Royal Highness, my brother, from carrying out this ghastly visit'.

The Prime Minister, Neville Chamberlain, had spoken directly to the Duke, who retorted, "I have abdicated the throne in the interests of this country, but I will not be deterred from doing what I believe is right. Whilst I may have given up my authority, my power, and, to some degree, my self-respect, I will not surrender my conscience nor will I give up my freedom. I am now free of your yoke and independent from the monarchy. After all, if Lloyd George, our former Prime Minister, can go to Germany, or Clement Attlee, the leader of the Labour Party, or others like Lord Halifax, who accepted a private invitation from Hermann Göring, then you people should exercise less hypocrisy and more respect." As a last resort, Colonel Menzies had called his old friend, Winston Churchill, who was close to the Duke and supportive of him, to see if he could intervene.

Churchill was horrified at the prospect of the visit, calling it 'the greatest propaganda gift we can give to this petty tyrant, legitimising his aims and strengthening his cruel resolve'. Churchill reported back to Menzies days later, saying, "The Duke of Windsor believes that he has a mission, which in my view is ill-advised, whereby he can help in averting the gathering clouds of war, whilst encouraging the improvement of workingclass conditions in Germany." Churchill had secured three concessions from the Duke: that he would not make speeches, not permit himself to be part of or associated with any rallies which the Nazis may plan and not allow the visit to resemble in any way, 'a state visit'. The

Duke conceded that it should be a low-key, private affair in order not to deliver the Germans a propaganda coup.

Frantic last-minute discussions took place on the itinerary and arrangements in the Paris Ritz during September 1937 between the Duke's assistant equerry, Dudley Forwood and members of the British government. Officials reported their frustration at being excluded from talks, which involved Deputy Führer Rudolf Hess, Joseph Goebbels, and von Ribbentrop. Dudley Forwood was twenty-five years old but had authority way beyond his years, defending the Duke and Duchess's interests with unswerving loyalty. When government ministers spoke with Forwood, he would politely say he needed to consult with the Duke and the German organiser of the visit, Captain Fritz Wiedemann, an adjutant to Adolf Hitler. Ministers reported feeling impotent whilst the Germans were striding around like peacocks with a triumphal arrogance, clearly enjoying the discomfort of the British contingent. The Duke and Duchess were staying at Hotel Le Meurice, on the Rue de Rivoli, about four hundred yards away from the Ritz, and, infuriatingly, papers had to be sent by hand to the British officials because, as the Duke said, 'walls have ears'. He was right, as Colonel Menzies had listening devices installed at the Ritz but had not been successful in accessing the Duke's hotel suite at Le Meurice.

Finally, Colonel Menzies had summoned Greta to his offices during the last week in September. He had tasked her with asking Charles Edward if he could clear it with Captain Fritz Wiedemann that she could attend the visit as a guest companion of Wallis Simpson. Charles Edward was delighted that she might be able to attend and ensured that she was accepted. He had already secured agreement that he would be meeting with the Duke during his visit, and the suggestion that Greta attend the trip was welcomed by the former King. He was concerned that there may be occasions where Wallis needed a companion, as she may not always be included in meetings he attended.

This particular day had been maddening. When Colonel Menzies had reported to Samuel Hoare his plans to mobilise agents in Germany and those in the British embassy in Berlin, he had not expected the response. "I'm sorry, old boy, but this is one show we are bowing out of," the Home Secretary stated to the incredulous head of intelligence. "Decision made at the highest level, I'm afraid. No British personnel are to risk security or exposing their cover for what is designated as a private visit which the Crown disapproves of. The government's position is that we distance ourselves from it entirely in order not to lend it any kind of legitimacy or importance. No staff from the British embassy are to be involved, and no agents from SIS either. There will be no welcoming party from any British officials, and no-one will accompany the Duke and Duchess other than their own staff. Goebbels is already rubbing his grubby little hands together, reaping what propaganda he can squeeze from this unfortunate episode. The government's policy is to act as though this is not taking place. You will accept this as a directive, Colonel. No involvement!"

Colonel Menzies knew that arguing this was pointless, as clearly the decision had been taken at cabinet level and, without a doubt, endorsed by the King. That did not prevent him from venting his anger at a decision that he felt had been taken out of petulant national pride rather than in the interests of national security. Whilst he did not take a directive from his political masters lightly, neither was he someone who would necessarily play by the rules.

When the phone rang, announcing the arrival of his loyal operative, Greta Atkins, Colonel Menzies felt that his next move would, at least, relieve his sense of having been emasculated. Noone in government knew her identity, which was customary as MPs were elected representatives, no matter how powerful. They were recognised as a security risk because of their politics and the fragility of their positions. Some home secretaries would attempt to change the status quo, which Colonel Menzies, together with military chiefs of staff, opposed absolutely. Greta was known as a society lady, unusual in that she not married, and, therefore, viewed as a tad eccentric by her peers, a reputation she enjoyed. She swept into his office in a loud if not garish tartan dress with enormous lapels, gathered tight at her waist with a thick belt, over which she wore a cloak in matching fabric fastened at the neck. To complete the look, her shoes were strapped, affecting the style of traditional Scottish footwear, complete with a matching handbag and a flat wide-brimmed hat worn at a jaunty slant over her hair, which was in ringlets to her shoulders. She walked to the colonel, offering him her hand to kiss, which he waved away, brusquely gesturing her to sit.

"I see you have dressed in a subtle manner so that you do not attract attention, Miss Atkins," he managed in a somewhat gruff manner.

"Why, my dear unflappable colonel, who on earth has ruffled your feathers?"

He was in no mood for her jocularity which, at best, he tolerated as being somewhat tiresome and frivolous. "Miss Atkins, can we cut to the chase? Next week, you are joining the Duke of Windsor and his former mistress for this absurd jaunt to Germany."

Greta suppressed a giggle at the colonel's disrespect and clear displeasure at the Duke's marriage, refusing to refer to Wallis as 'the Duchess'.

"I regret to say that, extraordinarily and against my advice, His Majesty's Government will not sanction any British Intelligence monitoring or involvement. As such, you may, of course, decline my request to accompany the visit, which I will deny having made." The colonel paused, looking upwards, as if he was not hearing the awaited response.

"My dearest colonel, I will always do whatever you ask of me," Greta breathed back in a teasing voice not unlike the actress Mae West, resulting in a grunt and a not-expected sigh from the colonel.

He continued, "You will not have the usual channels of communication available. However, an acquaintance of yours, Albrecht

Haushofer, has now, shall we say, come over to us via a friendship he has struck up through someone else you know, Douglas, the future Duke of Hamilton. He is anxious to avoid war and is very unhappy at the violence and excesses of Hitler's dreadful regime. Albrecht is working with his friend, the Deputy Führer, Rudolf Hess, in an attempt to curb moves which may provoke war. However, Hess remains a committed Nazi with unswerving loyalty to his Führer but sympathises with Haushofer's views. As such, he has assigned Albrecht to represent him at functions attended by the Duke, and Albrecht has agreed to pass on messages you may have via contacts he has at the British embassy."

The colonel stood, clasping his hands behind his back, and walked around the desk, to both add emphasis to his next words and a dramatic finality to the meeting. "Miss Atkins, we are informed that Hitler has invited the Duke to his private residence at the Berghof. You will be there with him. We think this will be where Hitler will make his move to secure some kind of agreement or pledge of loyalty from the former King. You need to keep your ear to the ground and note every nuance. Be careful, and good luck." He shook her hand, then, trying to affect a lighter note, he added, "Do please try to avoid any difficult messes like that last business at Cliveden. Frightfully difficult to cover up, my dear."

He was little surprised by her reply which, despite not showing it, lifted his spirits somewhat. "Why, Colonel Menzies, how is a girl to defend her honour when faced with your orders? I shall do my best to resist the temptation to carry out an embarrassing assassination of the Führer."

His instructions for her, which arrived the following day, were very precise.

Sunday 10th October 1937, 7.00pm
North East France

Greta was in a rail coach behind that in which the Duke and Duchess of Windsor were travelling, accompanied by the Duke's assistant equerry, Dudley Richard Forwood and Diana Mosley. They were joined by Prince Philipp von Hessen when the train stopped at Metz-Ville a couple of hours after leaving Paris. A smiling Edward and Wallis had announced, as dinner was being served on the train, that his cousin, also a great-grandson of Queen Victoria, was to join the party and accompany them during the trip. The Duke had stated, to the laughter of his guests, that they should not worry because even though he was German, his manners would be impeccable as he had been educated in England. Prince Philipp arrived in time for after-dinner cocktails, marching to the Duke's carriage door accompanied by four men in uniform who then snapped to attention, extending a full Nazi salute, before executing a smart military about-turn and leaving. As soon as he boarded, he bowed to the Duke, then again to Wallis, whom he referred to as 'Your Royal Highness', bringing a glowing smile to her face and an approving gesture from the Duke. It was the first time she had been so addressed, which he felt had been a gross slight to his position as former, and rightful, King.

After he had been introduced, the Prince stated loudly that it was his honour to announce that the Führer had gifted his personal train for the duration of the visit, bringing applause from those present. He was dressed in an impeccable dinner jacket, complete with white carnation to match his top pocket silk hanky, and wore the small round red and white badge of the NSDAP centred with a swastika on one lapel. He was a tall, slim man in his forties, his dark hair slicked back and having a small fashionable moustache. After cocktails, a handful of invited guests sat in the easy chairs of the saloon reserved for the Duke and Duchess. Greta opened a line of conversation directed at Prince Philipp, knowing that he was a highly valued state governor in Prussia personally appointed by Hitler, with whom he was a close confidante.

"Is it true that Germany's borders may change further to allow for expansion and, if so, might this not lead to war with France or Britain becoming unavoidable?"

The Prince smiled at her before addressing his remarks more towards the Duke of Windsor. "I think my cousin and I agree that we would not wish there to be any chance of another war." He raised his glass to the Duke of Windsor, who raised his own, allowing them to clink together. The Prince added, "We are, after all, from the same family and we both share German blood. War is unthinkable, but we need to make room for our people and give those Germans who live outside Germany the natural home to which they belong. We face a great threat in Europe from Bolshevism, and that should concern us more than the undisputable justice of our occupying territory in which Germans live and which has been taken from us. For example, our Führer was born in Austria and yet we are forced apart as separate countries and so, that will change. Expansion of Germany will be just, whilst we must also be strong enough to resist the greater threat from the East." The Duke of Windsor clapped the Prince, followed by a ripple of applause from the others present.

The Prince was sitting near to Greta, and as others became busy in separate conversations, he turned to her and kissed her hand. "My dear Frau Atkins, we have a mutual acquaintance in Albrecht Haushofer, I believe, and I have invited him to join us at a dinner in honour of the Duke and Duchess with my friend Reichsmarschall Hermann Göring. Another of your countrymen will also be there, at the invitation of the Reichsmarschall, His Grace, Squadron Leader Douglas-Hamilton, together with his companion, the renowned aerobatic ace Hanna Reitch. You will also meet my younger brother Christoph; we are both in the Luftwaffe. Göring likes to be surrounded by flyers."

The following morning, the train pulled slowly into Friedrichstrasse Station, Berlin, and Diana Mosley excitedly waved to crowds, who thronged the approach, their right arms raised, a salute Diana returned with her arm bent upwards at the elbow. Everywhere red flags and banners flew with the black swastika. As the steam hissed and the wheels clanked the train to a halt, Greta looked up to see Union Jacks alternating with the German flags along the station. She could hear the clamour of the crowd and watched through the window as a phalanx of German soldiers in black uniforms with white gloves stamped smartly to attention on command, their rifles topped with polished bayonets held ramrod straight. A band struck up the British national anthem, as Dudley Forwood popped his head through the door, telling them to follow the Royal party, maintaining a minimum respectful distance of five yards behind the Duke and Duchess.

As the Duke stepped from the train, a roar went up from the crowd which he acknowledged with a smiling wave, then he stopped, turning to offer his hand to the Duchess as she descended the step to the platform. A man stepped forwards dressed in a brown uniform, stood to attention, clicked his heels, then raised his arm before bowing, extending his hand to the Duke of Windsor. He introduced himself as Doctor Robert Ley, leader of the German Labour Front. Then, he gathered an enormous bouquet of flowers from an attendant, which he presented to the Duchess, again bowing deeply. "Your Royal Highness, welcome to Germany. The Reich is honoured by your presence." He stood aside as a smiling von Ribbentrop marched forwards, dressed in a grey three-piece suit and black tie, complete with a swastika tie pin, who repeated the salute, pausing for a second in front of the many press cameras, which repeatedly flashed. He bowed, placing his right hand formally across his middle.

"On behalf of the Führer, the Reich and the government of Germany, we are delighted to welcome Your Royal Highnesses. I am, of course, particularly thrilled to meet you both again, and, if I may say so, Your Royal Highness," he turned to the Duchess, "you look radiant in your outfit." His customary clumsy faux pas was ignored by the Duke, who turned to introduce his equerry, Dudley Forwood, who stood back to allow Ribbentrop to shake hands with Diana Mosley and Greta, as honorary guests of the visit. The party was then joined by the Gauleiter of Berlin, Artur Görlitzer.

The Duke was clearly delighted with his reception, as Dr Ley led the party towards the ranks of black-uniformed guards. On receipt of shouted sharp commands, they reacted with absolute precision as the Duke approached, their rifles moving from the shoulder to the front, then making a single thud in unison as the butts were brought to the floor. The officer commanding marched smartly forwards, a sword held in his right hand which he deftly placed in its scabbard after stopping in front of the Duke and Duchess. Then clicking his heels, he raised his arm, with a loud, "*Heil Hitler.*" The Duke returned the arm gesture, although less stiffly, as the cameras furiously flashed. The young officer bowed. "Your Royal Highnesses, the Leibstandarte SS Adolf Hitler humbly requests your inspection."

The reply from Edward was in perfect German: "*Ich würde gerne annehmen* ['I would be delighted to accept']." The Duchess smiled in acknowledgment but stood back with Dudley Forwood, von Ribbentrop and Doctor Ley, as the Duke accompanied the officer, who now redrew his sword, on a ceremonial inspection. After the Duke had walked down the ranks of soldiers, the military band struck up the German national anthem, joined by the lines of uniformed men singing a spirited 'Deutschland, Deutschland Uber Alles'.

Greta felt a deep sense of impending unease at the scene being played out in front of her, which was clearly not a 'private visit' and would not sit well at home, not least with Colonel Menzies.

18

A Mutual Deterrent

Thursday 20th February 2020, 6.00pm
Hotel Kempinski, Near Berchtesgaden, Obersalzberg, Bavaria, Germany

Darkness had enveloped the dramatic mountain view, whilst concealed lighting around the room almost added a sense of intimacy to their conversation. Göring was affable, even genial, but Hans sensed a ruthlessness in his demeanour that was displayed as he answered his mobile or when giving orders to those he summoned. They had been served a light meal of Weisswurst [Bavarian spiced sausage], soft pretzels, sweet mustard and a litre of Hefeweizen [light wheat beer].

Göring leant back in his seat. "Like you, I was brought up with little or no knowledge of my father, who had a brief association with my mother, but I was told of his identity at the age of seventeen. I was brought up by foster parents, but my mother did not hide from me and visited regularly. I was very lucky because she was warm and loving towards me, explaining to me in my early years that because of the war, she was not permitted to tell me a great deal about my family. My surname was changed to Heidemann when I was six after a man with whom my mother was having a relationship who was a journalist working for *Stern* magazine. My mother did not wish my life to be affected by having an identity that might prejudice opportunities which she had experienced. Although I knew her name when I was growing up, I never connected this with Hermann Göring being my grandfather. You and I were both spared the discrimination that followed the innocent children of the great visionaries of the Third Reich."

Hans almost choked over his food, exercising all the restraint he could muster not to argue with a heritage he despised. Discretion was needed, he surmised, in order to extract the most from this meeting. His natural instincts as a journalist were taking over and he had an overriding drive to be inquisitive. "Do you still see your mother?" he offered in polite interest. Göring's eyes saddened, as he grimaced, holding back an emotion that displayed a vulnerability.

"She died just over a year ago, which greatly saddened me as she was a good mother to me and I will always respect her memory." He lifted his glass to Hans. "To our parents and our heritage." Hans raised his glass in return, thinking of the genuine sentiment in his father's final letter, rather than dwelling on his misplaced loyalties. He also fleetingly thought of his mother whom he had neglected to contact since his last visit three days before and he suddenly felt very worried that she may be in danger.

Göring continued, "When my mother told me about her father, she spoke in warm terms of a man who had lavished attention on her. She informed me that he had been vilified at the Nuremberg trials and sentenced to death for crimes he did not commit. His wife actually assisted the Jews, and his ubiquitous brother, Albert, often sought his help in saving many people from the excesses of the regime. He was the stabilising influence between the vision of the Führer and the obsessions with order held by Reichsführer Himmler. My grandfather was a great man who had noble aspirations, with an appreciation for the finer things in life. He had a reputation for wit, style and impeccable manners. Moreover, he was a patriot who fought with enormous courage in World

War I as a fighter pilot ace, being awarded the Blue Max by the Kaiser. He supported the great policy of Lebensraum, recognising the enormous danger of Stalin's Russia to the world. Imagine if we had succeeded, and we very nearly succeeded in our great purpose, had we not been betrayed from within." He sighed, rising from his chair, and began pacing.

"Without that betrayal, we would have conquered Russia. Just think, there would have been no Cold War, no Iron Curtain, no Communist threat from the Soviet Union, no Cuban missile crisis, no partition of Germany, no Eastern European Bloc and no Warsaw Pact. We would have achieved freedom from the threat of nuclear war which has blighted Europe over the last seventy years. Even now, despite the so-called overthrow of Communism, this has been replaced by the endemic corruption of Vladimir Putin's regime and an emerging new Russian superpower causing alarm, once again, across Europe. Their cancer spreads as they support regimes like Assad's in Syria, give succour to the odious Erdogan in Turkey, wage war in the Ukraine and seize the territory of a sovereign state. He has carried out assassinations of those opposing him not only in his own country but also in other countries. Look at the poisoning of Alexander Litvinenko and Sergei Skripal in the United Kingdom. What does the world do? Nothing! Had the aims of *Generalplan Reich*' been fulfilled, all of this would have been avoided. Putin acts with impunity and has become the new Tsar. To think these vermin criticised the Führer!" He threw his hands in a gesture of astonishment, sitting back down with a sigh.

Despite the staggering irony of Göring's indictment of the Russian regime when Nazi Germany had murdered any dissenters, embarked on blatant unprovoked military aggression, combining this with a policy of horrific genocide, Hans chose again not to dispute his words. He had picked up on the word 'betrayal' used in Göring's tirade, and something was prompting him to find out more. He did not recall anything in the information left for him by his father which pointed to a betrayal other than the abortive bomb plot against Hitler in 1944. He knew he had to play his next move carefully in order that he was not seen to be seeking information that Göring may not wish to give. This, he thought, may become a cat-and-mouse game, as his 'host' clearly must have an agenda. He was still unsure of the reason why he had been 'invited' to this meeting but sensed he was being 'buttered up' for what was to follow.

Hans held up his hand for a moment, effecting a puzzled look, raising his right index finger. "Forgive me for interrupting, but are you referring to the betrayal by the Allies here in not sticking to what was agreed with Churchill in 1941, or the failed attempt on Hitler's life?"

Göring smiled for a moment, shaking his head. "*Nein, nein, nein,* it is the smallest things that sometimes have the greatest impact. The whole great endeavour collapsed due to traitors on both the British side and within German ranks, but all this was covered up after the war, as so much has been. We had the German traitor Admiral Canaris, who had been head of the Abwehr ['Military Intelligence'] until February 1944, when the SS took over and he was removed. However, Canaris maintained his contacts and was secretly plotting against the Führer, even meeting in France with British Intelligence operatives. He was appointed to the HWK in Berlin, which was a unit responsible for getting supplies through the Allied economic blockade of Germany. In July 1944, we had secured an agreement with the Allies for a ceasefire and Canaris was briefed about this, but he did not know what the final objective was. He was told that this was to allow for a negotiated peace settlement, which alarmed him as he did not want the Führer to remain in power.

"Our real plan in 1944 was that we commit to a counterattack against the Russians on the Eastern Front, supported by the Allies, enabling us to divert our reserves and our Panzer Divisions from France and Italy. The Russians had launched a major assault against us called *Operation Bagration* and we were too exposed because we were fighting on two major fronts. Operational Orders were signed by the Führer which would have ended hostilities between Germany and the Allies, enabling a massive new offensive to take place against Russia, backed by Britain and

America. These orders would have been carried out had it not been for the betrayal."

Despite having seen these Orders only three days before, Hans whistled in feigned astonishment. "*Mein Gott*, Herr Göring, you mean the war in Western Europe would have been over?"

His host looked at him quizzically. "This, I think, you know something of? No matter, there is more I will tell you. This is all covered by a protocol known as '*eins zu eins*'. Anyone who knows of this carries the secret to their grave and must never share it with anyone. The penalty for breaching this is death." Göring's eyes were steely, cold and unflinching as he looked at Hans directly, who sensed that this was no statement but a very real threat. "The plan was that we would lead a crusade against the Soviet Union to stop them seizing any territory in Europe and from spreading the cancer of Communism. Our forces would have been, ultimately, secretly under the command of the Supreme Allied Commander, General Eisenhower. The overall aim was to safeguard Europe from Russian domination, which, history now shows us, was the regrettable outcome of failure to execute the Operational Orders."

"Herr Göring," Hans interjected with genuine interest, deciding to be direct, "how did this betrayal you spoke of take place?"

Göring rose again from his chair and walked to the large window, peering at distant lights now showing on the mountains beyond. "Ach, it is of little matter because events overtook any plans that we made. Feldmarschall Rommel had been seriously injured in an air attack and was not expected to live. The Führer delayed moving on the Operational Orders plan because Rommel had the unswerving loyalty of our commanders and this was critical to the outcome. Three days later on 20th July 1944, the attempt took place on the Führer's life when the bomb exploded in the Wolfsschanze [Hitler's 'wolf's lair' military HQ in Rastenburg, East Prussia]."

Göring paced across the front of the large window, lost in thought for a moment. All he had said verified and added to what Hans had learned from Dr Friedman and the documents left by his father, but he still could not understand why Göring had brought him to this meeting. As if on cue, Göring spoke. "And so, Hans, you will be thinking, what is all this to do with me? *Ja?* Well, we searched for you after the good Dr Friedman came to see you. You should be pleased that we found you first because had it been the BND, things might have been very different. We know that your father kept many records from the days of the Reich and that Rommel gave him the German copy of the Operational Orders issued in 1944. When Dr Friedman came to meet with you, he handed over a case containing information and, for that, he paid with his life."

Göring's piercing eyes fixed him with a penetrating look of power. "I have shared much with you and taken risks to bring you here; you will realise that we are all after one thing. It is those Orders signed by the Führer and Eisenhower that you are now in possession of. That is all. Some more Cognac?" The invitation was added as a charming finish to what was now a demand.

"You see, Herr Schirach, you are, as I would expect, adept at covering up your reactions in the interests of gaining a story, but you missed something in our chat. You exhibited no surprise or reaction when I mentioned the Barbarossa Secret, which I knew meant you had been briefed because all of that is *'eins zu eins'*, and known only to a mere handful of people, now including you. This secret has been too dangerous to share with the world these last seventy-five years and remains so. Your great-grandfather and my grandfather were united in an historic movement for momentous change. Despite the tragic outcome of the war, we have triumphed, becoming powerful again, but it is not just in Germany where our movement flourishes: we have people in positions of power within the United States, Britain and across Europe. Germany now dominates the EU and we have succeeded in our aim of becoming the greatest economic power. We are rising, once again, and now, Hans, you can celebrate our unique ties of blood and heritage, joining with me and acting together for Germany." His voice had risen and Hans could see a fanatical look in his eyes. Göring looked at him directly. "So, perhaps you would please tell me where the Orders document is located?"

Hans felt adrenalin pumping, knowing that he was, despite the genial nature of his host, in grave danger. Suddenly he could see this man for what he represented, casting the shadows of one of the darkest eras of humanity on a world that, surely, had moved on; a world where there was no relevance to the perverted views of Adolf Hitler. He had previously believed that Nazi doctrines were an anachronism only pedalled by extreme right-wing groups. Yet, he now experienced a sickening realisation that the dark spectre of National Socialism was still pervasively real. Once again, he felt the need to delve further, his instinct for a story driving his question: "Why is this so important now, so long afterwards, when the war does not even exist in the living memory of most of us? What relevance does this all have today?"

Göring proffered a glass of Cognac to Hans, then extended his own, touching the crystal together as if in a mutual toast, which, despite himself, Hans accepted, recognising the need to keep the atmosphere relaxed. "My dear Hans, you are not aware of the reality of what has happened in the last seventy-five years since the end of the war. In 1945, the Führer travelled with Eva Braun to Spain, and then to the Eagle's Lair in Argentina. Our ace card guaranteeing the Führer's safety was the Barbarossa Secret, which Great Britain and America could not risk exposing to the Russians without this triggering another war.

"There were nine on the German side who originally knew the Secret, including the Führer. Gradually, that number dwindled. The first, Rommel, took his life in 1944, and we assisted Göring to do the same at the Nuremberg Trials. Reichsführer Himmler tried to make his own deal for power with the Allies and was assassinated by British Intelligence in an arrangement made with your father on the Führer's orders. Karl

Haushofer became a security risk, as he never got over his son's death, so we eliminated him in 1946. Martin Bormann was fiercely loyal to the Reich until his death in 1970. Hess was imprisoned under the highest security because he knew more than anybody, having held direct discussions with Winston Churchill with the backing of King George VI. He swore his ongoing allegiance to the Führer in a meeting he had with Albert Speer whilst in prison at Nuremberg and that he would never divulge the Secret or jeopardise the Führer's safety. He kept his word until his death, but we reminded him of his loyalty from time to time by 'briefing' him on his family's wellbeing. He was in Spandau Prison in Berlin with Speer and your great-grandfather, von Schirach. Speer too remained tight-lipped over the Secret, but after his release in 1966, he began to give press interviews and write memoirs, making good money. He was basking in the limelight, anxious to promote himself in a positive way, and started to talk too much. He was eliminated in a London hotel in 1981.

"Prime Minister Margaret Thatcher decided Hess was an unacceptable security risk and an obstacle to the reunification of Germany in 1987. His mental health was failing and he was the last remaining risk from those who knew the Secret. He was taken out by British Intelligence in 1987. They nearly screwed it up by reporting that he hanged himself, which was patently ludicrous. He could hardly walk and was ninety-three years old."

The information given by Göring left one single burning unanswered question. "Which, Herr Göring, leaves my father. He was the last who knew about the Secret from that time, so is that why he died?"

Göring leaned forward in his chair. "It was a terrible accident, Hans, and no-one wanted his death. He had been revered like a modern-day Führer, granted his power by the great Adolf Hitler himself. But Hans, we know he was in possession of the German copy of the Orders. You will understand that if the Secret was revealed today, it would have catastrophic consequences, destroying all we have worked for. All the institutions and structures we have in place across the world would be compromised."

Hans was thinking fast and a strategy was forming in his mind that would, perhaps, ensure his safety, but it was like moves played out on a chess board. His next would be critical to the outcome and he knew his adversary was aware of this. "So, what about the British and Americans?" Hans ventured. "Do they not have a copy?"

"Oh, *ja*," came the reply, "there were three. The Americans had one, passing the Orders from one president to another in the transfer of secrets such as the Gold Code for the launch of nuclear weapons. They have done this with the Barbarossa Secret since President Franklin D Roosevelt prepared the information in a secret file in 1945. After that, it was a standard part of the covert transition of executive power with only the President and his successor knowing of it. It was the same in the United Kingdom and all of those in the know recognised they had to take the Secret to their graves, which they did. That left Churchill, who deposited his copy of the Operational Orders with King George VI, who placed it in the Royal Archive. He passed the Secret on to Elizabeth II, giving the monarchy the power to brief incoming Prime Ministers but without copying them in with the Orders, removing them from the danger of British political control.

"In 2016, President Obama proposed to both the British and ourselves that we consign the evidence of what had taken place to irretrievable history by not passing on the information to anyone in the interests of humanity and security. He gave an undertaking to destroy their copy. The Americans were facing a presidential campaign with the unpredictable Donald Trump in the wings, who Obama saw as a threat to the integrity of the Secret, especially with his alleged ties to the Russians. British Prime Minister Theresa May agreed, and the Queen confirmed she would not pass the information on to Prince Charles, the future King. That left one loose end: the copy held by your father, which we requested from him. We agreed that our copy should be deposited in the British Royal Archive, which made all copies beyond the political sphere of control. I confirmed that we would surrender the original of our Orders document to the British in exchange for some minor favours, as it had fulfilled its original purpose of guaranteeing our security in the post-war period.

"We are now well established, with representation within the Bundestag, the British Parliament and we have members in both the US House and the Senate. We were the driving force behind the creation of the EU, recognising the potential for Germany to dominate Europe, as has become the case. Furthermore, we operate within the secret structure of the Bilderbergers and the New World Order, harvesting input from the greatest mindsets to set global policy and bypass democracy. Removing the last documentary evidence of the Barbarossa Secret ensures our future. Equally, we are concerned to prevent the political and financial market anarchy which would result if this ever came out. The Fourth Reich is already established and we will not allow our successful infiltration into modern institutions to be exposed or our existence to be placed at risk." Göring's voice had risen again with the last words, and he had an intense glint in his eyes, reminding Hans of films he had seen of fanatical Nazis delivering speeches.

Göring paused, reflecting for a moment before continuing, "We had a problem, as we were unable to obtain the original Orders document from your father and he was evasive whenever we contacted him. After the December 2019 general election in the United Kingdom, the former British Prime Minister was concerned about the whereabouts of the German copy of the Orders. She decided to take the German Chancellor into her confidence, who, up to that point, had no knowledge of the Barbarossa Secret. We tried to stop her, but she insisted because exposure represented a critical threat to international security. Despite repeated requests for the document, your father failed to comply. Now, tragically, he has lost his life, and for what purpose? It is so sad, unfortunate and regrettable. Hans, you are bright and gifted in your work. You should join us, because we need people like you and your pedigree is faultless." He once again fixed his unwavering eyes directly on Hans, his face smiling then hardening. "So now, please, you will tell us where the Orders are and surrender them to us, together with any other documents you have."

Hans felt a flush of anger at both the way in which the death of his father had been dismissed as 'unfortunate' and at the perversion of someone who could talk of him having a pedigree of which he felt ashamed. All he could now see was the corrupt, corrosive evil represented by the man in front of him, evoking terrible reflections of a very dark past.

This time it was Hans who rose from his seat. "I have listened, with interest, but I am right now in no doubt of the threat to my life and the reasons which cost my father his. Let me tell you, Herr Göring, yes, I have the Orders, but I took precautions in anticipation of being in this position before your commandos kidnapped me. The papers are all stored in a secure vault, but I do not know where. I contacted a number I had been given if I felt in danger, which turned out to be the Simon Wiesenthal Centre, named after a Jewish Holocaust survivor who became a relentless hunter of Nazi war criminals. I am sure you are familiar with his work. They are powerful, Herr Göring, with links to major Jewish organisations and an association with the Israeli secret service, Mossad. I need not remind you what they can achieve. I am sure you recall the demise of your Adolf Eichmann?" He watched as he saw the normally implacable look in his adversary's face turn to surprise and obvious irritation at the mention of Eichmann, who had been a prominent Nazi, kidnapped by Mossad in Argentina, taken to Israel, tried and hanged.

Göring reached for the phone on the table next to him. "One word from me, Herr Roche, and you will be shot and, believe me, you will not be found." The former geniality had disappeared. "There is too much at stake here that you will never understand." Hans raised his hand, as if protesting, then with a wry smile:

"I would advise you wait, Herr Reichsmarschall, until I have finished before threatening me. I told the Wiesenthal organisation that I was a journalist worried about highly sensitive documents that had come into my possession regarding Nazi activity which had been covered up. I informed them that my father had been murdered because of what he knew and that I was in fear of my life. They offered me safe, confidential and secure storage in return for my assurance that before I released any story, they would be fully briefed and given access to the documents which were sealed. I also drafted a legal codicil to my will which gives them full rights to the documents in the event of my death or incapacity. So, Herr Reichsmarschall, whilst I may be at your mercy, I think you might agree that I may have the upper hand here?"

Göring stood, walked over to him and spoke impassively. "Well, Hans, it seems we have what might be classed as a mutual deterrent? I let you go and ensure your safe return, but if you publish your findings, you become a target because, then, we have nothing to lose. I think this is stalemate." He called his men, asking that they escort Hans back to his hotel, then he handed him his camera, adding, "The photographs have been deleted and I might suggest you consider another angle if you wish to publish a story, omitting any reference to the Barbarossa Secret. I would investigate the part played by the British Royal Family, starting with the Duke of Saxe-Coburg in the 1930s. I will have something delivered to you which may assist. That way, you still get a scoop and we are both protected. I give you my word: your journey back will be safe." He surprised Hans by extending his arm. "*Gute nacht,*" and Hans surprised himself by shaking the extended hand.

Friday 21st February 2020, 10.00am
Weinfeldweg, Berchtesgaden, Bavaria, Germany

Hans was woken by Bernhard shaking him. Having been utterly exhausted and drained from the events of the last days, he had collapsed on his bed following their return to Bernhard's house. "Jesus Christ, Hans, there are two Mercedes outside, and men are hammering on the door." As if on cue, there came the sound of loud banging echoing down the hall. Hans became instantly awake; pulling the blue card from his wallet, he handed it to Bernhard. "Call this number and ask for Rubin Horowitz if anything happens to me. Try leaving by the back door and hide somewhere until they go."

He sprung up, still dressed from the day before, and approached the stout wooden door to the house. The hammering began again. "*Ich komme*, I'm coming," he shouted, gesturing Bernhard urgently to go. He slowly pulled back the iron bolt on the door, opening it slightly, knowing he may need to buy Bernhard time. Peering through the gap, he could see four men with Oberst Hoffman, his escort from the day before, standing in front of them carrying an attaché case. "What do you want?" Hans demanded.

The response was not aggressive but formal: "I have information for Herr Hans Schirach?" Then, as Hans opened the door: "Ah, *guten morgan*, Herr Schirach, I trust you slept well? I have a gift for you from the Reichsmarschall." He handed over the case and hardly had Hans muttered, "*Danke*," than the Oberst smiled broadly, clicked his heels, extending his arm and gave the Nazi salute, before he smartly turned and walked back to the waiting cars, which then rapidly drove away.

Hans took the case into the kitchen, placing it on the large wooden table. He called through the back door that all was safe and a white-faced Bernhard joined him. "*Mein Gott*, Hans, you certainly make life more interesting," he attempted to joke despite having felt terrified only moments before. Hans opened the case and, within seconds, both of them were staring open-mouthed at the contents. There was a handwritten note on top: *"Thank you for being my guest and for confirming our 'Mutual Deterrent'. These papers are my gift and were 'cleansed' from the Marburg Files after the war at the insistence of Prime Minister Winston Churchill, who ordered all records to be destroyed. We kept copies as insurance. If you need any more, I may consider assisting. Good luck."*

His signature was scrawled beneath – *'Manfred HA Göring'* – after which there was an email address. Underneath were two sheafs of papers contained in folders. Hans extracted the first; on the top left of the first page was the Nazi insignia of the eagle over a circular laurel surrounding the swastika, under which was printed 'Adolf Hitler'. The title was centred in Germanic Gothic letters:

STENG GEHELM ['TOP SECRET']
CHEF SACHE
['For the eyes of the Führer – literally for the boss']
Record of the meeting on 22nd October 1937

Between:

*His Royal Highness Prince Edward Duke of Windsor
formerly His Majesty King Edward VIII of Great Britain
and the British Dominions
And
Der Führer und Reich Kanzler: Adolf Hitler*

(Transcribed by Dr Paul – Otto Schmidt)

"*Oh mein lieber Gott*," Hans gasped, as he opened the second file, revealing a set of papers, carrying the same eagle logo which was centred above a title:

OPERATION WILLI
ADDENDUM 8(11)

ORIGINAL DRAFT: 1ST NOVEMBER 1937
AMENDED: 11TH MARCH 1940
REICHSKOMMISSARIAT GROSSBRITANNIEN

THE REICH ROYAL ACCESSION PLAN FOR GREAT BRITAIN AND THE BRITISH DOMINIONS

Following the abdication or departure or death of King George VI
For the Restoration of:
The Duke of Windsor and Rightful King Edward VIII and the Duchess of Windsor
who shall hereinafter assume the formal Title:
Queen Mary upon accession to the throne

As they read through each of the documents, they both uttered expletives in turn, staggered by what lay in front of them and, even more so, as they began digesting the contents. These alone, without the information they already had, represented an incredible, extraordinary prize which they knew could only make this the greatest story that either of them had ever worked on.

19

A Royal Reception

Friday 22nd October 1937, 1.30pm
The Berghof, Near Berchtesgaden, Obersalzberg, Bavaria, Germany

The long procession of motor vehicles wound its way up a twisting road, climbing higher from the town of Berchtesgaden, where the Duke and Duchess of Windsor had spent the night. Four motorcycles with armed soldiers in side cars led the way, followed by a Panzerwagen armoured vehicle, then a large open-topped Mercedes in which the Duke and Duchess were being driven. They were accompanied by Dr Robert Ley and General Bohle, who was leader of the NSDAP/AO, an arm of the Nazi Party for Germans who lived and worked outside Germany. Another Mercedes followed in which Greta travelled with Diana Mosley, Charles Edward, Dudley Forwood and Prince Philipp von Hessen. Behind this were four further motorcycles with armed outriders.

The Duke of Windsor's mood was improving as he discussed the developing network of support being given to German workers by the Nazi Party with General Bohle, who was extolling the idea of this becoming an international organisation. The Duke had not been in the best of moods, having received a note from George Ogilvie-Forbes, the chargé d'affaires at the British embassy in Berlin, advising him not to discuss anything political with Hitler.

He turned to Wallis as they left their hotel. "These damned people have the impertinence to tell me that they will have nothing to do with my visit and then interfere at every opportunity. They seem to ignore the fact that we have to deal with Hitler. One may not approve of the fellow, but he seems to be achieving a great deal and he is much admired by his people. Britain is missing firm leadership and direction. I would have influenced things very differently. I think my dear brother, Bertie, is too faint-hearted for the job. He's always been driven by that frightfully irritating Bowes-Lyon wife of his."

When they had arrived in Berlin at the start of their visit, his equerry had been handed a note from the Third Secretary of the British embassy telling them that the embassy would not be available to assist them during their visit, which had infuriated the Duke. In the privacy of their hotel, upon reading the note which Dudley Richard Forwood handed to him, he had exclaimed angrily to Wallis, "First, these bounders have the insolent temerity to demean my position, as former King and Emperor, by refusing to give you royal rank, then they have the affront to deny my visit diplomatic support or recognition. I will not be silenced, nor will I permit my rank to suffer further indignity. At least here in Germany, we seem to be treated as one would expect, and I am frankly beginning to feel I have more in common with these people than those purporting to govern my own country. Perhaps it is time I considered what role I can play in the future of Great Britain which, by divine right, was mine to rule."

Wallis chatted over drinks later that morning with Greta, reporting the Duke's remarks. "I sense David regrets abdicating in many ways, although we are deliriously happy. I rather think he feels he has deserted a sinking ship that, perhaps, he could and should have fought for. There are many who would still support him and who remain loyal, which is so kind of them, don't you think?" Greta agreed with her that loyalty was to be admired but made a mental note that she needed to pass this change in the Duke's views back to Colonel Menzies.

As the visit progressed with the arranged tours, the Duke of Windsor had appeared to be gaining in confidence, reasserting the outgoing characteristics and common touch that had earned him the admiration of the British people. As they had visited factories, he had conversed with workers, taking an interest in their conditions and welfare. Many enthusiastically spoke to him about improvements in their living standards and new opportunities, openly expressing admiration for the Führer, who had made all this possible. Dr Ley had been replaced as leader of the tour, resulting from his over-consumption of alcohol, even hitting a gate on one occasion as he drove the Duke and Duchess into a factory. However, although he no longer drove the Royal couple, as they were referred to by the Germans, he still accompanied the tour as chief of the German Labour Front. He acted as intermediary between workers and the Duke, who was fascinated by the ideas Ley espoused when sober.

Ley explained to the Royal party, in the early days of the tour, that the slogan of the German labour movement was 'Strength Through Joy' and that he was leading initiatives to massively improve the living conditions of workers. The Duke was particularly interested in the concept of a 'people's car', or *Volkswagon*, being introduced at the behest of Hitler, and which, Dr Ley informed them, had even been designed by the Führer. However, his humour was coarse if not vulgar and the Duchess found him odious, describing him as 'rather distasteful and somewhat of an idiot'. The Duke was more tolerant, accepting his ways as being a bridge to understanding the mindset of a German worker, having always felt, within himself, an empathetic bond with working people.

Hermann Göring had taken over the tour who was far more urbane and charming, much to the relief of the entire party. He conversed easily, with wit, being both entertaining and interesting with a grasp of literature, culture, politics and foreign affairs, engaging in debate without overtly pushing the Party line. His uniforms seemed to change daily and were immaculate with a touch of exuberance and flamboyance. The Duke of Windsor spoke enthusiastically of him and Greta noted that they were striking up a warm relationship, which needed reporting to the colonel.

During the week, they had dined with many leading figures, including Hitler's architect, Albert Speer, Foreign Minister von Ribbentrop, Deputy Führer Rudolf Hess and Propaganda Minister Joseph Goebbels, accompanied by his wife, Magda, whom the Duchess described as 'the prettiest woman I saw in Germany'. Greta was mentally taking notes all the time, gathering names of British members of society, about whom their Nazi hosts would talk of proudly and openly, who admired Hitler. Lord Rothermere, the owner of various national newspapers including the *Daily Mail* and the *Daily Mirror*, was frequently mentioned as a regular visitor, often meeting Hitler, whom he spoke of in glowing terms. In the privacy of her hotel room, she noted down the names, transcribing them into numbered code using a formula she had been given at SIS HQ in London. The list was placed in an inside back page of *Great Expectations* by Charles Dickens, a book which she had taken on the trip 'to read'. There were many on the list from the upper echelons of society, including HRH Windsor, to which she appended an exclamation mark with the words in code: "Gave Hitler admiration speech in public saying, '*miraculous achievements – one man one will*'." As the trip progressed, many more titled members of the aristocracy were added, including Lord Lothian, the Duke of Westminster, Baron Rothschild, Lady Ethel Snowden, a number of MPs and a dazzling socialite whom she knew of but had yet to meet, Princess Stephanie von Hohenlohe.

The Princess was becoming increasingly noticed in both British and German circles of influence. She was an imposing, attractive Austrian who had many connections and lovers within the establishment. She was a confidante and friend of Adolf Hitler and, therefore, detested by Unity Mitford, who saw her as a rival for the Führer's attention. Hitler had given her a castle in Salzburg, Schloss Leopoldskron, in recognition of her open and enthusiastic support of his policies.

Greta first met her at Carinhall, Hermann Göring's country residence, on a large estate north of Berlin, to which they had been personally invited for high tea, which was quite an ostentatious affair. They were greeted at the gates by a military band which then struck up the British national anthem. The band had then marched in front of the vehicles playing the 'Horst Wessel Lied' Nazi anthem, leading the procession into a huge square, at one side of which was a large Gothic front door where a beaming Göring awaited in full white dress uniform festooned with medals. Either side of the entrance, flaming torches added to the atmosphere which, Greta thought, was almost like a Hollywood film set. A guard of honour, with rifles, flanked the Reichsmarschall on either side of him dressed in the light blue uniforms of the Luftwaffe but with caps instead of the coal scuttle helmets they were used to seeing.

As they had alighted from their vehicles, the German marching band stopped and, surprisingly, began playing the popular dance and song hit of the year 'Thanks for the Memory', bringing a broad smile to the Duke's face and setting the atmosphere. Göring snapped to attention then bowed to the Duke, before turning and kissing the hand of the Duchess.

"Your Royal Highness, you do us a great service by visiting Carinhall, and we humbly place ourselves at your service." Both the Duke and Duchess beamed, once again sensing that here, at least, they were treated as befitted their Royal status. A female attendant in a traditional folk dress walked forwards and curtsied, giving the Duchess a small bouquet of flowers. Inside, a number of staff dressed in traditional Bavarian costumes lined the hall, bowing as the Duke and Duchess passed. The walls were lined with furs, antlers and various animal trophies. As they entered a large salon, there were a small number of people gathered who stood to applaud them. Greta noted that Deputy Führer, Rudolf Hess, was there, together with Albrecht Haushofer, whom she knew worked closely with him.

A string quartet played the music of Strauss in the corner, as Champagne was served by orderlies dressed in white tunics. Göring then introduced them to the guests, which included Douglas, the Marquis of Clydesdale and Douglas (the future Duke of Hamilton), who smiled in recognition as he greeted Greta. Von Ribbentrop was also there, who made great play of presenting Princess Stephanie von Hohenlohe to the party, accompanied by the Führer's personal adjutant who had organised much of the visit, Fritz Wiedemann. The Princess was clearly out to make an impression, dressing ostentatiously in a figure-hugging flimsy pink cotton dress with a matching shawl, worn slightly off the shoulders, with a plunging neckline and a large diamond pendant. Her dark hair was wavy, worn long beneath a wide-brimmed hat with a feather. Prince Philipp von Hessen, who had entered with Greta and Diana Mosley, steered them to meet the Princess, who greeted them both enthusiastically.

"Diana, your husband is doing marvellous things in England, spreading the awareness of our movement, but I think there is so much more we can do to promote the words and mission of our great Führer. Oh, and Greta, darling, I hear a great deal about your work for *Vogue* and I read with much interest your frightfully interesting interview with Baldur von Schirach. Quite a scoop for you, and it was very revealing."

Greta thanked her, recognising that she had been clearly well briefed, whilst feeling a little shaken, thinking back to the time when she had let her heart rule her head and the sacrifice that followed. Princess Stephanie then enthusiastically engaged the Duke of Windsor in a discussion about whether, in his opinion, there was sufficient awareness in the British corridors of power of the Bolshevik threat. She explained that her interest was because she had spent much of her time in Britain, having been partly educated there, stressing that Lord Rothermere, the press baron, was a great friend of hers. The Princess confessed that she was overwhelmed with admiration for the Führer and his achievements, to which another smartly dressed man present muttered a clear 'hear hear'.

Greta thought she recognised him, but it was Diana Mosley who assisted by whispering to her, "That's that dreadful man George Ward Price, who sneaks everywhere, ferreting around, sticking his damned nose in as the foreign correspondent of the *Daily Mail*. Be careful what you say, because it all gets put how he wishes it to be interpreted in the newspaper. Look at our Princess now, unashamedly giving David the eye; rumour has it that she is having an affair with Lord Rothermere. One of many she has ensnared, including, I should add, our trip organiser, Fritz Wiedemann. All very incestuous, don't you think?" Diana giggled, mischievously adding, "We are surrounded by awful, sycophantic people who are feeding off the marvellous words and deeds of the Führer, but I do love the gossip. Rather like the court of a King!"

They were interrupted by Albrecht Haushofer. "My dear Greta and Diana, two of the most beautiful girls in the Reich, yet both English!" He kissed both their hands, bowing. "I am anxious to learn more of your culture as I think our nations may be destined to stand together." Albrecht was dressed in a pinstriped suit with fashionable wide lapels and looked quite dapper, Greta observed, and, as always, she warmed to him. However, he now held more interest because she knew he was a reliable contact and conduit for messages to and from Colonel Menzies, resulting from both his increased disillusionment with Hitler's regime and his passionate commitment to peace. He was an invaluable source of information, being a close associate and friend of the Deputy Führer, assisted by the trust built through his friendship with Douglas-Hamilton.

"Dearest Albrecht," Greta smiled at him, "how is your poetry progressing? I have not forgotten my promise to widen your education and I brought you a book from which I think you may, indeed, learn a little of our culture." She reached in her bag, extracting her copy of *Great Expectations*, which she passed to him.

"My education is clearly lacking, despite my degree in geography," he countered, smiling, adding with a mischievous grin, "Perhaps I can add to yours." Opening the leather document folder he carried under his arm, he extracted a copy of *Mein Kampf*, with a somewhat menacing black and white photo of Hitler on the front cover, which he gave to Greta with a twinkle in his eye. "Maybe there is much you can learn from this," Albrecht added propitiously, with a wink.

A little while later, Reichsmarschall Göring took them on a tour of his home and was utterly charming to the small party, which included the Duke and Duchess, Greta, Diana, and Prince Philipp von Hessen. In one large room, there was an extraordinary model railway with a complex layout and scenery surrounding it, which the Duke took to, exhibiting an enthusiastic childhood fascination clearly matching that of his host. They both took control of separate trains, racing them with cries of genuine excitement like two boys, thought Greta. She inwardly reflected that so much seemed at stake in a Europe threatened by war yet here was such a contradiction when facets of power were dissolved by childish play. The Duchess had told Greta later, after their private meeting with Göring, that there was a map on the wall of his study showing Austria and Germany as one country. When the Duke had questioned him, Göring had replied that it was only what the Austrians wanted, especially as the Führer was Austrian.

Five days later, another social event had been hosted by Duke Charles Edward, at which he had invited Greta to be by his side. She refused, saying it would be a slight against his wife, Victoria Adelaide, who was playing the role of hostess. It was a sumptuous dinner, more like a State Banquet, held at the Veste Coburg, a vast medieval fortress in Bavaria, attended by over 100 guests. The Duke and Duchess were treated like royalty, escorted through the lines of guests, who bowed as they passed to the obvious delight of the Duke, who remarked later that he felt, once again, more respected in Germany than in his own country. A speech was given by Reichsmarschall Hermann Göring, during which the Duke was referred to as 'a King forsaken by country, yet recognised for His Majesty here in the Reich, where we honour leadership'.

Greta, once again, met with Albrecht Haushofer, to whom she presented the Shakespeare play *King Lear*, quoting loosely from it as she asked, "*Are we more 'sinned against than sinning'?* A question that affects more than a king, perhaps."

The night before, she had added more names to further list in code those she had reliably been informed were passing information to German intelligence, including Princess Stephanie von Hohenlohe and Lord Rothermere. The latter, she had learned, was holding regular meetings with Hitler, during which they discussed how to influence thinking in Britain through his newspapers.

The itinerary had been exhausting, leading up to today's climax which had been announced by Prince Philipp von Hessen as the highlight of an historic visit uniting the two nations as never before. Now, as the procession of cars entered between two large guard buildings, a line of troops in black uniforms stood to attention on both sides of the roadway leading towards the Berghof, which, as Prince Philipp von Hessen pointed out to them, was the Führer's favourite residence. As they passed, officers in front of the lines of men smartly raised their arms in the Nazi salute returned by General Bohle in the leading car. Greta merely waved whilst Charles Edward, Diana and Prince Philipp bent their arms at the elbow enthusiastically. The Duke's equerry, Dudley Forwood, did not join in and, Greta thought, looked somewhat wearily disdainful at what he was experiencing.

"Oh, Richard, you look frightfully bored," Diana taunted him, to which he replied, "One is, perhaps, a little wary of what may follow."

There was not the extravagance that they had witnessed on their visit to Carinhall. There were no military bands marching but a stiff formality and Greta sensed an almost fearful apprehension and nervousness in Prince Philipp von Hessen. She confessed to herself that she felt nervous at the prospect of meeting the Führer, but she certainly did not share the unswerving adulation or awe that others around her displayed. Instead, she felt a growing distaste and revulsion for all his regime represented.

The procession of vehicles slowed as they approached an enormous Alpine lodge complex built on the hillside but one which was constructed on a much grander scale than the norm for its architectural type. They forked left and up a short incline towards the buildings as their military escort left them, continuing on to the right. A low, long building on their left had an apex roof which intersected at right angles with a much larger and taller grand Alpine-style house with a timber upper structure, in the front of which was a flagpole flying the red and black swastika flag. On the right side, the hill dropped away, affording an unrestricted and magnificent view of the mountains. They halted by some steps and the doors were opened by guards, who then stood back, clicking their heels and jumping to attention. At the bottom of the steps, a smiling Rudolf Hess was standing together with Hitler's adjutant, Fritz Wiedemann, and both raised their right arms in the full Nazi salute as the Duke alighted from his car, offering a hand to the Duchess. Hess walked towards them and bowed.

"On behalf of the Führer of Germany and the Reich, I welcome your Royal Highnesses to the Berghof. We are deeply honoured by your presence." Above them, on a terrace, an officer shouted commands and a military band began playing the British national anthem. A line of black-uniformed guards with white gloves to their right presented arms then stood to attention. All those around them paused during the anthem, affording the Duke and Duchess all the ceremony and respect that might be accorded to royalty on a state visit.

The party were escorted up the flight of steps then right through an archway to a large panelled door which was opened by an orderly, who bowed deeply. Hess led them down a long corridor with low vaulted ceilings giving a majestic yet traditional feel to the interior. They entered a vast room dominated by a massive window containing squared frames overlooking the Untersberg Mountain and the peaks surrounding the Obersalzberg. On one side, a fire crackled in a huge red marble fireplace, in front of which were a number of easy chairs and a sofa. The ceiling had deep panelling, in which there were suspended large round iron chandeliers inset with numerous long candle-effect lights. The walls were hung with classical style paintings and tapestries, but it was the sheer size of the room with its open view which was as imposing as it was impressive.

"The Führer admires the monumental style in architecture which reflects his extraordinary vision," Hess informed them. "He has designed everything here, personally selecting the fittings and furniture. What started as a simple chalet has become both the Führer's retreat and headquarters where he likes to entertain heads of state. Incidentally, that massive window lowers to give a completely unrestricted view of the mountains. Perhaps it is a little cold today to demonstrate this."

As they peered around the room, a door opened at the far end and Unity Mitford entered, running over to greet her sister Diana, whom she embraced, before giggling. "Whoops, I'm sorry, David, I mean, Your Royal Highness, I quite forgot protocol."

The Duke responded, "My dear Unity, I would have been disappointed if you hadn't. Indeed, I might even have been deeply offended if you had forgotten to misbehave in front of me."

He smiled broadly as Unity curtsied before kissing the Duke on both cheeks. An officer marched in, bowing to the Duke and Duchess before speaking quietly to Hess, who then turned to the guests. "The Führer sends his apologies, but he has been delayed. He will join you very soon and extends his hospitality by offering you some refreshment."

As if on cue, a number of white-coated orderlies entered and they were offered glasses of Riesling wine but told by Hess that, as the Führer did not drink alcohol, they would be sharing tea with him when he joined them. The Duke of Windsor wandered over to the large window then turned to the room. "One has to admire this extraordinary man Adolf Hitler, who has not only transformed your country but who seems to possess talents in everything he touches or influences. His leadership seems to me to be inspirational and admirable. One can only wish we could emulate such qualities in Britain, where political direction seems lacking."

Diana Mosley quipped, "Then, darling David, perhaps you should take over what is, after all, your kingdom by right."

The Duke waved his finger at her. "That is treason, you know, and you could be taken to the Tower of London for such seditious talk."

There was polite laughter, but Rudolf Hess took up the theme. "Your Royal Highness has undoubted qualities which have been admired by many here in Germany, including the Führer himself. Here, we had to change the way government works to ensure decisions can be made by establishing strong leadership. Democratic government has inherent weaknesses whereas National Socialism delivers what the people need with decisive efficiency."

A discussion followed which, Greta noted, was clearly aimed at encouraging the view that the British government was weak. Hess stated his concern that Britain might fail to act if the threat was realised of aggression from Communist Russia, leaving Germany to stand alone defending Europe and civilisation. She could see that the Duke was not only in sympathy with the views being expressed but that he was being further persuaded by them. There was no question in Greta's mind that the discussion had been orchestrated leading to a conclusion that actions were needed more immediately to deal with the threat from the East. General Bohle seemed skilled at talking about international issues wherein he stated that many Germans were trapped inside borders unfairly drawn after the end of the Great War. Prince Philipp von Hessen agreed, nodding his head, saying that European strength and security would increase if Germans could be united under one flag. Charles Edward added that one leader was a more natural way than the confusion of democracy. He turned, as he spoke, to the Duke, who seemed to take confidence from ideas which were being endorsed by his aristocratic relatives, displaying increasing enthusiasm for what was being said.

Suddenly, the door opened up some steps to their right and an officer entered, clicking his heels. "Your Royal Highnesses, *meine Damen und Herren, der Führer!*"

Those in uniform around the group also clicked their heels, raising their arms in salute as Adolf Hitler walked to the top of the steps. He was dressed in a brown uniform tunic with the Iron Cross worn below the round Nazi Party badge on his chest. On his left arm was the red and white armband with a black swastika. He raised his arm from the elbow, the palm of his hand bent backwards, acknowledging the salute, pausing as he took in the scene.

The room hushed in respect; then, his guttural, unmistakeable voice broke the silence. "Today, the Reich honours the visit of Your Royal Highnesses and I believe this is a momentous time in our history in which we share a noble destiny. This is our great moment to seize and face the future, without hesitation, driven by resolve and purpose." His voice commanded attention but then he stopped and smiled, turning to an orderly: "I am sure my guests hear my voice too often, perhaps it must be time for tea," lightening the moment as he descended the steps, walking towards the Duke, briskly bowing before shaking his hand.

"Your Royal Highness, you are welcome to my humble home." He drew smiles and laughter before he turned to the Duchess, this time bowing more deeply. "Germany is deeply honoured by your visit, Your Royal Highness, and I hope you have enjoyed my train." He kissed her hand and the moment drew applause from those around them.

The Duke replied that he was grateful for the immense hospitality and that he was greatly reminded of his German family heritage and connections during the visit.

Hitler walked over to Diana Mitford. "*Meine engel*, there is only one who is as equally beautiful as you, which is your incorrigible sister Unity." He turned with a half-smile to Unity, who curtsied with a giggle. "We do not see enough of you and I always enjoy our discussions during which you challenge me. That is a rarity which I treasure." The Führer turned, with a smile, to Charles Edward. "My dear Duke, I am surrounded by royalty and aristocrats, I feel I am outranked." The remark caused much amusement. Then, addressing Prince Philipp von Hessen, he asked to be introduced to all the visitors, greeting each in turn with a brief bow and a handshake.

He stopped as he was introduced to Greta. "A journalist? My dear Frau, I am surprised you were permitted to travel with Their Royal Highnesses. It has taken me nearly a year before I was allowed to take a cup of tea with them, yet you will now have an exclusive story." More polite laughter, as he looked directly at her, and she felt his blue eyes piercing inside her as though he was reading her mind. There was no doubting the power and incredible charisma of this man. Greta was not nervous, almost surprising herself, although she sensed his utter hold on the room wherein those around him hung on his every word.

She replied boldly, "Sir, I am a friend of Her Royal Highness, and on this visit, I will never question or report on what happens because I am a guest."

Hitler responded, "A member of the press who does not question or report? We need more like you in Germany."

Again, there was laughter, but Greta sensed nothing but an intense dislike of a man who clearly revelled in his own status. The Führer walked away as tea was served on silver trays, shortly thereafter leaving the room, accompanied by the Duke, Dudley Forwood and Fritz Wiedemann.

20

All in a Letter

Friday 21st February 2020, 4.00pm
Weinfeldweg, Berchtesgaden, Bavaria, Germany

There was something gnawing in the back of Hans's mind as he discussed what he already knew with Bernhard. He tried to piece together the jigsaw of events taking shape in which pieces were missing. He was in possession of incredible information, that much he knew, but it needed fitting together. Where could he access further facts which may assist, especially in the background to the Barbarossa Secret? Was there someone in England who knew about the Operational Orders? Then, he remembered, in a flash of inspiration, something his mother had said.

"*Mein Gott*, Bernhard, it is staring me in the face, within my own family. My own *tolle Grossmutter* ['great-grandmother'] was a British Intelligence agent in the war. It was she who wrote a letter to my grandmother telling her about my family roots and how she ended up working directly for Winston Churchill. I need to return and see my mother because she has the original letter from her and I never asked to see it."

The two men, both journalists, had spent the day trying to make sense of the extraordinary elements of the story they were uncovering and, despite this being family and very personal, Hans could not prevent his natural instincts taking over to chase the leads. They had laughed over schnapps earlier in the day that they were like the legendary *Washington Post* reporters Woodward and Bernstein uncovering Watergate, yet somehow this was even greater.

"That merely removed the President of the United States," Bernhard had joked. "This could topple governments, and a crowned head of state to boot. *Himmel*, we are may be guilty of high treason!" Despite their humour, they were both very aware that lives had been lost and that danger surrounded them that could threaten their own.

Hans called his mother, who sounded distressed when she answered the phone. "Hans, *lieber Gott*, three men have been here today demanding I tell them everything or your safety may be compromised. They searched my house saying they had the authority, but I don't think they were BND. They never showed me any identity." She blurted the words out fast and Hans was taken aback, realising that his actions may have put his own mother's life in danger. "Hans, they took the photographs I showed you and said that I should tell no-one or they would be back. They were threatening me, it was terrible." She half sobbed, which Hans had rarely ever witnessed, as his mother had always been strong and very steadfast.

"Mother, I am coming to see if you are alright. I do not know how safe this call is so please say very little now until I see you. Can you just answer yes or no to my questions? Are you hurt physically?" Her negative answer was a genuine relief. "Was anything else taken?" Again her one word was welcome. "Finally, were they wearing long black coats?" It was a long shot, but he knew most in the BND favoured leather jackets or less formal attire. His mother merely replied, "*Jawohl*," and her inflection, as if giving an affirmative military response, raised his suspicions further that she was correct in that they were not German police or intelligence. Following the call, he made another, retrieving the number from the blue card he kept in his wallet. "Rubin Horowitz, please."

The next day, he left at 6.00am for the exhausting drive back to Hamburg, having given Bernhard strict instructions on what to do in certain circumstances, promising to keep him briefed. Bernhard Meyer was going to do some digging himself, calling in some favours from those he had dealings with in England. He knew exactly where to start, which was with someone who had actually known General Montgomery personally. In 2009, Bernhard had been given his first big assignment, working as a young reporter to cover a story about Germany fifteen years after occupation. This referred to the date the last Russian, British and American troops withdrew from the newly reunified East and West Germany. He had, during this time, built up a relationship with General Sir James Cranshaw, who, as a young British officer, had served with Field Marshal Montgomery in NATO in the late 1950s. Having retired from the army, he worked for the National Army Museum and was heading up a team compiling records relating to the withdrawal of British troops from Germany.

Bernhard had stayed in touch with General Cranshaw, who had been an ardent military historian, and who had assisted him in his research into the wartime activities of former Nazis. This was a subject which had gained Bernhard quite a reputation as an effective investigative journalist but also cost him some career opportunities with national journals. He was occasionally called upon to present TV programmes about the war, which had become his specialist area of expertise. Now, he knew he was involved with the greatest story of his career and he was enormously excited about the prospect.

At 6.00pm, Hans finally pulled onto the drive outside his mother's house, having occasionally checked to see if he was being followed by pulling off into side streets and waiting, before continuing. Despite being tired, he could feel the adrenalin mixed with a sense of anticipation as he approached the house, unaware that he was being watched from two vehicles parked close by. Eva opened the door gingerly, then her face lit up as she recognised her son, throwing her arms around him. She peered around the door before closing it quickly.

"I have only just finished tidying the house after their search. It was frightening, Hans, and I feared for my safety. What is going on?" They sat in the large kitchen as she customarily took out a bottle of Chablis, pouring them both a glass. Hans related to her the events that had taken place since he had left her only four days before. He told her of his father's letter, carefully omitting anything to do with '*eins zu eins*' or the Barbarossa Secret, concentrating on the secrecy surrounding the activities of the NSDAP and their infiltration into modern politics. He did not wish to endanger his mother further by giving her information which had already cost lives. He did relate the warm words that Gunther had written about her, at which she held a handkerchief to her eyes as tears of emotion showed. Upon hearing about the death of Dr Friedman, she became both angry and upset.

"These people, Hans, they are murderers and they are part of our own security!"

She broke down, remembering the way in which the doctor had kept in touch over the years giving her news of Gunther, ensuring that both she and Hans were cared for financially. They ate a meal she prepared of *eintopf* ['stew'], which he ate hungrily, having had nothing since departing Bavaria that morning. He told her of the events surrounding Gunther's funeral, his meeting with Göring, and the subsequent mutual deterrent that he had ensured. Further, he spoke of involving the Wiesenthal Centre in keeping the photographs and letter his father had left him, again avoiding any mention of the Barbarossa Secret or his copy of the Operational Orders. "There are so many gaps in this entire situation and I recall you saying that my great-grandmother had written a letter to your mother after von Schirach died. You said she had put some details in there about her time with Churchill. Can I see the letter?"

Eva rose from the table, saying that she had hidden it many years before because of the information it contained which her mother had told her was highly secret, warning that sharing it could be dangerous. Apart from Hans, she had told no-one of its existence, but now she felt relieved to share its contents with him. She took Hans upstairs to her bedroom, gesturing to a small access door to the roof space in one corner. "If you squeeze in there, there is a beam running across, and where it connects to the house wall, there is a gap where the letter is hidden in a plastic folder."

Hans manoeuvred himself into the darkened roof space with some difficulty, found the gap and, after some moments, felt the edge of the package, which he retrieved, backing out of the access door, which was barely wide enough to allow him through.

"Hans, what are you going to do with all of this?" she asked. It was a question to which he had no answer other than knowing he needed to fill in the gaps in the incredible information he already possessed. They went downstairs and shared a last drink before both deciding they should retire to bed, which would give Hans an opportunity to study the letter. He was very tired but knew he would not sleep until he had read it. In the comfort of his bedroom, he withdrew the folded-up pages of the letter and began reading. The words, written in neat, looped handwriting which slanted to the right, were in English in a royal blue-coloured ink.

Merchant's House
South Quay
King's Lynn
Norfolk
Friday 23rd August 1974

My dear Hanna,
 You do not know me and please forgive me for writing to you out of the blue, but I needed to contact you because I have on my conscience information about your late husband's family that I must impart to you. I was very sorry to hear that Siegfried had passed away; in fact, I was heartbroken, because he was my son. I realise this will be a great shock to you, and I have agonised over whether I should write but I have carried secrets with me for so long that you have a right to know. As you are aware, Siegfried was brought up under the auspices of the Nazi Lebensborn programme in which I was forced to leave him and for which I never forgave myself. I have lived with denying my son the right to a loving mother all my life since and this has haunted me so very much.
 Although Lebensborn was a twisted Nazi idea to generate perfect 'Aryan' children who would be bred to become the pure German race of the future, Siegfried was lucky to have wonderful caring foster parents. I am sure you will have met them. Apart from ensuring that they were always taken care of financially, there was no direct contact between us, nor did I ever see Siegfried again after he was born apart from briefly nursing him in the first month. I became hysterical when they took him and was grief-stricken for months; in fact, I have never come to terms with what I allowed to happen.
 The reason I gave him up was because of who I was and who his father was. I was a young journalist in the 1920s when I was recruited to join British Intelligence. I was useful, as my family was very well connected, and I was able to access and mix within the uppermost circles of society, but I did

not stand out because I was not 'titled'. I was even on first-name terms with the former King Edward VIII and Wallis Simpson before and after they were married. In the 1930s, I was spying in Germany for the Deputy Head of British Military Intelligence, and with my connections, I was accepted at the highest level, even meeting Adolf Hitler.

I went to the Nuremberg Nazi Party Rally in 1933 with the Mitford sisters, Diana and Unity, and our personal host was Baldur Benedikt von Schirach, who headed up the Hitler Youth. He was handsome, utterly charming, debonair and intelligent, and despite the fact I hated their loathsome regime, he certainly made an impression on me. I was granted an interview with him which included dinner. We abandoned principle and, as a result, I became pregnant with Siegfried, which had to be hushed up. This was not only because of von Schirach's position but because of his marriage to a bride Hitler had personally approved, which had taken place only eighteen months earlier.

I had to be hidden away in a private nursing home in the later months of my pregnancy where I isolated, pretending I had TB. When Siegfried was born, Baldur was very concerned to ensure that our child received the best care and I trusted him in that. We both agreed, although it broke my heart, that we could not see Siegfried after we had put him into foster care, although when we needed information, we could obtain it. Over the years, through my contacts in British Intelligence, I have been able to keep track on Siegfried's life. Even after the war, when Baldur was imprisoned by the Allies in Spandau Prison, Siegfried wanted for nothing until he left home and married you. Baldur always ensured that there was money provided for Siegfried's carers. I heard only once from Siegfried's father after the war which was when he was released from prison with Albert Speer in 1966. He wrote and told me he would never betray the secret we had. He also said he had only the happiest of memories about our meeting.

I realise all this will come as a shock to you, and forgive me, but there is a reason for writing because I know you have a daughter, Eva, my granddaughter. I would love her to know her real family roots so that, unlike

Siegfried, she can grow up with a real sense of identity. She can research about her grandfather, and I think she will find that although we were on opposite sides and that he was a National Socialist, close to Hitler, he was not guilty of all the terrible crimes that the Nazis committed. After the war, when he wrote to me, Baldur said he had many regrets and the greatest one of his life was being associated with those who could be capable of orchestrating slave labour, the death camps, and the systematic mass murder of the Jews and others. However, he still felt proud of instilling discipline and loyalty to Nazi ideals in the young. It seemed to me that he represented the confusion of a vanquished generation that had felt the pride of nationalism and invincibility but were blinded by the truth of the regime. My fear is that they will rise again. They have not gone away and I regret that I could have been complicit in that.

I feel as though I need to unburden myself of the guilt I have felt for so many years, not just in abandoning Siegfried, but in losing sight of what is right, surrendering truth, justice and integrity to expediency. The 1930s represented a confusing time of idealistic extremes, from Communism on the left to Fascism on the right. Many good people were genuinely confused, wondering whether National Socialism was, in fact, socialism of the left but with firm, centralised leadership. Good people joined both camps and those of us that believed in democracy and freedom were worried we may be disenfranchised, but, thank God, in England we were holding our own in the areas that mattered. I hated extremism and, having lost my dear father, my two uncles and my own wonderful brother, I so cared for, in the Great War, I would have done anything to prevent another.

Throughout the thirties, I worked for MI6, infiltrating those areas of society that were being seduced by the growth of National Socialism. Although I wanted to avoid conflict, I knew it could not be peace at any price and so, reluctantly, supported the Declaration of War in 1939. I regret that others, including the Duke of Windsor, together with many establishment figures, were still committed to appeasement with Hitler, even after the outbreak of war. They argued that the greater threat was from Russia in the

East. I was codenamed Marlene (after the actress Marlene Dietrich), and was considered valuable because of my language skills, speaking fluent German, and my contacts with many inside Germany at the highest level, even after 1939.

After war was declared, there was so much intrigue which was concealed afterwards. I can reveal that in May 1940 Hitler proposed peace terms with Britain, ordering German forces in France to cease their advance against us. He offered to withdraw from France in return for our neutrality as he pursued his goals in the East. The King was in support of these terms and Churchill wavered, but after the Dunkirk evacuation of our troops, made easier by the halt in the German advance, he hardened his resolve to stand firm against Hitler. This was all covered up, but it caused a major rift between the King and Churchill. The removal of the Prime Minister by the Crown was actively being considered, with staggering implications. At this time, I was seconded to work for Winston Churchill on the recommendation of the Head of SIS, Stewart Menzies, because of my many contacts in both British and German society.

I can tell you that we have been lied to about history, with the collusion of every government since the war, and the appeasement of my conscience lies in what I will tell you. There was a further attempt by the Germans to seek peace terms which was, subsequently, referred to as 'The Barbarossa Secret' named after the German plan for the invasion of Russia.

The flight by Germany's Deputy Führer, Rudolf Hess, to Scotland in May 1941 was all planned with the knowledge of both Hitler and the King. It was organised through me liaising between a contact I had with Hess's assistant, Albrecht Haushofer, together with Douglas, Duke of Hamilton. The proposal was simple from the German side: both sides cease hostilities, the Germans withdraw from parts of Western Europe and we back an invasion of Russia; an offensive which began in June 1941. This is highly classified; I was sworn to secrecy and I am bound by that to this day on pain of imprisonment (or worse).

Churchill was dead set against the German proposal to begin with but then it became apparent that if he stood in the way, King George VI might intervene and have him removed. The King himself had been persuaded that Churchill was a potential danger to the safety and wellbeing of the British people. At this time, German bombing of our cities was taking place and exacting a terrible toll in civilian lives and property which the King found intolerable. How do I know this? I was there and party to off-the-record personal conversations with Lord Louis Mountbatten, whose loyalties were divided.

I was reporting directly to the Head of MI6, Colonel Menzies, on everything I was hearing, and at this point, the fate or survival of the British government lay in his hands. The King had made it quite clear that if Churchill did not cooperate, he could not be held responsible for the consequences, but he dithered. My understanding from Haushofer in Germany was that there was a real threat from powerful elements of British society, supporting appeasement in Britain, that if the King did not take action against Churchill, he himself would be removed and his brother Edward put back on the throne. A compromise was reached to avoid the impending crisis which saved Churchill's neck. This was that if German forces succeeded in advancing within twenty miles of Red Square, the Allies would accept peace terms. These were being negotiated between Rudolf Hess, after his flight to Britain, and Churchill directly.

These were extraordinary times when the fate of our government, the Sovereign, and the outcome of the war were held in the balance, with Stewart Menzies at MI6 working flat out to influence others. He was ably assisted by Lord Louis Mountbatten, who stated to me that giving in to the Germans was unthinkable. I also played a role, using whatever powers of persuasion I had, to deter those tempted into the appeasement camp after the war had started. I did eventually accept, in 1941, that ceasing hostilities and facing up to Stalin's Russia might be the lesser of two evils, but under strict guarantees of there being no threat of German aggression or invasion. There are many who would worry if any of this came out, but please tell Eva that I did what I believed was right.

The talks with Hess stalled with the changing fortunes of the war, and as a result of Lord Louis Mountbatten warning others that a constitutional crisis would be catastrophic. Churchill's hands were strengthened, and, eventually, he and the King repaired their relationship.

By July 1944, the tide of war had turned against Germany and we had invaded France. After D Day, there were further moves by Germany to sue for peace. Churchill approved a plan, put forward by Hess, that there be an unofficial surrender of supreme command of the German forces to the Allies. German Army command structures would remain and an immediate withdrawal of their forces from France would be undertaken enabling them to counterattack against the Russians on the Eastern Front. Allied forces would provide logistical support to Germany and Hitler would remain as Führer. Eisenhower favoured a joint German/Allied offensive to take the Russians by surprise, but Churchill refused, saying that any aggression must be seen as Germany's alone. Initial peace terms were drafted which were known as 'Operational Orders'. These were signed by Adolf Hitler, Eisenhower, as the Supreme Allied Commander, together with General Montgomery and Field Marshal Rommel as commanders in the field, but the entire initiative collapsed due to a betrayal on both sides.

Shortly thereafter, there was an assassination attempt on Hitler by his own people and no further cooperation was proposed with any credibility, although many Germans tried. The Allies were approached by Himmler, but it was clear he did not have the support of others. Last-minute attempts were made with proposals by Hess for a cessation of hostilities, protection of the existing German regime and Allied intervention to avoid the Soviets entering Berlin, but the situation on the ground was changing too quickly and all came to nothing.

I witnessed attempts by Churchill to halt Russian occupation and territorial aggression, but it was too late. I was appalled by their subsequent seizing of territory and the setting-up of pro-Communist regimes which resulted in the Cold War. Hess's final concession was to surrender German scientists, top-secret weapons and rocket technology to America and Britain in exchange for Hitler's freedom to leave and live in South America. British and American intelligence at the highest level joined in the cover-up that followed. You should also know that the Germans had already partially developed an atomic bomb and the surrender of their atomic research was the final bargaining chip. We knew that their scientist, Wernher von Braun, had developed a ballistic missile that could have potentially resulted in a nuclear attack on Britain or the US had Hitler not been allowed to escape. Von Braun was taken by the Americans and subsequently designed the rocket that took men to the moon.

We had an extraordinary impasse in that Hitler, the US and the UK each held the threat of making public the Barbarossa Secret thus ensuring mutual cooperation. It was the Nazi's ace card because, apart from the Operational Orders, nothing was ever signed by anyone on either side nor any minutes taken of meetings between Hess and Churchill. The Operational Orders provided the only evidence which, as Churchill said at the time, if released, would have caused the potential collapse of our government and that of the United States. It would have been enough to tip us into war with Russia, a war we may well have lost. The whole affair was all terribly 'hush-hush'.

I know that the Nazis had one copy of the Orders, the Americans another, and I believe the British copy was passed from Churchill to the King in 1946 in order to remove all evidence from the fluctuations of political control. Lord Louis Mountbatten told me the British copy was put into the Royal Archive, where I believe it remains.

I am sworn to secrecy on this. However, I am now seventy-eight years of age and Eva is my granddaughter and my only surviving relative. Someone needs to know the truth about the lies that regrettably I helped to cover up all those years ago. Please tell Eva that my decisions were not easy and my conscience was tested to the limit, albeit I could just say I was acting under orders. There were no easy choices for any of us, including Churchill, who *agonised over the direction we took. I felt it was right that I leave behind something that tells Eva of her heritage and why I could never have been there for Siegfried, or for her. Siegfried was my only child and it is my greatest regret that I never held him again after those first precious days following his birth when he was taken from me. Part of me died at that time and I was never the same again.*

I hope you will tell Eva her and I am happy to answer anything you or she might wish to know. I am sending you some diaries I kept covering the war years which contain my reflections. Even now, I am worried that it would be dangerous if our family history became public and, for that reason, it may be better if we keep all this secret.

Thank you for being a wonderful wife to Siegfried, as I know you were, from contacts I still keep, and thank you also for all you have done, as a mother, to make Eva's life so secure.
I have so many regrets now and can only wish that Eva is spared all that has shadowed and blighted so many lives. Love always,

Greta
Greta Anne Maude Atkins

She had put her name in full, Hans presumed, to give her a traceable identity. He sat back in his bedroom, letting out a whistle of astonishment. This filled in many gaps, but it was the staggering information it contained relating to the British Royal Family which added an extraordinary element to the unfolding story. As if the confirmation of all his father had written was not enough, to hear the British perspective gave the historical context depth and horrific reality. The irony of his great-grandmother's last words was not lost on him as, clearly, his mother, Eva, had been steeped in secrecy all her adult life for the same reasons Greta had been.

"*Mein Gott*, does this never end?" he said out loud before calling Bernhard on his mobile.

21

The Heir Apparent

Friday 22nd October 1937, 3.30pm
The Berghof, Near Berchtesgaden, Obersalzberg,
Bavaria, Germany

Hitler led the way into his study, ushering the Duke of Windsor through the large doors, followed by the Duke's equerry Dudley Richard Forwood, the Führer's adjutant Fritz Wiedemann and Doctor Paul Schmidt, who was introduced as an official interpreter. Hitler waved towards some timber-framed low easy chairs, as a white-uniformed orderly entered with a tray of tea, biscuits and small cakes, which he placed in front of them. The room was quite long with wood-panelled walls to one side and a number of windows to the other. Ceiling lights were relatively simple square glass fittings. There were classical-style oil paintings in decorated gold gilt frames providing a contrast to the simplicity of the décor. A large desk was at the far end with a standard lamp on each side and inset bookshelves behind. A further desk intersected the room halfway down, on which was a large desk lamp. The Duke positioned himself to one end of a green-coloured sofa, and Hitler sat at the other with a small round table between them. Their three companions settled into matching armchairs set back from the table, giving the Duke and the Führer centre stage.

Hitler turned to his adjutant, saying that the talks needed to be shared with a minimum number, and Wiedermann immediately left the room. Surprisingly, Hitler then picked up the tray of biscuits and cakes, smilingly inviting each to take one. Turning to the Duke, he began, "I would like to speak in German, Your Royal Highness." It was more a statement than a request but made in English, to which the Duke replied in German, "I do speak fluent German, but I may slip into English; however, I feel sure our interpreters can ably assist."

Hitler responded that that they should each speak in their own language to ensure there were no errors in the understanding of their words, which, he indicated, he had asked his interpreter to record. He motioned to Dr Paul Schmidt, who reached for a leather folder, from which he took a pad of paper and a pen. The Duke stated that he would not require his equerry to take minutes but was happy for Dudley Forwood to jot down the odd note, stressing that he spoke fluent German also.

Hitler began, "I have admired your work with ex-servicemen and the unity you have promoted between former enemies. I think we share a belief that there is strength in unity and that worker's welfare is of great importance. We call it '*kraft durch freude*' ['strength through joy'], which is the motto of our national workers' union, the German Labour Front. Your Royal Highness, there is so much that unites us being far more than that which divides us."

The Duke readily agreed, saying he had come to admire the achievements within Germany, which he had to attribute to be the inspiration of Hitler himself. He stated that he felt the affinity between the two nations was natural, if not historically based. "We are, after all, of the same stock; the Germans and the British races are as one and they should always be as one because they are of Hun origin. My firm belief is that we need stronger leadership and, if I may say so, you have demonstrated this admirably."

Hitler smiled, making a denying gesture, but thanked his guest. "Your Royal Highness is most kind, and I concur that our races are united by blood, culture and purity, and that is what I wish to protect. We have become contaminated and we need to foster an improvement in our genetic health through a return to our racial origin. Eugenics is being studied in the United States and many other leading cultures. Here, in Germany, we believe in the concept of *ein volk*.

"I will unite the German races which have been separated, our territories seized and our nation corrupted by those who insidiously poison our race. Strength, Your Royal Highness, which I believe you represent to your own people, is the modern way of leading nations. This new leadership strategy is spreading, as we see in Italy, Spain, Portugal, Japan, South Africa, China and Slovakia, with many other nations admiring our model, such as Bulgaria, Yugoslavia, Hungary, Romania and Greece. We are growing and gaining power but recognise the threat from the communist evil of Bolshevik Russia. Who will stand in Stalin's way? Who will prevent his vile poison from spreading? Who will seize the historic moment that Providence gives us to stand up for humanity?" Hitler's voice had risen and his arms were outstretched in a dramatic gesture, pausing as if in a divine trance.

The Duke responded, "Herr Hitler, there is an undoubted threat from the East and we recognise and understand your concerns about a situation which must be addressed."

Schmidt translated the words for the Führer, who listened and nodded in acknowledgement of the Duke's firm support, but at that point, Dudley Forwood interjected. "Falschübersetzt! ['Mistranslated!']" he blurted, raising his hand, taking both the Duke and Hitler by surprise. "Sir," he turned to the Duke, "the words you used have been changed to say that you believe the threat from Russia and you will support Germany in facing up to this by whatever means."

The Duke was swift to calm the situation. "My dear Dudley, I speak German fluently, and I am content in that I am aware of what is being said to Herr Hitler. I would request, however, that we be allowed to speak frankly to one another, as I am sure Herr Hitler would prefer."

He translated his words back into German and Hitler responded by nodding his head with a sardonic smile and a further nod to Schmidt, who looked uncomfortable.

"Your Royal Highness," Hitler began, and the Duke interrupted, "I am happy to be referred to as 'sir', although my dearest friends call me David."

Hitler smiled. "Then I think protocol should be observed, sir, if I may speak frankly as you request. It is my belief that you are the rightful King of England. You seem to understand the German view of matters and I regret your abdication. There are many in my country and yours who believe that your abdication was unwarranted, wrongfully forced by those whose attitudes belong in the past. I think there is a question of succession here which should be addressed."

Dudley Forwood interrupted, "Sir, I am concerned about your constitutional position here and how this may be reported."

Edward immediately apologised to Hitler for the interruption then turned icily to Dudley Forwood. "I will speak with Herr Hitler in the manner that I feel is correct and I will not be challenged on that, not by you, not now nor afterwards. I trust I make myself clear!" The latter was not a question but an order.

Hitler then stated in an equally terse manner, "This meeting is private and will not be reported on. I will speak as I wish and His Royal Highness may say whatever he wishes to me. I hope there will be no more interruptions." Hitler's tone echoed the Duke's and left the room in no doubt that the two men would speak openly.

Hitler continued, "If anything happened to your brother, you should be in no doubt that Germany would support your right to accede to the throne with your Queen by your side. No-one, in our view, has, or had, the right to make it otherwise. We believe in blood ties and you are the rightful King of your country. Please remember that many of your family live here in Germany, not least the Duke of Saxe-Coburg and Gotha, and Prince Philipp von Hessen, both of whom are here today. Even the former Kaiser, the grandson of Queen Victoria, is resident here and would support you."

At that moment, the doors opened and a white-coated orderly sought permission to serve more tea, summoning another to clear away. A replacement pot of tea appeared and was placed in front of them with fresh cups.

The Duke spoke warmly. "I am grateful for your words and I know many support my right to the throne not only here but more especially at home. I have given my position much thought and I do recognise that I am the rightful King. If anything does happen to my brother, then I shall exercise my Divine Right of accession to the throne. In that, I would be supported, I am already assured, by most of my peers, many of whom sit in the House of Lords and, indeed, by a large number in the House of Commons."

Hitler went further. "If there was an attempt to restore you in a revolution, driven by the people's will, designed to overthrow the government, what would be your position?"

The Duke immediately responded that he would have no hand in such action, nor under any circumstances would he endorse such a move.

This gave Hitler the opening he wished for. "If the people voted for a change in government which endorsed you as the rightful monarch, where would your loyalty lie?"

The Duke thought for a moment, then: "I would never become involved in any kind of action that may be judged as treason, nor could I countenance any action against my brother, but if the people spoke, then that would be a democratic change and one would be forced to consider it."

Hitler clapped his hands together, saying, "Then, sir, you would be in a position, not unlike mine, when the people spoke, desiring a change under my leadership."

The Duke took a sip of his tea, then leant forwards, replacing the cup in a gesture which reflected a decision he then made to speak with frankness about his own passion. "Herr Hitler, I am an admirer of your undoubted achievements, but there is one area of concern relating to social matters upon which I must speak. I have always wanted to foster improvements for the working classes, but my concern lies in the need to support those who may be less fortunate. There are disturbing stories about removal of the under-privileged to centres where their rights and freedoms are compromised. In addition, sir, it has been brought to my attention that those not showing unswerving loyalty to your regime may suffer from loss of property, punishment and even imprisonment. My view is that some dissent is healthy and that to undermine the status of those who disagree weakens the morality and justice of government."

Hitler showed no sign of annoyance, as he had been prepared for such an eventuality through an earlier briefing by von Ribbentrop, who had accompanied the royal visit for a time and held discussions with the Duke over his concerns.

"There are many sacrifices," the Führer countered, "that we must make to re-establish order and take the difficult decisions necessary to rebuild Germany. I have the burden of this great responsibility on my shoulders, and the decisions I take are not made without conscience, but boldness must give the courage to carry the torch which is bringing new hope to the workers and great benefits to families across the Reich. We arrange holidays for workers, improve their conditions, their healthcare, their education and their pay. We have even made available to the masses a people's car, the *Volkswagon*, which I partially designed. I do not know of any country that has made such advances, not even your own."

The Duke replied, "Touché, sir, I cannot deny what you claim but I trust you respect that I must express my views." He bowed slightly, and Hitler extended his hand, which the Duke shook warmly.

The Führer, considering the matter was closed, moved to his desk at the top end of the room, extracting a paper and returning to address the Duke. "I like to keep a close eye on what is happening inside Russia for two good reasons. We have a policy plan called Lebensraum which is the natural settlement of Germans to the east, in many cases taking back territory which was historically ours. It is colonisation to make room for our people, expand our economy and give us more security within Europe, whilst also bringing a cultured civilisation to these areas. Secondly, there is a threat to us and to the civilised world from the vile aggression of Communism. Fortuitously, there are Russians who want no part of Stalin's oppressive and brutal regime, which even includes former Bolsheviks and revolutionaries. They await their liberation from this tyrant and here in Germany may lie their salvation."

Hitler laughed as he announced, "Even their artists admire us. One of those that Stalin thinks he can manipulate is the actress Olga Chekhova, but she is a good friend to Germany and has pledged her loyalty to me.

"This paper contains a secret list prepared by their Jewish Foreign Minister, Litvinov, of countries the Soviet Union intends to occupy if we agree not to take action and reach a peace accord. He has given this to Olga to sound us out and see whether we would allow their aggression. The list includes Poland, Finland, Estonia, Latvia, Lithuania and Romania. This man Stalin, he represents the worst of the abhorrent collection of mongrel scum governing Russia. There are those who would join us in a great crusade to rid the world of this vile threat to peace. Germany will rise and fight this aggression; the great Reich will defend Europe from the toxicity of these filthy Slavs. Forgive my language, Herr Duke, but I am a passionate believer in protecting the world and our cultures against the scourge of Communism." The Führer sat down wiping a shock of his hair back from where it had fallen over his brow during his passionate outburst.

The Duke of Windsor felt his conviction, which touched him and struck a chord within. "My dear Führer, please do not concern yourself about speaking directly, an attribute I admire in our workers, with whom I have enjoyed mixing from the time I met many on the Western Front in the Great War. We shared that dreadful experience, which must never happen again. War between our countries is unthinkable; I will do whatever is in my power to ensure that we remain at peace, and I concur that the Soviet Union is our greatest threat. I think that in many areas, your ideas and those I espouse meet very comfortably, and I cannot deny that your Lebensraum policy seems admirable in its aims to achieve order in Europe."

Hitler rubbed his hands together, feeling that the meeting could not have gone any better, picking up a plate of cakes, which he offered smilingly to those present, insisting they each take one. The Führer then thanked both Schmidt and Dudley Forwood for their attendance, asking them to invite the Duchess to join them.

A moment later, a smiling Duchess entered with Rudolf Hess, General Bohle, Prince Philipp von Hessen and Charles Edward. Conversation was light as Hitler asked the Duchess for her observations about the tour, smiling benignly as she spoke about how well they had been treated. He laughed when she informed him that meeting Göring was like a state visit.

"The old rascal, he loves drama and being the showman. I think he has a uniform for every day of the week." The mood was light as Hitler showed them his private terrace overlooking the mountains before they joined the rest of the party and descended the steps to the waiting cars.

The line of guards along the side of the drive to the Berghof snapped to attention, the officer in front raising his right arm in salute. A beaming Hitler shook hands with each guest in turn and was obviously in very good spirits. He bowed again to the Duke and Duchess, then shook their hands, before placing both of his over theirs.

"Today has been historic, giving our two peoples the foundations on which to build. I am honoured by your visit and in you I have found friends who really matter and understand our position."

The Duke replied, "Herr Hitler, I am delighted we have had this opportunity to meet and I cannot thank you enough for the kindness you have shown to both Her Royal Highness and myself."

The Führer stood to attention, stiffly extending his arm in salute, which the Duke returned as the cameras flashed, setting in motion what was to follow.

22

The Scottish Connection

Wednesday 20th April 1938, 3.00pm
Dungavel Castle, Near Strathaven,
South Lanarkshire, Scotland

Albrecht Haushofer felt torn between his loyalty to his friend whom he respected, his country and his conscience. Four weeks had elapsed since German troops had marched into Austria, in direct contravention of the Versailles Treaty, being welcomed, in the main, by the Austrian populace. In some ways, Albrecht understood the move and supported it, but he could no longer support the regime of Adolf Hitler, which he despised. He had held many meetings with his friend Rudolf Hess, sometimes turning into heated debates about the excesses of the Nazis and the brutal treatment of anyone who dared to oppose them. Hess was adamant that his loyalty was to the Führer, no matter what, whether his policies appeared good or bad. Only Hitler had the vision which could carry the people because he uniquely possessed the strength and great purpose to ensure the ultimate fate of the Reich. It was as though Hess had lost objectivity and that he was seized by a religious-like fervour in his admiration of the Führer.

His unswerving obsessive belief, and that of so many others, Albrecht likened to that of the medieval Catholic dogma, still held, professing the Divine infallibility of the Pope.

He had walked miles that day in the company of the man with whom he had built a close association and friendship over recent years, the Marquess of Douglas and Clydesdale, Douglas DouglasHamilton. He had loved sharing the breath-taking scenery, the bracing air and the openness of the countryside contrasting with the confines of Berlin, which had become somewhat claustrophobic of late. Albrecht was artistic of mind, loving music, poetry, fine literature and classical art. His proximity to the ruthless doctrines being applied by the Nazi Party had a depressing influence on him. Here, in this stunning Scottish location, he felt a sense of liberation and freedom which had disappeared from his life at home.

Dungavel House, his host told him, was a step down from the grandeur the Hamiltons were used to. They had owned the magnificent Hamilton Palace which was, the Duke declared, more grandiose than Buckingham Palace. The approach drive alone had been three miles in length and the palace was sumptuously furnished, but regrettably, the very wealth in the coal mines they owned was the ironic reason for the demise of their home. The palace suffered from extensive mining subsidence and eventually repairs were impossible to sustain, forcing the family to move to Dungavel House, which had previously been a hunting lodge and summer retreat. Nevertheless, they were comfortable enough and Douglas proudly displayed the aircraft runway he had designed behind the house which he used regularly, as a result of his passion for flying and his position within the RAF.

This was supposed to be a holiday for Albrecht, but the reality was that Hess had sensed war with Great Britain may be the inevitable outcome of the current situation. There was a need to persuade those with influence in Britain of the positive aims of Germany and gather support. Hitler wanted to 'liberate' Germans living in parts of Czechoslovakia, which was causing a sticking point with both France and Britain. Hess had told Albrecht that anything he could do during his visit to foster sympathy for Hitler's aims might help avert war. As he walked with the Marquess across the Scottish moorland that day, the two men discussed the deteriorating relationship between Germany and Britain.

Albrecht painted a very dark picture, "Hitler has taken back the Rhineland and effectively invaded Austria last month, although they call it 'Anschluss' ['political union']. Whilst those outside Germany may view these actions as tyrannical conquests, Hitler sees them as liberation. Now he has designs on the Sudetenland, but he will not stop there. I know this because Hess has told me that the Führer's Lebensraum policy requires annexation or conquest of lands to the East. My belief is that Russia will ultimately be his target. My primary concern is that we try to avert a war with Britain in the short term, and, in the longer term, I am building up an alliance with those who oppose Hitler."

Douglas pointed out that there were many in Britain who supported Hitler, including some fellow MPs within his own Conservative Party. "In terms of the upper echelons of society, I am aware that there is admiration for what has been achieved in Germany. The hawks in Parliament, led by Mr Winston Churchill, are warning that war is inevitable and that we must prepare. Churchill has powerful royal allies and we should never underestimate the power the Royal Family still have. My sources say that our new King dithers despite two of his brothers, the former King and Prince George, both wanting to adopt a more pro-German stance to resist the danger from Stalin's Russia. Frankly, it's a bloody mess, old chap, but for my part, I think the lesser of two evils is to try and do business with Herr Hitler, at least for now."

They had reached a small crofter's shelter in which they sat, uncorking a bottle of Chablis and sharing beef and salad sandwiches prepared that morning by the butler at Dungavel House. Albrecht spoke earnestly. "I need to confess something to you, my friend, which is that, although I am genuinely here because of our friendship, I am also acting on the orders of Hess. He has tasked me with finding out whom we may rely on to resist going to war with Germany. My conscience dictates that this is a mission I should fulfil, because I want to avoid war, and that is why I hesitated in telling you. As you are aware, I have already been passing information to British Intelligence through you and via a mutual acquaintance, Greta Atkins. However, I still have loyalty to my country." He lit a cigarette, drawing deeply, embarrassed by his admission.

The Marquess turned to him, smiling. "You are a double agent, old man, I should have you shot, but as you have confessed, I will, on behalf of His Majesty, confer a royal pardon upon you. But listen, we can have some jolly fun here and give our Nazi friends a little misinformation that, perhaps, will assist both of us. In the meantime, have you any last requests, in case I change my mind about the pardon?" They laughed, taking alternate swigs from the wine bottle, sharing ideas and both feeling a tad mischievous as they hatched a plan.

Later that evening, after dinner, they had played a game of snooker during which they finalised those they would target in their plan, which Douglas stated he would have to put to Colonel Menzies at British Intelligence. It was effective in its utter simplicity. They would list those that they knew had overt Nazi sympathies and sow seeds of doubt about their real loyalties in the report, which Albrecht would file upon his return to Hess. After their game, they sat enjoying large brandies discussing their joint wish to avoid war, and began creating a separate list of those they felt they could rely upon to promote a peaceful solution with Germany. By the end of the evening, they had two agreed two lists. The first contained those who would support appeasement and, hence, if necessary, a peace initiative, and the other, with which they had more fun, listed those who Albrecht would report, upon his return to Germany, were questioning their support for Hitler's regime. The lists contained names, some of which they could scarcely believe they were adding, but they knew the enormous gravity of their task.

Friday 22nd April 1938, 2.00pm
HQ SIS, 54 Broadway, Westminster,
London Office of the Deputy Director

"Enter." The voice of Colonel Menzies reacted to the knock on his door.

"Wing Commander Douglas Douglas-Hamilton MP and Herr Albrecht Haushofer, sir," his secretary announced, allowing the two men entrance. Colonel Menzies rose from his desk, walking over to shake their hands given in a brusque military fashion.

"I think you both know Miss Atkins." He gestured to a chair, where Greta was sitting, dressed in a dark blue suit edged with cream silk, almost giving it the appearance of a uniform, together with a beret and net worn angled over her eyes from her auburn hair, which she wore long. The two visitors briefly bowed to her, and she smiled, looking upwards at them, breathing that she was delighted to meet them both again.

"Albrecht, darling, I must educate you further in order to ensure your literary tastes have risen beyond *Mein Kampf* since we last met during the state visit of the former King," Greta said with a smile.

The colonel interrupted, "Please let us not be reminded of that dreadful business, and if you will forgive us, Miss Atkins, we have work to do." Greta feigned a hurt look. The colonel continued, "We need to establish peace options, both acceptable and otherwise, and for that, we must be in control of the strategy. What have you got, Douglas?"

The colonel listened carefully to their plan, interrupting at one point to ask Albrecht how far he was trusted by senior Nazis, the reply to which set aside any doubts or concerns he may have. "I am now working directly for the Deputy Führer in his Berlin office. The extraordinary thing is that although he knows I disagree with what National Socialism has come to represent, he values my friendship, in which I think he sees an honesty he does not find elsewhere. My father is included in briefings which Hitler holds with his inner circle, advising the Reich on, and legitimising, Lebensraum. These people like to justify all they do with a historical, social or geographic perspective to give impetus to their ideology. I can tell you, without doubt, Herr Colonel, they do not want war with Great Britain, which the Führer sees as a natural ally. However, they will not shrink from it, if necessary, as they believe they have almost a Providential Divine Right to execute their plan."

Douglas retrieved the two lists they had prepared and passed them over to the colonel, who scanned the first, which contained the names they had compiled the night before who were purportedly questioning their loyalty to Hitler. He looked up more than once, smiling and thinking for a moment, before continuing to study the list. "Ah, we are to discredit Princess Stephanie von Hohenlohe and her insipid lover Fritz Wiedemann. He is Hitler's adjutant and was utterly odious when he was organising the dreadful visit of the Duke of Windsor to Germany. His dismissal would be a coup indeed. If we nab those two, that may also serve to destabilise Hitler's relationship with that damnable newspaper man Lord Rothermere, who also holds a candle for that wretched Hohenlohe woman. I see you name many society figures; we have that misguided Tory MP Sir Arnold Wilson; Lord Mount Temple, who heads up the absurd Anglo-German Fellowship organisation; former foreign secretary Sir John Simon; plus two influential aristocrats, the Duke of Westminster and the Duke of Buccleuch." The colonel looked up again with a wry smile. "You might end up in the Tower of London for this. You have several German generals too: Runstedt, Kleist and Kluge. Take the list back with my blessing, Mr Haushofer."

He turned to the second list of those who would support a peace accord, raising his eyebrows. "Good Lord, you have headed it with His Royal Highness the Duke of Windsor, you could get hung for less. Ah, hmmm, then we have his brother, Prince George; are you sure, Douglas?" The colonel looked across at Greta, his eyebrows raised.

She was suddenly serious. "Colonel, I have had very little contact with the Duke of Kent who is, as you know, aide de camp to the King. He does his own thing socially and I regret to say there are certain rumours of his proclivity for, shall we say, Bohemian tendencies."

The colonel waved his arms as though not wishing to hear this.

Douglas-Hamilton took up the subject. "Sir, the Prince is well known to me professionally as a fellow RAF officer, and I can say he is a damned good pilot but he is somewhat sympathetic to the Nazis. There is no doubt that he would be drawn to support a treaty with Germany."

The colonel continued perusing the list, remarking that Lord Louis Mountbatten was not shown, for which he was thankful. However, there were many other names that did cause him concern on the list, including the current Prime Minister Neville Chamberlain; the Home Secretary Samuel Hoare; the Foreign Office spokesman RAB Butler; Horace Wilson, Senior Civil Servant and advisor to the Prime Minister; Henry Channon MP, private secretary to RAB Butler; and even Lord Halifax, the Foreign Secretary. There were also several senior army personnel, all of whom were people of considerable influence.

The colonel furrowed his eyebrows. "Whilst we may be forced by circumstance to consider peace negotiations with Germany, and we must prepare for that eventuality, we must not deliver to the Germans anything which suggests we are weakened. You must stress the power of the faction led by Winston Churchill, to add balance, and include Mountbatten as a royal supporter of resistance to German expansion. We really need to be in on any communication between Germany and those whose support they seek, especially if it is covert or unofficial. It seems to me critical that we maintain the ability to stand up to Hitler, if the time comes, and be wary of those who may resist that."

Douglas-Hamilton leant forward. "Sir, my belief is that there are many both here and in Germany who would welcome a peaceful solution, not least the Deputy Führer, which may prevent further military aggression. I think we should convene a meeting between Albrecht here and the Foreign Secretary Lord Halifax, and see if we can knock something together for Albrecht to take home."

The colonel made a call and, after a few perfunctory exchanges, replaced the receiver. "I regret that Lord Halifax is in France, and unless we have him onside, there can be no plan to put to Germany. Let us hope this does not cost us peace."

At that moment, Greta interjected, "I know these people and Germans like clear, precise facts presenting. I recommend we use the connections we have here. I suggest Albrecht approaches Hess and says that, through you, Wing Commander, he has access not only to the establishment but to members of the Royal Family. I will say to Charles Edward that I want to play a part supporting Hitler's aims by influencing decisions through our social contacts. I will stress to dear Charles the high-level connections which Douglas has, whilst you, my dear Albrecht, can send much the same message separately to your superiors. We could then open a link via Douglas here, which gives us a feel of Germany's intentions and a peace route, if necessary."

Albrecht clapped his hands together, smiling warmly at her. "Bravo, Greta, I think this will work, with your approval, of course, Herr Colonel. I know that both Hess and Hitler want to avoid war, but Hitler is also the more aggressive and will not hesitate to attack anyone who stands in his way. Hess will do all he can to avoid this. I also believe that Greta is uniquely well placed as she is known to many people of influence in Germany."

The colonel concluded the meeting by summing up the strategy. "Whilst I'll be damned if we ever considered appeasing this wretched Adolf Hitler, we must be pragmatic and consider all options. We will continue feeding names to you, Mr Haushofer, of those in Germany we, ahem, 'hear' are becoming disloyal or disillusioned with Hitler via Douglas-Hamilton. I will authorise that we open a channel of communication through you, via Douglas, with Hess, but no-one in government here will know, and if this gets out, it will be denied absolutely. What we have agreed here today must not be communicated to or discussed with anyone outside these four walls, and that includes anyone working in government. For the avoidance of doubt, that will also include anyone holding ministerial office, and even the Prime Minister. For once, I might agree with National Socialism that sometimes democracy can be a nuisance, if not a liability."

Greta coughed in a dramatic manner, then said in a girlish voice, "Why, Colonel, I am deeply shocked. When I signed the Official Secrets Act, I thought I was working for His Majesty's Government, and now I am being asked to betray my country out of my unswerving loyalty to you."

In the ensuing laughter, the colonel gave his expected sigh before shaking hands with Albrecht and waving the others from his office.

A week later, invitations were sent out by the Duke of Saxe Coburg and Gotha to an Anglo-German dinner being held at the Savoy Hotel, London, in mid-May. Greta was delighted when the Royal Family accepted, stating that they would be represented by Prince George. The German Ambassador, von Ribbentrop, also confirmed his acceptance, together with Lord Louis Mountbatten, Lady Astor, the US ambassador Joseph Kennedy and the Italian ambassador Dino Grande. Regrettably, Lord Halifax was unable to attend, denying Haushofer of a useful connection in the heart of the British government. However, RA Butler (RAB Butler), the Under-Secretary for Foreign Affairs, was to be sent in his place. A substantial number of MPs and members from the House of Lords agreed to attend from across the political spectrum, whilst the press baron, Lord Rothermere, also accepted. Winston Churchill was a surprise guest, whose invitation was organised via Lord Louis Mountbatten. Churchill had indicated a desire to meet his adversaries. As he eloquently put it: "Better to know your enemy before they take up their weapons, in order that one might learn of their weaknesses, and, thus, be better prepared to disarm or defeat them later."

23

Following Orders

Saturday 22nd February 2020, 12.05am
Strandtreppe, Treppenviertel Blankenese, Hamburg, Germany

"Hello, Bernhard, I have hit gold here." Hans spoke excitedly into his phone. "The letter I told you of covered all the blank spaces and, my friend, it is the original so no accusations of a false story. *Mein Gott*, she was quite a lady, my great-grandmother, with contacts in all the wrong places. You know what? They gave her the codename Marlene, after the vampish singer Marlene Dietrich. She even worked for Winston Churchill!" He told Bernhard the letter revealed that in 1940, a peace offer had been made by Germany which was under serious consideration by the British.

"The letter corroborates the Operational Orders of 1944, and also confirms Churchill's involvement in the Barbarossa Secret from as early as 1941. When this comes out, they will try discrediting us as a hoax like the Hitler Diaries in the 1980s. Trust me, this is far bigger and we have proof it is all genuine."

His friend interrupted with expressions of astonishment as Hans confirmed what he had uncovered, adding, "The real bombshell in all this is that my great-grandmother says King George VI was ready to dismiss Churchill in 1941. As if we have not got enough, Bernhard, this is far bigger than Watergate ever was. It is the story of the century, if not the most incredible ever."

The voice at the other end was equally excited. "Hans, I also have amazing news. I spoke with my old friend General Sir James Cranshaw, and, get this, he related to me that he was speaking to Field Marshal Montgomery in 1958 when 'Monty', as he was known, said he had information that James may be interested in. Apparently, Monty wanted his legacy enhancing but, equally, was concerned it may be tarnished if certain matters were exposed by others. When he had found out that James was writing a history of the war after D Day, his vanity encouraged him to reveal his role in our story. James kept notes of his conversation and was able to accurately relate to me what was said."

Friday 10th January 1958, 12-00 noon
Headquarters of NATO, Rocquencourt,
Near Versailles, France

The answer to the knock on the door was swift and customarily abrupt: "Come!" Lieutenant James Cranshaw of the Grenadier Guards entered to see the field marshal looking down at papers in front of him. He did not look up but waved the young officer to a leather armchair opposite his desk. There was silence for a few minutes as Field Marshal Sir Bernard Law Montgomery finished perusing the document, before attaching his signature with a flurry, then, looking up, he gave a brief smile.

"Sorry to keep you, Lieutenant, but one has to ensure that our American masters do not overstep the mark. I have never been an easy man, most certainly not a pushover, and I do not intend to change now.

Eisenhower is a good man but lacks field command experience, as I told him after D Day when he was making some rather silly choices. I had to point out to him that we were fighting the war before they came along, and many of his American subordinates were under my command at the personal behest of Winston Churchill."

He made a grunting noise, as if ensuring there could be no argument, and James knew his reputation for accepting few alternatives to his own ideas. The field marshal pulled on his beret with the two badges for which he was renowned. The first was the general's insignia and the second, a Royal Tank Regiment badge he was presented with by an admiring soldier when he climbed into a tank to obtain a better view of the front line in the war.

He rose from behind his desk, strode over to James and shook his hand briskly. "Now look here, James, this book you are writing on the war; I want you to be clear on two counts. The first was that I remained loyal to my principles throughout, and the second, that I did not accept orders without debate, unless I agreed with them. Nearly cost me my job, but I stuck to my guns, for which I was knighted and promoted to field marshal by Churchill. You may not quote me on this but whilst admiring the Americans, they needed to listen more and speak less. I think we should adjourn to the officer's mess for lunch. I should bring a notepad if I were you." This was clearly an invitation being given as an order.

They walked to a nearby building, Monty always returning salutes smartly to subordinate officers as they passed. He directed an orderly that they be given privacy and they were shown into an ornate dining room hung with portraits, where Monty sat at the head of one of three tables, gesturing James to take a seat to his left.

"I have thought a great deal about this interview, and I have decided to be frank in the interests of historical accuracy. Further, I wish to ensure that somewhere there is a record of my reluctance to sign an order about which you will say nothing unless my name is, one day, being discredited to protect the reputations of others." The soup arrived, which was an excellent beef consommé. Monty directed that they finish their soup before he continued in earnest.

"In July 1944, we had successfully consolidated our positions with American and Canadian Forces, having landed on the beaches in Normandy, but we had problems with the Germans holding Caen. I devised a perfect battle plan which allowed us to break out from where we were, greatly weakening the German position by stretching their forces on a broader front. The problem, Lieutenant, was Eisenhower, who had little understanding of military tactics on the ground." The field marshal went into great detail about his master battle plan which had resulted in the 'extraordinarily successful outcome in France' on a timescale that had, as he put it, 'greatly shortened the War, but for which I am often not given enough credit'.

After a main course of roast chicken with much more generous side dishes than were customarily served in the officer's mess, Monty completed a long summation of his strategy which, he claimed, had resulted in a victory which rivalled if not exceeded his triumph at El Alamein earlier in the war.

"I was facing defences devised by the same damned enemy commander as at El Alamein, that wily old 'Desert Fox' Field Marshal Rommel. Now, to the pieces of this jigsaw which I will order you to keep secret unless, as I previously inferred, my name is being used to protect others or, indeed, if history is being perverted."

Monty arose from the table and strode to the long eighteenth century window overlooking the grounds. "We are now engaged in a Cold War against Russia which could have been averted but at a price. I am a military officer and it is not my place to question political decisions. However, I do debate them with my masters where necessary. In July 1944, in the middle of my plan to liberate France, I was called to a meeting with Eisenhower at which he informed me that the Germans were willing to surrender. They would cease hostilities, begin withdrawing from France and their forces would be placed secretly under supreme Allied

Command. However, their own command structures were to remain in place. Eisenhower further informed me that Churchill had agreed we would not prevent their forces continuing to attack the Russians to the East. Germany would retain its nation status, with Hitler and his gang remaining in power. I must tell you now that I was opposed to this plan as treachery. However, I accepted the orders I was given, although I stated that if I was asked to commit British forces against the Russians, I would refuse. Eisenhower shook my hand and said that he respected my honour with the words, '*History may judge our actions if this ever surfaces*.'"

Monty paced the room as though wrestling with his conscience as, indeed, he was, and the young officer sensed the burden this icon of military leadership carried. He repeated the words as though reflecting: "History may, indeed, judge us one day, but I am now in the final year of my military service, facing a Russian threat which, had events not taken another course, may have been averted. The day after my meeting with Eisenhower, we met the Germans in Colombelles, Normandy, to sign what were termed Operational Orders. This was not, for both military and political reasons, to be classed as a surrender by the Germans. Eisenhower was driven in a separate car to me, for security reasons, signing the Orders without conversing with any of the Germans before immediately leaving. There was only one staff car on the German side, with no escort, which I thought was frightfully trusting of them.

"There, I met Erwin Rommel and it was a rather strange affair as we were old adversaries from our time in Africa three years before. We shook hands and smiled, recognising the extraordinary irony of the position in which we had been placed. We spoke for a short time, sharing some coffee, reminiscing about the fortunes of war. He seemed a rather pleasant chap and I felt more at ease talking to him than some of my own officers. I would have liked to have known him better as there was an affinity between us. I frankly felt he was rather like me. The Orders were signed by both Rommel and myself, then he shook my hand, stepped back, saluted and left. I kept the signed Orders, but they became irrelevant as matters took another course. However, in May 1945, the day after the German surrender, I was visited in Germany by a rather charming woman working for MI6 who stated that I needed to return immediately to Britain and meet with the Prime Minister at Downing Street. I was told by her that I must take my copy of the Operational Orders and that no-one should be made aware of their existence, nor should I delegate this task to anyone else. Strange business, but she insisted on accompanying me, which I found rather tiresome.

"When I met Churchill, he politely requested that I hand the Orders to him, confirm that there were no copies and then asked me to deny all knowledge of them. I was told that there were only a handful of people remaining alive who knew of them and that he was surrendering the document to the King, after which he would deny its existence. I felt thoroughly uneasy about the whole business, which, for the record, I had never agreed with."

Monty sighed deeply, walked across to the young officer and reminded him that he had signed the Official Secrets Act stating that he hoped this information would never be needed as he feared the consequences. He then retrieved his beret and placed it firmly on his head, before saluting and shaking James by the hand. He never referred to the matter again.

In December 1975, James received a Christmas card from him, inside which was written, "*Delighted to hear you made colonel, and from a regiment I relied on at El Alamein too! Remember that although we obey orders, they are sometimes executed with conscience. BL Montgomery.*"

Field Marshal Montgomery passed away three months later in March 1976. James knew that Monty had not wished his role in the 1944 agreement with the Germans revealing, and had kept the matter secret. However, on hearing some of Bernhard's revelations regarding the Barbarossa Secret, he felt the time was right to disclose what he knew.

Saturday 22nd February 2020, 2.00am
Strandtreppe, Treppenviertel Blankenese, Hamburg, Germany

Despite being very tired, Hans was consumed by all they were unravelling. As any journalist knew, obtaining a story was one thing, but to have witnesses or irrevocable evidence was another. He had been busy scribbling during the long phone call.

"This is incredible, Bernhard; let us consider the key elements supporting our story." He read from his list. "I have summarised the clear evidence we have:

1. An original letter from an MI6 agent stating that Hitler had offered Britain peace terms in May 1940, over which the King and Churchill clashed.
2. Two written sources confirming a potential armistice and nonaggression pact between Germany and Britain in 1941.
3. Records of direct meetings between Rudolf Hess and Churchill.
4. Evidence showing that Britain and the United States would indirectly support an attack on Russia in 1941 and again in 1944.
5. A contemporary witness of a plot to remove Churchill by King George VI.
6. Embarrassing minutes of the meeting between the Duke of Windsor and Adolf Hitler.
7. An original copy of the Operational Orders signed by Adolf Hitler, Eisenhower, Rommel and Montgomery in July 1944.
8. Clear and irrefutable evidence of Allied support for a German offensive against Russia in 1944.
9. Confirmation that a deal was struck between Nazi Germany and the Allies just before the war was ended for the safe passage of Hitler out of Germany in return for access to German scientific research and technology.

10. Complicity between Britain and the USA in covering up the Barbarossa Secret."

These were just the main evidential facts, but they also considered that there were other areas which their investigation was uncovering such as the involvement of British Intelligence in assassinations, including those of Albert Speer and Rudolf Hess. There was the existence of a neo-Nazi organisation run by Göring's grandson which had infiltrated government, security and political institutions. They considered the minutes of the meeting between the Duke of Windsor and Hitler in 1938 which alone, under normal circumstances, would have given them a scoop. They both agreed to sleep on what they had exchanged between them and then decide how best to proceed. Despite his excitement, Hans felt pangs of guilt as he thought about his father losing his life as a result of what they were uncovering, but then, he thought, as his eyes closed, perhaps his father may have been proud of him. Something was missing from the puzzle which was nagging at him, and he was wracking his brain trying to put it all into focus. He was struggling to make sense of the enormity of all they had already discovered and which leads they should follow up in which order. The big question which was also facing them was what they should do with all they had already uncovered.

His sleep was very deep as exhaustion took over, and so he did not initially feel the muzzle of the Mauser pistol being pressed into his temple, although he was alarmingly aware of it as he awoke to a torch being shone in his face.

"You will not shout, you will not make any noise or I will end your life now," the voice hissed. "Get up immediately and move to the lounge."

As he walked from the room, he could feel the gun painfully pressed against his back, pushing him forward. His mother was sitting on a couch with her face in her hands. Behind her stood another man in a black leather jacket with a shaven head, giving him a menacing look and also holding a gun. Eva looked up as he entered. "Oh, Hans, what is happening? They say they are Bundesnachrichtendienst but will not reveal who they are nor what they seek."

The man behind him had a voice which was familiar to Hans as he spoke. "Be silent or your son will be hurt!" He emphasised his point by raising his knee sharply into Hans's back, sending him sprawling to the floor, gasping for breath. Hans looked back over his shoulder, recognising the man as Karl Schmidt from the roadblock in Berchtesgaden two days before, recalling in a flash that this was the man who had shot and killed his father.

"You will surrender the papers given to you by Dr Friedman, please. You will know already that I do not make empty threats, Herr Schirach, which your father failed to appreciate."

Hans felt an almost uncontrollable wave of anger course through his body, but he suppressed the urge in an instinct of selfpreservation. The other man moved towards his mother, who was trembling in fear, his weapon pointed to her head.

"You will tell us now where we can locate these papers and anything else given to you by Friedman. If you do not, she will die now, shortly to be followed by you. For me, it is nothing whether you live or die, as I am merely following orders." His voice was cold, toneless, and Hans recognised in the man's aloofness lay an utterly ruthless streak which made his threat real. He also realised, in a flash, that the men threatening them had not, remarkably, searched his room, as he had hidden his notes and the letter from Greta Atkins behind a wardrobe. Something had told him to conceal the letter, recognising its critical importance in corroborating much that he had already surmised or read in the information left by his father.

"I would give you everything, if I could, and I will tell you where the documents are because they are not here. I have deposited them for safekeeping with the Simon Wiesenthal Centre. They are instructed not to release them, but they have legal power of attorney to take ownership of them if anything happens to me with instructions to release copies to the British, American and German press, together with the Russian TV station RT. You may wish to think carefully, therefore, about pulling the trigger of your gun." Hans was shocked at the calm delivery of his words despite being gripped inside by a feeling of utter terror. He continued, keeping his voice steady, "Are you ready to take responsibility for your actions, Herr Schmidt? You may, perhaps, not realise the implications if these documents are made public. I suggest you contact your superiors, I mean at the top of your organisation, and mention these words, '*eins zu eins*', and wait for the reaction. I would urge you to think very carefully." Hans stood up slowly, looking directly into the eyes of the man facing him.

"I know of these words," Schmidt countered calmly, then, more surprisingly: "Then, perhaps, you may not realise the implication if we accept that these documents may be made public and face the consequences. You see, Herr Schirach, I have no loyalty to the current state of Germany." Schmidt turned sideways and two shots were fired from his gun, taking his accomplice completely by surprise, who fell backwards, his face contorted in pain and shock before he crumpled to the floor.

Eva screamed, then sobbed in shock, looking up, saying, "Why, dear God in heaven, why?"

Schmidt was unmoved as he looked back at Hans. "I work for the BND, but I am an SS Obergruppenführer in the Fourth Reich taking orders directly from Reichsmarschall Göring, our Führer. We have this place bugged and your words sealed the fate of my colleague, who heard too much during your phone call to your friend. If necessary, I will kill you because we are prepared for all eventualities. If the governments fall in Germany or the United States or Britain, it would be inconvenient, difficult even, but not insurmountable. We will be part of the reconstruction as we were back in 1945, when they needed our organisational, financial and administrative expertise, and, just as before, we shall be there. Do you realise that ten years after the war, former Nazi Party members formed the majority of those in positions of power in both East and West Germany? In the Justice Ministry alone, they represented nearly eighty per cent of senior officials.

"Nazis continued to run Germany after the war, but it was just not spoken about, and those at the centre of power wanted to keep it that way. We even named bases after leading military figures under Hitler, such as the two Rommel Barracks at Augustdorf and Dornstadt, the General-Thommsen base in Stadum, the Feldwebel Lilienthal base in Delmenhorst, the Marseille barracks in Appen, and the Adelbert Schulz in Munster. We remain powerful and our influences are everywhere, and, I can tell you, we are growing.

"Herr Schirach, your Jewish friends may not be as much of a threat to us as you think because the Jews are a strange race. They are warm-hearted, good family people, but they cannot resist the lure of a good deal. This is where pragmatism overrules principle. We have been providing Israel with arms for decades, and they had no problems trading with Germans after the war. They knew they were often dealing with former Nazis, but they put business first. Everyone has their price, even Jews."

Hans watched, with derision, as Schmidt began texting on his phone. "We know about your Simon Wiesenthal connection, but we will see whether principle or pragmatism holds sway, shall we? Our people are making contact with the Wiesenthal *schweine* and negotiations will commence. Who is your contact within the organisation?"

Hans hesitated and watched, horrified, as Schmidt turned to point his gun directly at his mother, who buried her head into the cushions of the couch. Without hesitation, he immediately revealed it was Rubin Horowitz. As Schmidt continued texting on his phone, Hans's mind was racing as he tried to absorb what he was hearing and the implications of who Schmidt was working for. He recalled Göring informing him that he was not responsible for his father's death, yet now it all seemed very different.

He decided to play for time and pose the question: "My father, why did he die?"

Schmidt looked unblinkingly at him, his thin mouth betraying no emotion as he responded, "That is simple: he refused to surrender the documents when requested by Göring. Matters came to a head when the issue was raised with the Chancellor of Germany, who demanded we retrieve the documents held by your father using force, if necessary. Göring was equally clear that we should get there first and, therefore, that became my task. Your father was killed by accident, but please be assured that my orders were clear from the Führer; he had become a security risk we could not afford." Schmidt shrugged his shoulders. "He made his choice, so he had to be removed."

He walked towards Hans until he was just a couple of feet away, fixing him with a cold stare. "That is not why I am here. What was it the British said in the war? 'Careless talk costs lives', and you chatter like a canary on your phone. You have a letter from your great-grandmother which you will now hand over, please. You see, today I am in a similar position as I was with your father and so, if you wish to avoid a similar accident, you will cooperate by surrendering the letter."

Hans realised then that if they had bugged his phone, he had little choice but to comply.

Suddenly, there was a huge crash from the entrance hallway, and as Schmidt moved to investigate, gun held close to his chin, the glass on the patio doors smashed. A man in a balaclava appeared dressed in black, holding an automatic weapon at shoulder level, shouting, "Stop where you are or die! Drop your weapon, now! Lie on the floor, *schnell!*" Schmidt let his gun fall, placing his hands behind his head as he dropped to the floor. Another figure appeared in a balaclava from the hallway, walked forward and kicked Schmidt's supine body. He then frisked him roughly, telling him not to move or his life would end.

He took Schmidt's mobile phone and read aloud from the screen. "*BND officer down. Need to clean house. Make contact with Efrayim Fineberg at Wiesenthal Center. Code: Arc of Covenant – suspect docs with Rubin Horowitz. Suggest offering up to two million Euros. Advise elimination of Rubin.*" The dark figure stood up.

"What a pity, you did not click 'send' on this message, or I may soon not have existed."

He slowly reached up, removing his balaclava to reveal a tanned, smiling face, neat moustache and dark curly hair. "Shalom." He bowed briefly. "My name is Rubin Horowitz."

24

Peace at Any Price

Sunday 26th June 1938, 11.00am
Reich Chancellery, Wilhelmstrasse, Berlin

Albrecht Haushofer felt the hands of history weighing heavily on his shoulders. He had spent weeks cultivating contacts in Britain, building up useful allies and providing elements of dis-information to Germany. He had two conflicting motives in his desire to pursue peace: the first, to find those who were broadly supportive of the Nazi regime; the second, to establish which members of British society were supporters of appeasement and who may stand against the hawkish elements, like Churchill advocating war as the only way of stopping Hitler. This eventually led him to compile three lists – supporters, appeasers and opposers – only two of which he shared with Rudolf Hess and German Intelligence. The third list included those in both Britain and Germany who were strongly opposed to Hitler and his regime. By now, Albrecht had been briefed by Hess that, in the unfortunate event that Germany was forced to go to war with Britain, it was critical that they knew those within the British establishment who might be relied upon to collaborate in a strategy for peace. Hess had also stated that all eventualities had to be considered, including invasion of Britain, in which case, it was made clear to him that the Führer would not want to establish an occupying government. Hitler preferred that Britain became an autonomous nation under a regime supporting German objectives.

From his discussions with his old friend Hess, Albrecht was convinced that the Deputy Führer genuinely wished peace unlike others within the inner circle, although Göring also sought to build more ties with Britain, believing that it would create an insuperable alliance. However, the Führer's patience was running thin, wishing to progress his policies of Lebensraum without delay, and had no time for petty bureaucracy. He wanted the Sudetenland Germans liberated from Czechoslovakia and he was adamant that the Danzig Corridor of German lands, controlled by Poland, was integrated to the Reich. His declared mission was to rectify the injustices whereby land had been unfairly seized, as he proclaimed, under the Treaty of Versailles. By the end of May 1938, Hess informed Albrecht that his mission assumed a new urgency as Hitler had already authorised by a secret directive the invasion of Czechoslovakia, to take place by October, despite ongoing diplomacy.

Albrecht spent more time in Britain building connections and was drawn to add Prince George to the first list of Nazi admirers after meeting him at the Anglo-German dinner in May 1938. The younger brother of the King enthused to Albrecht his admiration for Hitler, which was indicative of the strong leadership that was sorely needed in Britain. He took him to one side to share a quiet whisky, where he stated,

"My brother, Bertie, is a fine chap, but he never wanted to be King and, frankly, his heart is not wholly committed to the challenges the job presents. In my view, David should never have abdicated. There are many amongst us that believe in increasing the power of the Royal Prerogative and thereby create a more ordered society, as you have done. There is no doubt that Edward VIII as King was the legitimate line of succession and many in England would welcome his restoration on the throne. As far as standing up to Hitler, as this rather tiresome man Winston Churchill advises, I am utterly opposed to any concept of war with Germany. On the contrary, we should support Germany in establishing a bulwark against the wretched Bolsheviks in Russia." It was, therefore, clear that many who were on Albrecht's first list would also appear on the second.

The third list that Albrecht compiled, he only shared with Douglas Douglas-Hamilton. This contained the names of those he met in both British and German society who were utterly opposed to Hitler's regime. Whilst those names on the British side were of passing interest, they were not altogether surprising to Colonel Menzies in SIS Headquarters and Greta Atkins, with whom he consulted. It was the growing list of German names on the list that demanded more critical attention. As time progressed, the names became increasingly intriguing. The aims of SIS were based on a threefold strategy: the first, to look at the potential for a German coup to remove Hitler; the second, to influence decisions from within; and the third, to obtain useful intelligence. The third list began to grow, containing some of those who were prominent amongst Hitler's inner circle or associated with it. Colonel Menzies and Greta highlighted those that were potentially the most valuable, which included:

- Albert Göring – the younger brother of Hermann
- Admiral Wilhelm Canaris – Head of German Military Intelligence
- General Hans Oster – Deputy Head of Military Intelligence
- Ernst von Weizsäcker – Under-Secretary of State
- General Franz Halder – General of Artillery
- Generaloberst Ludwig Beck – Chief of the General Staff
- Konstantin von Neurath – former Foreign Minister, now Minister without Portfolio
- Carl Friedrich Goerdeler – former Economics Advisor to the government and ex-Mayor of Leipzig

Albrecht was becoming increasingly concerned at the excesses of the Nazi regime and he was hearing of 'camps' in which anyone opposed to Hitler were incarcerated without trial. There were rumours emerging of Nazis committing appalling atrocities, including mass killings. As he mused that June morning, he decided that his conscience should be clear in that he was not betraying his country but defending it from an evil shadow that was enveloping all aspects of life.

Monday 29th June 1938, 11.00am
HQ SIS, 54, Broadway, Westminster,
London Office of the Deputy Director

Colonel Menzies and Greta Atkins pored over the growing list of those opposed to Hitler in his office over tea but regrettably concluded that a coup, for now, was not a likely prospect. There were many on the list, including bankers and diplomats, but despite their influence, there were competing factions with aims varying from a desire to overthrow the regime, to the removal of Hitler or merely whatever was needed to avoid war. The most valuable amongst those on the list, they concluded, were Admiral Canaris and General Oster. Whilst they were not considered good enough yet to develop into double agents, the colonel stated that connections with them should be maintained and encouraged.

"I believe that our surprising ally in proving to this scoundrel Hitler that we mean business and thus, perhaps, avoid war, may lie with the intransigent views of our friend Mr Winston Churchill. He's a good chum of Lord Louis Mountbatten and I'm sure I can rely on you to exert your inimitable influence to organise a meeting. I think we should arrange to pay Churchill an unofficial visit, Miss Atkins?"

Greta pouted at him. "Colonel, I presume that you are exercising the royal use of the term 'we', and, moreover, that you are expecting me to place my reputation at stake, as I so often do for you."

Raising his eyes to the ceiling, his response was short but not without good humour: "Miss Atkins, I'm sure your reputation speaks for itself, good afternoon."

Albrecht had announced to Douglas Douglas-Hamilton the previous November that Hess had confided in him that, in his view, war was inevitable in Europe. Hitler had called a meeting with his top generals outlining that Germany's economic future was only guaranteed by territorial expansion and Lebensraum. This was not a negotiation position but a decision by order of the Führer. Any diplomacy would be window dressing to this decision. Hess had decided that he would do whatever was in his power and influence to promote peace with Britain, hence the role he had required Haushofer to perform. Albrecht subsequently reported to Hess that, despite his attempts to seek out those who would oppose war, it was a challenge to prevent the increasing influence of those like Winston Churchill who would not entertain any appeasement. However, Prime Minister Chamberlain was utterly determined to avoid war and attempt negotiation.

Thus it was that Albrecht wrote to von Ribbentrop on 26th June 1938: *"Britain has still not abandoned her search for chances of a settlement with Germany… A certain measure of pro-German sentiment has not yet disappeared among the British people; the Chamberlain-Halifax government sees its own future strongly tied to the achievement of a true settlement with Rome and Berlin (with a displacement of Soviet influence in Europe.)"*

Having despatched a copy to Douglas-Hamilton, he was informed that a meeting was being set up with Winston Churchill, which he could attend. This resulted in him leaving Berlin for London two days later. Rudolf Hess had given him a full briefing before he left which, he stressed, was not to be communicated to anyone in Germany and which he would deny all knowledge of if asked.

Tuesday 30th June 1938, 2.00pm
11 Morpeth Mansions, London

The chauffeur-driven Rolls-Royce, courtesy of Lord Louis Mountbatten, swept from Trafalgar Square, down Parliament Street, passing the House of Commons with Big Ben, onto Victoria Street approaching Westminster Cathedral. "I am a little nervous meeting this man, Mr. Churchill; he has quite a reputation," Albrecht stated as he looked through the windows at the buildings of the capital he had seen very little of on his previous visit.

"Dear boy," Douglas-Hamilton responded, "this from a man who meets Hitler! It will be a piece of cake."

Greta, who was sitting next to Albrecht in a long fur coat and beret, grasped his hand. "He's usually quite charming," she said, "and a fine wit if he's in a good mood. He likes a cigar and a scotch too if he's relaxed. If he offers you a drink, I think it would be a good sign, so do accept."

Albrecht looked round with a wry smile. "Then he is different to Adolf Hitler, who never drinks alcohol and rarely offers any. The Führer has said he would rather deal with Churchill than Chamberlain, so maybe I have nothing to fear."

The glass panel behind the driver lowered slowly and the chauffeur, in dark blue livery, spoke. "We are approaching your destination now; I will alight first, and once Mr Churchill's man appears, I will return to open the doors." The panel whirred back up, settling with a low thud against the roof. They had discussed their strategy briefly before they had been collected during lunch with Champagne at Claridge's. Lord Louis had arranged the meeting and, therefore, Churchill would have been given a brief, but it was decided that Douglas-Hamilton would make the introductions and set the scene. Greta would then take over to outline intelligence and Albrecht could then state his case for peace. Churchill was a man who commanded considerable respect in Parliament and they all recognised that they needed to impress upon him that there was an alternative strategy to war which was backed by many people of influence within Germany.

They stopped outside a tall, patterned, red-bricked building. A few moments later, the car door was opened smartly and the three of them alighted, being guided towards a man standing in the doorway immaculately dressed in a black jacket, silver tie and waistcoat. "Good afternoon." He smiled briefly. "My name is Inches, and I will escort you to meet with the Right Honourable Mr Winston Churchill." He led them through a large white portico with stone carvings on either side, then, under a suspended Victorian lantern, into a spacious hallway, from which they mounted ornate, circular marble stairs. They climbed three floors, finally reaching a double dark wood door with polished brass handles. The maroon carpet had been thick on the stairs and was no less so as they entered. The hallway had a small table on which was a lamp with a gathered silk shade. There was the smell of cigar smoke in the air, and an elaborate crystal chandelier hanging overhead gave an imposing yet welcome atmosphere. Inches bade them wait for a moment before knocking on a panelled door. They heard the growled, "Come," then, after they had been announced, a commanding, "Please enter, as time and tide wait for no man."

They entered a long room with easy reclining chairs and a sofa, the walls adorned with landscape paintings with a wide bookcase on one side, beyond which was a large Adams-style fireplace in which coal was stacked. There were windows to the other side with long velvet curtains and ornate swags and tails, giving the room an almost stately appearance. By the far window was an easel, in front of which Churchill was poised in an overall with a brush in his right hand and a cigar in his left, staring at a painting.

His gruff voice continued, "Or, indeed, *'For thogh we slepe, or wake, or roam, or ryde, Ay fleeth the tyme; it nyl no man abyde.'* I believe that we can attribute this to Geoffrey Chaucer in *The Prologue to the Clerk's Tale* around 1365, unless you wish to correct me?"

He put his brush down and shrugged out of the paint-stained overall whilst puffing on his cigar. Beneath he was wearing a dark waistcoat, a large watch chain around his middle and his signature spotted bowtie. His trousers were dark with a barely visible pinstripe, and he pulled on a black jacket as he turned, then, removing his cigar, he smiled broadly.

"I am deeply touched that an emissary from Germany should wish to honour me with a visit after my somewhat unrestrained words which some would, perhaps, describe more colourfully." He walked over, bowing to Greta, and shook hands vigorously with Douglas-Hamilton and Albrecht Haushofer. "I believe we met at the Anglo-German dinner, although I think that Dickie Mountbatten had me on a tight leash that night so that you could exercise your Machiavellian skulduggery in weeding out those amongst the guests you could select for your nefarious intentions!"

Their previously planned strategy was somewhat derailed as Churchill motioned them to sit in comfortable chairs positioned near the fireplace. "Dickie Mountbatten tells me that it is imperative I listen, not a trait for which I am renowned, but let me understand the position." He remained standing, relighting his cigar and puffing for a moment before continuing, "I do not underestimate the determination of Hitler, nor do I seek, despite how I may be represented, to go to war. However, we cannot stand idly by whilst unfettered aggression is unleashed, creating a tyranny in Europe, and so, Mr Haushofer, whilst I applaud your desire for peace, I will never join those who will shrink from adversity, sacrificing honour, abandoning allies and, thus, compromise the integrity of mankind." He stopped as though his words were a final summary and conclusion.

Greta decided this was her moment. "Sir, we understand there are great principles at stake here, but we are not here to represent the appeasers but to explore all options. Albrecht Haushofer is known well by me personally, and both Colonel Menzies and myself can vouch for his utter integrity. He is not the mouthpiece of Hitler, nor would he wish to be so; however, he does have a message from Germany which is endorsed by the Deputy Führer, but which is not official policy." Greta knew that by confirming the endorsement of Colonel Menzies, Churchill would immediately recognise Haushofer was working with British Intelligence.

Churchill looked at each of them in turn, as though inspecting minions but without demeaning them, his eyebrows raised. "Miss Atkins, I shall defer to your intervention which, I hear, I would be wise not to ignore, not least from Dickie, who says you have quite a wit. That may allow us, perhaps, to duel on another occasion. The word of Colonel Stewart Menzies puts a different perspective on this discussion and, indeed, Herr Haushofer, I admire your courage in the face of the ruthless repression of Hitler's regime and I will listen." He stood by the fire with his hands behind his back, his cigar in his mouth.

Albrecht began, "Sir, there are many of us in Germany opposed to all that the Nazis represent, but we have to face up to realpolitik. Our beliefs will not triumph right now and we must wait for our moment, which will come. However, we are facing the terrible possibility of war, opposition to which unites many strange bedfellows from both inside and outside Hitler's circle. The one matter on which most agree is that we face a threat to civilisation from the blight of Communism ready to spread from the East. Russia, Mr Churchill, will be our common enemy one day, and if we ignore this, it will be to our cost. Rudolf Hess has been my friend for many years. Does that surprise you? My opposition to the Nazis has not, surprisingly, destroyed our friendship. I have a Jewish grandmother and it was the intervention of Hess that saved me from persecution. He is not a bad man, misguided, perhaps, but he tries to make a difference from within, although he is utterly captivated by the Führer, which, regrettably, is an obsession shared by so many of my countrymen."

Churchill moved to a seat opposite Albrecht, looking at him directly. "I have no quarrel with the German people, and, moreover, my family has many ties with them, not least my sixth cousin, Elizabeth Bowes-

Lyon, who is married into the Saxe Coburgs, and is Queen of England. I agree that the Russian threat of aggression is real and menacing and one which, inevitably, in time, will occupy much of our attention. However, we are faced with the more pressing threat of Nazi-driven ideals to attack, subjugate and conquer, against which we have to stand and, once again, with ancient vigour, rise up and save civilisation. If not challenged, countries will fall one by one to this great, dark menace to civilisation, and then we may face alone this tyranny as an island nation resolute in the protection of our people and our Empire."

This time it was Douglas-Hamilton who spoke. "Sir, I have been to Germany many times and there is no desire for war except by those fanatics who say that any opposition to their great Führer's will must be crushed. If we can reach a common aim as two nations, it seems, from what I have heard from Albrecht, that their ultimate goal is the destruction of the Soviet Union, enabling German colonisation to the East and the removal of the Communist threat. If we appeal to both the avowed wish of Hitler not to go to war with Britain, with a non-aggression pact, in the event he attacks Russia, whilst also securing guarantees from him governing the rest of Europe, we might avert war and deal with the Russian problem."

Churchill held his hands up in a mock surrender. "I think I may be surrounded and require sustenance to defend my position. Shall we partake of some scotch? My dear Lord Marquess of Douglas and Clydesdale, whisky is one of the greatest blessings bestowed upon us by your great country. I have some fine Johnnie Walker Red Label, which I recommend we take with a dash of soda, unless, my dear Greta Atkins, you prefer that we suffer Champagne?"

The moment broke the ice, and there was laughter as Greta said she had few words to counter his renowned skill as a statesman, knowing when to concede. Moments later, Inches entered the room with a tray of glasses already filled with generous measures of scotch.

Albrecht seized the break in tension to put forward Hess's proposal. "The Deputy Führer says Hitler may be persuaded that if we grant them the concession to their demands in Czechoslovakia, he will forgo any further territorial demands in Europe and turn his attention to Russia. If there is no danger of a second front, Hitler and his generals believe they can overrun Russia in less than six months."

Churchill was sitting nursing his glass of scotch, in which he swirled the contents round and round. He took a deep breath and spoke. "I have done what few accept I ever do, which is to consider the views of others which may not necessarily coincide with those of my own counsel. The difficulty we have here and the great unknown is the mind of our enemy. As Napoleon Bonaparte said, *'There are but two powers in the world, the sword and the mind. In the long run the sword is always beaten by the mind.'* The problem we have here is whether we are dealing with the mind of Adolf Hitler, who possesses the mentality of the sword. Whatever we agree now with Germany, you may mark my words will be undone by this tyrant. He is not driven by honour or principle, nor by the finest of values, but by a dark purpose that knows no boundaries nor recognises any bastions. Napoleon also said, *'Those who failed to oppose me, who readily agreed with me, accepted all my views and yielded easily to my opinions, were those who did me the most injury and were my worst enemies, because, by surrendering to me so easily, they encouraged me to go too far... I was then too powerful for any man, except myself, to injure me.'"*

Churchill stood up with his glass held out and turned to them, proposing a toast. "Let us seek peace but not at any price and never yield too easily."

25

L'Chaim – To Life

Saturday 22nd February 2020, 9.00am
Israelitischer Tempel, Pool Strasse, Hamburg

They were in the kitchen of a small apartment in an outer building that Rubin Horowitz had arranged through an acquaintance working there, reasoning that no-one would expect they would stay near Hamburg centre. An hour before, Schmidt had been taken at gunpoint from Eva's house by two men working with Rubin for interrogation. Rubin had then turned to Eva saying that it was important she did not remain at her home and asked if she knew anyone outside the city with whom she could stay for a few days until matters quietened down. Eva called an old friend, who lived half an hour's drive away, Johanna Weber, who readily agreed. Ironically, Johanna had served with her in the NSDAP over thirty years before, but though Eva knew that she still retained rightwing ideals, they rarely discussed politics. Within fifteen minutes, Hans had bid his mother farewell as she was driven in a car Rubin arranged for her to Johanna's farmhouse in Tangstedt, a quiet municipality thirty-five kilometres away.

Hans was bundled into another car with Rubin and a man introduced as Levi. He was told to keep his head down as they sped the twenty-five-minute journey to the Israelitischer Tempel less than a mile from where he lived. On their arrival, Rubin had ordered his accomplice to check the part of the complex where they were to stay. Levi hid his automatic weapon beneath his coat and walked slowly to the building as Rubin covered his progress with a handgun at the ready by his shoulder. Within seconds, Levi had entered and re-emerged, waving them to join him. Rubin had walked behind Hans, telling him not to run, turn round or hesitate and that he would ensure his safety. Once inside the modern outbuilding, Levi led them through a pine-coloured door into a short corridor, opening another door which led into what was described as a student apartment. Rubin informed Hans that he could remain there for the time being until another safe house was found.

Although Hans had already given Rubin some information on the documents he had previously entrusted to him, he now decided to give a complete briefing on the contents. He went on to describe to an increasingly astonished Rubin the events of the previous days from his attendance at his father's funeral, through to meeting Manfred Göring, the revelations obtained by Bernhard and his great-grandmother's disclosures. He spread out on a table his jotted notes of the key features of the story he had discussed with Bernhard, Greta's letter and the information gifted by Göring. Rubin read the letter first, then studied the minutes of the meeting between Hitler and the Duke of Windsor together with the Operation Willi documents, whistling and shaking his head in disbelief as he looked.

"My friend, what you have uncovered is staggering and the value is priceless, not only in financial terms but for humanity. We lost more than six million Jews as a result of what happened in those years, and for what? So much could have been avoided with the right will and a little more integrity, but we were just Jews. I despair at the failure of my own country, Israel, to act after the war and uncover more, but our security as a new nation was the first priority, plus a desire to build economic ties. I regret political expediency overruled justice."

He reached into his bag and pulled out some Schnapps with a wicked grin. "It is morning, but I think a drink and then, perhaps, we must discuss what we can do with all this." They sat round a kitchen table.

"What will happen to Schmidt?" Hans asked as he sat back with his drink, trying to relax his frayed nerves. "You know, that is the man who killed my father."

Rubin leant forward, grasping his hand. "I did not know this; I am very sorry and I could have finished him for you if I'd known."

Hans thought for a moment then gave a dry laugh. "The ultimate irony here is that I am the son of the second Führer and I am rescued by a member of an organisation founded on hunting Nazis. Yes, I wish that man was dead, but you know what, I always argued against the death penalty."

Rubin touched Hans's glass with his. "I had ideals like that once, as a young man, but my country has hardly had any peace during my lifetime. I did my first bout of military service on the Gaza Strip, which kind of wears away ideals. I experienced much I care not to remember for values I was unsure of, but I still have some principles. I work now in any way I can to do what I instinctively know is right, although I regret that I have not turned my sword into a ploughshare."

Hans related to Rubin all that Schmidt had said, including the claim that the Wiesenthal Center had been infiltrated.

Rubin smiled ruefully. "I have worked in the military and in intelligence. I am still affiliated in my work to Mossad and I have contacts all over the world in other intelligence agencies, and you know what, Hans, there are many who would sell their own mothers if the price was right. That is, I'm afraid, the way of the world. Politicians, civil servants, police, intelligence and the military are all corrupted, but it depends to what level and whether the corruption is sanctioned by the state, as we see in Russia. No country is immune from this, not Germany, the United Kingdom or the USA, nor for that matter, even Israel. Schmidt is right in that there will always be those who will sacrifice their morality for a price or for gain. So, it is all a game where we try to infiltrate and gain the upper hand, and all this at a time when Europe is meant to be at peace. I think of a quote from Proverbs in the Bible: '*Whoever trusts in his riches will fall, but the righteous will flourish like a green leaf.*' So, Hans, I am hoping my contribution is for the righteous."

Rubin walked to the window, gazing towards the sky as if in deep reflection. "You know what, my family was German once, but now they are Jews living in Germany because of what happened here under Hitler, but I have made Israel my home. Nearly all my family died in the concentration camps, but my great-grandmother managed to escape to England and spent the war in an internment camp. We must fight for what we believe in or we will, once again, lose our sense of what is righteous."

Hans voiced his concern regarding his mother's situation. Rubin reassured him. "Just like them, we have friends everywhere in our constant battle, including within the local police and the BND. Evidence will be removed from the house and, within days, once we decide what to do, your mother can return. I think it is time we prepared all our evidence. The Nazis will not want this to come out, despite what Schmidt told you, and neither does the state, and so it seems you may still have all the aces here."

Monday 24th February 2020, 9.30am
Office of the Prime Minister, 10 Downing Street, London

"Christ, is this virus going to be some kind of biblical Armageddon plague?" The PM was pacing, which was not a good sign. The papers were already predicting that a lack of action over the coronavirus was going to potentially lead to a pandemic and headlining that time was running out.

"Prime Minister, there is just one more thing." The Cabinet Secretary had just completed his briefing on the first cases infected with the virus to be reported in the UK. He recognised the frustration being exhibited by a man who was impatient to, in his words, 'get it done', referring to his agenda.

"Yes, what is it, Mark?" The Prime Minister ran his hand through his blonde hair, making it even more unkempt than his hallmark look. "I have a Cabinet meeting in an hour and God knows I need to get my head round this."

Sir Mark Sedwill closed his file and reached for his briefcase. "I have just been chatting with 'C' [the director of MI6] about a couple of things and he's asked if he can pop his head round the door. I haven't a clue what he wants and I never ask. Probably something and nothing, but you know what these chaps are like. Mum's the word and all that."

The PM waved his hand in the air, which was a customary affirmative, shook Sir Mark's hand and continued pacing.

Moments later, the director of MI6 knocked and entered. "I won't keep you, sir, but thought you should know. Something is kicking off in Germany rather big style; but the strange thing is, no-one seems to know exactly what, which is highly unusual. The director of the BND has been a frequent visitor to the Chancellor, and there has been talk of lives lost on some highly covert operation. There have been a number of top-level briefings involving the security services, but no-one dares speak of what other than, and this is the strange part, it seems to involve something that happened during the war. The Chancellor has placed it all on the highest level of secrecy and she is directing this personally. Our chaps can't get anyone to talk about it other than to say it may seriously impact both the UK and the US, so it looks interesting. I'm on the case and I'll keep you briefed; tallyho and all that."

The PM thanked him, mumbling, "Yes, yes, please do that. If something has got Merkel's knickers in a twist, it must be big. I may have to mention this to Her Maj during my weekly grilling on Wednesday just in case something comes out."

He agreed with the director that, under the circumstances, it should not be shared at Cabinet or at the forthcoming COBRA (national crisis response body) meeting convened to consider the coronavirus, nor, indeed, with anyone else.

Monday 24th February 2020, 10.00am
The Oval Office, The White House,
Pennsylvania Avenue, Washington, DC

The President was sitting with his son-in-law watching the British Prime Minister giving an afternoon statement on the coronavirus to the House of Commons on Fox News. "I think this China virus is getting blown up into more fake news." The President leaned back, putting his hands behind his head. "Hell, though, maybe these guys in China have cooked this up to get back at me for kicking their asses on trade. Someone had to have the courage, and it was a tremendous thing to do, but we did it and we sure delivered on that… but the press don't see it that way."

Jared Kushner nodded, letting out a sigh, "Those guys never give you a rest, but our 'fake news' message is getting through, oh, yes, sir. We're getting a whole lot of coverage on social media, considerably assisted, Mr President, by your, er, discreet, tweets."

They both laughed as an intercom buzzed and the President's secretary announced, "Mr President, I have the director of the CIA here asking for a brief moment of your time."

Moments later Gina Haspel entered wearing a smart, light grey suit and scarf, carrying a folder under her arm.

"Always good to see you, Gina." The President stood to shake her hand warmly, followed by Jared Kushner. He motioned her sit and she began, "Mr President, I need to bring to your attention a little whispered detail from Europe, but, sir, this may be regarded as highly sensitive." She looked across at Jared, but the President smiled.

"He's OK, Gina, I can personally vouch for him. He's a tremendous asset doing a tremendous job." He laughed and the moment was lightened.

She continued, "Mr President, my British connections are telling me there is some kind of heavy stuff going on in Germany right now which is so secret that, for once, the Brits have yet to crack it, which they normally do, and the Chancellor appears to be exercising personal control over it. People have been killed in security operations and, get this, what we do know is that it involves World War Two and matters of concern to Germany, the UK and the US. Everyone is very tight-lipped and no-one has dared to speak out, yet. We will get there, Mr President, but it will take time, and the Brits have more connections than we do."

President Trump leaned forwards in his maroon chair, placing both hands on the brown leather-topped desk between them. "There is a lot of stuff from that time we kept quiet on, an awful lot of stuff which would be terrible if it were all known. They had to take a lot of tough decisions back then, very tough, so we may need to watch this one. I think we keep it under wraps for now, Gina, and, er, noone outside this room apart from us should be involved, not even the USSS Director [United States Secret Service]. Too sensitive, just a little too sensitive until we know more." The President looked wryly across at the bust of Winston Churchill sitting on a table to his right. "I guess we still need his wisdom, and his great courage."

**Tuesday 25th February 2020, 9.00am
Office of the Bundeskanzlerin (Chancellor),
Bundeskanzleramt, Willi Brandt Strasse, Berlin**

The large, airy, grey-carpeted office seemed to dwarf the three people sat at the elliptical desk of the Chancellor of Germany, watched over by a large portrait of the first post-war Chancellor, Konrad Adenauer. The meeting had been called at short notice with a curt message received at 9.00pm the previous evening. The mood was icy but business-like and the Chancellor was driven by a ruthless need to achieve the fastest resolution to a crisis that was adding to the growing problem posed by the coronavirus. She found out that the journalist behind her new headache had been the very same one responsible for fielding annoyingly incisive questions to her via a colleague at a press conference the week before. She now had a growing file on this Hans Schirach and it was increasingly worrying. He had quite a reputation as an investigative journalist and it was time to bring order back into chaos.

"As I often say, there are few quotations I repeat from my life in East Germany before unification but there was one which was '*Ordnung muss sein*'. If this debacle continues, we will lose control and it will be made public, which must not happen."

The three men opposite looked very uncomfortable, knowing that failure to achieve a resolution could all too easily lose them their jobs and their reputations. They included the President of Bundesamt für Verfassungsschutz, (the Federal Office for the Protection of the Constitution – BFV), the President of Bundesnachrichtendienst (Federal Intelligence Service – BND) and the President of Militärischer Abschirmdienst (the Military Counter Intelligence Service – MAD). The Chancellor made it clear that there must be an end to what had occurred and that it was critical a lid was placed over the incident. "We already have too many involved and fatalities which are down to sloppy planning and controls. Your task, *meine herren*, is to stop all this now so that we can continue as before. If it takes money, this will be found, but with no trace, please. We do not want to see another debacle where state money is tracked to source, as happened when we paid that Iraqi scientist who lied to us about WMD. *Mein Gott*, that made our BND look stupid after Colin Powell used our intelligence to justify invading Iraq.

"In Europe, we have peace and stability, which it is my life mission to promote and sustain. Already, we are losing power and influence because of Britain leaving the EU, and we do not want anything that could further rock the boat. I strongly suggest you three work together to find a solution which will resolve this mess. You are all now in possession of information which, until recently, even I was unaware of. This information will not be shared with anyone. It is, and has been for many years, protected by a convention known as *'eins zu eins'* and needs never to be spoken of again. The future security of Germany and possibly Europe rests in your hands. I hope I can rely on you to tell me that this has been dealt with."

Tuesday 25th February 2020, 11.00am
Israelitischer Tempel, Pool Strasse, Hamburg

They heard the motorcycles which had accompanied the car in which Bernhard Meyer was being driven from the airport. He had been met the night before, told to leave lights on in his home, before being taken to a safe house where he was given false identity documents by Wiesenthal agents. He then travelled from Munich International on the 8.00am flight and was met at Hamburg Airport by another agent who drove him, protected by armed motorcycle outriders, to the temple. He was escorted into the building where Hans greeted him with an embrace. He introduced him to Rubin Horowitz, with whom Hans had spent most of the previous three days, then showed him the 'dossiers' that they had created using a scanner, printer and laptop. There were files set around a long table; on the front of each was the Nazi eagle clutching a swastika in a wreath emblem under which, in German Gothic, was written:

THE BARBAROSSA SECRET

(Generalplan Reich und Unternehmen Willi)
Chef Sache – Streng Geheim – Top Secret
'Eins Zu Eins'

BESTELLUNG VOM FÜHRER

ADOLF HITLER

Bernhard looked incredulously at what appeared in front of him. The others left him for an hour to study what they had already seen. He sifted through the photos of Gunther Roche; his letter to Hans; the signed Orders of 1944; the notice of the Nazi Congress of 1984 held in Argentina; the minutes of the 1938 meeting between Hitler and the Duke of Windsor; documents regarding Operation Willi; and Greta's letter confirming the involvement of Britain in talks with Germany in 1941, 1944 and 1945.

When they returned to the room, Bernhard was clearly both astonished and excited by what he had seen. "*Mein Gott*, this is incredible and represents more together than I have ever seen on any story; but why not electronic file copies instead of all this?"

Rubin tapped the file nearest to him. "This is my doing because I can tell you that physical evidence has far more impact than what appears on a computer screen, plus it is not easily deleted. We learned the value of this in raising press interest in many of the later cases we pursued against Nazi war criminals."

As a newspaper journalist, Bernhard appreciated the point recognising the power of print. "Well, I have something we can add to the dossiers." He looked at them with an element of triumph. Opening his briefcase, he produced a letter. "This was sent to me by General Sir James Cranshaw, and look, maybe he appreciates the power of print too. He has signed and dated his statement before scanning and emailing it." Rubin and Hans studied the document, which was a detailed summary of the meeting Cranshaw had held with General Bernard Law Montgomery on 10th January 1958, complete with notes he had made at the time.

"Two things strike me from reading all this." Bernhard was trying to think objectively, struggling to suppress his journalistic instincts to simply go with what they had. "No matter how good this seems to us as extraordinary evidence of a cover-up at the highest level, we must remember that because it goes to the very pinnacle of power and threatens our trust in democracy, it will be challenged. They will stop at nothing to prevent this getting out, and if any of it does, the establishment will close ranks to discredit the facts. Even the most credible evidence can be dissed and we must remember that there are so many interests that will be threatened by this."

Rubin pointed at the Operational Orders signed by Hitler, Eisenhower, Montgomery and Rommel, which lay on the table. "Surely this is enough to convince anyone, because we have the original."

"We must remember," continued Bernhard with a rueful smile, "that the authorities need to protect themselves. The evidence will be examined by experts, who will then discredit it. They will field the most eminent they have and, I regret to say, anyone may say anything if they feel it is either for the greater good or for a price. The establishment strategy, in such circumstances, is to create an information fog whereby conspiracy theories are encouraged to thrive, including those that support the evidence but sweetened with additional claims that put the truth into the absurd. The general public initially become excited, then disillusioned with what is then seen as a damp squib or a fraud. There are huge interests at stake, with both big business and power threatened. Remember the saying: '*All power corrupts, absolute power corrupts absolutely.*' They will stop at nothing to protect themselves. I learned this to my cost as a young man. I traced Nazi war criminals, finding that they held high positions either here in Germany or in the United States. I had to be stopped and they blocked my work, stifling my attempts to publish. Regrettably, I had to make a living and so I had to report on 'safer' issues to remain in employment. The reality is we all have to live and, therefore, everything has its price.

"There have been cover-ups of the part the Pope played cosying up to the Nazis in the War, the top German politicians and their former connections, the shooting of JFK, spy scandals such as the Russian assassinations abroad, Vietnam, and the Princess Diana affair. Then there were the total lies spread surrounding the Gulf War involving our BND, Prime Minister Blair, the UN and President George W Bush.

"The list goes on covering anything the authorities are concerned about. From UFOs to some in the British Royal Family having pro-German sympathies in the war; and now the nonsense we are being pedalled about this coronavirus. Only the establishment could dream up bullshit like it came from a bat after a mutation in illegal Chinese meat markets. Tell a partial truth admitting illegality, add nonsense re bats, flood the media with more conspiracy theories involving Chinese biological weapons research and it diverts the public's mind away from the truth."

Hans had listened to his friend, recognising the sense of what he was saying, recalling that he too had sacrificed much of the truth in his reporting under the guidance of editors who knew what could happen if they overstepped the mark.

"So, Bernhard, you said there were two things that stood out to you? These dossiers are still dynamite in my view and guarantee a major story irrespective of what the authorities do."

Bernhard stood and walked over to the Aga cooking range, warming himself, holding his hand up in deep thought as he put what was needed in order. "OK, my two issues. We have no real evidence about the royal connection apart from Greta's letter. I think we need more to back up the story, although the minutes of the Duke of Windsor's meeting with Hitler are incredible but a little circumstantial. Secondly, there is mention of a great betrayal, yet we do not know what this was nor who was involved."

"So, Hans," Bernhard looked at his old friend with a mock quizzical expression, "are you part of the cover-up or have you missed an important third element? Your great-grandmother mentions diaries, does she not? We have not seen them."

The response was instant: "*Gott im Himmel*, I am losing the plot here!" Hans exclaimed. "I had totally missed that or not thought on it. We need to contact my mother."

He reached for his phone, but Rubin stopped him. "Not by that route, my friend, unless you wish to place your mother in more danger. They will monitor every call from your phone and Bernhard's, plus you may be traced. I suggest we vacate this place and move to another safe location. We know where your mother is and we can visit her later today." He left the room saying he needed to arrange for some protection.

An hour later, the door opened and a tall man with greying blond hair entered in a rollneck sweater and jeans, followed by Rubin, who introduced him: "This is Major Moshe Feldman who works for the Israeli Secret Service, Mossad. I can vouch for him as a true friend."

The major smiled briefly, shaking each of them by the hand. He then turned to Rubin and spoke briefly and tersely in Hebrew. Rubin then stated, "Moshe is concerned that there are roadblocks being set up around the city. They have put out that it is an Islamic terrorist incident, but I am afraid they are looking for us."

Rubin spoke again in Hebrew to Moshe, explaining to Hans and Bernhard he was seeking safe transport. Moshe left the room, saying he needed to make some calls. Five minutes later he returned with a smile on his face, announcing triumphantly in a deep accent, "We are in business. We have friends here in Hamburg and I have arranged to, er, borrow the consul's car from the United States Consulate. This will fly the US flag and has the benefit of one-way glass, plus," he added ruefully, "the glass is bulletproof. We will not be stopped or it would cause an international incident." He grinned as though mischievously enjoying himself. "*L'chaim.*"

26

"This Could Bring Peace"

Friday 24th May 1940, 10.00am
Office of the Director of SIS, 54 Broadway,
Westminster, London

"Awful business, this." The colonel sighed, shaking his head. "After only two weeks, the German army is advancing rapidly, our army is trapped and it looks like France will inevitably fall. I knew nothing good could come from Nazism and that appeasement was misguided."

Greta, for once, was conservatively dressed in a dark grey threequarter-length dress with black stockings and shoes, over which she wore a trench coat-style mackintosh. Her hat was a stylish and fashionable addition but still a sombre black with feathers adding a hint of class. The news from France was simply awful and she felt quite depressed. She barely noticed the unusually personal way in which the colonel had addressed her on arrival, when, in a tired voice, he had said, "Come in, *my dear*," a term of endearment he had never used before. He now spoke earnestly.

"I'm afraid we also have a pressing problem with the new PM which could not have come at a worse time. Whilst his legendary determination may be laudable, he is on a collision course with the King. Yesterday, we received via our embassy in Spain a personal message from Adolf Hitler to Winston Churchill which was copied to the King. The Germans are declaring a unilateral halt on their advance for seventy-two hours with an offer of peace. Their proposal is to cease military operations in France and withdraw all their forces, making no further territorial claims, with the exception of Alsace and Lorraine. Further, they will also withdraw from Belgium, Holland, Denmark and Norway if we accept peace with Germany and enter into a non-aggression pact in the event of there being any hostilities with Russia or other Eastern European nations. They have also offered a form of independence to Poland as a German protectorate."

Greta was utterly shocked. "My goodness, sir, this could mean the war is over, and so quickly too."

The colonel leant forward. "I regret, Miss Atkins, it is not that simple. Churchill says the price is too high and we cannot do business with a 'gangster', as he calls Hitler. The King, on the other hand, is adamant that we should accept peace in the interest of saving lives. Yesterday, Churchill effectively walked out of a meeting with His Majesty at Buckingham Palace when he was informed that he might be dismissed from his post if he did not comply with the King's wishes.

"Miss Atkins, we could have a constitutional crisis on our hands because if the King acts, this could trigger a catastrophic series of events with many influential people in society remaining loyal to the Crown whilst Parliament could take a very different view. There has been nothing like this for three hundred years since Charles I and Cromwell."

Greta felt a sense of bewilderment. "Which side are we on, sir?"

"We are patriots of this country, Miss Atkins, and my job is to ensure that we control the demands of the PM whilst steering a careful constitutional course with the King."

At that moment, the phone rang on the colonel's desk. "Ah, just in time, do tell my guest to join us, please."

Seconds later, the door swung open and Lord Louis Mountbatten entered in naval uniform. The men exchanged salutes and shook hands, then Lord Louis turned, smiling at Greta and kissing her hand. "Ravishing as always, Greta, absolutely delighted you could join us." Greta felt a touch of amusement at his customary way of taking over any situation. After all, he had joined them. The colonel sat down and Lord Louis took a seat by the side of Greta, balancing his cap on his knee.

"Miss Atkins," the colonel looked at her, his eyebrows furrowed, "we need a mole at the centre of power. That is where you come in. I need to know what is happening at the heart of government and, coincidentally, the new Prime Minister has requested an intelligence officer as a liaison to work closely with him. We want to put your name forward. You have met Churchill previously and he spoke highly of you after that business when Haushofer was still attempting peace negotiations. Dickie here has Churchill's ear and he endorses your appointment."

"Naturally, Colonel, I am flattered and I am more than happy to accept your proposition, if you will forgive my choice of words."

The colonel ignored the humour in her riposte. "Well, that is all arranged then, I had already told the Prime Minister that you would accept. Please report to 10 Downing Street tomorrow morning at 10.00am. You might enter via No 12 actually, as we don't want to draw attention to your presence."

Greta could not resist. "Why, Colonel, how utterly forward and presumptuous of you. I am deeply shocked."

Once again, the colonel failed to react, looking at her earnestly. "Miss Atkins, Dickie and I have a plan which is damned simple and could save a hell of a lot of lives. Your job is to report the PM's actions directly to me as this unfolds. Hitler has given us a window of three days to consider his offer. We have tens of thousands of men retreating in France and they have been ordered to make for the port of Dunkirk. We will put every ship we can lay our hands on to sea and save as many lives as possible. If we succeed, Churchill can go back to the King, with Dickie, and persuade him that we have achieved our objective and that we can defend Britain and the Empire."

"I know Bertie well," Lord Louis interjected. "He will see reason but will have no brook with Winston's perceived impertinence. If we succeed at Dunkirk, then we can avert a rift between King and Parliament which would rip this country apart, allowing Hitler in through the back door. I think Hitler's peace plan may ultimately be worth consideration, but not, I think, at the price of a split between Crown and state, and certainly not right now."

Greta responded, "Forgive me, Dickie, but why not peace with Germany now? Surely ending the war is preferable."

"I'm afraid, my dear Greta, that this chap Hitler is no respecter of agreements or treaties, as has already been proved when he invaded Poland in direct contravention of the Munich Agreement he signed in 1938 with poor Neville Chamberlain. Hitler knows of the divisions in our society, which were there, as you were aware, in the 1930s. This is a German strategy to exploit those divisions, leaving us weakened and divided. We need to build unity here against the menace of the German threat, which will derail his plan. Hitler's intention is to grow his Reich and achieve territorial domination. If we accept terms now, we would merely be delaying an inevitable attack in the future wherein he may be in an even stronger position. We are still mustering forces from across the British Empire in order that we can stand up to this threat against not only our country but the civilised world. If we delay negotiations now, we can build up our own strength in order that Hitler does not dictate the terms of peace."

The colonel took up the theme. "We will buy time over the next three days as Churchill considers Hitler's peace offer. As we do so, we will assemble an armada of ships to rescue our troops from Dunkirk. Everything depends on a successful outcome because we can be sure that if France falls, we will be next. We also have very disturbing news from Washington that the Germans are persuading the Americans to stay out of the war in exchange for a commitment by Germany to topple the Communists in Russia. We also have the American ambassador here, Joe Kennedy, telling the President that he thinks we will be overrun. President Roosevelt may be swayed not to commit America by the argument that if he does nothing, the Russian threat will be removed. Believe it or not, the idea was floated to the President by your old friend the Duke of Saxe-Coburg and Gotha on a visit to Washington in March. To add to our royal complications, the Duke of Windsor is still in France and heaven knows what our former King's thoughts are."

Greta raised her eyes in exasperation. "I am utterly disappointed in Charles Edwards's supplicant obsession with Hitler, but I confess that I am equally frustrated by the fact we are at war and that America is even considering approaches from Germany, quite apart from failing to come to our aid at our time of need. I broke off contact with the Duke, sir, after war was declared."

The colonel looked at Lord Louis. "The PM says the Duke of Windsor is welcome to return home, but there seems to be an issue with the King on that too. However, we cannot have him cosying up to the Germans."

"Sometimes, its dashed awkward being part of the Royal Family." Lord Louis drummed his fingers on the desk. "I know David very well, and he can be damned stubborn if he feels he is being disrespected. I believe the return of the former monarch may help rally morale here a little, especially if the Duke and the King appear side by side. The trouble is that Bertie's wife, our dear Queen, has said she will not countenance any contact between the King and his brother, and most definitely not if Wallis is involved. I regret to say that in many ways the Queen seems to rule the roost. I think, perhaps, the solution lies in removing David from Europe altogether. Perhaps, we could find him some kind of useful job abroad out of harm's way. I'll call Winston and suggest it."

The colonel coughed, clearing his throat as he nodded. "Turning to the subject of the PM, Miss Atkins, you will report to me and only me.

Your loyalty must be absolute even beyond that which you give to the PM. Is that clear? You will meet with me here every week on a Wednesday morning. You will be my eyes and ears on everything, including that which is top secret."

For once, Greta was business-like. "Sir, how shall I communicate with you if I have something urgent to report that can't wait?"

He looked up, gathering his papers, nodding appreciatively. "I thought you might ask. I have made it clear to Churchill that you must have freedom to travel between our respective offices whenever I may require you. For security reasons, you should only call me from the Chancellor's offices in No 11. The administration is spread through a number of connecting offices and, therefore, any time you spend there should not attract attention." Then in a rare attempt at humour, he added, "One last thing, please try not to use your weapon defending yourself from the PM's interest. I would hate having to explain to His Majesty why you had despatched the Prime Minister."

"My dear colonel, I must protect my innocence," she replied, lightening the mood, drawing the expected sigh from her boss.

The meeting was over and they all shook hands. As Greta left, she had reserved a last comment: "Congratulations on your promotion to Head of Department, sir. From now on I shall call you 'C'. How simply delicious."

He could not resist a smile as the door closed.

Tuesday 25th June 1940, 2.00pm
El Bohio Restaurant, Illescas, Spain

Five days had passed since the Duke and Duchess of Windsor had arrived in Spain, and already their presence was stimulating more attention from England than Edward had experienced in the previous eighteen months. He reflected how tiresome it was that, since his abdication, he had been afforded meagre respect from his country; respect that, as former King, he felt he rightfully deserved. Even his old friend Churchill seemed to have vanished until now. Then, two days before, Sir Samuel Hoare, another friend and the British ambassador to Spain, passed him a message from Churchill instructing him to return to England. He felt somewhat affronted, and this was made worse when he learned arrangements had been made for him to leave from Lisbon, in Portugal, on 24th June without any discussion. The Duke was a little more persuaded by Dickie Mountbatten, who had written informing him that he was sorely missed and that his presence would make an enormous difference to the people, who loved him. However, he was not being afforded the status or deference he felt was appropriate, even being asked to live away from London. The Duke of Westminster had offered him a house 'up north somewhere' at Saighton Grange in Cheshire. Edward was feeling utterly undervalued and needed assurances that, at very least, Wallis would be given some regard if they considered any possible return. Further, he expected that they would be regularly received at the Palace, but Sir Samuel Hoare had informed him that this may not be possible.

"Well, dash it all," he had exclaimed to Wallis. "Apart from the dreadful way they treat me, if I go back and Britain loses this damn war, what then?"

They had decided not to leave and now sat and chatted, sharing a jug of Sangria on the bar terrace of a delightful restaurant overlooking the countryside beyond. The Duke and Duchess of Windsor were guests of Don Javier 'Tiger' Bermejillo, an acquaintance and diplomat whom they had known from his time with the Spanish Embassy in London. He had been carefully instructed by the Spanish leader, General Franco, that he should explore how the Duke and Duchess felt about their country and the situation unfolding in Europe. This information had been requested by both Admiral Canaris and von Ribbentrop in Berlin.

That morning, the Duke had given a press conference pledging that he believed Britain would prevail in the war, despite his misgivings, but now as they sat drinking in the warm afternoon, he spoke his thoughts openly to his friend, Don Javier. "You know, old chap, that this beastly war could probably be resolved by Germany more quickly if one executed an effective bombing campaign; this could bring peace. Dreadful thought, I know, but the prize would avert the loss of life that might then be avoided. My brother is just not strong enough and, frankly, I am beginning to believe that it would be better if he abdicated. If I had remained King this damned war could have been avoided and jolly well would have been. I would have stood up to Mr Churchill, avoiding the carnage and terrible loss of life we are suffering."

That night, Don Javier reported the Duke's comments directly to his opposite number in the German Embassy, and by 9.00am, the following morning, the Führer had been informed. The German ambassador was instructed to use all possible means of persuading the Duke of Windsor to remain in Spain. At 4.00pm, the same day, an aircraft from Berlin bound for Madrid had been boarded by an elite SS commander, Walter Friedrich Schellenberg, with a team of five men on a mission Hitler termed '*Unternehmen Willi*'.

27

Unternehmen Willi

Friday 28th June 1940, 9.30pm
'The Rectors Club' Jazz Lounge, The Hotel Palace,
Madrid, Spain

The jazz band was in full swing playing a new Duke Ellington release, 'Cotton Tail', as the Duke of Windsor in a dinner jacket sat with his feet tapping beside the Duchess, dressed in a silver evening gown, with their guests, Alexander Weddell, the American ambassador; his wife, Virginia; Colonel Juan Beigbeder y Atienza, the Spanish Foreign Minister; and his English socialite companion, Rosalinda Powell Fox. Champagne was flowing and the Duke was regaling his companions with the story of his escape from France the week before.

"Your damned people nearly caused my capture by the Germans, by refusing to let me cross into Spain," he exclaimed in good-natured banter with Beigbeder. "Doubtless your revenge for the defeat of the Armada." There was laughter as the Duke, in a fine mood, lit a cigarette, passing it to Wallis, who inserted it in a cigarette holder, before lighting his own. "There we were, fleeing the Nazis, and these blighters would not let us into Spain. I said to them, '*I am the former King of England, I demand entry to Spain*,' but this consul chappie said he could not move without orders. It took a telegram to the British ambassador to Spain and another to my friend the Spanish consul in Bordeaux to sort it out. The next thing the wretched man knew, he had an order from General Franco himself to let us pass. Suddenly, he was all smiles, bowing furiously and apologising, even offering us drinks. Poor fellow got the fright of his life."

The jazz band moved to a slower number, 'All Too Soon', and as the words were sung, the Duke turned to Wallis. "A sad song which makes me think of home, and if it wasn't for that damned silly brother of mine, we could have remained, although I'm afraid England may now lose this war if we do not sue for peace."

At that moment, the hotel manager appeared. "Your Royal Highnesses, Your Excellencies, ladies, forgive me, but His Excellency the German Ambassador, Baron Eberhard von Stohrer, requests the pleasure of your company with your guests in the Palace Lounge for vintage Champagne."

The Duke of Windsor raised his glass, smiling. "Well, speak of the devil, we are invited to carouse with the Hun, and why not?" He raised his eyebrow to his table, seeking their approval, before rising.

They walked from the room, Edward acknowledging the bows of guests they passed with a brief wave, to the lift which took them to the Palace Lounge. They entered the room, which was an opulent area with an extraordinary glass dome over the centre, surrounded by pillars, and from which hung a huge chandelier which would have been the envy of any palace. The manager led the way to a cordoned-off table, where a smiling man in his fifties rose to greet them dressed in a white militarystyle double-breasted jacket and tie over black trousers. Wallis noted that he looked quite attractive with his finely trimmed moustache and movie-star, swept-back hairstyle. He was sitting with two other men, one of whom Edward recognised, who was reintroduced as Albrecht Haushofer, attached to the office of the Deputy Führer, and Ramón Serrano Súñer, the Spanish Interior Minister, who was also General Franco's brother-in-law. They all bowed to Edward and Wallis before shaking hands. The party were immediately offered seats, with the Duke being guided to the head of the table, and then vintage Champagne was poured by attentive waiters.

The ambassador raised his glass. "Your Royal Highnesses, you do us a great honour, and I would like to propose a toast to peace between our countries."

Edward immediately rose to his feet and glasses were clinked together. As they sat, Edward remarked, "Mr Ambassador, I trust you will not now attempt to restrain or kidnap me, as we are, after all, at war?"

The ambassador laughed and tensions eased as he immediately responded, "My country does not desire war with Britain and, sir, I must remind you that we did not declare it. We simply wished to reverse the injustice of the Treaty of Versailles and liberate our people. We seek peace and Mr Haushofer here can speak for the Reich, as he has just arrived with a message from the Deputy Führer. We can talk privately, Your Royal Highness, if you would prefer." Edward declined, stating that he wished any discussions were openly shared amongst friends.

Albrecht then spoke after briefly reminiscing over the visit of the Duke and Duchess to Germany in September 1938, when they had previously met on a number of occasions. "Your Royal Highness, we do seek peace and merely wish to share informally our thoughts. If we are forced to continue this war and we prevail, it is our belief that Britain should govern herself and that any discord might be reversed with the restoration of the rightful monarchy. However, the war could be stopped. We believe that Britain should be our natural ally as a bastion against Communist Russia and know that many in your country and in the United States share our views. Why should we continue in a war over disputed territory when there are greater issues at stake? Sir, it is our belief that if you spoke out at the right moment, that could be the catalyst for change in Britain. Put simply, Your Royal Highness, you could be pivotal in an historic moment to change history." He then raised his glass as he had been instructed by von Ribbentrop in a briefing before he left Germany that morning. "I propose a toast to the rightful King of England, Edward VIII and his Queen." Albrecht raised his glass and the other guests followed suit.

The Duke felt profoundly ill at ease but was inwardly warmed by the display of loyalty and friendship. He had not believed that war with Germany was either right or justified, but he could not be seen to be betraying his country nor could he consider displaying disloyalty to his brother. Wallis whispered in his ear, "David, at least say that you are moved."

He did so, expressing his gratitude, but also indicated that, as his country was at war, it would not be correct for him to say more, concluding with, "I neither supported nor wished for this war, and I will do all I can to seek a peace which is justified." There was applause around the table; then, in an effort to deflect from the issue and lighten the tone, the Duke added, "However, I am mightily concerned about my homes in Paris and my villa at the Cap D'Antibes on the Cote D'Azur. I mean, it would be simply dreadful if we are unable to maintain certain standards of propriety enabling one to have a house in both Paris and the Med. Perhaps Germany might assist in maintaining my standards." More laughter followed and the evening passed with shared conviviality.

After the German ambassador departed, Juan Beigbeder took the Duke to one side. "Please, Your Royal Highness, I can offer you a wonderful place to stay here in Spain where you will be afforded all respect. I can arrange for a palace to be made available to you in beautiful Andalusia." The Duke responded he had much to think upon before making a decision.

12.00 midnight
Portman Square, London

Greta was ready for bed, having stayed up to listen to the Home Service on the radio, relaxing to swing music and imagining better times. The phone rang, and it was the Foreign Office, giving her a predetermined code, to which she replied with a recognised word. The voice at the other end simply said, "Rosa says Ted is being compromised or seduced by Charlie – urgent withdrawal essential." Ted was the code for Edward and Charlie was a term for the Nazis after the comic actor Charlie Chaplin, who sported a Hitler-like moustache.

Greta frowned and dialled; the phone was picked up in seconds. "Menzies."

Saturday 29th June 1940, 9.30am
The Ritz Hotel, Madrid

The following morning, there was a call on the Duke of Windsor's room phone informing him of a telegram. He agreed to take delivery, pulled on a dressing gown and walked to the door of their suite, seeing a paper had been pushed under the door. He picked it up and saw the eagle and swastika symbol on the wax seal of the fold. He ripped it open and there was a typed two-line message. *"Your Royal Highness, the Führer himself has ordered that your properties in Paris and on the Cote D'Azur are to be guarded twenty-four hours per day. Compliments, Baron Eberhard von Stohrer, Reich Ambassador to Spain."* His signature was on the note. At that moment, there was a knock on the door, and he took and opened the telegram.

Telegram from: the Prime Minister to the Duke of Windsor
Your Royal Highness – Stop – Please leave Spain immediately – Stop – Report to the British Embassy Lisbon – Stop – Do not delay – Stop – Winston

The Duke made a phone call to the British Embassy, demanding to speak with Sir Samuel Hoare, the ambassador. "Sam, I will not beat about the bush, but you will inform Winston that I am capable of making my own decisions and, furthermore, I am not about to surrender to his petty whims. I will return to my country when my country learns to deal appropriately with the former Sovereign. I require assurances in that regard. In other words, Winston can go to blazes." In any event, he thought after the call, it was impossible to leave as he had a dinner and reception to be held that night for five hundred guests at the British Embassy at which he was to be the guest of honour.

The irony of being both lauded by the guests at the British Embassy and yet be at loggerheads with the Prime Minister came to a head twenty-four hours later. The Duke was not pleased to be disturbed after an exhausting night of dancing coupled with fine Champagne. However, on answering his phone, he was, once again, informed that there was message from the British Embassy which needed immediately conveying to him personally. Moments later, there was a knock on his door, and as the Duke opened it, he was surprised to see it was Sir Samuel Hoare himself standing in the hotel corridor. "Why, Sam, what on earth is going on? I thought you would be far too hungover after last night to be out of bed."

The ambassador did not smile and looked grave. "Your Royal Highness, I regret I must deliver this message personally, sir." He looked entirely uncomfortable. "I am instructed to give you a direct order from the Prime Minister to return to England at once, and that this is not a matter for debate." The Duke felt utterly affronted, barely concealing his anger as he spluttered he would consider whether he would be making appropriate arrangements. Re-entering his suite, he did not restrain himself with Wallis. "Who the hell does this man Churchill think he is? He swears loyalty to me then abuses it. Supports my right to retain the crown, then insults both my position and my integrity. I ask that you be treated properly if I consider returning, and my request is ignored. Maybe I should pack my bags and go to Germany."

2.00pm
The Reich Ambassador's Office, the German Embassy, Madrid

"I will not be party to some gangster-like plot to kidnap someone I have invited as a guest for dinner, who not only enjoys immunity because of the status of this embassy, but because of who he is and, *verdammt alles*, out of decency." Baron Eberhard von Stohrer was not in a good frame of mind.

The SS officer spoke in a precise tone. "Then I suggest you persuade your guest to accept your proposal and remain here in Spain for a while. We will even pay for his accommodation at our expense, which is, I think, a generous gesture. We would prefer he is a willing guest, but if not, it is of no concern to me. Ultimately, Herr Baron, although I would not wish to be harsh, you will obey my orders as I am instructed directly by the Führer. You will cooperate, please."

This was not a request but a threat. The tall man in the menacing black dress uniform, with the Iron Cross at his neck, loved the fear he engendered in others. He placed his hands on the ambassador's desk, fixing him with an icy stare. "To spare your bourgeoise embarrassment, we will take him after he leaves the reception. It is merely a military matter of planning to me." SS Brigadeführer Schellenberg did not ever consider failure, nor would he accept that anyone could challenge the wishes of the Führer. He walked brusquely to the door, turned, clicked his heels, extending his arm – *"Heil Hitler"* – then marched out triumphantly.

"*Leiber Gott*, the arrogance of these men!" The ambassador sighed, reaching for his pen.

Later that day an embassy courier arrived at the Ritz with a personal handwritten invitation for the Duke and Duchess of Windsor from the German ambassador to an intimate private reception in their honour to be held on Wednesday 3rd July 1940 at the house of the Spanish Interior Minister. The note explained the venue had been chosen to avoid embarrassing publicity. The invitation slightly improved Edward's demeanour, and he went to his desk and wrote: "*Dear Prime Minister (Winston), I am considering my options, but my final terms for returning must be clear. I require that due respect is given to both Wallis and I by my brother, the King. I further require a minimum fifteen-minute audience with both the King and Queen for the Duchess and myself. I have decided that to avoid further embarrassment to the British Government, I shall leave for Portugal imminently, where I await your considered reply. Edward.*"

At 4.00pm, the phone rang in Edward's suite, and his equerry informed him that a friend of the Spanish Interior Minister, Rosalinda Powell Fox, was in reception. Moments later, the Duke opened the door to his suite. She was as beautiful as she was imposing with long wavy blonde hair, a petite pretty face that was vivacious and pouting lips that made her look ravishing. The Duke was to later say, "Her voice was enchanting, but her looks simply took one's breath away." On this day, she appeared flushed and, despite the softness of her face, she displayed a seriousness that commanded attention.

"Your Royal Highness, I must abide here only briefly and, if asked, please confirm that the Duchess invited me in for afternoon tea. Sir, I regret to say that there is a plot which may put both your life and that of the Duchess in danger. You must leave Spain immediately, but you cannot explain why or my life will be threatened. There are SS special forces here, and on Wednesday, when you attend the private dinner with the German ambassador and the Interior Minister, they plan to take you. You must request extra guards from the British ambassador when you leave, but just tell him it is because of rumours. Whatever they may say of me in time, remember, I loved my country."

The Duke was lost for words and, as she said she could not stay long, he kissed her hand and promised that, when the time was right, he would put in a good word. She looked at him, her large eyes meeting his. "Sir, these are terrible times; you must not trust anyone, but if you need to believe me, ask Lord Louis Mountbatten, because he is the only one in your family who knows about me."

Despite himself, the Duke embraced her, sensing her sincerity, and as she left, he said simply, "I shall never forget you."

28

Revelations

Tuesday 25th February 2020, 4.00pm
Tangstedt, Scheleswig Holstein, Germany

The large black Mercedes with the stars and stripes flags on the front wings had been driven past a number of police checks and waved through as they left Hamburg behind. They had packed all the papers they had been working on to take with them and move to a new secure location. Moshe was driving with Rubin next to him in the front seat, an automatic weapon by his legs plus a handgun he had donned in a shoulder holster before they left, making Hans feel both reassured and nervous. Within thirty minutes they had left the B432 main road and were slowly travelling west of Tangstedt down Dorfstrasse towards the house where Eva had sought safety. As they turned into a track, they approached what appeared to be a converted old farmhouse.

Moshe slowed the car to a stop twenty metres before the end of the drive and Rubin climbed out, walking slowly towards the heavy slatted wooden entrance door whilst Moshe took out a handgun, which he held close to the window. Rubin reached the entrance and used the knocker. Within seconds, the door was opened and a woman spoke with him, and he waved the others to join him. Moshe turned the Mercedes round and reversed into one side of the courtyard space in front of the building. They left the car, walking through the cold, crisp, late afternoon wind to the welcome warmth of the house. The woman, introducing herself as Johanna, led the way into a comfortable room in which logs were burning in an open fireplace. Hans walked over to Eva, who rose out of a large armchair, and embraced her.

"Mother, everything is good and we are piecing together an incredible story, but I need to find my great-grandmother's diaries you told me of. She mentions them in her letter. They may hold the key to so much."

Eva looked at him, cupping her hands around his face. "You know, I escaped this world thirty-five years ago and I am frightened to go back. Perhaps we should leave this."

"Mother, I need this because my father left me his testament and died for it. I must know why all this has happened and what has been going on. It is time to uncover the truth. Please help me; for the sake of my father, for Gunther, for you."

Eva sat back in the armchair, looking into the distance. "There have been so many bad things happen to Germany and too many secrets, some of which I was involved in back in the 1980s. Hans, I helped some escape justice because of what I believed, arranging passports, false papers and bribing officials, but I kind of hoped it was all over. When you were born, I wanted to find a new life." Hans sat by her whilst Johanna left the room to make coffee.

Eva looked up at Bernhard, Moshe and Rubin. "I'm sorry, but it is difficult to bring all of this back. Yes, Hans, I have the diaries, but they are in safe storage. Mutter first showed them to me when I was a student, but they didn't really interest me then. After she passed away, I found them and then it really hit me just how incredible they were. When I read various sections and saw some of the documents, I knew they were dangerous, so I kept them in the roof for a while then decided I needed to keep them more secure. I nearly destroyed them, but I could not bring myself to do it, realising that would not have been right because they are historically significant. I tried to get my head around it all and understand the motives of those involved. My grandmother and my grandfather may have been on separate sides, but they both had values, however misguided some may have been."

Eva then told them she had placed a box containing the diaries and documents in a safe storage facility called 'Storebox' based four kilometres from Hamburg centre. When Hans stated it was too late in the day to retrieve the box, Eva told them she had twenty-four-hour access via a code on her mobile app. There was a sigh of relief in the room as Hans obtained the access credentials from his mother and then looked up. "As you said earlier, Moshe, I think we are in business."

At that moment, Johanna entered with coffees and suggested that as they had not eaten, they should wait and have a meal. Although he had an overriding sense of anticipation with his body full of adrenalin, Hans agreed there was no pressing need to leave immediately. Johanna returned minutes later with beers and a bottle of wine. The TV was switched on and they watched the unfolding story of the spread of coronavirus dominating the news. Somehow, the story that Hans had been covering a week ago about the virus seemed pointless in the light of what they had unearthed. The reports were concentrated on a debate by the World Health Organization as to whether the outbreak might be termed a pandemic. Limited lockdown restrictions on movement were being introduced in Italy and containment policies put in place elsewhere. A welcome dinner was served of *Pichelsteiner Eintopf* (Bavarian stew) and they entered into discussion on the best way of dealing with the story they already had.

"For me it is not the financial value of all this," Rubin said, "but that people understand what was going on and how so much has been covered up. I am happy to help protect the information and act as your life insurance. I owe it to my race and what happened to us. It is time for the truth to be told."

Hans recognised his professional instinct to follow the story but also felt an emotional attachment. "This involves my father without whose bequest to me, none of this would have occurred. Maybe I should be grateful or maybe I should wish it had never happened, but he was murdered before I could meet him. It also involves my great-grandfather and I have a need to understand what drove him to be a leading Nazi. Then there is the extraordinary work of my great-grandmother as an agent of British Intelligence. I feel personally conflicted in a way, as they are family yet this is a story which must be told for other reasons."

Bernhard sat back, his hands in an open gesture. "My career was compromised because I told the truth and, you know what, that makes me even more determined that we get this story out. Remember Woodward and Bernstein, whose lives were in danger because of Watergate, yet when the story broke, it protected them."

Headlamps on the darkened hill in the distance behind the farmhouse momentarily flashed through the windows, prompting Rubin to indicate that it was time they left. As he was reaching for his weapon, he was utterly taken by surprise. "No-one move, please, I mean it." Johanna's voice cut in sharply; they turned to see her standing in the doorway of the dining room, holding a gun in both hands pointed at them. "I am truly sorry, Eva, but I have remained loyal to the Party and its ideals. I run the political Kommissariat and report directly to the Reichsmarschall. You will please all remain seated until we are joined by some of my colleagues, and be in no doubt, I have had military training and know how to use this."

"You have shocked me, Johanna, I thought I could trust you as a friend. Why are you doing this?" Eva said weakly.

"What I do I do for Germany," Johanna responded. "Look at what is happening in the world. We need order now more than ever in a new and powerful Germany with stronger, more principled leadership. Our government is weak, pandering to liberal forces, diluting our nation with uncontrolled immigration contaminating our cities. There is anarchy on the streets with rising crime and disorder. After fifteen years under one chancellor, there is stagnation and corruption at the top. You believed in us once when we worked together for a cause we shared. Our influence has helped ensure that we dominate the EU and expand through our economic strength. We are friends now with Israel and they are great intelligence partners. The days of anti-Semitism are over and what you are doing will stoke it all up again; for what reason? What purpose will all this serve other than to rekindle memories that are best forgotten? I am still your friend and have no quarrel with any of you. If you want to tell or sell a story about the British Royal Family, you will make a lot of money, but leave what has happened in Germany alone. We need to move on."

"I regret Johanna is correct and that we are with her." Moshe now stood up, reaching inside his jacket, producing his own handgun. "I am afraid that realpolitik has taken over the world. As you know, Mossad works for the state of Israel, and our business ties with our friends in Germany are just too important to be placed at risk. For that reason, it has been decided we cannot permit this story of the war and what happened afterwards to be published. We always consider, and cover, all options because it is good for business and, therefore, we are forced to deal with the devil, although, perhaps, Manfred Göring may not welcome that description. After the war we built up a huge business relationship with Germany, which is now our largest trading partner in Europe and second only to the USA in the world. Sadly, it is money and business that decide policy, not ethics or history. I believe it was Goethe who said in his great wok about Faust who sold his soul to the Devil: *'By Fortune's adverse buffets overborne... Myself at last did to the Devil give!'* I am sorry, my friends, but I need to obey orders and, therefore, we can collate your story and release elements of it relating to the British Royal Family only, from which you will still obtain benefit." He turned to Johanna. "What is the plan?"

She pulled a chair out and sat, keeping her gun trained on Eva, Rubin, Hans and Bernhard. "I spoke with the Reichsmarschall and he is sending two cars over. We are to retrieve all the documents, including, most importantly, any copies of what he calls the Operational Orders. Then you will go with Eva to the storage centre, obtain the diaries and any other documents, taking them to his offices. Once we have everything, we can release these people, but Rubin is to be held hostage until Schmidt is released by the Wiesenthal organisation, together with the original documents deposited with them by Herr Schirach. All documents and any copies are to be destroyed, which will be overseen by the Reichsmarschall himself, together with the director of the BND. I am told that the former US President, the former British Prime Minister and the British monarch will then be informed. No-one will be permitted to read the contents of any documents. Nobody needs to be hurt if the Reichsmarschall's orders are obeyed."

Moshe moved slowly over to the fireplace, warming his back, rocking on his heels. "You know the strange thing about literature," he began, as he walked back round the table. "There is often more in the meaning than in the first interpretation of the words as it is often in life. So, the great English playwright Christopher Marlowe carried on the tradition of Faust and gave his Dr Faustus these words after he realises the terrible price he must pay for selling his soul: *'For the vain pleasure of four and twenty years, hath Faustus lost eternal joy and felicity.'* Now, I don't know about you," he said, almost quizzically, as he paced around the table to stand at Johanna's side, "but I rather like the thought of eternal joy, so today I will not be selling my soul and for that reason," he paused and turned, placing the barrel of his gun against Johanna's temple, "you will place your weapon on the floor, then move to the couch." His voice hardened. "Now, Frau Weber. *Schnell!*" Johanna was startled, her look betraying her shock as she slowly lowered her arm, placing the gun by her feet.

"Apologies for the interval, *meine herren*, but normal service now resumes." Moshe grinned. "A regrettable delay, but I needed to find out what was being planned, and as I suspected, they want to close the door on history, but in Israel, there are forces that will never let that happen. I never trust anyone; I never obey orders from superiors except for the director and, you know what, I can always cover whatever I do with an inventive story. That is why I am a good Mossad man, huh?"

He shrugged as Rubin let out a deep sigh, picking up Johanna's gun and reaching for his automatic weapon, which was propped against the wall. "Moshe, you are *momzer* ['devious']." Eva was asked by Moshe to gather anything she had brought with her, which Rubin loaded into the Mercedes, running back as he saw the headlamps of approaching vehicles.

Moshe was looking out and now took command of the situation. "OK, here is what we will do: I shall shoot out their tyres, then the outside lights. Rubin, you will run to the car and drive like the wind to Hamburg. They do not know where you will be going until I am taken and our nightingale here sings, so you have no time. Take whatever Eva has deposited there and go to one of your safe houses." He turned to Johanna. "If you move off that chair, I will shoot you without question or conscience." She looked ashen-faced as she lowered her head.

"What about you?" Eva asked.

"Oh, I shall be fine because they dare not harm me as an officer of the Israeli government, plus they want Schmidt. Shalom." He grinned again like a mischievous schoolboy and went to the window, where he crouched with his weapon at the ready as the cars approached on the track leading to the house.

"Come, come." Rubin's voice was agitated. "Follow me now, and when I say go, run like hell to the car. Hans, protect your mother."

Rubin switched the light off in the room and then in the hall standing close to the entrance door, which he opened slightly. Suddenly all hell broke loose with deafening gunfire, exploding the headlamps of the approaching cars, and then the glass shattered on the outside lights, plunging the scene into darkness. Repeating shots continued and sparks flew off the front of the vehicles outside. More gunfire erupted, and there were shouted commands as Rubin led them around the side of the house to where the Mercedes was parked. The front of the car faced the way out; a tactic which Moshe had earlier insisted he always employed as a safety measure for a fast getaway. There was more thunderous firing from the house which was returned with flashes from men lying on the floor by the cars, and the smell of smoke hung in the air as they piled into the Mercedes, Rubin telling them to crouch to the floor. The engine roared into life, the wheels span and then there were sounds of rounds hitting the body with loud bangs as the powerful consular vehicle shot forward, lurching sideways onto the drive, a wing catching the open door of one of the parked cars, which was wrenched backwards and left hanging at a crazy angle as they sped past.

Gunfire continued from behind them, and there were deafening metallic crashes with the Mercedes being hit again and again as Rubin drove from side to side on the narrow lane. Then they swerved into the intersecting road and suddenly there was quiet apart from their gasping breaths as they raced down the highway.

"There will be a heavy tip added to your taxi fare," Rubin called out cheerfully as he told them to climb back into their seats. They were still all trying to catch their breath with a mixture of fear and panic as Rubin explained that, despite being bulletproof, some shots might still have penetrated.

"Well, thank you for that reassurance," Hans remarked sardonically.

Rubin added, "The car is a bit of a mess so I'm going into Hamburg by a back route to hopefully avoid roadblocks." He asked Eva if she knew exactly where the box of diaries was located, which she confirmed, as she had seen it only recently when depositing some old furnishings there.

Rubin began speaking into his mobile phone, and after a brief conversation in Hebrew, he announced they would be changing cars on the outskirts of Hamburg, stating he had arranged their stay in another location just outside the city. After twenty minutes, Rubin turned off and weaved through a number of small, winding side roads, before driving onto a business park, then swept into a large industrial unit with the entrance shutters open. There were three men there who gestured to a black Lexus SUV with dark windows. Rubin leapt from the vehicle as one of the men held the doors open for Hans, Eva and Bernhard who grabbed their bags and files from the boot of the Mercedes. One of the men, who was obviously known to Rubin, shook his hand. "*Sohn einer hündin* ['son of a bitch'], Rubin, what have you done to the American consul's car? We have to return this!"

Rubin gave orders quickly to him. "David, you drive the Mercedes to the Storebox on Herderstrasse, arriving there in twenty minutes, no sooner. Then enter with the app credentials Frau Schirach will give you now." Eva texted them to David as Rubin continued, "Look as though you are carrying something out from the storage unit to the car, and then speed away as I think you will be followed. Lead them outside the city before losing them or dealing with them."

"I think we can handle them," David responded, smiling, as he opened his jacket, revealing a handgun in a holster and pointing to two menacing-looking automatic weapons leant against the wall which his colleague went to pick up.

Rubin continued, "We shall enter the unit five minutes after you leave. *Viel glück* ['good luck']."

The tyres shrieked as the two men left in the Mercedes with bare metal dent marks pocked in the paintwork all across the body and cracks in the rear window. Rubin followed minutes later at a sedate pace, which calmed them all a little. "They will be expecting us, but not in this vehicle," he murmured.

"The things I do to get you a scoop, eh!" His remark broke the tension and they all laughed. Minutes later, they parked about one hundred metres short of the Storebox and watched as the Mercedes approached the entrance and stopped just outside. David left the vehicle and entered the facility. They noticed lights being switched on in two cars parked not far away. "No-one has followed him to the entrance, which is good," Rubin remarked. A few moments later David emerged carrying a box, placing it in the boot. He then looked around as if checking he was not being watched, then climbed back in the vehicle and drove away. Within a second, both cars, which had previously put their lights on, followed.

Five minutes later, they drove slowly to the entrance and, after Hans had taken careful note from his mother of exactly where to look, he entered the building. They waited for what seemed like ages before they saw him emerging with a box carried in both arms. He climbed into the SUV, placing the box between Eva and himself. She nodded as he looked at her for reassurance that he had correctly identified it. Then he took a key from his pocket, running it along the brown packing tape, securing the lid, as Rubin drove the car a few blocks, turning off into a side street and stopping to watch. Hans switched the interior light on and opened the flaps of the box gingerly, peering inside, where he saw a number of A4 diaries neatly piled with a box file to one side, which he opened. There was a note on the top written on a sheet of paper which he recognised as the handwriting of his great-grandmother. Underneath were photographs of documents with a number of letters. Then his eyes were drawn to a memo to a Colonel Menzies of British Intelligence from Greta Atkins which made him gasp. "Oh, *mein Gott*, it is the proof we needed."

He passed it to the others and there were further gasps of astonishment as they read the contents:

TOP SECRET – TO BE READ
BY NAMED RECIPIENT ONLY
MEMO

To:	*Colonel Stewart Menzies – OIC and Chief of SIS*
From:	*Greta Atkins – Intelligence Attaché to the Prime Minister*
Date:	*Thursday 8th May 1941*

I am informed that, weather permitting, Deputy Führer Hess will attempt flight to Dungavel Castle either tomorrow 9th May or Saturday 10th May 1941, weather permitting. We will know by twelve noon on the day it is to happen. Trusted officers in air defence may now be briefed.

In the event of capture, the cover story will be that visit unauthorised by Hitler. German invasion of Russia planned for 22nd June 1941. Urgent that peace talks take place. Albrecht does not believe that Hitler will delay much beyond that date in order to avoid a winter campaign.

"There is another letter here from Winston Churchill threatening the Duke of Windsor with arrest and court martial if he doesn't leave Portugal!" Hans exclaimed. At that point Rubin interrupted, telling them they needed get to the safe house as it may not take long before it was discovered the wrong car had been followed from the storage unit. Within fifteen minutes, they had arrived at a secluded house set back from the road on Pinneberger Strasse, around ten kilometres north of the city. Rubin told them it was owned by their organisation and was normally rented out. "We will arrange for you to return home tomorrow, Frau Schirach. You will be guarded for the moment, but our people have influence, which will ensure your safety. In any event, I do not think you have any information of value to them now."

Not long after arriving, there was a knock on the door and take-away food was delivered by one of Rubin's men together with some Mosel wine. He also dropped off a laptop and printer/ scanner. Eva made coffee for Bernhard and herself whilst Hans and Rubin opted for the wine. They all agreed that they would examine the contents of the box in detail the following day, but in the interim, they laid out the files of documents, as they had prepared previously, before leaving the Israelitischer Tempel. Hans could not resist reopening the box they had recovered, taking out the note on top of the diaries his great-grandmother had left forty-six years before, which he read to them:

Dearest Hanna,

I hope you find these records of some interest, or that my granddaughter will, or even future generations. I began taking photographs of important documents in 1940 because I was worried about what was happening. There was so much deception and counter-deception, but though I wanted peace, I found some of the terms suggested intolerable and that they were even considered was utterly disgusting to me. I also realised that so much was being, or would be, covered up or hidden using the Official Secrets Act to shield the world from the truth.

I hated the part I played in all this, especially in 1944 when there was a real chance of peace, saving thousands of lives, but I could not bear the terms and I assisted in sabotaging the plan, after which Churchill was insistent on complete victory over Germany. I suppose the photos were a way of easing my conscience so that someone would one day find out. I have witnessed some awful things and the thought that those in authority could act with impunity appalled me. I lost an entire generation of my family, including my father and brother in the First World War, and what I have done is for them and in their memory.

Please do not think badly of me,
God bless you always,

Greta x

29

Divided Loyalties

Monday 1st July 1940, 11.00am
The Berghof, Obersalzberg, Berchtesgaden,
Bavaria, Germany

Von Ribbentrop was enjoying his moment as he stood in front of the enormous window of the great room, framed by the Unterberger mountains behind him, relishing the attention and glowing with self-satisfaction. Göring found him utterly loathsome, sharing his distaste for this 'sycophantic' man with many there that day. The inner circle of power grouped in the room listening included Hermann Göring, Rudolf Hess, Martin Bormann, Heinrich Himmler, Joseph Goebbels, Admiral Canaris and Albert Speer. Adolf Hitler was standing behind a large table facing them, on which was spread a map of Europe. Standing at either end of the table were Field Marshal Walther von Brauchitsch (Commanderin-Chief of the German Army) and Generaloberst Franz Halder (German High Command Chief of General Staff), whilst General Erich Marcks (the field general tasked with drafting military plans) stood next to Hitler. Ribbentrop was in full flow after a tiresome introduction.

"After discussing our Lebensraum policy with the Führer, I recognised that Russia would stand in our way and so I began preparations. First, I needed to nullify the threat from the Russians, so I entered into talks using the division of Poland as a bait last year. In September, I succeeded, despite critics saying it was impossible, in securing the Molotov–Ribbentrop pact which is, gentlemen, a non-aggression pact between our two countries. This gave us the opportunity, under the Führer's inspirational leadership, to invade Poland, Norway, Denmark, Belgium, Luxembourg and the Netherlands, and now we have conquered France, expanding the Reich to the West, knowing we were secure in the East. I then decided that we needed to obtain a moral blessing for our great purpose, so I sought talks with the Pope in Rome. In March this year, His Holiness Pope Pius XII approved the plan I submitted for peace, acknowledging our rights to central European territory and our great crusade to liberate Russia from Communism."

"Then, we have God on our side, so we have nothing to fear," quipped Göring, drawing some laughter and a look of disdain from Himmler.

Ribbentrop ignored the interruption. "In Britain, I have been fostering covert peace talks with many, but we are hampered by the war-mongering Winston Churchill. However, we have, perhaps, an interesting ally in the former King, who has displayed sympathy with our position, and he is still enormously influential. Herr Admiral, you may wish to say something?" He turned to Admiral Canaris.

The admiral stiffened to attention, always formal, then saluted Hitler. "*Mein Führer*, by your leave."

Hitler was in an ebullient mood. "We are blessed at this historic time by the hand of Providence, once again, and you all may be relieved by the fact I am not doing all the talking today!" There was greeted by much more laughter, this time including Reichsführer Himmler.

The admiral continued, "*Meine Herren*, the Duke and Duchess of Windsor are currently residing in Madrid. We have made a number of social contacts with them. This week, they were sharing Champagne with our ambassador." There were expressions of surprise as he spoke. "We have despatched a team to persuade the former King to openly support a peace initiative with Britain by issuing a public statement sweetening this with an offer of fifty million Swiss Francs. If he does so, it may prompt those who have influence to force Churchill to negotiate. The Duke has made it clear that, in his opinion, we should commence bombing England because, and I use his words, '*That will bring peace.*'"

This time the murmurs of surprise were more vocal. "I think I can assist there, and my Luftwaffe squadrons are ready," Göring confirmed, looking towards Hitler.

The Führer spoke again. "We offered Britain peace, but Churchill stood in our way. Destiny will judge his error harshly, which will exact a terrible cost."

He waved Canaris to continue. "If we are unsuccessful in persuading the Duke – or, perhaps, even if we are not – we may take him into protective custody to prevent him leaving Spain. Our greatest hostage could assist in bringing peace which, I believe, *mein Führer*, will strengthen your great purpose." The admiral stood back, bowing.

"We are not primitive barbarians." Hitler now took command of the room. "I do not want any harm to come to the Duke and Duchess, and they are to be afforded the best treatment with deference and respect. Is that clear?" He pointed his finger, stretching his arm. It was not a question but a command, and both von Ribbentrop and Admiral Canaris clicked their heels, raising their arms in the Nazi salute. Hitler continued, "I am announcing Operation Otto. I have already tasked our generals to prepare outline plans for this. I now want detailed plans drawn up for the invasion and conquest of Russia, which will commence in 1941 after we have either subdued Britain or made peace. The Duke of Windsor may be the key to peace, which will also free us from the threat of involvement by America. We can then direct all resources to a Russian campaign. Perhaps we should consider the removal of King George VI in order that there can be a restoration of the rightful monarchy. This will secure an unshakeable alliance with the British, who should be our natural allies against the vermin in the East.

"Reichsmarschall Göring, prepare your Luftwaffe for operations against British military targets initially. We shall move on to bomb cities, if necessary, and I want attacks on Buckingham Palace when the sovereign is in residence. If the King is removed, we shall cower the British will to fight. I recall my conversation with the Duke of Windsor during his visit when he said that if anything happened to his brother, then he should assume the throne."

Hermann Göring stepped forward. "*Jawohl, mein Führer*, the Luftwaffe will subdue Britain into seeking peace within four weeks." With that, he snapped to attention and gave a salute.

Hitler moved to the map, sweeping his arm across Russia and the East. "Our mission is now to cleanse the world of the Jewish evil that has infected not only Western Europe but allowed Communism to thrive amongst the Slavic scum that contaminate the East. The time we have waited for is upon us and destiny awaits. The purity of our Aryan race will thrive and prosper. We shall conquer and destroy all opposition to our great purpose, to which we will commit millions of our infantry and Panzers in a momentous Blitzkreig."

As so often, his voice had risen, filling the room, following which there was silence as he looked upwards. Then, quietly, he turned to General Erich Marcks. "Now, tell us your initial thoughts and I shall arrange for tea to be served."

Monday 1st July 1940, 4.30pm
10 Downing Street, London

Greta picked up the phone in her office. Colonel Menzie's voice was unmistakeable. "Miss Atkins, Ted must depart and cannot wait. The admiral says Gerald is willing to take him now and keep him here with his child asleep. Tell PM." She knew what his coded message meant, being used to his cryptic style, although she took a moment to understand that sleeping child referred to kidnap. Moments later, she was knocking on the Prime Minister's door. Winston Churchill was sitting behind his desk, in a dark double-breasted suit and bowtie, black half-moon glasses perched on the end of his nose, over which his lively, searching eyes now peered at her, eyebrows raised.

"Greta, my dear, what is it?"

She cleared her throat. "Sir, the Germans are planning on kidnapping the Duke of Windsor imminently."

The Prime Minister removed his glasses. "How good is your source?"

She looked directly at him. "Sir, it comes from the Head of German Intelligence, via Colonel Menzies."

The Prime Minister snatched up his phone. "Gerald, message the British Embassy in Madrid, right now. I want a major guard detail on the Duke with the highest security level. I will inform him of the reason and telegraph him. Do it immediately." He put the receiver down and lit a cigar, puffing out a large cloud of smoke, before picking up a crystal glass and taking a couple of sips of whisky. "We must get him out of Spain. Mobilise any of his friends we can trust and find him secure accommodation in Lisbon." Within five minutes, Churchill had penned his message to the Duke of Windsor:

"Your Royal Highness, I must respectfully demand you leave Spain forthwith with the Duchess. You may understand, although it pains me, that this is an official

order which, if not obeyed, will result in your detention and court martial. Please proceed to Portugal with all haste and cancel further engagements.

With all due respect, Winston."

Wednesday 3rd July 1940, 10.00am
The Ritz Hotel, Madrid

Six cars pulled up outside the front of the hotel, and moments later, the Duke and Duchess of Windsor emerged, surrounded by a number of armed British Embassy staff. Luggage was to follow, and the cars had left within six minutes of arriving. Such was the speed and secrecy of their parting that even the press were unaware and did not find out for over two hours. As he left the hotel, the Duke handed a note to Sir Samuel Hoare, the British ambassador, who had come to ensure the operation went smoothly. The message was forwarded to the Prime Minister within the hour:

"Dear Winston, I have accepted your orders without question, but might I suggest that a position be found abroad wherein I may play a useful role for the country I love and to which I shall wholeheartedly dedicate myself serving faithfully with tireless commitment. This would prevent the embarrassment of our return either to myself or to the nation without compromising your authority as Prime Minister.
Yours, Edward."

A letter was hand-delivered to the German Embassy late that Wednesday afternoon apologising that, because the Duke and Duchess had been unavoidably detained, they would be unable to attend the reception. Upon reading this, the Reich ambassador smiled to himself before writing a cable to von Ribbentrop.

On that evening there was a message from the Foreign Office for Greta. "Rosa says Ted has left for his gal."

Tuesday 17th September 1940, 1.00pm
The Savoy Grill, The Savoy Hotel, London

Looking as dashing as ever in his naval uniform, Lord Louis Mountbatten rose to meet Greta as she entered the hotel, folding the newspaper he had been reading. "Hello, my dear, you are looking as utterly ravishing as ever. Frightfully nice to meet you again, but in such beastly times, I'm afraid." He kissed her hand gallantly, motioning her towards the grill room. The head waiter fussed over them, taking their order for a drink, before motioning them to a quiet alcove around which was a red rope hung loosely from posts, giving them more privacy. Champagne was served almost immediately and Lord Louis proposed a toast. "Here's to better times and a world free from Hitler." They touched their glasses together. They both ordered a smoked salmon starter, laughing over the carefree days they had enjoyed in the thirties, which seemed a lifetime away.

"I suppose you've heard we got David and Wallis safely settled in the Bahamas," Lord Louis started. "It was not without drama. Churchill threatened him with a court martial if he did not agree to return to the UK at one point. Poor old David is pretty damned bored out there as governor, but he needed a job to make him feel useful. The Germans tried to kidnap him again in Portugal after we rescued him from Spain, but we kept him well guarded. However, he still thinks we can make peace with these blighters and that is why I needed to see you. This is all very hush-hush, you understand, but I know you are well versed in such things." He paused as the waiter recharged their glasses.

"I cannot countenance doing business with Hitler, but I am afraid not all in my family are convinced. Dear Bertie has been traumatised by the civilian losses we have sustained in London from the German bombing these last weeks. What started in July as bombing of ports and airfields was bad enough, but this Blitz business has unnerved him and, at the weekend, I became extremely concerned. A week last Sunday, the

Jerrys bombed Buckingham Palace, fortunately just missing the wing where the King and Queen were. Then, last Friday, they hit the Palace again, this time with several large bombs. Five members of the Palace household staff were injured, one of whom has since tragically died."

Greta interrupted, exclaiming, "Oh, how utterly dreadful. How are the King and Queen?"

"They are fine but shaken up pretty badly. They are both stalwarts and have indomitable spirits. Churchill suggested they leave the country, but they will not even consider it, saying their place is with their people. Very admirable of Bertie; however, I regret that these attacks, combined with the enormous loss of life, have made His Majesty, once again, question whether Churchill is the right man for the job. He feels that the awful suffering and destruction of property could be avoided if we, at least, talk to the Germans, but Churchill will not hear of it."

Lord Louis looked round to make sure no-one was in earshot. "Bertie thinks Churchill is obsessed with the war and the cost of his policy is too high in human life when it could all be stopped. As a result, he is considering the unthinkable: that of having Churchill removed from office. I shudder to think of the consequences. I have to say there are many who would support the King, some of whom are high up in the military; plus he has spoken to the Duke of Hamilton, whom he knows has connections within the Nazi regime. Bertie tells me that the Duke is still in touch with a number of people in Germany and has offered to help."

Greta was utterly taken aback as she considered the threat to the Prime Minister. The exercise of such Royal power had not been used for hundreds of years, and she knew the danger that it could divide the nation. Dickie took hold of her hand as he spoke, "I think we need to be seen to be exploring options, and I regret to say that this may mean, at least, being seen to be talking with the enemy. If I can reassure the King, then I think we have a chance of nipping this in the bud. The last thing we need right now as this Battle of Britain is being fought, is for our leaders to fight each other and let Hitler in through the back door." Greta looked into his eyes, seeing the complete concern and sincerity in a man she had really come to respect, both as a friend and for his patriotism. She told him she was aware of ongoing contact between certain people in Britain and those seeking peace in Germany, indicating it was essential they brief Colonel Menzies, to which he agreed. "I am just relieved to get this off my chest," Lord Louis added, "before I was asked to take sides in a situation I would wish to avoid at all costs."

After they parted, Greta made two calls from the hotel, the first to Colonel Menzies and the second to Downing Street, informing them she would not be returning that day as she had an urgent meeting at SIS HQ.

Tuesday 17th September 1940, 3.30pm
SIS Headquarters, Westminster, London

Colonel Menzies had listened to Greta's briefing and was decisive with his response. "The lists we were given by Hamilton and Haushofer may be critical now, Miss Atkins. Clearly, we need to open an avenue for discussion with the Germans and let the King be aware. I think that to involve the PM at this stage would be a mistake. He will not have any part of discussing terms with the Nazi leadership, which he now refers to as '*a gang of thugs and criminals*'. If we play this like English gentlemen, we will lose the game, so it is time to employ the basest Machiavellian instincts, with which I am sure you are familiar." Despite the seriousness of the situation, the colonel had a twinkle in his eye, which their long relationship now justified.

She responded, "My dear colonel, I have rarely ever met a man whom I could class in the same sentence as both English and a gentleman, most being bounders and scoundrels. Perhaps if we adopted female wiles, we might do better." The colonel coughed in mock apoplectic shock. "Sir, it seems to me," she carried on earnestly, "that we have three powerful allies in Berlin to a potential strategy. Admiral Canaris, their Head of Intelligence, who is feeding information to us through a desire for peace coupled with a regime change as long as it is not betraying, as he sees it, his country. Then we have Deputy Führer Hess, who has already voiced his opposition to war with Britain and attempted to avoid it, although he has total and unshakeable loyalty to Hitler. Finally, there is dear Albrecht, who wants no part of National Socialism and who is helping to form a resistance which may topple Hitler. He desires peace but on no account allowing the Führer or any Nazi-led government to remain. The one word that unites all three is '*peace*'.

"Those who would back peace in this country, even now, include the King, his brother Prince George and, of course, the Duke of Windsor representing a very powerful faction. There are a phalanx of others, including the Duke of Hamilton; the Foreign Office Spokesman, Rab Butler; our current Spanish Ambassador, former Minister and Home Secretary, Sir Samuel Hoare; the distinguished and influential Head of the Royal British Legion, General Sir Ian Hamilton; and the former PM, Neville Chamberlain…" She stopped, as the colonel was gesturing.

"Please, Miss Atkins, I am aware that we have powerful factions at work here. Your point, please?"

"Colonel, I am merely stressing the need to be seen to be making moves. I suggest we make immediate contact with Albrecht Haushofer via Douglas-Hamilton, requesting that he involve both Canaris and Hess in examining peace options, saying this has Royal backing. That way, we are fully in the loop with what is going on. We know that the Germans have ambitions in the East, and if they come into conflict with Russia, they will not want another front in the West. If you sanction this, I can inform Dickie, who, in turn, can placate the King. When we have moved matters forward a little, we can then brief Winston Churchill, who, despite his instincts, may be forced, by recognising the power at play here, to accede to the strategy."

The colonel stood up, walked around his desk and shook Greta's hand. "Good Lord, Miss Atkins, if you were not a lady, I would say you would make a damned fine politician," to which she replied,

"Sir, it is because politics is so dominated by men that we are in this mess, and so, I should, perhaps, accept your compliment." The colonel laughed, a rare occurrence, leading her to the door.

"Do not delay, Miss Atkins, we have no time to lose, and you have my full blessing and authority. Keep me posted daily. Oh, and try not to use your pistol."

She looked back, giving an exaggerated, shocked expression as the door closed.

One month later, Greta was able to submit a top-secret report back to Colonel Menzies:

To: Colonel Stewart Menzies CIC SIS
From: Greta Atkins
20th October 1940

Sir,

It appears events covered at our last meeting may have overtaken us. I held a meeting with Douglas-Hamilton on 20th September, securing his confidence in the benefit of us working together. He informed me that Albrecht Haushofer had a meeting with Deputy Führer Hess on 31st August, during which he declared that the King, backed by British supporters of appeasement, was already considering the removal of Churchill. Hess reported to the Führer in early September that if the planned invasion of Britain was postponed, and heavy bombing continued, these measures may be sufficient to secure the agreement of the King to dismiss the PM and sue for peace. Hitler was already greatly concerned about Germany's heavy air losses in the Battle of Britain and so Hess's intervention came at a good time. As a result, Hitler ordered that the invasion of Britain be postponed on 17th September. Albrecht Haushofer reported to Hess that he had secured an indirect connection with the King via

Douglas-Hamilton, backed by the Head of the British Legion, General Sir Ian Hamilton.

On 8th September, Haushofer, on Hess's instructions, wrote to Douglas-Hamilton proposing a meeting between them in either an accessible area in Europe or Portugal. Albrecht's father, Karl, who is very much part of Hitler's inner circle, despite being outspoken, has indicated that both Hess and himself may be willing to secretly participate in peace talks. Karl has stated that Hitler will not wish to be seen being part of this process.

As you know, the contacts between Albrecht and DouglasHamilton were intercepted by our friends in MI5, and the Head of the Double Agent Section, Colonel Tar Robertson, has liaised with me on this, on your instruction, for which I'm grateful. I am submitting a request that we appoint Douglas formally to continue in this role and effectively act as a double agent as he meets with Albrecht and others.

Sir, I must point out the dangers of not informing various political people about this, such as the Foreign Secretary and, indeed, the PM. If Churchill hears about this from another source, he may, at best, block continued communication and, at worst, class our actions as treason.

I suggest we do this on a 'need-to-know basis'. There are too many people becoming involved and if we are to prevent the PM becoming aware of the King's potential intention, we need, at very least, to give a story which is credible, of covert 'peace talks'. In order to keep Churchill on side, the process could be couched in terms such that we are exploring peace options with those who are disillusioned with Hitler's regime which, in reality, is partially true.

I can also tell you that Karl has informed Albrecht that there is a secret military operation being worked on in Berlin named 'Unternehmen Otto', which is a plan for an attack on Russia, possibly in 1941. We have little information and this is being kept very hush-hush, restricted to the closest of Hitler's associates. More to follow and, subject to your authority, I shall ensure arrangements are put in place for Douglas to meet Albrecht as soon as can be arranged.

I have two final concerns. There are many powerful players involved here and hence we must tread carefully. The first is that I am informed the former Foreign

Secretary, Lord Halifax, has indicated to the Duke of Hamilton that he is broadly supportive of reaching a peace accord and may support Churchill's removal if he gets wind of the King's position. As you know, he is now in Washington as British ambassador but carries a lot of weight both here and in America. The second is a matter of some delicacy. An old friend of yours, Violet Roberts, the wife of Walter, with whom I believe you went to school, is another very influential person in the appeasement camp. She has made it plain she wishes, on behalf of others of influence, to be involved in any talks. I think we should try and secure a top-level meeting, excluding such third-party involvement. Deputy Führer Hess is anxious to pursue peace because it frees the Germans from fighting on two fronts, allowing them to concentrate on their Russian venture. He may wish to personally lead direct talks with Britain.

There is no doubt that there is a serious possibility of peace with Germany, but clearly, the conclusion of this, if not handled delicately, may be utterly unpalatable, strengthening Hitler.

We must consider how all this might sit back at home. I recognise there will be those that would welcome the overthrow of the Russian government. These are political matters and not areas upon which I can make a judgement, but I do think we can build bridges and alliances with connections in Germany that may eventually result in weakening Hitler or, at very least, assist in obtaining regime change.

Finally, sir, I confirm that I have briefed Dickie, and he has informed me that, although the patience of the King is wearing thin due to the appalling loss of civilian life in the bombing, he has undertaken that he will not consider, at this point, any move to oust Churchill.

Subject to confirmation of your instructions, I shall continue in my role and look forward to our next meeting.

Respectfully,
Greta Atkins

The reply, when it came, made Greta smile, although she knew the colonel would pursue his stated objective with ruthless efficiency.

My dear Greta, your wiles are worthy of your gender, of which, no doubt, you are enormously proud. I can only observe and admire with not a little awe. Continue as instructed, and authorise Hamilton to arrange talks immediately, preferably in Lisbon. I have requested an urgent briefing with the PM today and I will ensure our (stated) strategy is both approved and executed.

Yours,
Stewart Menzies

30

Flight of History

Wednesday 18th December 1940, 9.00am
The Reich Chancellery, Wilhelmstrasse, Berlin

The room was absolutely silent, despite there being a dozen men present, after Hitler had slammed his fists down on his desk; his voice raised to a crescendo, asking, then demanding to know if his great vision was being betrayed. General Erich Marcks had nervously began responding, "With the greatest respect, *mein Führer*—" but Hitler silenced him, banging his fist down yet again.

The Führer was now pacing in front of a map of Europe taking up a large part of the wall, tapping the map with a long pointer. "My generals, I remind you that I am a decorated soldier and that I fought in the Great War. Although we are a superior race and vastly more developed than the Bolshevik scum, they have huge numbers and we must overwhelm them quickly on a broad front with a force of an unimaginable size. This must be the greatest military operation ever undertaken in history."

Hitler strode in front of his audience, who nodded approvingly if not dotingly. He folded his arms, staring at Bormann, Göring, Goebbels, Canaris and Himmler. "Can I rely on you, and you and you and you?" Then to Rudolf Hess: "And you, Herr Deputy Führer? Is this not our greatest policy for which we have striven? Our purpose, our destiny?" His voice rose again, and Hess stood up, raising his arm in salute and approval. He turned towards Karl Haushofer. "This massive landmass of Europe should yield to our might so that we can take back our Germanic heritage. Is this not ours by right, supported by history, Herr Professor?" Haushofer nodded as Hitler marched to Field Marshal Walther von Brauchitsch and Generaloberst Franz Halder, who were standing, looking uncomfortable, to one side of the map. "Have we the numbers to make up the most overwhelming invasion force ever known, not in thousands, or tens of thousands, but in millions? Not one million, not two million, not even three million, but four million?" The Führer's voice rang out loudly, clearly stressing every syllable. Both officers clicked their heels, nodded and bowed. "Then why did you bring to me a plan two weeks ago that was without strength of numbers, initiative or imagination? This is the realisation of our supreme mission, for which we need force and ingenuity. We will seize territory on which we can build grand cities designed to celebrate the superior culture of our race modelled on principles of National Socialist design." This time Hitler swung round, looking directly at the architect, Albert Speer, with a shrug as though seeking approval, which was affirmed by the smiling, enthusiastic nod he received.

The Führer strode back to the map. "You brought with you *Unternehmen ['Operation'] Otto'*, but that was clearly conceived too small. You will rethink on a grand scale, beyond anything you have imagined, and this shall be called *'Unternehmen Barbarossa'*. We will invade on a front stretching three thousand kilometres; that is our task and this momentous endeavour will match the scale of my vision. I want the plans redrawn and preparations made for an attack in May 1941. We will fulfil our great purpose and rid mankind of the Communist vermin, earning the gratitude of the whole world." Hitler wiped away the hair that had fallen across his brow, then walked purposefully back to a seat behind the desk.

"*Mein Führer*, please?" Hermann Göring rose to his feet, and, after receiving a nod from Hitler: "What is to become of our campaign against Britain?"

Hitler leaned forward. "My Reichsmarschall, that was your task, but you left their air force too strong." He raised his finger in the air. "However, when we defeat Russia, they will want peace and that snivelling, drunken warmonger Churchill will come begging. Continue the bombing, as it will weaken their resolve. I recall it was their ex-King who said so."

Tuesday 25th March 1941, 2.00pm
Office of the Prime Minister, 10 Downing Street, London

Churchill sat, having listened to the arguments for over an hour of Rab Butler, whom he had recently moved from the Foreign Office to become Minister of Education, and the Duke of Hamilton, which had not been well received. Colonel Menzies, who was also present, had remained relatively silent. Churchill's voice rose with passion. "You expect me to conduct negotiations with these gangsters, these Nazis, whose perfidious deeds have cost our country dear in life and property. Their treachery and insatiable desire for conquest has led to incalculable misery, the subjugation of nations and the cruel trampling-upon the rights of mankind. Countless lives have been lost within the ranks of our brave men in this time and you now suggest we betray not only them but their fathers who stood and fell before in the trenches of Flanders within our lifetimes. Hitler has threatened not only our Empire, but was also poised to invade our country just a month ago. We continue to be threatened as never before since the Armada, with modern weaponry of unimaginable cruelty, indiscriminately destroying civilian life and homes." He lit another cigar, puffing large clouds of smoke, before sighing disconsolately, sitting back in his chair.

They had argued that a peace accord was a real possibility; Germany had offered to cease hostilities, immediately withdraw from the Channel Islands and acknowledge Britain's territorial rights over her Empire and all her sovereign territories. Churchill was almost beside himself. "You watched as this pariah tore up treaty after treaty, made a fool of my predecessor with the Munich Agreement, the terms of which he then blatantly ignored, and now you tell me he has designs on Russia!" Churchill's voice had become a thunderous growl. "They only signed the Molotov-Ribbentrop Non-Aggression pact in Moscow eighteen months ago. I will not give succour to this foul dictator." The Prime Minister stood up, walking to the long window overlooking the rear garden, and there was an awkward pause before he turned to face them.

"I am reminded of many wise words, but I think Shakespeare assists me, gentlemen, *'There's no trust, no faith, no honesty in men; all perjured, all forsworn, all naught, all dissemblers.'* I will resign before I agree to negotiate peace terms."

Colonel Menzies knew that if he could not rescue the position, then the Duke of Hamilton may force a constitutional crisis by warning that they had the support of the King, which would make Churchill even more intransigent. This was the time to act. "Sir, please might a humble old soldier speak with some inner knowledge of the machinations of the German government. I think we can trust Albrecht Haushofer. Albrecht is utterly opposed to Hitler and we know he is establishing a network of those who support removing him from power. We are aware, sir, of many senior officers in the Wehrmacht who would support a coup. If we have faith in Albrecht, we should be seen to be negotiating, which will increase his influence with those opposing Hitler. Although the risk of invasion has receded for now, it has only been postponed. We need to buy time whilst we attempt to encourage the United States to enter the war. I must stress that, in my view, this is a question of the survival of our country. Hitler will not make further moves against us whilst there is a chance of peace, and if he becomes engaged in a war against Russia, he will need to dedicate all his available military resources to the East." Churchill was now sitting forward in his chair, his face set in a solemn but determined, resilient look, as he listened, weighing up the arguments being advanced.

"I think, sir, it would serve our purposes to, at least, permit a covert meeting to take place with those seeking peace. This will strengthen Haushofer's standing and, if the prospects are favourable, may lead to Hitler's downfall. If we are not talking with them, then the Germans who would otherwise be persuaded to join the dissidents will think otherwise. The German mind is not easily given to betrayal, especially the military, who have taken an oath of loyalty to the Führer. If we are not perceived as the enemy, then many will feel that they can join those who are seeking to remove Hitler or deter his territorial aggression. I am not one easily given to quotations, sir, an attribute best left to you; but I think, '*Adversity makes strange bedfellows*' may fit here."

Churchill put his cigar down in a slow, deliberate way and cleared his throat. "I recall the words of Napoleon, '*Never interrupt your enemy when he is making a mistake*', and, it is for that reason, and your wise words, Colonel, that I shall permit some discussion to take place. Although, I stress, I will not, either directly or indirectly, negotiate a peace with this appalling pretentious potentate. Perhaps, therefore, we can despatch someone of note without attracting attention. I shall ask Sir Samuel Hoare, our ambassador in Spain, who has been quite well in with the Germans after the affair with the Duke of Windsor." The Prime Minister rose from his seat, shaking hands with each of them. "I believe we have agreement in the room and you may, therefore, join me in a drink."

Tuesday 1st April 1941, 3.00pm
Buckingham Palace, Westminster, London

The car being driven up the Mall was not ostentatious by any means, nor did he wish it to be, in order not to draw any attention to his visit. The Duke of Hamilton was being driven in the Morris 10-4 towards Buckingham Palace gates with some trepidation. This was not going to be an easy meeting, he thought, holding his homburg hat on his lap. Gazing through the windows, he could see the grey skyline interrupted with barrage balloons which hung over the city like huge unwieldy leviathans at varying heights. To the left there were anti-aircraft guns, the fingertips of their barrels pointing skywards at varying angles surrounded by soldiers. Surprisingly, there were sheep too, grazing in the grass of Hyde Park, seemingly totally oblivious to the activity around them. They passed a marching column of soldiers in khaki, all wearing helmets, and there were uniforms everywhere, a stark reminder of wartime Britain. Further back, he could see palls of smoke arising from the East End of London, which had taken a pounding from the bombing of the night before.

As they approached the tall iron gates, which had been opened, they swerved to avoid three huge craters in the road in front of the Palace, which, he knew, had taken a number of hits. The King had to be admired, he reflected, for staying in the capital despite the constant danger of German bombing. The car swept under the portico, where a footman was waiting, complete with top hat. The door was opened and he was led in by a smartly dressed man in dark topcoat and tails through an entranceway into a reception area where Greta Atkins, dressed in a smart black suit and matching hat worn at an angle, with feathers, smiled a greeting. They were led up a semi-circular stairway with empty alcoves and gold cornices which surrounded spaces where huge portraits were normally hanging. The brighter-coloured paper beneath showed where pictures had formerly been before being removed because of the danger of bomb damage. As they walked down a large ornate corridor, this too had been stripped of paintings and was bare of the many statues which Douglas Hamilton recalled from pre-war visits. They were ushered into a room where they were asked if they would like to take tea, which they both declined. They waited near a white marble fireplace in which a coal fire burned, adding a touch of homeliness to a room that was grand despite being modest in size. Ornate antique furniture was spaced around including a number of small tables on which were vases, photo frames and ornaments. There were decorative Georgian-style white plaster mouldings in neat, rectangular patterns set against soft, green-coloured walls, almost like a piece of Wedgwood pottery, Greta thought, as a tall door opened and King George VI entered, followed by his brother, Prince George.

Both were dressed in dark suits, but Prince George was wearing a three-piece with wide lapels and a striped tie, whilst the King's was more sombre with a plain grey tie. "Delighted you could make it, old boy, and the delightful Miss Atkins too." The King smiled as he shook the Duke's hand, then kissed Greta's. "How is the frightful world of counter-espionage? Pretty damned busy, I should think?"

Prince George also extended his hand but gripped the Duke's with both of his as if to emphasise his welcome, then bowed to Greta, who had curtsied. The King motioned to chairs around the fireplace and then stepped to the wall, pressing a bellpush. Seconds later, drinks were being served. They had settled on having port, which arrived in a crystal decanter together with four cut glasses carried on silver trays by two footmen.

Prince George poured the drinks as the King began. "I understand that peace discussions with the Germans are stalling because our dear Mr Churchill is not giving them enough credence. We cannot delay further,

Douglas, too many are dying here night after night needlessly and we will not permit this to continue."

The Duke looked from the King to Prince George. "Your Majesty, sir, I think we need to inform the Prime Minister that he has no choice but to accept direct face-to-face peace talks, however unpalatable. For that I will need to impress upon him the support I can muster politically and back that up with your authority; however, I regret he may still refuse. Sir, the Germans clearly desire peace because they are to attack Russia. They are prepared to guarantee our Empire, with the exception of former German colonies, and the absolute security of Great Britain. They have also given an undertaking that they will immediately withdraw from the Channel Islands and will consider withdrawing from some occupied territories in Western Europe, whilst creating a protectorate in Poland."

Prince George voiced his approval, then asked, "What about other territory they have seized?"

The Duke responded, "Their annexation of Austria and the Rhineland they regard as part of Germany. They are prepared to withdraw from Norway, and Denmark. They will negotiate over Belgium, Holland and France subject to a guarantee of nonaggression. However, annexation of territory in Eastern Europe is a non-negotiable part of their policy."

Greta raised her hand as if to stress her next words. "Your Majesty, I know this is important to you, the Germans have offered one more concession. They will cease bombing London in return for secret face-to-face negotiations with Churchill. If the Prime Minister refuses, then they suggest with you or an appointed Royal representative. They would be represented by the Deputy Führer, Rudolf Hess. They propose secret negotiations are held here in England immediately."

The Duke then added, "Albrecht Haushofer knows my estate and has suggested, in order to keep this absolutely under wraps, that Hess, who is an accomplished pilot, flies from Germany using the landing strip behind my home in Scotland. Finally, sir, the Führer will only permit the talks if you personally guarantee Hess's safety and if he is received by a member of the Royal Family. He does not trust politicians."

The King stood up, walked over to a desk and opened an ornate box, from which he extracted a cigarette. Picking up a silver lighter, he clicked it down deftly, and a lid popped open, revealing a flame. He took a deep draw on his cigarette, exhaling the smoke with a long sigh, drumming the fingers of his hand on the table. Then he straightened up, his face set. "Look here, we must immediately take decisive steps and seize this moment. I will give this peace initiative my blessing and I think it is high time we showed our colours. We will commence negotiations now and, if necessary, bypass Churchill, but, and I stress this, it is on condition that the bombing ceases. I will tell Churchill, personally, that I will act in my capacity as Sovereign if he ignores my advice. He must be made aware of the support we can muster from many influential people in both the military and within Parliament whom we shall call upon if it becomes necessary. I know those I can rely upon. If he does not want a constitutional crisis, then my advice to him is to accept terms of peace. George, you will travel to Scotland and meet with Hess. If Churchill fails to cooperate, I regret he may find that he is removed from office, and sent to Canada; by force, if necessary."

Saturday 10th May 1941, 10.08pm
Chain (Radar) Early Warning Station, Ottercops Moss,
Near Newcastle upon Tyne, North East England

"Sir, I think we have something." the Young WRAF operator was watching a screen intently. "The target came on my screen about twenty minutes ago and has appeared to cross the coast a few times now."

Squadron Leader Lawrence Gibbs came over to look, although he had been expecting something to crop up. Before he had come on duty, he had taken a call from the Air Ministry and been informed that there was a bit of a hush-hush operation going on. Nothing to worry about, but he was not to over-react if any single 'bandit' aircraft were detected from around 9.00pm. He was ordered to inform only the senior officer at RAF Bentley Priory and no-one else. A little unusual in being so alerted and, even more so when the person he spoke to was none other than Air Commodore and Acting Air Vice-Marshal John Andrews, Air Officer Commanding No 13 Fighter Group. He had only seen him once from a distance at a ceremonial parade. Whilst he thought it curious, he was flattered that such a senior officer would take an interest and when told it was 'hush-hush', he felt quite proud.

He replied to the WRAF operator, "Keep an eye on it. HQ will not want to be wasting time on a single bandit at this time. There's a huge show with enemy aircraft down south right now and our orders are to hold back." Moments later, the operator announced that the bandit had crossed over the coast near the Farne Islands and was heading north very low and at high speed.

"OK, I'll notify RAF Bentley Priory myself." The WRAF operator thought it a little strange but shrugged her shoulders, giving him the information.

"Air Commodore Gill, please." Gibbs felt a moment of importance, asking for such a senior officer. "Squadron Leader Gibbs here, sir, Chain Station Ottercops – expected bandit heading north very low and fast, crossed coast at 22.10."

Saturday 10th May 1941, 10.12pm
Royal Observer Corps Station, Chatton, Northumberland

Sergeant Ian Walker was astonished and his heart raced; the sound of an aero-engine turned to a roar as he spotted the twin engine aircraft heading directly towards him. Within a few seconds, it had flown past with black crosses identifying it as German, and he actually saw the pilot waving.

"Cheeky little blighter," he muttered as he wound his phone handle. "Solitary bandit Messerschmitt 110 heading on a course 0010 – height fifty feet," he stammered.

Saturday 10th May 1941, 10.13pm
RAF Fighter Command, 72 Squadron,
RAF Acklington, Northumberland

Wing Commander Herbert John Pringle answered the phone and the words, "Scramble – single bandit identified Messerschmitt 110," made him sit up with a jolt. The duty officer at HQ suggested scrambling two spitfires. He had been expecting the call but still felt a rush of adrenalin reacting to the situation as he had been ordered earlier. The AOC (Air Officer Commanding) had been specific. "You will not scramble, John, and I'm afraid mum's the word. Hush-hush and all that. Perhaps, wait a while and send up a Spit for a nosey round and that sort of thing. Don't worry, old boy, I'll back you up if necessary. But, Wing-Co, this conversation has not taken place. Do I make myself absolutely clear?" The tone was final, commanding, and he knew there was to be no discussion, nor was it expected.

He waited another five minutes before popping his head round the door to the duty room. "Sergeant, I need you to scout around, old chap, some lone bandit has been spotted heading towards Glasgow. It's getting pretty dark, so be careful. The chances are we won't find him, but have a dash up that way, see what you can find and report in. Just in case you see him, our orders are to confirm, before engaging, as we want to see what he is up to. Good luck, Maurice." Within a minute, Maurice Pocock had reached his Spitfire and was ready to taxi onto the runway.

Saturday 10th May 1941, 10.17pm
603 Squadron, RAF Turnhouse, Near Edinburgh

"Sir, there seems to be a bit of a fuss brewing over a bandit straying towards our sector. 72 Squadron at Acklington are on it, but HQ requested we keep you briefed."

Wing Commander Douglas Douglas-Hamilton was in the duty office and had been expecting some news. He moved to his private office and called his home. "Hello, Granger, Douglas, please can you ask our guest to come to the phone." Seconds later, he recognised Prince George's familiar voice: "Johnnie here," which was their prearranged code. "Johnnie, I can confirm that delivery of the Horn is expected and should be with you soon." Douglas hung up, returning to the duty office. Observer Corps were calling with updates and he felt a sense of elation that the plan was being executed.

Saturday 10th May 1941, 11.04pm
Floors Farm, Waterfoot, Near Eaglesham,
East Renfrewshire, Scotland

David Maclean felt and heard the explosion at the same time inside the farmhouse, which shook the building, echoing into the early night sky. He rushed to the window and moments later saw the white shape of a parachute floating down towards his fields. "I'll see to this," he said to his mother, grabbing his shotgun off the wall. He broke open the barrels, inserting two cartridges. On entering the fields, he could clearly see the outline of a parachute on the ground. Walking closer, he saw a figure, half lying on the floor, wrestling to rid himself of the harness. In the bottom field he could see wreckage on fire which he presumed to be an aircraft. A smell of burning rubber and aviation fuel hung in the air.

"Stop what you are doing and identify yourself," he called out.

The reply was crisp but well-spoken in clipped English: "I am Hauptmann Albert Horn. I have flown from Germany and I need to reach Dungavel House. I have an urgent message for the Duke of Hamilton."

The airman undid his flying helmet and finally released himself from the parachute. He had a square face, prominent eyebrows and deep, staring eyes. The farmer could not help but think there was something familiar about him. "I think you should come to the house and we'll give ye a cup of tea and you can rest." He motioned Horn to get up, but as the man tried to rise, his foot gave way.

"I caught my foot on the tail of my aircraft. Perhaps it is broken." He managed to struggle up and limped with some discomfort as Maclean directed him to the farmhouse. Horn bowed to Maclean's mother, apologising for any inconvenience, but declined her offer of tea, asking if they had water which she gingerly gave him. They began chatting about family and the German produced photos of his wife, Ilse, and son, Wolf, whom he said he nicknamed Buz. He seemed relaxed and stated that he had many British friends, and that the war was a tragedy which should never have happened. After thirty minutes, there was the sound of engines and a truck entered the farmyard. There was a loud thump on the farmhouse door, which Maclean opened to a uniformed man holding a revolver.

"Captain William Ferguson, Home Guard, where is the German?" He walked in with two armed men.

"You are here to take me to the Duke of Hamilton?" Horn asked.

The officer replied in German asking him about his reasons for being there. Horn responded that he had urgent information for the Duke, but he could not discuss it with them. They took him away, after Horn had thanked David Maclean and his mother for their kindness. It was not for some time that the Scottish farmer and his mother realised they had, in fact, taken into their home and been conversing with the Deputy Führer of Germany, Rudolf Hess.

Sunday 11th May 1941, 1.30am
603 Squadron, RAF Turnhouse, Near Edinburgh

The phone rang in the duty room and Douglas-Hamilton was informed it was the police. An officer explained that the Home Guard had captured a German pilot by the name of Horn asking for him. The police officer further informed him that they had secured the services of an interpreter from the Polish Consulate in Glasgow who was helping them to interrogate him. The Duke's heart sank. The entire operation had called for absolute secrecy. The capture, involvement of the Home Guard, police and others now completely changed the position. He ordered the police to cease interrogation forthwith, to secure the prisoner and not to speak to anyone until he arrived in the morning. Following the call, he phoned Dungavel House and, on speaking to Prince George, he said briefly, "Package intercepted, please find alternative accommodation immediately. Inform Burt. I will speak with him later." The latter name referred to the King.

That night was the last night of the Blitz in which the Germans launched a massive final bombing raid on London: 1,436 people were killed and 12,000 made homeless.

31

Diaries and Documents

Wednesday 26th February 2020, 9.30am
Pinneberger Strasse, Hamburg

They sat around the sitting room of the house attempting to place documents into some kind of order. There were twelve diaries labelled with dates covering the period 1940–45. Hans proposed that Bernhard, Rubin and himself took four each whilst his mother placed the photographed documents in order. Their excitement was palpable as more and more evidence emerged corroborating everything they already had from Gunther Roche, the information given by Manfred Göring, the revelations from the SS sergeant who had served under Roche and the contents of Greta's letter to Hanna.

"*Mein Gott*, listen to this," exclaimed Hans. "A showdown, my great-grandmother calls it, between King George VI and Churchill after Hess had flown to Britain and been discovered. She writes that Douglas-Hamilton was instructed by Colonel Stewart Menzies, the Head of British Intelligence, to immediately brief Churchill. He was ordered to inform Churchill of the purpose of Hess's flight, and reveal the involvement of the Crown. Churchill had then, apparently, demanded an audience with the King."

Monday 12th May 1941, 11.00am
Meeting of the War Cabinet, 10 Downing Street, London

The Duke of Hamilton was feeling decidedly uncomfortable as he presented the position to the seven members of the War Cabinet, as he had been instructed by Churchill. The Prime Minister was watching him intently as the Duke told them the agreed story despite knowing that more than one person present was aware of the truth. "I believe that Hess has flown here under the illusion that he could broker some kind of peace arrangement with me. This is because I had social ties with a chap called Haushofer before the war who was a friend of his and who now works for him. We had tried, in 1939, to avoid war if at all possible and build bridges with more reasonable Germans, resulting in some off-the-record discussions but nothing more. I had absolutely no idea he was going to attempt this as, indeed, I believe it will come as something of a surprise to Hitler." *My God, if these people only knew,* he thought, wondering nervously how the next meeting would go; an audience with the King scheduled for 2.00pm at the Palace. So much was happening so quickly.

He had held a private meeting with Rudolf Hess the previous day, during which he had to explain to the Deputy Führer that matters had taken a new course because of his capture. Now his visit had been discovered, which meant that matters could no longer be kept secret as too many people were already involved, including the police, the Home Guard, the chain of command and the local community. He had been contacted by Prince George the night before, who had left Dungavel House after learning of Hess's capture, hurriedly travelling to Balmoral Castle. The Prince informed him that the King had decided Churchill needed to be fully briefed on the planned peace negotiations. This had triggered a chain of events starting with a call to Greta Atkins, who, in turn, consulted with Colonel Menzies. The colonel had called him, giving orders that he spoke directly with the Prime Minister. The Duke then had made contact with Churchill's private secretary, John (Jock) Colville, stating that an urgent matter of the highest national importance had come to light about which he needed to personally inform the Prime Minister. Churchill had then summoned him to a meeting, instructing him to leave immediately and meet him at his weekend retreat at Ditchley.

After flying down from Scotland to nearby RAF Kidlington, the Duke of Hamilton had spent a very uncomfortable late afternoon and evening explaining to an enraged Churchill that he had acted on the direct authority of the monarch.

"Have you and your mistaken conspirators – nay, I would refer to you as plotters, no less – presumed upon yourselves to bypass the government? By God, sir, this may not only be classed as treacherous sedition but treason. Never, since Charles I sought to seize power against the wishes of Parliament elected by the people in 1642, has any monarch presumed upon themselves to overrule the elected government. I am, indeed, related to the Royal Family, but I am elected by the people. I will never surrender the powers that are mine by right and privilege, nor should the King exceed his. He will never need to utter the words, '*The birds hath flown*,' for I shall face this crisis and, in so doing, will look the King in the eye, albeit I am ever loyal to the Crown."

Douglas-Hamilton, angered by Churchill's words, responded forcefully, "Prime Minister, there are many sharing your benches, and, indeed, within your government who support the course of action suggested by His Majesty. Might I remind you that it is hardly treason if I acted with the authority of the King. I will not be termed a conspirator, nor should I be castigated for doing what, in all conscience, I believe to be right for my country. I will, however, do all in my power to establish a resolution to this issue and, to that end, I will do whatever you may require of me."

Churchill grunted an acknowledgement and said they had much to do in order to prevent a challenge to the authority of Parliament, which, in wartime, was unthinkable. After dinner at Ditchley, the Duke produced a file containing proposals from the Deputy Führer for peace. It was emphasised that these were merely outline proposals to form the basis of negotiations. The Duke explained to the Prime Minister that Hess had authority from Hitler to negotiate peace and, importantly, he stressed to an incredulous Churchill that he had the guarantee of the protection of the British Crown.

Now, after his exhausting weekend, Douglas-Hamilton was facing a series of awkward questions, mainly from the Minister of Labour, Ernest Bevin, who was doubting, if not suspicious of, the events as described. Douglas stated with conviction that to anyone it would appear unbelievable, no less so than to himself. Knowing what had been agreed with Hess beforehand, in the event of capture, the Duke knew that Germany would disassociate itself from the mission. He could, therefore, state that time would undoubtedly show that this was a clandestine attempt by Hess without any authority from Hitler. However, as he had agreed with Rudolf Hess the day before, the reality was that being discovered could, in a way, make the process of secret negotiations easier because open accessibility to him would not be seen as suspicious. Clement Atlee, the Lord Privy Seal, wanted to establish what would be done with the prisoner because the people would need to know. Churchill responded he would put Hess where many had been placed throughout history who had stood against the British Crown. "I shall have him thrown into the Tower of London," he announced triumphantly, despite his own unease on what was to follow that afternoon.

Monday 12th May 1941, 2.30pm
The Audience Room, Buckingham Palace

They had travelled to the Palace together and Churchill's mood had vastly improved from the day before, becoming more sanguine about matters. In the Rolls-Royce being chauffeured up the Mall, he smiled through puffs of smoke at Douglas-Hamilton. "I am not entirely surprised, nor, indeed, unduly perturbed, nor even perplexed by what has been revealed to me, albeit belatedly and, doubtless, judged as ill-timed by history. *'Heaven is above all yet; there sits a judge, that no king can corrupt.'* Queen Katherine in *Henry VIII*, old chap. Hopefully, both our heads are safe. I do sometimes feel that this is like being summoned before the headmaster, despite the fact that I am the chair of the governors." He laughed, looking in the vanity mirror and adjusting his bowtie.

Once inside a great anteroom at the palace, they were only waiting for around a minute before they were summoned. "His Majesty will see you now," announced Sir Alan 'Tommy' Lascelles, gliding out from the room, immaculately dressed in a dark suit, grey silk tie, his hair swept back, with a neatly trimmed moustache. Outside a tall door, he paused, shaking hands with Churchill and bowing to the Duke.

"I trust he is in fine spirits, Tommy?" ventured Churchill, with a wink at Douglas, drawing the response, "Protocol denies that I answer you, Mr Churchill, but my advice is constant, rarely requiring voice, although today may warrant an exception in that you should act with deference and be as extremely well prepared as your position, perhaps, warrants." He smiled briefly, before stepping aside to allow their entrance. Churchill went first, walking towards the King, who stood from behind an ornate desk with intricate gold decoration above narrow legs. They both bowed before Churchill shook the King's hand. He gestured them to two large, upholstered Georgian armchairs.

"Mr Churchill," the King started, "we shall not keep you long as you must be very busy, but do please inform us of the reasons for your somewhat pressing request?" His tone was strong and commanding.

"Your Majesty," Churchill started slowly, "I feel sure that my loyalty to my country and, indeed, the Crown, may never be doubted. Sir, many have judged my reputation for intransigence as a failing, but I believe my record will show that my steadfast spirit has served me well. My reasons for the request are many, but my doubts about the need, I am hopeful, will far outweigh my concerns after this audience."

The King lit a cigarette, standing up and moving from behind his desk. "Mr Churchill, we will dispense with Royal protocol for a moment and we will speak frankly." His eyes fixed Churchill with a steely look, his manner clearly causing the Prime Minister some unease and surprise. "I have known you for many years and you may know that you might not have been my first choice for Prime Minister, but because of my respect for my constitutional position, I would not, nor did I, interfere with the process of your selection to serve as my Prime Minister. I may, however, have one power that is inalienable, which is to advise my ministers. I gave you my advice, Mr Churchill, very clearly, which you chose to ignore and, I regret, that this may have cost this country very dearly. Please do not interrupt until I have finished."

Churchill dropped his hand, which he had raised as if he was about to speak. The King continued; his voice was unwavering, despite the difficulty he had in expressing some words, showing an absolute authority and command. "Peace, Mr Churchill, peace. That was all I proposed, not blindly, not weakly, but as a realistic prospect. You, however, did not wish to listen. Peace was my advice and remains my advice. Two nights ago, there was a crushing, cruel air raid on London in which so many tragically died, whilst thousands more were displaced. Your House of Commons was bombed and burned to the ground. As a result of my intervention, I have secured a reprieve in bombing attacks, for now, and I am advising that we do the same. This action, alone, will save many lives.

"I realised that many of those wanting peace in Germany did not support Hitler, yet we ignored them. I was informed that a member of Hitler's government, who held power, wanted to talk, but you refused to even consider this. I am advising you, Mr Churchill, as I advised others, that we should, at least, listen. I offered my protection to Mr Hess; that is also my prerogative and you will respect this. I have not commanded or given orders to anyone but merely given advice and my support. My advice to you, Mr Churchill, is clear, and that is to listen, not surrender, but to listen. Many of those within your party, including your ministers, agree with me. If they wish to force a situation in which I have to act, then so be it, but I would rather there is no constitutional crisis, nor would I wish for one. I merely want my Prime Minister to listen to my advice, that is all. I trust I make myself clear?" It was not a question but a statement of authority.

Churchill pulled out a cigar. "Your Majesty, might I prevail upon you to allow me to smoke?" The King gestured with a resigned smile as he sat back behind his desk. "Your Majesty, I have always served the Crown diligently and I shall continue to do so. I recognise that I am not infallible, despite my gift of er… intransigence." He indulged himself a look of amusement, to break the tension. "If I have failed to heed your advice then that might be judged, in the fullness of time, and doubtless with hindsight, to have been a grave error. However, we must recall the pact that my late predecessor signed, with good faith, the Munich Agreement, despite my own advice to the contrary; a treaty which, I believe, was viewed by Hitler to be indicative of our weakness. Hence, as we now know, he invaded Poland, flying in the face of civilised international justice." Churchill puffed on his cigar, pausing as his last words rang out; perhaps a tad inappropriately, he mused, bearing in mind this was not Parliament.

"Your Majesty, I have viewed with some disquiet, trepidation and, indeed, not without some deep reservations, the peace proposals put forward by Deputy Führer Hess. Whilst there may be some welcome elements, including the German withdrawal from occupied territories and the guarantee of your Empire, Hitler demands that we do nothing upon his exercise of his territorial ambitions into Eastern Europe. I am given to believe that, despite yet another of their treaties, the so-called Molotov-Ribbentrop pact, Hitler will invade Russia this summer. For that reason, notwithstanding the wisdom of your gracious advice, I may be persuaded that this is the time when we have the best hand." Churchill sat back in his seat as though he had concluded the issue.

The King leant forward, addressing him informally. "Winston, I am not known for my lack of intuition, but forgive me, I appear to be missing the point here?"

"Your Majesty, Hitler and his generals do not wish to fight a war on two or more fronts. Hitler's goal is the overthrow of Communism, a desire that, dare I say, might be one of the very few I may share with him. For this reason, we hold, perhaps, more aces in our hand than we could have hoped might have been dealt. Furthermore, it appears to me that talks with the enemy, no matter how illusory, may give us more time in persuading President Roosevelt to commit America to come to our aid. Public opinion there is undoubtedly beginning to turn our way."

"Mr Churchill," the King resumed a more formal address, "are you telling me that you will now be accepting my advice?"

Churchill opened his hands, feigning surprise. "I believe, Your Majesty, that my loyalty to the Crown has never before been called into question, and propose that is an impossible supposition to even contemplate. My terms for peace, however, will be uncompromising in that we should not cease hostilities until we are assured of the success of their purpose. Why play a hand, if I may again use the metaphor, when the result is not without too much risk? I propose that if the Germans are within, say, twenty miles of Moscow, we consider concluding a treaty with them."

The King looked across at the Duke of Hamilton. "Douglas, what is your assessment of this chap, Hess? Can we rely on his sincerity? He is, after all, a committed Nazi, is he not?"

Douglas-Hamilton responded, "Sir, my connection in Germany also works for British Intelligence and feeds us invaluable information. Despite his political differences with the Deputy Führer, which Hess tolerates, they are trusted friends. I have, through him, previously already been in contact indirectly with Hess pursuing peace options and even met with him last month in Portugal when he stated both he and the Führer now sought peace.

"Your Majesty, I think it worth mentioning that in a visit to the White House last year, Charles Edward, Duke of Saxe Coburg and Gotha, proposed that the Americans participate in a joint German/American offensive against Russia. The President indicated that he might be prepared to consider this if we joined them."

The King winced and looked irritated. "That damned cousin of mine is always stirring things up and causing trouble." He turned for a reaction. "Mr Churchill?"

Churchill raised his right hand as if waving this away. "Let us dwell on how matters proceed as Hitler pits his so-called invincible forces against the might of the Russian bear. As Napoleon said, *'I am sometimes a fox and sometimes a lion. The whole secret of government lies in knowing when to be the one or the other.'* If our enemies weaken themselves, then any subsequent position we take may be strengthened enabling our endeavours to be those of a lion. I think Your Majesty may be relieved that, for once in my life, I have listened to advice."

The King stood up, giving Churchill a wry look. "I did say I would not keep you long as you will be busy, but to add to my advice, Winston, might I suggest a pause in the bombing of German cities as a gesture to match that given by Germany to cease raids on London. Thousands of lives will be saved as a result." The Prime Minister bowed, shook the

King's hand, muttering that he was delighted to be a servant of the Crown.

Later that day, Churchill issued a memorandum to Sir Charles Portal, the Chief of Air Staff, instructing him to cease bombing operations against German cities.

In the morning of 22nd June 1941, over three million Wehrmacht soldiers, the largest invasion force in the history of warfare, invaded the Soviet Union along a 1,800-mile front, with five hundred thousand motor vehicles and over six hundred thousand horses for non-combat operations. Hitler addressed the German nation on the radio, proclaiming that he was a man of peace forced into the steps he had taken, whilst Goebbels termed Barbarossa 'a European crusade against Bolshevism'.

Wednesday 26th February 2020, 11.00am
Pinneberger Strasse, Hamburg

Hans was flicking through page after page of his great-grandmother's diaries which, as he said, traced a clear period of the talks taking place with Hess in May 1941. They were trying to piece together the essential elements of what had taken place. "She says here that Hess is pretty miffed with the way he is being treated. Apparently, Churchill ordered that he be shut in the Tower of London in May 1941, but she says it was a token gesture for publicity." Then he announced, "Ah, this is quite poignant, I never realised. The entry is dated 23rd May 1941."

He read it out: *"Terribly sad news today. Poor Dickie Mountbatten has been dive-bombed on board his ship, HMS* Kelly, *off Crete. The ship went down, but he has survived, thank God, but had to be pulled from the drink. One hundred and twenty-eight men were tragically lost. Only thirty-eight survived. I felt like crying; he is such a nice chap and really cared for his men. Strangely, I was with Hess when I got the news who had just arrived at Ditchley and he offered his condolences. He stressed this was all awful and unnecessary, saying it just added more reason to achieve peace. I do hate Hitler and all he stands for, but Rudolf seems quite nice and unlike a Nazi, although he is utterly obsessed with his Führer. He has been moved nearer to here so he can conduct talks with the PM secretly at weekends. We even have a young chap who has started flying here from Germany in a British-marked plane, and he lands on the lawn with messages for Rudolf. He comes in and has tea with us for half an hour whilst his aircraft is refuelled from a bowser. It really is quite bizarre taking tea with the enemy. Winston says we are a bunch of rogues and fifth columnists and refuses to join in, although I know he shares a whisky with Hess. What a crazy, beastly time this is.*"

"Oh, dear God." Hans's words were broken. "That pilot was my father."

Eva went to him, placing her arms around him. "He would be so proud of you now, Hans, I know he would."

Hans looked at her. "Oh, Mother," he sighed, "I am proud of him, but should I even feel that? He was a brave man led into madness; but then he became part of it all. What am I meant to feel? We must continue; we must unearth all we can because it matters to so many."

Eva squeezed his hand and returned to the table. She was to have left the house to return home that morning, but she had now become fascinated and excitedly immersed in all that was coming to light. She was sifting through the photos of documents that had been with the diaries. "I have a copy of a German military report from the Russian front dated December 1941 from Field Marshal von Brauchitsch to Hitler which is quite extraordinary:

'To: The Führer, Adolf Hitler
'From: Generalfeldmarschall Walther von Brauchitsch
'5th December 1941

'Mein Führer,

You asked that I inform you when German forces are within thirty kilometres of Moscow. I can report that one of our forward battalions today occupied Khimky which is only twenty-eight kilometres from Moscow. Our 2nd and 7th Panzer divisions are within thirty kilometres and making good progress. We have other forward reconnaissance units within sixteen kilometres of Red Square.

We are meeting unexpected resistance from Russian divisions who have been transferred from the far-eastern border of Russia with Japan. A high-ranking Russian prisoner has told us that Moscow was given reliable intelligence assurance that Japan would not attack Russia. This has allowed Ivan to reinforce their defences. Rumour says the source is from a German double agent.

Despite the stiffening resistance, I am confident we can take Moscow, although the weather is deteriorating and slowing our advance. Nothing will stop us achieving complete victory.

'Heil Hitler.'"

She added, "There is a handwritten note from Hess to Churchill clipped to it dated 9th December 1941." Eva continued, "'*Prime Minister, I believe we have achieved our objective and fulfilled all conditions. We can complete the annihilation of Stalin's regime but we desperately need more divisions to defeat their counter-attacks. I trust we may now have the treaty signed? Respectfully, Rudolf Hess, Deputy Führer.*'"

They agreed that copies of both documents should be added to the dossiers as Hans commented, "Hess slipped up there and broke the '*eins zu eins*' principle by putting something in writing. That nicely ties up additional evidence of the British role in clandestine peace talks using the German invasion of Russia as a bargaining chip."

This time, it was Rubin who spoke. "What date is on that military report?" he asked quietly, placing his finger on a page in the diary he was holding.

Eva looked. "5th December 1941."

Rubin looked triumphant. "Hans, check your great-grandmother's entry for 7th December 1941. Does that date not ring a bell?"

Hans was puzzled as he flicked through the pages then the realisation hit him as he read out loud for that date. "'*Today, the Japanese attacked Pearl Harbor, creating a dreadful rumpus here. Winston charged through Ditchley, shouting, "Damn them, but now America will be with us." He summoned me and said that he believed the peace accord negotiated with Hess need not be considered further. I advised that we should discuss other options and allow talks to continue for the moment. I discussed this with Menzies and he agrees that we need to keep Hess on side as he may have more uses. Poor Hess arrived here for talks but Winston said he hadn't time to see him. I had lunch with Rudolf but I suppose I have got to know him quite well. We had a chat about his wife and son, but he was genuinely distressed that peace talks seemed to have stalled. He says he has done all he can but feels that he has been used by Churchill. Winston has delegated the task of further discussions with him to others and peace negotiations are definitely off the Prime Minister's agenda for now.*'"

"I feel sorry for Hess myself," said Eva. "He flew here trying to make peace and fell victim to intrigue and circumstance."

"He was part of their appalling regime." responded Rubin. "Never forget the terrible abuses, the concentration camps, the genocide, the military aggression that killed so many. Anyone who opposed them or spoke out was killed or imprisoned."

"There is more of interest here on 10th December 1941," announced Hans. "'*My goodness, today saw what Winston has been praying for. America have declared war on Germany. Well, actually, Germany issued a declaration first but only because they wanted to declare before the US. Apparently, Roosevelt is happy for another peace initiative with Germany but only if the Germans actually take Moscow. However, they will not consider joining an offensive against Russia. Reports are saying the Germans are close to taking Moscow and many here are secretly hoping they do.'"*

Bernhard turned to Hans. "Is there any evidence of actual terms agreed with Churchill before Pearl Harbor?"

Hans flicked back through the pages carefully as if treating them with reverence. "In June 1941, it looks as if they were close to agreement," he announced, "just before the Germans launched their attack on Russia. Listen to this:

'21st June 1941 – Great excitement as Rudolf Hess has told us the invasion of Russia will commence within the week. Winston arrived at Ditchley and spent the afternoon in discussion with him. At around 3pm, they were joined by Douglas-Hamilton and then Prince George. Douglas joined me afterwards and told me the meeting had been tense. Hess was insisting on a signed agreement, but Churchill refused. Apparently, he said, "Twenty miles is the trigger, take it or leave it," referring to the Jerrys getting near Moscow. Prince George tried to soften things, but Churchill would have none of it. Rudolf has asked for better accommodation and was told he will be moved when the fuss has died down. He is to be allowed drives in the country and even visits to restaurants and pubs provided he keeps it all low-key. I do so hope we can achieve peace.'"

They continued looking through the information, gradually adding the odd scan of a document or diary entry to the dossiers. Bernhard suddenly erupted. "I think we have it; the missing piece of the story, Hans, that was haunting you, *'the great betrayal'*. This is incredible, and to think that British Intelligence didn't cotton on until the 1960s."

32

Plots and Conspiracies

Monday 21st January 1944, 10.30am
HQ SIS, 54, Broadway, Westminster,
London Office of the Director

Greta swept in to meet her chief, surprising him by wearing a uniform for the first time. She marched to his desk, stopped and saluted. "Major Greta Atkins would like to offer her personal congratulations to the general on his promotion, sir!" She had been given her rank upon entering service with the Prime Minister to give her more authority, but she never wore a uniform. General Menzies gave the customary sigh but coughed, mumbling a slightly embarrassed 'thank you' before gesturing her to a chair.

"Miss Atkins," he started, "perhaps I should defer to Major. To business. Yesterday, our man in Madrid intercepted a message from Joachim von Ribbentrop to General Franco asking whether the Spanish would lend their military support on the Eastern Front if the Germans secured a treaty with the Allies. Our friend Albrecht, despite being under surveillance, has managed to get a message to us that there are a growing number of high-ranking Germans who are seeking to make an agreement with the Allies but from varying factions. At the top of the pile are those seeking to depose Adolf Hitler and form a new government. A number of plots have already been hatched, but the Führer is incredibly well guarded. We have even been sent a proposed new German government structure by Carl Friedrich Goerdeler, their former advisor on finance, with named candidates for key positions. Then we have those that wish to negotiate peace in order to prevent Russia from invading Germany. There are others who seek a military alliance between America and Britain against the Soviet Union. I think there is a uniting factor behind all factions in Germany which is the hatred, if not fear, of Russia. I have to say, erm, Major, that there are many here in positions of influence who share that sentiment. Last month, it was agreed by Stalin, Roosevelt and Churchill that Germany should be divided after the war between the major powers, which has put the fear of God into the Jerrys, whilst many in America and here are equally ill at ease. So, perhaps now we have the strongest card to play for peace since the war began. As the old proverb says, '*The enemy of my enemy is my friend*', but, Miss Atkins, who is our enemy?"

"Oh my goodness, sir, surely we cannot be even thinking of making peace or even siding with Hitler now, not after all we have fought for. That is utterly unthinkable to me and I could not countenance such a course."

"Expedience, Miss Atkins, expedience. After all, there are plots afoot in Germany and Hitler may well be removed. We must ask ourselves whether we might wish to live under a constant Russian threat of war or, even worse, a Communist regime in Britain. That too would be unthinkable."

Major General Menzies walked to his bookcase. "Have you ever read Gibbon's *Rise and Fall of the Roman Empire*?" He pulled a large book down, leafing through some pages. "There is a direct parallel here of the fear of barbarian invasion coupled with the collapse of virtue, and as he puts it, '*acquiring the vices of strangers… under a deluge of barbarians*'. No matter." He replaced the book. "Roosevelt and Churchill are wary of the Russian threat in a postwar era and want to explore alternative strategies. Churchill is coming under pressure from the King again because of appalling war casualties, plus a dreadful new German threat from advanced weapons, including pilotless flying bombs. Hitler has announced that these flying bombs will rain on London and the King is appalled at the possibility. We must seize the initiative here and be seen to explore these varied interests using the Russian threat as a bate. To that end, we need to revisit old friends. Rudolf Hess is now staying at the Maindiff Court Centre at Abergavenny, so you may wish to visit."

"After the peace talks floundered in 1941, I thought he was staying at Mytchett Place, near Aldershot," Greta responded.

Menzies looked at her, askance. "Good Lord, do you mean we actually, for once, successfully kept something secret! We had a slight problem with Mytchett. Damned Polskis at a nearby barracks decided to have a go at kidnapping Hess. Rather unfortunate, but we ended up with the British Army defending the Deputy Führer against our Polish allies in a gun battle. There were casualties on both sides, but, thank goodness, no fatalities. We had to move him, but the King insisted he had to be given absolute security as he had given him an assurance of Royal protection."

"Then, sir, I suggest we move him back to Wilton Park Manor House in Beaconsfield, where we had him previously during his negotiations with Churchill. The PM is now using Chequers again as his weekend retreat, which is less than an hour's drive away."

They agreed that Greta should visit Hess and prepare the ground for new negotiations, whilst Menzies would brief Churchill, suggesting covert talks with Germany, using Hess as an intermediary. He stated this would, at very least, satisfy the varying factions whilst avoiding a repeat of any tensions between the King and the government.

Sunday 21st May 1944, 10.00am
Chequers, Buckinghamshire, England

Rudolf Hess sat forward, his brow furrowed, looking intently at the Prime Minister, who frowned back, his jaw set in a resolute look, with a lit cigar in his hand. "Our proposal is simple, Mr Churchill. We propose an immediate armistice and ceasefire on all fronts with the exception of the East. We will surrender all our armed forces to the overall supreme command of the American and British Allies, retaining existing operational command and military structures under the direct authority of the Führer. We will revoke any further territorial claims in Western Europe, and immediately withdraw from Italy and Greece, including the Island of Crete. Further, we will surrender the Channel Islands and allow British forces to operate from there unimpeded. In return, we propose that American and British forces join with us on a great crusade against Soviet Russia. We will be unstoppable, removing the cursed evil of Communism from humanity forever. Mr Churchill, we already have Russians fighting with us who want to liberate their people from the vile dictator Stalin. Surely, it is time for peace between us to spare the pointless loss of life and fight a common foe."

The Foreign Secretary, Anthony Eden, had sat quietly making notes, and he now lowered his glasses to the small table by the side of him. He was dressed impeccably in a suit, a white shirt with a winged collar and dark tie, whilst a neatly folded handkerchief in his top left breast pocket added to his look.

"I must say, Herr Hess," he spoke in a clipped English accent, expressing his words with a preciseness and in a forthright manner, "that whilst one might acknowledge your proposal has some substance, it contains less, in territorial considerations, than you offered in 1941, which causes me some surprise. I would submit that your bargaining chips, shall we say, have been reduced by quite a margin. Indeed, you are, of course, aware that we are poised to launch an invasion which will liberate Europe, forgive my directness, from the tyranny of your country's oppression. Might I suggest, therefore, that you leave out one important matter: that is the question of France and what you propose there?"

Hess looked at the British Foreign Secretary with a disdainful expression. "France is not, using your betting terminology, Mr Eden, on the table." His response was uttered in a ruthless, unyielding manner. "The French declared war on Germany and they would be a threat to Germany if we withdrew whilst we fight to free the East from what you might, more accurately, describe as oppression. You forget our Atlantic Wall, and the impregnable nature of our defences. We are ready for you but," his voice softened, "we want to avoid conflict and the appalling losses that your invasion would cost. The Führer desires peace."

Churchill cut in briefly with a strong, growling voice. "Peace at any price is not peace, Herr Hess, but a capitulation, and you may mark my words, oft repeated, 'We shall never surrender,' which also applies to principle. Now, as we are poised for the greatest of endeavours, it is not beholden upon you or your Führer to dictate any terms, but it is, perhaps, time for you to accept ours. You may tell Mr Hitler that we shall proceed, whatever the cost, unless he concedes to our demands, which, at very least, would require the immediate withdrawal of all your forces from France. That, sir, remains my unwavering position from which I shall not be moved."

As they lunched, before his departure, Hess felt a sense of relief that his proposals were not being turned down by Churchill in their entirety, and that there may be grounds for further discussion. He was only glad that it was not he that would personally present the proposition of a withdrawal from France to the Führer. There was a lively debate over lunch, to which Major General Menzies had been invited, over history and the part that Roman, British and Germanic influences had played in the foundation of the modern world. It was extraordinary, Hess reflected, that they could hold such a civilised, friendly debate, yet they represented two nations at war.

Just over two weeks later, on Tuesday 6th June 1944, in Operation Overlord, the largest seaborne invasion in history took place, in which the combined Allied forces landed on the Beaches of Normandy, France, in what became known as D Day.

Saturday 15th July 1944, 2.00pm
Field Marshal Erwin Rommel's Headquarters, Château de La Roche-Guyon, Northern France

The field telephone rang on his desk and Rommel immediately straightened as he heard the voice at the other end say, "Herr Feldmarschall, this is Berlin, I have the Führer for you. Seconds later, the unmistakeable voice of Adolf Hitler greeted him curtly before speaking of his wish to regain the initiative on the Eastern front and pursue the glorious mission to overthrow Soviet Russia. There followed a lengthy preamble as Hitler outlined the critical need for Lebensraum in order that land could be liberated for an expansion of the Reich. He thanked Rommel for his loyalty and said that he would be rewarded for his steadfast commitment to the protection of Germany, finishing with a summary:

"The resolve of the Allies, shaken by the onslaught of our V1 vengeance weapons, has softened. Their former King Edward was correct in 1940 that effective bombing could 'bring peace'. Three weeks ago, we began hitting London and the weak King George's backbone has failed him. Hess has met with Churchill, whose war-mongering bellicose belligerence has been quelled by our titanic resolve. Now, they have weakened and we can secure the future of the Reich against the satanic tyrants in the East. I am authorising the pact with the Allies of which we have spoken previously. Although I was initially opposed to this, I must concede to a monumental purpose guided by a higher authority. Our great mission is to oppose the world of barbarity in the East, resist the Central Asian flood and free the world from the foul Bolshevik poison. Our momentous struggle can only be compared with the greatest historic events of the past and now I am called to lead this for the future. Eternal Jewry forced on us a pitiless and merciless war. Should we not be able to stop the elements of destruction at Europe's borders, then this continent will be transformed into a single field of ruins. For this ultimate purpose, we must dedicate our unshakeable resolve making sacrifices that would once have been unthinkable even to me. The Operational Orders for this have been prepared and will be signed by myself then flown to you by a trusted courier, SS Sturmbannführer Gunther Roche. These orders will be signed by General Eisenhower, the Supreme Commander of the Allies, and by the commander of their ground forces, General Montgomery. You will sign on behalf of the forces of the German Reich. You will then make plans for the withdrawal of German forces from France and prepare for a massive offensive in the East. This time, the weather will be with us as we execute a new Blitzkrieg with overwhelming superiority and take Moscow within two months. I want that criminal Stalin arrested and put on trial in Berlin. I will be appointing you our supreme commander to plan and execute my orders."

Rommel felt a surge of pride despite having mixed feelings about what was being proposed. He had been made aware of many officers being involved in a plot to remove Hitler from power but had turned down an invitation to join them. He was fiercely loyal by nature and felt the timing for an attack on the leadership was not right when Germany was fighting for survival. He had assured the conspirators that he would not oppose them but could not be complicit in the plot, nor would he put in place contingencies to assume any interim command whilst the coup was taking place. However, he felt that when the time was right, Hitler should step down and a new leadership put in place. Despite this, there was always something about Hitler that commanded his respect with his clarity of vision and purpose which could be inspiring. When he told the Führer he would carry out his orders, he did so with a genuine commitment.

Only that day, Rommel explained, he had written to Hitler proposing that urgent peace talks were undertaken, to which the response was, "Providence, Herr Feldmarschall, providence."

Saturday 15th July 1944, 5.00pm
Reich Chancellery, Wilhelmstrasse, Berlin

Admiral Wilhelm Canaris drove away from the briefing at the Reich Chancellery; his mind in a turmoil. Of course, he wanted an end to the war but could not bear the thought that Hitler might remain in power. But then, he balanced that against what had been described as a great opportunity to save lives and remove the Russian threat to the Fatherland. Russian invasion was unthinkable with the reputation of their troops for brutality against civilians. Whilst he had heard reports of the behaviour of the German SS, which appalled him, his concern was the best outcome for Germany. He knew about the plots against the Führer and reasoned that it was unlikely Hitler would survive for long, but the proposed peace strategy risked strengthening his hold on power.

No-one was safe anymore and he himself had been under house arrest until just a month before. He had been dismissed as head of the Abwehr by Hitler in February 1944 following a series of poor intelligence reports and failures in command. He was under investigation at Himmler's behest, who suspected his loyalties. He was surprised, in many ways, that he had survived after having deliberately falsified intelligence reports with the aim of derailing plans for further mass Jewish extermination. Only six months before, he had secretly met the head of British Intelligence, Major General Stewart Menzies, in Switzerland, to establish areas they could share intelligence with the aim of achieving an end to the war. Yet, the Führer still had faith in him and he was rehabilitated in June and appointed chief of the department for

Economic Combat Measures, known as HWK. With offices in Berlin, it had been responsible for resistance to the Allied economic blockade of Germany. As the war progressed, the role changed to one of miscellaneous administration and coordinating non-combatant military operations.

Canaris had been summoned to a meeting that afternoon with the Führer and leading members of government. They were briefed on an extraordinary secret meeting which had been arranged for two days later between the German military commander in France, Field Marshal Rommel, and the ground commander of the Allied forces, General Montgomery. An agreement would be signed by both commanders whereby hostilities would cease and a military alliance formed against Russia. Germany had agreed to withdraw from France in exchange for unopposed Lebensraum in the East. Hitler had announced, in a dramatic speech, with animated gestures, that it would be a glorious and victorious end to the war resulting in triumph over the Soviet Union, whilst securing the future for the Reich.

Rommel was central to the plan, having previously agreed to coordinate an immediate ceasefire and, on the Führer's command, to surrender the supreme command of the German Forces to General Eisenhower. Canaris knew that Rommel had both the respect and loyalty of his troops and senior officers in the field to ensure the orders were implemented. Hitler had made it plain that anyone in High Command who resisted could be executed under his authority.

Canaris was tasked with organising a covert demilitarised safe area around the scheduled meeting place at Colombelles, in Normandy, where there would be no military activity, without alerting any field commanders of the reason. Weighing up the position, he now decided to divert to the Bendlerblock Military HQ on Bendlerstrasse. Recent times had become increasingly stressful and he had, long ago, abandoned any belief in Hitler and the other current leading figures in government. He had been feeding information for many years on an ad hoc basis to the Allies and was particularly appalled at the treatment of the Jews, many of whom he had helped escape persecution through his Abwehr network. Himmler was watching him like a hawk, wanting to take him down, and he was a dangerous, ruthless adversary. However, his leadership and organisational qualities were considered useful. As he approached the Bendlerblock, he became aware of a brown military Kubelwagon which seemed to be following. He pulled in past the guards, who saluted smartly, and as he left his car, he saw the Kubelwagon stop just outside the parking square and three men in SS uniform approach the guards.

On entering the lobby, he spoke briefly to the receptionist, asking for General Friedrich Olbricht, and moments later, a smiling figure in uniform emerged from the corridor opposite. "Wilhelm, you old sea dog, do you never cease working? I thought you had given up all the cloak-and-dagger routine and now worked regular hours."

As they moved towards the general's office, Canaris spoke softly. "Friedrich, are any involved in Valkyrie here? We need to consider our position urgently in the light of some news I have; but first, I need to fire off signals to commanders in Normandy."

General Friedrich Olbricht was head of the General Army Office and controlled an independent system of powerful communications transmitters which could reach forward positions whilst telephone communication was available for some of the high command operating away from the front. Olbricht stated that he could summon some of those behind Valkyrie to be there within thirty minutes.

Canaris went to the central communications area where an array of around thirty transmitters were positioned on long desks at which sat signal operators in a large room. The noise of tapping could be heard as coded signals were being sent, some to relay stations who could forward messages to German forces on any front. There were Luftwaffe, Kriegsmarine and Wehrmacht operators but no SS, as they had a separate network in another building. Canaris first went to the glass-fronted office overlooking the transmitting stations, where a line of telephones were situated. He barked an order to one of the two operators in the room: "Get me Feldmarschall von Runstedt, *bitte*."

Within minutes, he was speaking to von Runstedt, commander of all German forces in the west, explaining that highly secret testing of the latest new weapons, pilotless flying bombs, was to be undertaken at 0600 hours on 17th July on the Normandy Salient, operating from mobile launchers. All troops were to be cleared from the sector where the firing was to take place. He told the field marshal the weapons programme was being speeded up on the Führer's orders and that no-one was to be informed what was happening. The orders were that Wehrmacht forces evacuate the town of Colombelles, pulling back two kilometres, and that no military action should be taken within that area. He further informed him that Feldmarschall Rommel was supervising this operation and would be visiting.

He made a similar call to General Leo Geyr von Schweppenburg, the commander of Panzer Group West, to be sure that none of his roving units might be in the wrong place at the wrong time. Then, striding back into the main communications centre, he passed a message to one of the operators for local commanders. This said that there was to be a two-kilometre pull-back from Colombelles for regrouping and a counterattack. Within seconds she was tapping the code keys on the Enigma transmitter and Canaris knew the clock was ticking.

He was unaware of the events unfolding outside the building, although it might have added to the imperative of the steps he was taking. Generalfeldmarschall Erwin von Witzleben, the former overall commander of German forces on the Western Front, was arriving in a chauffeur-driven Mercedes approaching the guarded entrance to the complex. Two uniformed SS men approached the vehicle, led by an officer who shouted, "Halt!" followed by two men with their Schmeisser machine guns held at the hip. Von Witzleben was a man who had a reputation, established over forty years, as a ruthless officer who would never suffer a challenge to his authority. He wound his window down. "*Was zur hölle ist los?* ['What the hell is going on?']"

The SS officer looked at him with insolent arrogance. "I will ask the questions and you will answer them. If you do not, then I will have you shot like a dog. I am here with the authority of Reichsführer Himmler. Understand?"

The field marshal exited the car, exclaiming loudly, "You are insubordinate, Major, I outrank you and I am the holder of the Knight's Cross awarded to me by the Führer himself. Get out of the way or I will have you arrested."

The field marshal reached towards his pistol; there was the sound of machine guns being cocked and the two men behind the SS officer raised their weapons. The major responded icily, "We have heard your traitorous words criticising our great struggle against the Russians in the East and your betrayal of your oath of loyalty to the Führer. You will answer my questions. What is the purpose of your visit and who are you meeting?"

The field marshal responded in a raised voice that it was a matter of state secrecy and that if they persisted, he would have them shot. As the SS major reached into his holster for his Luger, the field marshal turned his back on him. At that moment, a sharp voice rang out: "Herr Major, if you draw your weapon, you will die instantly."

The two men behind the SS officer swung round to face a young lieutenant colonel in a grey uniform with a patch over his left eye, behind whom was another officer; both had their handguns drawn. Six more soldiers stood in line behind, all holding their rifles at shoulder height in the firing position.

"You will lower you weapons now. *Schnell!*" The commanding voice was unwavering, and the two SS soldiers immediately complied. "Listen to me carefully, Herr Major, I am Oberst Claus von Stauffenberg. I am assigned to High Command and I have today been in a meeting with the Führer personally. With just one phone call, I can have you arrested and executed, if I do not do this myself now, which I am tempted to do. You will now salute the Generalfeldmarschall and apologise."

The younger officer behind him had now wandered to the side of the SS officer and was holding his handgun with his arms outstretched pointed at the SS major's head, who said curtly, "With respect, Herr Oberst, we have our orders."

Stauffenberg walked within two feet of him, staring directly at him. "You have exactly five seconds to salute and apologise before I allow my men to open fire."

The major clicked his heels and turned to von Witzleben. "Herr Generalfeldmarschall, please accept my apologies. I follow orders. *Heil Hitler.*" He raised his right arm stiffly. His two men followed suit and they were escorted to their vehicle. Stauffenberg told them that if they returned, he would immediately inform the Führer.

As they entered the Bendlerblock, Stauffenberg turned to his fellow officers. "This is what the Fatherland has become which makes our mission even more pressing." Moments later, they entered General Olbricht's office, where the general was talking to Admiral Canaris, who knew all three officers well. Generalfeldmarschall Erwin von Witzleben had a distinguished military career which included commanding the campaign to invade France. Oberst Claus von Stauffenberg was a senior staff officer who was accompanied by his adjutant, Oberleutnant Werner von Haeften. Stauffenberg was organising a coup with the codename Valkyrie, which was to commence with the assassination of Hitler; an action he intended to execute personally. The men in the room were all party to the conspiracy. They briefly considered the altercation in the parking square.

Stauffenberg summarised: "I think we need to have our discussion quickly before the Reichsführer learns of this and has apoplexy."

Within half an hour, after Canaris had briefed them on the planned meeting between Rommel and Montgomery, they had agreed intervention was essential. Whilst peace with the Allies was desirable,

Hitler's position would be strengthened if he was seen to be in an alliance against Russia, attracting many would-be insurgents who saw Russia as a threat. The date for the planned assassination of Hitler had already been set, and they agreed it was vital that the coup, involving many senior commanders, could not be compromised. The action they decided upon was simple to speak of but more difficult to contemplate.

Saturday 15th July 1944, 9.30pm
Holligenstrasse, Bern, Switzerland

Halina Szymańska received the coded message on her short-wave radio. She read it with enormous alarm. Canaris, an old and intimate friend, had guessed correctly that, as she was Polish, she would instinctively oppose any plan that kept Hitler in power, and he knew she worked with British Intelligence. She directly left for the British Embassy, where she gave the required code to gain immediate entry as an intelligence operative needing access to deal with a matter of the highest priority.

In the communications centre, she worded her message carefully to one of her contacts in SIS in London. He worked in communications, and she already knew that he had major Communist sympathies from debates they first had in Switzerland in 1943 when he had accompanied Colonel Menzies for a clandestine meeting with Admiral Canaris to consider peace. The talks had been an opportunity for those opposing Hitler to establish what prospects there may be for an ending of hostilities if there was a coup by the German military. Churchill had refused to even countenance such a strategy and had sent a message back to Canaris stating that his terms for ending hostilities were 'unconditional surrender'; a simple message which had disappointed and frustrated the conspirators against Hitler. Yet now, she thought bitterly, there was an act of utter hypocrisy taking place in that the Allies were prepared to '*do a deal with the devil*' with the prize of an alliance against Russia. She hated both Hitler and Stalin, who had plundered Poland, carving up her homeland between Russia and Germany, in 1939.

Halina had occasional contact with the polite Englishman, who, despite working with SIS, professed that he believed in Marxist doctrines. She had no sympathies with Communism, but she had enjoyed debating the issues with him. She liked to develop useful relationships. This had been an invaluable tactic in her espionage work and she had recognised that he may be useful as someone in British Intelligence whom she could trust if the need arose. The message she typed for transmission was direct, but she was confident it would be sufficient to achieve the objective. She gave a code that identified her as the source then sent: "Critical! On 17th July 1944, at 3.00pm, Rommel will meet Montgomery to sign a ceasefire agreement at the Norman Tower in Colombelles, Normandy. The Allies will form an alliance with Germany against Russia. May prevent imminent plot on Hitler. Rommel will become German Supreme Commander. He must be eliminated. Suggest air-strike on Rommel. Contact Squadron Leader Tadeusz Kotz, in 303 squadron. He knows me and will act on this codeword – *'Powstanie'*." She added some essential details for her plan and watched the clattering teletype, praying that her instincts were correct.

33

The Great Betrayal

Sunday 16th July 1944, 10.00am
Press Section, The War Office, Whitehall, London

Guy Burgess had a hangover and was feeling somewhat irritated that his Sunday morning should be interrupted in this way. The night before, he had gone out to one of his favourite haunts, the Bunch of Grapes, with his manservant Jack Hewitt, returning at around 10.30 to the house he shared on Bentinck Street with an old university friend he had met at Cambridge thirteen years before, Anthony Blunt. On entering the house, Blunt gave him an 'important message' that there was a telex awaiting him at the office from the British Embassy in Berne. By this time, after having consumed a large number of gin and tonics, he was in no mood for work. "What on earth do those blighters want at this time of night? More secret service mumbo-jumbo from the damned Jerrys probably. I wish they would just bump off Adolf like they keep promising instead of being all talk and no action. It can bloody well wait." He then partied the night away with Hewitt and Blunt, drinking cocktails until 2.00am, when he passed out in the drawing room. He had joined Hewitt in bed at around

7.00am but awoke two hours later, recalling the telex, realised that he had better go in and meet '*the call of duty*', and took a taxi to the War Office.

"Oh my dear God," he cried out as he read the words from Halina. The enormity and the implication of her message were staggering, but what she proposed set his mind in turmoil. If he authorised the actions, they would need to be covered up and an appropriate fog created. Fogging was a method used by SIS to cover up actions taken by releasing varying stories or misinformation, some with strands of truth to encourage rumours and speculation, whilst hiding the reality. There would be enormous ramifications and yet he knew that whilst there was a pressing urgency, there needed to be a coherent plan. If he notified his Russian handlers, this could lead to staggering repercussions for which he did not wish to be held responsible. Of course, he wanted peace, but his allegiance was to Communist Russia and had been since his time at Trinity College, Cambridge, when he had accepted the utter bankruptcy of capitalism.

Friendships forged at Cambridge allowed him to be recruited as a Russian spy, when he was tasked with penetrating British Intelligence. He had joined the BBC in 1936, a useful cover, which enabled him to build up a network of contacts in politics. Having successfully infiltrated British Intelligence through social connections, he carried out freelance assignments for a number of years, providing an information conduit to Russia. The message from Halina, if revealed to his handlers, would potentially lead to a Russian military attack on the British, which, despite his loyalties, he could not countenance. Instigating the action required must not compromise his cover as a Russian spy. Finally, he decided on a direction and dialled a number.

Greta Atkins had been planning a quiet Sunday after an exhausting week attempting to coordinate the signing of the Operational Orders. She had been liaising between Hess and Downing Street, effecting a strategy to which she was utterly opposed. She too desired peace but could not accept any policy which would leave Hitler in power and potentially betray those who sought to remove him, which included her old friend Albrecht Haushofer.

"Greta, its Guy Burgess. I'm at the War Office and I need to see you urgently. Can we meet somewhere?"

Sunday 16th July 1944, 12.00am
Wiltons Restaurant, Jermyn Street, St James, London

Burgess had called Jimmy Marks, the proprietor, known affectionately as 'mine host', and secured a private dining room. He arrived first and had ordered two Mary Pickford cocktails, instructing the head waiter how to mix the rum, pineapple juice, grenadine and maraschino liqueur. Greta arrived shortly afterwards, looking immaculate in an angled large wide-brimmed hat with a net over her eyes, a cream double-breasted mackintosh, under which she wore a three-quarter-length black dress with a thick white belt and shiny patent leather high-heel shoes. Burgess could not help but admire her, always appearing beautiful no matter the occasion. He was dressed more simply in a subtle pinstriped three-piece suit, blue and white striped tie, and a white silk handkerchief in his breast pocket. His hair had a wave at the front but was neat and shone.

As he began to tell her his news, she interrupted him, "Guy, it is my department who have been organising this. Only yesterday, I was with Mr Churchill and Rudolf Hess at Chequers finalising the dreadful details for this ill-advised plan. The crazy thing is that we know there is a plot to kill Hitler, and this, in my view, may well backfire on us uniting Germans behind Hitler in a common purpose of defeating Russia."

"Listen, old girl, I have more for you. Halina has Polish contacts in RAF Fighter Command. She has passed on the name of a squadron leader who does intelligence reports for her from time to time. That woman seems to have her finger in even more pies than you!" He smiled for a moment at the mock shock on her face before continuing. "Awful business, really, but she suggests we make contact with this RAF chap, give him this codeword *'powstanie'* and tell him the location of Rommel. She says he will organise a strike but then we will need to fog this because no-one must know the source of the information nor who is responsible. Clearly, the Germans will blame the British for the breaking of the promise we gave of safe passage. Churchill will be livid and Hitler will believe he has been betrayed. Halina is certain that if Rommel is taken out of the equation, this plan will fail, and trust me, I know these Poles: if they sniff a German target of such prominence, nothing will stop them."

Greta agreed that she would make contact with the Polish officer and follow it with the fogging of operational information for the day. She assured Burgess that she could rely on the involvement and covert support from the head of SIS, Major General Menzies, who was also opposed to the planned ceasefire. They ordered Irish coffee after finishing a raspberry pavlova, which they agreed added a delicious sense of decadence to the day, making light of the grim operation they were putting in motion.

Sunday 16th July 1944, 4.00pm
Office of Squadron Leader Tadeusz Kotz, RAF Westhampnett, 303 Squadron, Near Chichester, West Sussex

The day had already been too long with sorties that had started at 7.00am with the continuation of daylight bombing raids of new German rocket weapon-launching facilities being constructed across occupied Europe. Their missions were to escort bombers, but the fighters were also ordered to engage any targets on the return leg over France, especially over Normandy, where fierce ground fighting was raging after the Allied landings nearly six weeks before. Kotz had already flown three sorties that day and he was tired. He was nearly thirty-one years old but would have passed for forty. There was a constant need to keep a sharp and wary eye open for Luftwaffe fighter aircraft that would await over the Channel at high altitude. There they would dive out of the sun, using speed and surprise as their key tactics, attacking from behind and catching British pilots unaware. His eyes were heavy and strained, and the last weeks since D Day had been demanding and relentless. Despite this, he remained a cheerful figure on the base, inspiring those around him to 'never give up', a phrase he borrowed from a speech he had heard Winston Churchill give.

He had just lit his pipe, puffing thick clouds of smoke into the air, when the phone rang. "*Do chelery!* ['Damn it!'] Not more missions today," he said as he picked the phone up. "Squadron Leader Kotz."

Then his posture changed and he stiffened in his chair as he heard one word in a strong female voice: "*Powstanie.*" It was not pronounced correctly, but he recognised the codeword immediately. "Squadron Leader," the voice continued, "I am a major from British Intelligence. Please listen carefully. This message is from Halina Szymańska, whom you know, and she is working with us. On Monday 17th July 1944, Field Marshal Rommel will visit various bases in Normandy. He is scheduled to leave the town of Colombelles at 5.00pm and will proceed, driven in his staff car, down the N179 heading back to his HQ at La Roche-Guyon. He will not be escorted because he is on a highly secret assignment. The mission is to attack and eliminate. We suggest the deployment of two aircraft only, but you should not inform anyone of the purpose of the sortie. As the source of this intelligence could be identified, this must not be recorded nor must you divulge that you have been given this information. British Intelligence will deny that we contacted you. You may discover in coming days that many claim they were involved in the attack. You must never do so. Do I make myself clear, Squadron Leader?"

As he was gathering his thoughts, he replied in Polish, despite speaking English well: "*Tak* ['Yes'], Major."

Greta's voice had assumed an edge of authority. "This is your chance to make history and help shorten the war. Good luck."

Monday 17th July 1944, 4.00pm
Colombelles, Normandy, France

Feldmarschall Erwin Rommel rose from the makeshift table looking at General Montgomery directly. "We are in the hands of those who manipulate our fate, I think," he remarked acidly.

General Montgomery also stood, straightening his beret with the two distinctive badges giving him an individual much-admired identity with those under his command. "'*Ours not to reason why,*' old chap, I'm afraid, '*ours but to do and die.*' We just obey orders." Rommel chuckled. "Your poet Alfred Lord Tennyson, I believe. We are old foes, but just maybe we will now join forces and fight a common enemy. Perhaps history will say we made an invincible partnership."

"I doubt that," Montgomery retorted. "I'm told that I am insufferable, if not impossible. However, I have come to respect you and I do hope we will meet again in better circumstances."

They both left the building, each holding a briefcase containing the signed Operational Orders. Rommel clicked his heels, then shook hands with his old adversary, adding, "'*He alone is great and happy who fills his own station of independence, and has neither to command nor to obey.*' Johann Wolfgang von Goethe, a great German writer, *ja?*" He saluted and executed a smart about-turn, walking from the base of the tower to his waiting car.

Montgomery turned to his adjutant, who had been waiting outside. "At least we didn't have to suffer the banality of a *Heil Hitler.*"

As Rommel was driven away in the front of his open Horch staff car, he turned and remarked grimly to Major Neuhaus, who had accompanied him for the day visiting troops in the forward lines. "I wonder whether we will still be able to drive here tomorrow or, soon perhaps, anywhere in Normandy." As he was expected for a meeting with von Ribbentrop that evening, he asked his driver, Feldwebel Daniel, to get them back fast, then, turning again, he spoke to an aircraft spotter he had brought with them, Feldwebel Hoike, "Please watch carefully, the Allied aircraft are operating everywhere."

As they were approaching Livarot, Hoike alerted them to a number of aircraft that he could see diving in the distance and there was rising smoke ahead. They heard the sound of explosions and decided to divert onto a back road leading to Sainte-Foy-de Montgomery, three kilometres north of Vimoutiers.

Squadron Leader Tadeusz Kotz banked his Spitfire Mk IX to the left, heading away from Caen, where he and his chosen wingman, Flight Sergeant Stanislaw Czezowski, had attracted both flak and small arms fire, then dropped down to four hundred feet, scanning the main roads heading towards Vimoutiers. He had informed Czezowski that their mission was to test two newly modified Spitfires that they had picked up a few days before in order to acclimatise themselves before the entire squadron was equipped with them. As they had left RAF Westhampnett four hours before, they had climbed to over forty thousand feet, way above the operating ceiling of their previous 'Spits'. They had dived down as they approached the French coastline, trying out differing manoeuvres and enjoying a rare moment of freedom from the normal disciplined requirements of an operational sortie. They had refuelled at the temporary airfield at Bény-sur-Mer, where they lunched with Canadian pilots stationed with 412 Squadron which was tasked with flying strafing missions to soften up German defences facing the Allied invasion force.

Taking off at 1600 hours, Kotz had informed Czezowski that they should seek out ground targets and trial the new heavier armaments with which the new aircraft had been fitted. He ordered his No 2 to follow him above and behind to watch his tail whilst he scanned the roads for targets. As they reached Falaise, they roared east towards Vimoutiers, where he turned to circle south of the town, intending to double back and then follow the road west to Falaise. Just as they were about to change course, he noticed a vehicle travelling fast up a tree-lined road to their left side. He rocked his wings from side to side and turned, diving down to 150 feet. As they approached, he could see it was an open-topped staff car and he felt the adrenalin rush as he flicked the safe off his gun and cannon buttons. The vehicle had turned off into a more densely wooded lane but was clearly in view as he banked steeply, turning in an arc, bringing his height even lower. He levelled his sights and felt his aircraft judder as he fired a long burst of his 20mm cannon, seeing the flashes as his shots hit the car, which veered left then right before turning over on its side, smoke already pouring from its engine, with one occupant thrown clear. He climbed, turning again, then shouted into his radio, "Let's finish this." Both aircraft banked, then swooped down, opening up with heavy machine guns as flames began erupting from the car. Two bodies were clearly visible on the grass verge with a third slumped over the wheel. As they climbed away, wingtip to wingtip, Kotz looked across at Czezowski, who was clearly visible, excitedly giving a thumbs-up.

By the end of the following day, the Allies had taken Colombelles giving a prophetic truth to Rommel's words as he had been driven away from his meeting with Montgomery. Two days later, on 20th July 1944, Oberst Claus von Stauffenberg detonated a bomb at the Wolf's Lair headquarters at Rastenburg, East Prussia, in a room in which Hitler was meeting senior officers. The plan was to detonate two bombs simultaneously but due to the meeting starting early, there was only time to prepare the time fuses on one, reducing the effectiveness of the blast. The plot very nearly succeeded. Three senior officers were killed, plus a stenographer, and thirteen others were wounded. The wheels had already been set in motion for a coup which failed, with terrible consequences for the conspirators. Hitler survived despite sustaining injuries including two punctured ear drums, blisters, burns and two hundred wood splinters in his hands and legs.

Feldmarschall Erwin Rommel suffered serious head injuries in the air attack with multiple skull fractures and glass fragments imbedded in his face. He spent several weeks in a French hospital before returning to Germany to recuperate but was forced to commit suicide on 14th October 1944 for his suspected involvement in the plot to kill Hitler.

The Barbarossa Secret was never raised by the Führer again except its secrecy being used as a bargaining chip to gain him safe passage to Argentina in May 1945. He vowed that the treachery of those around him would be avenged which had robbed the world of the chance to eliminate the Russian threat.

34

Pandora's Box

Wednesday 26th February 2020, 2.00pm
Pinneberger Strasse, Hamburg

They had sat open-mouthed as Bernhard had read entry after entry from Greta's diary of 1944 learning of the great betrayal. "There is a poignant entry here dated 18th July, Hans, which is quite personal. You may wish to read it."

Hans took the diary from him, reading out loud slowly, bringing a very real emotional connection to their endeavours. "'*Yesterday, I feel as though I betrayed my conscience. We have heard news that Rommel is fighting for his life after an air attack. In one sense, his involvement would have led to peace, but at what cost? I have blood on my hands and, if he dies, it will have been because I was complicit. Strange how I can be part of the 'war effort' and yet I am concerned about the death of someone who was, or is, part of the enemy. Many will die because of what I have done, and that feels unbearable. Russia is saved and we will eventually have victory, but tonight I have cried. I can only hope that the plot to remove Hitler succeeds, but Winston says he will not allow any further negotiation with the Germans. What have I done and how will I be judged?*'"

Hans felt his voice falter as he finished, sitting back down in an armchair with a long sigh. It was Eva who spoke first. "Grandmother was a wonderful person and you have inherited many of her qualities Hans. You can be very proud of what she did, I think."

Bernhard had picked up a diary for 1945 which contained references to further discussions with Rudolf Hess on the safe passage of Hitler out of Berlin. Entries described how arrangements were initially put in place for him to escape via his own private aircraft which the Allies guaranteed they would not attack. He read a further passage out loud: "*'The Russians are not involved in the discussions over Hitler, and Churchill states it is imperative that he does not fall into their hands. If the Barbarossa Secret is revealed, the Prime Minister said it would lead to another war and any agreements negotiated on the post-war make-up of Europe would be meaningless.'*"

Eva, who was sifting through further photographs, suddenly exclaimed excitedly, "There is a handwritten letter from King George VI here to Churchill, which is dynamite. Listen to this:

Buckingham Palace
Friday 20th April 1945

'My dear Winston,

'I want to raise some final questions that will, no doubt, continue to be a concern to both of us now and after this war is over.

'We must take every precaution to secure the secrets we share and one, in particular, carrying the words of our arch-enemy, which I am loathe to repeat but to which we are bound, "eins zu eins". We have here a mutual deterrent that secures Europe and assures survival of certain parties, despite one's natural distaste for this after the dreadful carnage we have endured.

'Hitler is making demands which, under any normal circumstances, as vanquished to victor, would be unreasonable, but he does hold, to use a simile that you have oft employed with myself, some of the ace cards here. I understand his plan is for Germany to dominate a new post-war Europe economically rather than militarily. We may, at very least, be thankful that, at last, they appear to be abandoning their military aspirations.

'I would urge that we use every endeavour to obtain German scientific research papers into nuclear fission which must not fall into Soviet hands. Additionally, the Americans are keen for certain scientists to be given over to them, especially those involved in the V1 and V2 rocket projects which, I think, is perfectly reasonable and to which purpose, we should give every assistance.

'I am assured by my contacts within Argentina that safe haven will be offered to certain guests and I am delighted that one, in particular, has given an assurance that he will remain silent to the world after his departure from Germany.

'There are, of course, other sensitive papers that we must urgently secure concerning the dealings with my family, the Saxe Coburgs and, not least, my brother.

'Might I suggest you place the Orders of which we are both privy into the care of the Royal Archive which will secure them from political scrutiny for all time, or, at least, until they have no relevance.

'Finally, I have spoken to a dear friend, Hugh Trevor Roper, a highly respected historian, who has agreed to give the official version of the impending demise of "the Reich" his personal attention, ensuring the facts meet the historical narrative. He is also known personally to Major General Menzies, who will give the necessary intelligence input. I trust you will agree that he is the ideal candidate.

'I now think it utterly critical that every effort is made to protect our position and ensure safe extraction and delivery of what might be described ironically as our asset before it is too late.

> *We have navigated troubled waters together, and whilst I may not have always agreed the direction, the destination is, undoubtedly, one of which we can be justifiably proud, not least because of your steadfast leadership.*
> *Believe me,*
> *Your very sincere friend,*
>
> *'George R.I. (Rex Imperator – King and Emperor)'."*

Hans walked over to where some bottles of wine stood. He opened one and poured out four glasses with a smile of relief. "I think our story is nearing completion or, perhaps, just beginning. To our future. *Prost.*" Rubin's phone began buzzing, and he spoke rapidly in Hebrew for a minute; after terminating the call he announced,

"That was our friend Moshe, who has been released without harm by Göring after Mossad's intervention in return for an assurance regarding the release of that low-life Karl Schmidt. Moshe has been speaking with Schmidt, who knows nothing of this arrangement. He is suddenly becoming very cooperative, having been told he can either be flown to Israel and turned over to Mossad central for interrogation or released to Göring if he talks to us now. He has confirmed that specific orders were given to kill your father by none other than Reichsmarschall Göring, even if he had surrendered the Orders."

Hans turned to his mother. "At least we now know and that has made the decision, which I now wish to make, much easier. We need this story releasing in England not Germany, where it will be hushed too easily. This is a decision for my father, for the civilised world and for those who died for the greater good. Each life is one precious individual."

Wednesday 11th March 2020, 10.00am Offices of The Daily Telegraph, 111 Buckingham Palace Road, London

The motorcycle courier entered, proceeding to the plush reception area. "Package for the editor. Needs signing for and, blimey, it looks like something from the war." Across the front was an eagle clutching a wreath but without the swastika in the centre. Underneath in gothic letters were printed the words '*Bestellung vom Führer*'. The receptionist took one look and called a number on her phone, bidding him wait. Then, after explaining what was on the front of the package, she turned to the courier. "Has your company looked after this since despatch, and, if so, can you identify the sender?" He replied that it was a franchise operation and that they could only trace it back to a source location, which was a depot in Munich, Germany. There was no return address given. Moments later, two security guards arrived to look at the package, which was labelled '*Papiere*'. After putting the parcel through a scanner, they took it to a lower room, where it was gingerly opened by an operative in protective clothing, mask and helmet. As he opened the outer covering, there was an inner wrapping, which he peeled back to reveal a thick black file, on the front of which was the eagle and swastika logo of the Third Reich; below which was written:

THE BARBAROSSA SECRET

(Generalplan Reich und Unternehmen Willi)
Chef Sache – Streng Geheim – Top Secret
Eins Zu Eins

BESTELLUNG VOM FÜHRER

ADOLF HITLER

The security operative's expletives were clearly picked up by those watching him open the package on camera. "Christ, guys, we need to show this to the managing editor now."

Similar scenes were occurring at the offices of the BBC, ITN, *The Guardian*, the *Daily Mail*, *The Independent* and *The Times*. The Director General of the BBC called his opposite number, the CEO of ITN News, both agreeing to do nothing before calling a number they used rarely and only where matters of national security were at stake.

Wednesday 11th March 2020, 11.00am
Office of the Head of MI6, Sir Alex Younger AKA 'C',
HQ British Intelligence, SIS Building, Vauxhall Cross, London

Tony Lord, the Director General of the BBC, was studying one of the two files he had brought with him, having borrowed the other from the offices of ITN on the promise he would return it. This was open on the table in front of the Head of MI6, who was leafing through it methodically, every now and then turning pages back to cross-reference dates and information. The phone buzzed, which he snatched to his ear. "Which national newspapers? Jesus Christ, contact every editor and state that this is being declared a matter of national security. From the top, the advice is to issue no statements. Get special branch to seize every file they can find now." He slammed the phone down, returning to his file. They were thick ring binders containing plastic wallets in which documents and photographs were placed in date order, starting with a letter from the Duke of Saxe-Coburg and Gotha to King George V dated June 1932. "Oh my Lord, Tony," C muttered as he scanned more of the content, then again: "Oh, for Christ's sake, you must be joking, this is staggering stuff." He moved to his desk and pressed a button; a voice on loudspeaker answered within seconds. "Mark, it's C, I need to see the PM now. This is code red. No, it can't wait until then, I mean in thirty minutes. Get him out of Cabinet. Thank you."

Within minutes, he was being driven in an emergency vehicle with blue lights flashing over Vauxhall Bridge then weaving in and out of traffic heading towards Westminster, passing the Houses of Parliament into Whitehall, then past the police guards through the already open gates to Downing Street. The journey had taken eight minutes and the polished black door of No 10 was swiftly opened to let him through. Met inside the door by the Cabinet Secretary, Sir Mark Sedwill, he was ushered down the simple maroon carpet flanked by the black and white tiled floor through double doors, down a corridor and straight into the PM's office.

As he entered, the PM rose from behind his double pedestal desk to greet him, shaking his hand. Boris Johnson appeared tired and his face showed the strain of recent days as the impact of the forthcoming coronavirus pandemic was becoming a stark reality. However, he still managed a smile. "I can't say I'm delighted to see you, Alex, what's happening?"

C extracted the black file from his case, handing it to the PM. "Please peruse this lot, sir, I'm afraid it's a big one. Involves the Royal Family as well, unfortunately."

"Holy Mother of God" was the response after just a few seconds. In the ensuing minutes there were further expletives. The Prime Minister called in his Cabinet Secretary, giving him a summary briefing. The reaction was complete and utter astonishment from a man who was renowned for remaining calm in any crisis. The PM pointed out a couple of the documents, including the April 1945 letter from George VI to Churchill confirming royal collusion in a historical cover-up. Then, he stood upright and assumed a commanding tone. "Mark, we are issuing 'D' notices to all media preventing publication in relation to this damned file."

C interjected, "I have taken the liberty to request the police to seize all copies they can, and all social media have been ordered to block anything that might be related to this, particularly content containing the word Barbarossa. I think we can contain this, as no news outlet wants to breach a 'D' notice issued in the interests of national security. They know the kind of repercussions that may result."

Within seconds texts and emails were being sent from the intelligence office of Downing Street, and within two hours of the packages being delivered, all media had been contacted and restrained by the orders of the UK government and British Intelligence. The Prime Minister was nervous and paced his office, discussing the position with the Head of MI6. His head was buzzing as he had received the latest briefing on the alarming spread of the coronavirus. He had decided to make a broadcast to the nation the following day which would be the most difficult speech of his political career. He needed this on top like a hole in the head. He had been horrified to see the first draft of his speech in which he had been advised to inform the population that they would lose loved ones before their time.

As he dwelt on the ramifications of the file he had been perusing, a call came through to C, who paled visibly, then he rose from his chair. "Sir, we have a problem: someone by the name of Rubin Horowitz, who is a freelancer loosely connected to Mossad and the Wiesenthal centre, has tweeted that Britain and America were involved in a secret deal brokered with Adolf Hitler to keep him in power, supporting an attack on Russia. The tweet says that Churchill was being threatened with dismissal by the King if he did not cooperate." The PM was burying his face in his hands, shaking his head. "I'm afraid there's more," C continued gravely. "He has put a video up claiming that the Allies actually offered to join forces with Germany in 1944 and turn on Russia. Even worse, he states there is a secret Führer operating in Germany. The whole thing has gone viral and although the content has been taken down, it is too late to put a lid on it."

At that moment, the Cabinet Secretary entered. "Prime Minister, I have had the Israeli Prime Minister on the phone demanding to speak with you. I regret, sir, I have also taken a call from RT, who are saying they must have a statement from you or they will release the story in the UK on their news."

The PM ran his fingers through his unruly blond hair, then muttered the word, "Containment," before turning to the waiting Cabinet Secretary. "Get Premier Vladimir Putin on the hotline. Now! Oh, and tell Benjamin Netanyahu I will speak with him in thirty minutes" He turned to 'C'. "This is going to cost us so much, and Putin will love the leverage it gives him. God help Ukraine and other Eastern European states. How the hell did they manage to keep this thing secret for so long?"

'C' looked up from the file he had been studying. "I think, sir, it was called *'eins zu eins'*."

Epilogue

Monday 21st December 2020, 1.00pm Eilat, Southern Israel

"You see how we look after our own people." Rubin Horowitz smiled at Hans, who had just returned from receiving his covid-19 vaccination courtesy of Israeli intelligence. "You receive yours only two days after Prime Minister Benjamin Netanyahu!"

"Only because you need what I have agreed to share with you," Hans countered, touching Rubin's glass in a mock toast. Rubin had taken him for his jab and they had returned to take delivery of an appetising lunch prepared by Omer's, a local restaurant, which they had enjoyed on the outer terrace overlooking the sea on what was a warmer-than-average day. They were now sitting on the veranda of the villa both Hans and Bernhard had been living in since their escape the previous April. Initially, they had been given personal protection from Mossad agents in Germany, but the situation had become untenable as the BND had demanded they be handed over for questioning on espionage charges. They had been taken to an airstrip in Bavaria, from where they were flown out by private jet to Israel. Eva had elected to stay behind and try to live her life normally. She had agreed to cooperate with the authorities and, after suffering initial questioning, they realised that because matters were now being dealt with on a damage limitation basis, they had to tread carefully, releasing her without charge.

Bernhard had decided to settle in the USA, where he continued to write on a freelance basis with a new identity arranged for him. Hans had opted to remain under the protection of Israel until matters settled but was intending to publish the complete story in conjunction with Bernhard, with whom he was in daily contact. They had already been offered very large sums of money for exclusives but were taking the time to assimilate the enormous amount of material they had gathered. In addition, the covid-19 crisis had overtaken global imperatives and they had concluded that the world could wait a little longer.

Rubin and Hans sipped the Recanati Winery Special Reserve Cabernet Sauvignon, looking out across to the port through the palm trees and shrubs bordering the villa. Hans leant forward, sighing deeply.

"You know, I often think of how much this all affected my great-grandmother, Greta. She never really got over the contradictions in her role or the personal compromises she had to make. She stayed on working for SIS until 1952 when the chief, Menzies, retired. I think there was possibly something going on between them, reading between the lines. Her father left her a tidy sum and she settled in King's Lynn in Norfolk, living out her life quietly. She rarely mixed with those she had known before the war although she stayed in touch with Diana Mitford in Paris. Isn't that an ultimate irony considering Diana was married to Mosley and socialised with Hitler?"

"Was it all worth the sacrifices you have had to make, Hans, or do you regret exposing the greatest cover-up in history?" Rubin asked.

"So many lives lost, so many betrayed," Hans replied ruefully, "and then there was the hypocrisy of those who were supposed to be dedicated to a higher purpose but who put their own agenda before principle. I cannot help but paraphrase the words of that poor man Albrecht Haushofer, in the sonnet he wrote in his cell before he was shot by the Nazis: many 'should have more sharply called evil evil'."

Rubin stood up to go. "I think, my friend, that is the way of all humanity, that we fail to call evil evil loudly enough. *Shalom chaver.*"

In Memoriam

To The Following German Opponents Of Hitler
(List covers those mentioned in this book only)

Generaloberst Ludwig Beck – Chief of General Staff from 1935 - 1938. Opposed many of Hitler's policies but was initially tolerated. Resigned in August 1938 after disagreements with Hitler over his military expansionism. After resignation, plotted with others to overthrow Hitler and would have been Head of State had the July 20th plot succeeded. Arrested on 20th July 1944 and attempted suicide with his pistol, and after seriously wounding himself, was shot by his captors in the back of the neck

Admiral Wilhelm Canaris – German admiral and chief of the Abwehr, the German military intelligence service from 1935 to 1944. Involved in secret peace negotiations with the Allies. Helped many Jews escape persecution. 9th April 1945 – executed by hanging naked, Flossenbürg concentration camp.

Carl Friedrich Goerdeler – conservative German politician, Mayor of Leipzig, executive, economist, civil servant and opponent of the Nazi regime. Planned post-Nazi government. Assisted Jews to escape Germany and avoid deportation. 2nd February 1945 – executed by hanging, Plötzensee Prison, Berlin.

Albert Göring – German engineer and businessman and the younger brother of Hermann Göring. Albert was opposed to Nazism, and he helped Jews and others who were persecuted in Nazi Germany. He survived but was shunned in post-war Germany because of his family name, dying without any public recognition in 1966. His humanitarian efforts were not recognised until decades after his death.

Oberleutnant Werner von Haeften – a decorated officer in the Wehrmacht. After being severely wounded on the Eastern Front in 1943, he became adjutant to Oberst Claus von Stauffenberg. 21st July 1944 – executed by firing squad, Bendlerblock Army HQ, Berlin. At his execution, he threw himself in front of shots meant for Claus von Stauffenberg.

Karl Haushofer – German general, professor, geographer, and politician. Imprisoned in Dachau concentration camp for eight months. 10th March 1946 – poisoned in grounds of his estate at Pähl/Ammersee, Bavaria (possible suicide).

Albrecht Haushofer – son of Karl Haushofer. German geographer, diplomat, writer and member of the German resistance to Nazism. Arrested in Bavaria, 7th December 1944. 22nd April 1945 – shot in the neck by the SS outside Moabit Prison, Berlin, after which his body was left in the street.

General Friedrich Olbricht – German general during World War II and one of the conspirators involved in the 20th July plot to assassinate Hitler which he personally planned. 21st July 1944 – executed by firing squad, Bendlerblock Army HQ, Berlin.

General Hans Oster – general in the Wehrmacht of Nazi Germany and a leading figure of the German resistance to Hitler from 1938. 9th April 1945 – executed by hanging naked, Flossenbürg concentration camp.

Generalfeldmarschall Irwin Rommel – German general and military theorist. Popularly known as the Desert Fox after commanding the Afrika Korps. In command of German Defences on D Day. Highly popular with troops. Passive opponent of Hitler but would not participate in plot with conspirators. 14th October 1944 – forced 'suicide' after being suspected of supporting 20th July plot on Hitler. Given choice of taking poison near his home in Herrlingen, Southern Germany, and being given a state funeral with his family looked after, or face trial in Berlin with disgrace and consequences for family.

Oberst Claus von Stauffenberg – German army officer, decorated for bravery fighting in Russia. Transferred to North Africa and fought in panzer division. Lost one eye, a hand and two fingers of his left hand. A staff officer in 1944, he helped plan and execute the plot to kill Hitler. On 20th July, he placed the bomb next to the table leg where Hitler was sitting. 21st July 1944, 1.00am – executed by firing squad lit by the headlights of a truck, Bendlerblock Army HQ, Berlin.

Generalfeldmarschall Erwin von Witzleben – German field marshal in the Wehrmacht during World War II. He commanded part of the German force invading France in 1940 but was a critic of the invasion of Russia in 1941. He was a leading conspirator in the 20th July plot to assassinate Adolf Hitler and would have become supreme commander of the German army had the plot succeeded. 7th August 1944 – hanged with a thin hemp rope-like piano wire at Plötzensee Prison in Berlin. Filmed for Hitler's pleasure.

In addition to those mentioned in this book involved in the assassination attempt on Hitler in 1944, a further twenty thousand were tragically executed by the Nazi regime in the purge following the 20th July plot. (There were over forty plots on Hitler's life, some of which came close to success, including a bomb planted on the aircraft in which he was flying which failed to detonate on 13th March 1943.)

To the estimated six million Jews and eleven million others (Russians, Slavs, Poles, gypsies, those with disabilities, holders of certain religious beliefs, homosexuals, repeat criminal offenders and opponents of the regime) who perished in the Nazi concentration camps – *each life is one precious individual.*

To all who sacrificed so much in the course of World War II.
"We will remember them."

Postscript

Extract from Moabit Sonnets by Albrecht Haushofer – written at Moabit Prison in April 1945 just before his execution by the SS.

I am guilty,
But not in the way you think.
I should have earlier recognized my duty;
I should have more sharply called evil evil; I reined
in my judgment too long.
I did warn,
But not enough, and not clearly enough;
And today I know what I was guilty of

Biographical Index

(Alphabetical)

Nancy Witcher Langhorne Astor, Viscountess Astor: 19th May 1879–2nd May 1964. An American-born British politician who was the first woman (seated) Member of Parliament for Plymouth Sutton from 1919 to 1945. Divorced her first husband in 1903 and married Waldorf Astor in May 1906. She espoused many causes, including equal treatment of English-speaking peoples in an expanding empire. She organised a group of intellectuals called the Cliveden Set (named after her home), who embraced some aspects of National Socialism which von Ribbentrop reported to Hitler. After the war, she continued to espouse beliefs that were considered outdated or politically embarrassing. She became increasingly isolated after the death of her husband in 1952.

Clement Attlee: 3rd January 1883–8th October 1967. 1st Earl Attlee. Prime Minister of the UK from 1945 to 1951 and Leader of the Labour Party from 1935 to 1955. He was three times Leader of the Opposition (1935–40, 1945, 1951–55) Served as officer in World War I. Attlee took Labour into Churchill's wartime coalition government in 1940, initially as Lord Privy Seal, and then as Deputy Prime Minister from 1942. Under his Government the NHS was formed, worker's rights improved and the welfare state established. Voted against joining EEC.

Colonel Juan Luis Beigbeder y Atienza: 31st March 1888–6th June 1957 A Spanish military and political leader served as Minister of Foreign Affairs between 12th August 1939 and 16th October 1940, during the rule of Francisco Franco. A major participant in fighting for Franco in the Spanish Civil War. His mistress was Rosalinda Powell Fox, who assisted British Intelligence.

Ernest Bevin: 9th March 1881–14th April 1951. A Labour politician, and General Secretary of the Transport and General Workers' Union. Served as Minister of Labour and National Service in the wartime coalition government. Served as Foreign Secretary in the post-war Labour government under Clement Atlee and helped in the adoption of the atomic bomb. He strongly opposed Communism, oversaw the end of British rule in India, and the independence of India and Pakistan.

Anthony Charles Lynton Blair: born 6th May 1953. A British Labour politician. Prime Minister of the United Kingdom from 1997 to 2007 and Leader of the Labour Party from 1994 to 2007. Led Britain into war against Iraq claiming that they had weapons of mass destruction (WMD) which turned out not to be true. He subsequently became Special Envoy to the Middle East in a diplomatic post until 2015. He now works for the Tony Blair Institute for Global Change, established in 2016. He is the only Labour leader to form three consecutive majority governments.

Obergruppenführer Ernst Wilhelm Bohle: 28th July 1903–9th November 1960. The leader of the foreign organization of the National Socialist German Workers' Party from 1933 until 1945. Born in England, he moved to South Africa with his father. Later education in Berlin, where he forged a career in commerce. Joined Nazi Party 1932. Was a member of the Reichstag from 1933 until 1945.

Reichsleiter and Obergruppenführer Martin Ludwig Bormann: 17th June 1900–2nd May 1945? Head of the Nazi Party Chancellery. He gained immense power as Hitler's private secretary from 1935, controlling access to Hitler. Joined the Nazi party in 1927 and the SS in 1937. Overseer of renovations at the Berghof, Hitler's property at Obersalzberg. Controlled aspects of Nazi finance with reports saying he amassed a fortune used to finance post-war activities. Last time officially seen May 1945 outside Hitler's Berlin bunker. Reports from Argentina claim sightings in the 1950s and 1960s. DNA evidence from a body found in Germany claimed to be Bormann's was later discredited.

Eva Anna Paula Braun: 6th February 1912–30th April 1945? Mistress to Adolf Hitler, with whom she lived from 1936 until the end of her life, although some reports claim they parted in the late 1950s. Married Hitler in the Führerbunker in Berlin on 29th April 1945. Official version of death is that they both committed suicide on 30th April 1945. Their bodies were never found.

George Walker Bush: born 6th July 1946. An American politician and businessman. Elected forty-third president of the United States from 2001 to 2009. A member of the Republican Party, he had formerly been governor of Texas. His father, George HW Bush, was the fortyfirst president of the United States from 1989 to 1993. Considered a reforming Governor of Texas in education, energy and justice. Took America into second Gulf War against Iraq claiming they had WMD, which later proved not to be the case. Launched the Global War on Terror in the wake of the terrorist attacks on the World Trade Center, New York, on 11th September 2001.

Guy Francis de Moncy Burgess: 16th April 1911–30th August 1963. A British diplomat, BBC broadcaster and Soviet agent. He was a member of the Cambridge Five spy ring that operated from the mid-1930s to the early years of the Cold War era. Recruited to Russian Intelligence 1934–35 and infiltrated British Intelligence, 1937. His defection in 1951 to the Soviet Union with his fellow spy Donald Maclean had major repercussions for the sharing of intelligence with allies. Burgess acted as a confidential secretary to Hector McNeil, the deputy to Ernest Bevin, the Foreign Secretary.

Admiral Wilhelm Franz Canaris: 1st January 1887–9th April 1945.
Fought in the German Navy in World War I, seeing action, evading capture and carrying out intelligence work. Initially attracted to National Socialism for opposing Versailles Treaty and opposition to Communism, he became disillusioned by the early years of World War II. Served as German admiral and chief of the Abwehr, the German military intelligence service, from 1935 to 1944 when he was removed by Hitler and his function replaced by the SS. He was involved in the opposition to Hitler and his intervention helped many Jews escape persecution. Met Allied Intelligence operatives in Spain and Paris to

discuss terms for peace if Hitler was deposed. Executed in Flossenbürg concentration camp.

Arthur Neville Chamberlain: 18th March 1869–9th November 1940. A businessman then Conservative politician with posts including Postmaster General, Minister for Health and Chancellor. Served as Prime Minister from May 1937 to May 1940. Supported appeasement and signed the Munich Agreement on 30th September 1938, pledging guarantee of protection for Poland whilst conceding the German Sudetenland region of Czechoslovakia to Germany. Following the German invasion of Poland, Chamberlain announced a declaration of war on 3rd September 1939. Resigned as Prime Minister on 10th May 1940. Lost confidence of many in his party and Labour refused to join government under him.

Olga Konstantinovna Chekhova (née Knipper): 14th April 1897– 9th March 1980. A Russian-German actress. Her film roles include the female lead in Alfred Hitchcock's *Mary* (1931). Married Mikhail Chekhov (Anton's nephew) in 1914. Moved to Berlin in 1920. In the 1930s, she rose to become one of the brightest stars of the Third Reich and was admired by Adolf Hitler and Joseph Goebbels. Continued as successful film actress after the war and was also a director and producer.

Randolph Frederick Edward Spencer Churchill: 28th May 1911–6th June 1968. A British journalist, writer, soldier and politician serving as a Conservative Member of Parliament for Preston from 1940 to 1945. He acted as both army officer and journalist in World War II, exhibiting some bravery. The only son of British Prime Minister Sir Winston Churchill and Clementine Churchill. His relationship with his parents was often tempestuous and volatile, which caused upset to Winston in later years. Had a reputation for social outbursts under the influence of alcohol. He was writing volumes about the life of his father when he died.

Sir Winston Leonard Spencer Churchill: 30th November 1874–24th January 1965. Distinguished army officer, statesman, politician, writer, historian and artist. Served as a soldier seeing action in India, the Sudan and in the second Boer War. Also worked as a war correspondent. First elected as an MP in 1900 and was an MP over a period of sixty-four years. Served on the Western Front in World War I before being recalled to government where he served in various ministerial posts including Home Secretary, President of the Board of Trade, First Lord of the Admiralty and Secretary of State for War. British Prime Minister from 1940 to 1945, and again from 1951 to 1955. Leader of the Conservative Party from 1940 to 1955. Served continuously (apart from two years, 1922–24) as an MP from 1900 to 1964. Led Britain throughout most of World War II and was accredited with possessing highly effective leadership skills whilst inspiring the nation. He passionately argued against 'appeasement' with Hitler in the 1930s, warning of the inevitable outcome of war. Recognised as one of the greatest Prime Ministers, although not without controversy, he was given a state funeral. He was seventh cousin one time removed to Queen Elizabeth II..

Sir John Rupert Colville: 28th January 1915–19th November 1987. A British civil servant who served as secretary to Winston Churchill during the war about which he kept diaries. He served in World War II as a pilot in the Royal Air Force Volunteer Reserve (RAFVR) from 1941–44. He was Private Secretary to Princess Elizabeth 1947–49 and was Joint Principal Private Secretary to Winston Churchill from 1951–55.

Flight Sergeant Stanislaw Jacek Czezowski: 22nd August 1919–20th August 1996. Born in Olkusz, Poland, and served in RAF during World War II, joining 303 Squadron 20th July 1942. Flew spitfires. Last posting with 315 Squadron. After the war, settled in the UK.

Sir Robert Anthony Eden: 12th June 1897–14th January 1977.
1st Earl of Avon. Served with distinction as an officer in World War I. Conservative MP elected for Warwick and Leamington 1923 aged twenty-six. Foreign Secretary three times and was a skilled diplomat. Served as Prime Minister for two years from 1955–57 and presided during the Suez Crisis, which led to his downfall resigning as Prime Minister on 10th January 1957. Bred cattle in his retirement and was Chancellor of Birmingham University.

His Royal Highness Edward VIII, Duke of Windsor: 23rd June 1894– 28th May 1972. King of the United Kingdom and the Dominions of the British Empire and Emperor of India from 20th January 1936 until his abdication in December of the same year. Christened: Edward Albert Christian George Andrew Patrick David. Known as David to close family and friends. Proposed to a twice-married American, Wallis Simpson, in 1936, causing a constitutional crisis resulting in his abdication. He then became Duke of Windsor, marrying Wallis Simpson in 1937. In 1937, he visited Adolf Hitler during a tour of Germany. Served as Governor of Bahamas in World War II, then lived in France until his death.

Charles Edward, Duke of Saxe-Coburg and Gotha, Leopold Charles Edward George Albert: 19th July 1884–6th March 1954. Grandson of Queen Victoria and Cousin of George V. Partly educated at Eton. Had British royal and other titles stripped after fighting for Germany in World War I. He served as a member of the Reichstag representing the Nazi Party from 1936–45 and as president of the German Red Cross from December 1933–45. Held various diplomatic roles, even visiting President Roosevelt in the White House in 1940. He spent the last years of his life in seclusion and died in poverty, the Russians having seized most of his property, and having had to pay large sums in fines for his part in Nazism.

General Dwight David Eisenhower: 14th October 1890–28th March 1969. American military officer and statesman, popularly referred to as 'Ike'. Thirty-fourth President of the United States from 1953 to 1961. During World War II, he became a five-star general in the Army and served as Supreme Commander of the Allied Expeditionary Force in Europe for Operation Overlord on D Day. He was responsible for planning and supervising the invasion of North Africa in Operation Torch in 1942–43 and helped plan the successful invasion of Normandy in 1944–45. In 1950, he became Supreme Commander of NATO, resigning in 1952 when he ran as a Republican for President. He was inaugurated as thirtyfourth US President in 1953, serving two terms, presiding over the escalation of the Cold War adopting nuclear arms control as opposed to disarmament, recognising the need for nuclear weapons.

Her Majesty Queen Elizabeth II: born 21st April 1926 and christened Elizabeth Alexandra Mary. She is Queen of the United Kingdom and fifteen other Commonwealth realms. The Queen is the longest-lived and longest-reigning British monarch, her reign commencing on 6th February 1952. Her coronation took place on 2nd June 1953, which was the first to be fully televised in a major national broadcast. Elizabeth is the longest-serving female head of state in world history. In 1947, she married Prince Philip, Duke of Edinburgh, who died in April 2021, aged ninetynine. The Queen served in the Auxiliary Territorial Service during World War II. The Queen is a keen horse rider and also takes great interest in horse racing, owning a number of horses. Elizabeth is the first monarch to address a joint meeting of the Unites States Congress. The Queen has a deep sense of public and religious duty, whilst attempting to make the monarchy more open, undertaking popular 'walkabouts' to meet people.

Her Majesty Queen Elizabeth, eventually the Queen Mother (Angela Marguerite Bowes-Lyon): 4th August 1900–30th March 2002. Married the then-Duke of York in 1923. Queen of the United Kingdom and the Dominions from 1936 to 1952 as the wife of King George VI. She became estranged from Edward VIII after his abdication and refused to countenance Wallis Simpson. During the Blitz, she toured areas affected with King George VI, which made her popular. After her husband died, she was known as Queen Elizabeth the Queen Mother. Her daughter is Queen Elizabeth II. Related to Winston Churchill as sixth cousin one time removed, she continued to make public appearances throughout her life until she died aged 101.

Sir Dudley Richard Forwood: June 6th 1912–January 2001. He was a soldier, diplomat and equerry. In 1934 he was appointed Honorary Attaché at the British Legation in Vienna, where he met the Duke of Windsor, then Prince of Wales, after which he was attached to the Prince's ADC Sir Walford Selby. After the abdication he was asked to become equerry to the Duke of Windsor (former King Edward VIII). Served in the Scots Guards during World War II but remained in close contact with the Duke and Duchess of Windsor.

Rosalinda Powell Fox: 1910–2006. Born in India, she married at sixteen but developed bovine TB and her husband left her. Lived in England briefly before being sent to Switzerland, where she was told she had limited time to live. Left for warmer climes and ended up in Spain, and was known for her beauty, becoming mistress of Colonel Juan Luis Beigbeder, Minister for the Exterior in the Government of Francisco Franco. Passed intelligence information to Britain in World War II and praised by Winston Churchill. Lived out her life in Spain until the age of ninety-six.

His Majesty George V: 3rd June 1865–20th January 1936. King of Great Britain from 6th May 1910–20th January 1936, the British Dominions and Emperor of India. Son of Edward VII, he was christened George Frederick Ernest Albert. His elder brother, Prince Albert Victor, died aged twenty-eight in 1892 of influenza. His hobbies included stamp collecting and game shooting.
During his reign, major political upheavals with new movements for change were emerging.

His Majesty George VI: 14th December 1895–6th February 1952. King of Great Britain from 11th December 1936–6th February 1952, the British Dominions and Emperor of India. Christened Albert Frederick Arthur George. Second son of George V. Great-grandson to Queen Victoria. Known as Bertie to family and close friends. King from 11th December 1936 until his death. Father of current Queen Elizabeth and brother to the Duke of Windsor, the former King Edward VIII. He favoured seeking a peace agreement with Germany, causing friction with Churchill. Refused to leave London during the war and boosted morale by touring areas devastated by bombing with Queen Elizabeth (later the Queen Mother).

Prince George, Duke of Kent: 20th December 1902–25th August 1942. Christened George Edward Alexander Edmund, was the fourth son of King George V and Queen Mary. He was the younger brother of Edward VIII and George VI. Served in the Royal Navy in the 1920s and became Duke of Kent in 1934. In the late 1930s he served as an RAF officer and was known to favour reaching a peace agreement with Germany. There is speculation that he was to meet German Deputy Leader Rudolf Hess when Hess flew to Britain in May 1941. He died in an air-crash travelling to Iceland in an RAF Sunderland flying boat. There were fifteen on board and only one survivor. The purpose of the flight has been a matter of conjecture with one passenger's name never released. This was the first death in over 450 years of a member of the royal family on active service.

Paul Joseph Goebbels: 29th October 1897–1st May 1945. German Nazi politician, Gauleiter of Berlin and Reich Minister of Propaganda in Nazi Germany from 1933 to 1945. Fanatical admirer of Adolf Hitler. Skilled public speaker and held extreme anti-Semitic views. Joined the Nazi Party in 1924. Known for clever use of media for propaganda purposes. On 30th April 1945, he was appointed Chancellor of the Reich under the terms of Hitler's will, but on 1st May 1945 Goebbels and his wife committed suicide after poisoning their six children with cyanide in the Führerbunker.

Carl Friedrich Goerdeler: 31st July 1884–2nd February 1945. A German politician, businessman and economist. Fought in World War I. After initial support for Hitler, he became an opponent and prominent amongst those opposing the Nazis. Was Mayor of Leipzig but resigned over Jewish statue dispute. Passed some information to British Intelligence and was part of 20th July plot against Hitler. He was opposed to the Holocaust. Goerdeler would have served as the Chancellor of the new government if plot against Hitler had succeeded.

Mikhail Sergeyevich Gorbachev: born 2nd March 1931. Russian politician and last leader of the Soviet Union before the end of Communist rule. General Secretary of the Communist Party of the Soviet Union from 1985 until 1991. Head of state from 1988 until 1991 and president of the Soviet Union from 1990 to 1991. An idealist, he transformed the Soviet Union with sweeping policies of reform, resulting in many Eastern bloc countries seeking freedom by holding democratic elections and ousting communist control. He decided not to intervene in an historic moment when the Berlin wall came down in 1989, whilst many former Soviet Republics declared independence both of which signified the end of the Cold War. This was aided by the tough stance against communism adopted by British Prime Minister Margaret Thatcher and US President Ronald Reagan.

Reichsmarschall Hermann Wilhelm Göring: 2nd January 1893–15th October 1946. Decorated air ace in World War I being awarded the Pour le Mérite (Blue Max). Served with legendary ace Manfred von Richthofen. Joined Nazi Party in early 1920s. Elected President of the Reichstag in 1932, a post he held until 1945. Became Commander in Chief of Luftwaffe (German Air Force). Given rank of Reichsmarschall, which gave him seniority over all officers in Germany's armed forces. Was seen as Hitler's successor at the height of his power. He died from taking poison the night before he was due to hang after being sentenced at the Nuremberg war trials.

Dino Grandi: 4th June 1895–21st May 1988. Ist Conte di Mordano. Italian Fascist politician and ambassador to Britain 1932–1939. In 1939 tried to broker a peace between Britain and Italy and was removed from his post by Mussolini. In 1943 after total disillusion with Mussolini, he was instrumental in moves which for the King reassuming power. Later helped organise the resistance to Germany. Later, he fled to Spain and, after the war, he did not return to live in Italy until the 1960s.

Lord Halifax, Edward Frederick Lindley Wood, Ist Earl of Halifax: 16th April 1881–23rd December 1959. British Conservative politician and diplomat. He held senior ministerial posts including Viceroy of India from 1925 to 1931 and Foreign Secretary between 1938 and 1940. He was one of the architects of appeasement working with Prime Minister Neville Chamberlain. After Germany occupied Czechoslovakia in 1939 he abandoned policy. Advocate of peace talks through Italy in 1940 and disagreed with Churchill. Sent by Churchill, as a result, to become British ambassador to Washington 1941–46.

Air Commodore Douglas Douglas-Hamilton, 14th Duke of Hamilton and 11th Duke of Brandon: 3rd February 1903–30th March 1973. Scottish aristocrat, politician, RAF officer and aviator being the first to fly over Everest in 1933.

Served in the RAF, becoming the youngest Squadron Leader of his day at twenty-eight and served in World War II, becoming responsible for air defence of Scotland. Unionist MP for East Renfrewshire from 1930–40. Rudolf Hess, the Deputy Führer of Germany, parachuted near his estate at Dungavel House on 10th May 1941, requesting to be taken to see him. Later served as a privy counsellor and held many senior positions in business.

Sir Ian Standish Monteith Hamilton: 16th January 1853–12th October 1947. Was a British Army officer with a distinguished career in the Victorian and Edwardian eras. He commanded the Mediterranean Expeditionary Force in the Gallipoli Campaign of the First World War. He was a founding member of the Anglo-German Association before and after Adolf Hitler's rise to power, initially being an admirer of the Führer. He was a senior official in the Royal British Legion.

Karl Ernst Haushofer: 27th August 1869–10th March 1946. Was a German general, professor, geographer and politician. He taught and influenced his student Rudolf Hess at Munich University in ideas known as Geopolitik which influenced and justified the development of Adolf Hitler's expansionist strategies. Although he advised Hitler, he was not an overt supporter of National Socialism and did not join the Nazi Party. Committed suicide by poison in March 1946?

Albrecht Haushofer: 7th January 1903–23th April 1945. Was a German geographer, diplomat, author and active member of the German resistance to Nazism. He was a friend of fellow student Rudolf Hess at university and worked for Deputy Führer Hess and the propaganda ministry in Berlin. He assisted Hess in acting as a peace intermediary with the British up to and after the outbreak of war. He visited Douglas Douglas Duke of Hamilton at Dungavel House before the war which was where Hess flew on his peace mission in 1941. He was executed by the SS outside Moabit Prison in April 1945 for his part in the plot to assassinate Hitler.

Deputy Führer and Obergruppenführer Rudolf Walter Richard Hess: 26th April 1894–17th August 1987. German politician, becoming Deputy Führer in 1933. Served as military officer and decorated in World War I. In December 1933 he became Minister without Portfolio in Hitler's cabinet. Favoured peace with Britain and on 10th May 1941 flew to Britain on a mission to seek a treaty. He was arrested and there is confusion about his role in subsequent talks, which were covered up and denied. Sent to Spandau Prison, Berlin, after the war, serving life imprisonment, and was reported to have committed suicide by hanging there in 1987 at the age of ninety-three.

Reichsführer-SS, Heinrich Luitpold Himmler: 7th October 1900– 23rd May 1945. Joined Nazi Party in 1923, and the new SS (paramilitary elite guard organisation) in 1925. Appointed Supreme Commander or Reichsführer-SS by Hitler in 1929. Built this up to become a huge military organisation of fanatical dedicated troops. The SS were attributed with many atrocities and war crimes. Himmler attempted late negotiations with Allies in 1945 when Germany was facing defeat. He was poisoned or took cyanide whilst captured by the British on 23rd May 1945.

Adolf Hitler (born Schicklgruber): 20th April 1889–30th April 1945? Politician, soldier, leader of the German NSDAP (Nazi Party) and Führer of Germany. Elected Chancellor 1933, assuming dictatorial powers and becoming Führer in 1934. Born in Austria, he was decorated with the Iron Cross in World War I. In 1921 became leader of the Nazi Party. Attempted to seize power in 1923 in Munich *putsch*. Jailed and wrote *Mein Kampf* in 1925 whilst in prison. Adopted policy of Lebensraum (expansion in the East). Directed military aggression across Europe and Africa, causing World War II. His regime was responsible for genocide, including the extermination of Jews. Official version of death is that he committed suicide in his bunker in Berlin with his wife Eva (formerly Braun) on 30th April 1945 as the Russian forces were closing in. Their bodies were never found there and even the Soviet leader, Joseph Stalin, believed they had escaped.

Sir Samuel John Gurney Hoare, 1st Viscount Templewood: 24th February 1880–7th May 1959. A senior British Conservative politician who served in various Cabinet posts in the governments of the 1920s and 1930s. Posts included Secretary of State for Air, Secretary of State for India, Foreign Secretary, First Lord of the Admiralty and Home Secretary from 1937 to 1939. A leading appeaser, his removal from office was a condition of Labour joining the coalition government of Winston Churchill in May 1940. He was British ambassador to Spain from 1940 to 1944.

Princess Stephanie Julianne von Hohenlohe: 16th September 1891– 13th June 1972. Christened Stephany Julienne Richter. An Austrian princess by her marriage, she was a Hungarian national. She relocated to London after her divorce and was suspected of being a German spy in the 1930s. She socialised with Hitler, who called her his 'dear Princess' and awarded her the Gold Medal of the Nazi Party. She also mixed with leading members of British society. Interned in the USA during World War II, after which she returned to Germany developing many influential relationships including connections with Presidents John F Kennedy and Lyndon Johnson.

Alexander Boris de Pfeffel Johnson: born 19th June 1964. Attended Eton College and read Classics at Oxford. Elected President of Oxford Union in 1986. Political correspondent for the Daily Telegraph from 1989 and Editor of The Spectator until 2005. Elected MP for Henley serving from 2001 – 2008 and Mayor of London from 2008 - 2016. Re-elected as MP for Uxbridge and South Ruislip in 2015, serving as Secretary of State for Foreign and Commonwealth Affairs becoming Prime Minister and Leader of the Conservative Party in 2019. Known as a Euro Sceptic he was credited with achieving a vote in a divided Parliament to leave the European Union in 2020 after calling a snap election in 2019. He led the country through the pandemic drawing diverse criticism for both being over draconian and failing to act decisively enough. He has a reputation with some for being colourful and is considered by others to be entertaining, Survived a no confidence vote in 2022 within the Conservative Party.

Joseph Patrick Kennedy Sr: 6th September 1888–18th November 1969. A prominent American businessman, investor and politician. He is the patriarch of the Irish-American Kennedy family and is the father of President John Fitzgerald Kennedy (JFK) and Robert Kennedy. He served as American ambassador to Britain from March 1938. Resigned on 22nd October 1940 after declaring, during Battle of Britain, that democracy in Britain was finished. Had some reportedly anti-Semitic views.

Squadron Leader Tadeusz Kotz: 9th August 1913–3rd June 2008. A decorated Polish RAF pilot and fighter ace of World War II. Fought with the Polish air force during the German invasion of 1939. He escaped to Britain, serving with 317, 308 and 303 Squadrons, flying the Spitfire. In 1943 Kotz was shot down over occupied France but evaded capture and returned to England. He moved to Africa after the war and then to Canada.

Jared Corey Kushner – born 10th January 1981) – A US business man running various investment organisations. Also active as a real estate developer and publisher. He was a senior White House advisor to his father-in-law, Donald Trump, the 45th President of the United States. He is married to Donald Trump's daughter Ivanka Trump. He assisted President Trump's media campaign for election. He formulated contraversial pro Israeli policies in the Middle East peace process. Advised the President on the response to the covid-19 pandemic claiming the threat was exaggerated.

Yola Letellier: 1908–? Born Yvonne Henriquet. Wife of a newspaper owner, she was a French socialite in the 1920s and 1930s meeting Lord Louis Mountbatten at a dance in 1932. Became Mountbatten's mistress and was also a family friend including his wife, Edwina. She remained close to Lord Louis Mountbatten until his death in 1979.

Theresa Mary, Lady May (née Brasier): born 1st October 1956. A British politician who served as Prime Minister and Leader of the Conservative Party from 2016 to 2019. Elected MP for Maidenhead in Berkshire in 1997, she was Home Secretary from 2010 to 2016. Elected Conservative Party leader and became the UK's second female prime minister after Margaret Thatcher. May increased NHS spending in a long-term plan and committed the UK to a climate change target. She began the process of withdrawing the UK from the European Union after the 2016 referendum. Presided over Brexit negotiations but after versions of draft withdrawal agreement were rejected by Parliament three times, she resigned in December 2019, remaining in the House of Commons as a backbencher.

Mona Maund: 1897–1966. Worked for SIS in the 1930s, mainly identifying Soviet spies through activities within Trade Unionism, particularly the AWCS – Association of Women Chartered Secretaries. She was recruited by arch spymaster Maxwell Knight (Head of MI5 section for infiltration into subversive groups) and was able to penetrate the Communist Party. She eventually worked for Communist Party HQ, where she helped to identify a Soviet spy ring and famously correctly identified Melita Norwood as a strong suspect. Retired in 1940 to Worcester to look after her ailing father.

Major General Sir Stewart Graham Menzies: 30th January 1890–29th May 1968. Educated at Eton, after which he joined Grenadier Guards. Decorated Army Officer in World War I, during which he received DSO from George V. Fought in first and second battle of Ypres. Wounded in 1914 and again in 1915, when he was gassed. Joined British Intelligence in 1917 and then MI6 or SIS (Secret Intelligence Service) after World War I. Served on British delegation to Versailles peace conference. Became Deputy Director of MI6 in 1929 and Director from 1939 to 1952, achieving rank of major general. His work, particularly in organising information obtained from code-breaking, was considered a massive contribution to victory in World War II, during which he had over 1,500 meetings with Churchill. He participated in active contact with anti-Nazi elements in Germany during the war.

Angela Dorothea Merkel (née Kasner): born 17th July 1954. A German politician who has been Chancellor of Germany since 2005. She lived in former Communist East Germany until unification in 1990. She served as Leader of the Opposition from 2002 to 2005 and as Leader of the Christian Democratic Union (CDU) from 2000 to 2018. Merkel is the first female chancellor of Germany and, in 2018, became the first Chancellor to be elected for a fourth term. She has been described as the most powerful person in the European Union, whilst she is considered one of the most influential leaders in the world.

Diana Mitford (Lady Mosley): 17th June 1910–11th August 2003. An aristocrat, writer and society socialite, she married Bryan Guinness in 1929. She became the mistress of Sir Oswald Mosley, the leader of the British Union of Fascists, whom she married in 1936 at the house of Joseph Goebbels attended by Adolf Hitler. Interned during the war, after which she lived in Ireland, then France. She met Hitler many times, who called her 'my angel'. Despite attracting much criticism, she also mixed with Winston Churchill and other leading society figures. Became a friend of the Duke and Duchess of Windsor after the war, whom she claimed shared her views of Hitler.

Unity Valkyrie Freeman-Mitford: 8th August 1914–28th May 1948. An aristocrat and socialite. She travelled to Germany in 1933 with her sister Diana and became infatuated with Adolf Hitler and then a prominent supporter of Nazism. She became part of Hitler's inner circle and was rumoured be in an intimate relationship with him. After the declaration of World War II, Mitford attempted suicide by shooting herself in the head. She survived but never recovered from the extensive brain damage. Hitler paid her medical bills in Switzerland and safe passage was arranged for her return to Britain in January 1940.

Sir Oswald Ernald Mosley, 6th Baronet: 16th November 1896–3rd December 1980. Fought in France in World War I then became a Conservative Member of Parliament for Harrow at age twenty-two before turning independent then joining Labour. Mosley's Knighthood title was inherited. Formed and led the British Union of Fascists (BUF), known as the Blackshirts, in 1932. Mosley married his mistress Diana Guinness, née Mitford, secretly in October 1936 in the home of Germany's Minister of Propaganda Joseph Goebbels. Adolf Hitler was guest of honour. Disgraced by his association with Fascism, he spent most his later life in Paris.

Field Marshal Bernard Law Montgomery, 1st Viscount Montgomery of Alamein: 17th November 1887–24th March 1976. Senior British Army officer who served in World War I, the Irish War of Independence and World War II. In command of British 8th Army in first major victory of World War II at El Alamein in North Africa. He was in command of all Allied ground forces during the Battle of Normandy (Operation Overlord), from D Day until 1st September 1944, then in command of 21st Army Group. After the war, he served as Chief of Imperial General Staff and then with NATO until his retirement in 1958.

Admiral of the Fleet, Lord Louis Francis Albert Victor Nicholas Mountbatten: 25th June 1900–27th August 1979. Born Prince Louis of Battenberg, he was known by friends and close family as 'Dickie'. He was a British naval officer and statesman. Related to royalty as second cousin once removed to Queen Elizabeth II and uncle to her husband, the Duke of Edinburgh. In World War II became Chief of Combined Operations, then Supreme Allied Commander South East Asia. He was the last Viceroy of India and the first governor-general of independent India. Assassinated by the IRA with a bomb planted on his boat when out with family in Mullaghmore, in the Republic of Ireland.

Benjamin Netanyahu: born 21st October 1949. Longest-serving Israeli Prime Minister. Raised in Jerusalem and attended high school in Philadelphia, USA. Saw active service in the military in the 1967 six-day war and later served in special forces. Graduated in science, he entered politics in the 1980s after serving a period as permanent representative to the UN. In 1993, he was elected Chairman of Likud and became youngest Prime Minister of Israel in 1996 but was defeated in 1999. Served as Minister of Foreign Affairs and Finance under Ariel Sharon and is credited with successful economic reforms. In 2009, he became Prime Minister a second time and remained so until 13th June 2021.

Barack Hussein Obama II: born 4th August 1961. Civil rights attorney, academic and served as the forty-fourth president of the US from 2009 to 2017. A Democrat, Obama was the first African-American President. Introduced Affordable Care Act and legislation to stimulate the economy. He increased US troop levels in Afghanistan, reduced nuclear weapons and ended military involvement in the Iraq War. He ordered military intervention in Libya contributing to the overthrow of Muammar Gaddafi. He ordered the military operation that resulted in the killing of Osama bin Laden. He increased LGBT rights, attempted gun control legislation and authorised action against so-called Islamic State. Other foreign policy initiatives include tackling global warming, normalised relations with Cuba and the brokering of a nuclear treaty with Iran.

George Ward Price: 1886–22nd August 1961 was a journalist who worked as a foreign correspondent for the *Daily Mail* newspaper. He interviewed both Mussolini and Hitler in the 1930s. War correspondent from 1942. Initially refused to condemn or blame Nazism for concentration camps. Later covered Korean war.

Vladimir Vladimirovich Putin: born 7th October 1952. Russian politician, former KGB intelligence officer and FSB Director. President of Russia, 1999 to 2008, then Prime Minister 1999 to 2000 and 2008 to 2012, before reassuming powers as President. Sixteen years serving as KGB officer, he then worked for President Boris Yeltsin before being appointed Prime Minister. When Yeltsin resigned became Acting President, then President. Re-elected in 2012 and 2018. Promotes conservative policies based on traditional Russian Soviet-style values with little tolerance of dissent. Reduction in democratic values has taken place under his leadership which has strengthened his hold on power which some describe as dictatorial.

Ronald Wilson Reagan: 6th February 1911–5th June 2004. An American actor, union leader and politician who served as the fortieth president of the United States, serving two terms from 1981 to 1989 and became influential voice of conservatism. Initially worked as radio commentator, then an actor starring in some Hollywood movies. He became president of the Screen Actors Guild, where he rooted out communist influence. As governor of California he built a reputation for firm leadership and sound economics. Reagan was the oldest person, at the time, to become President at sixty-nine. Reagan implemented sweeping economic reforms dubbed 'Reaganomics', advocating tax rate reduction to spur economic growth and deregulation. Helped end the Cold War through meetings with Soviet General Secretary Mikhail Gorbachev, supported by the British Prime Minister Margaret Thatcher, with whom Reagan had a strong relationship. In later life suffered from Alzheimer's disease. His approval ratings made him one of the most popular US presidents.

Hanna Reitsch: 29th March 1912–24th August 1979. A German aviator and test pilot. She set many world glider flying records before World War II. Tested many of Germany's new aircraft during World War II and received numerous honours. A committed National Socialist, she was an admirer of Hitler and was awarded Iron Cross with diamonds by him. Flew last plane out of Berlin before the German defeat in April 1945. In the 1950s she set up a gliding centre in India, even flying the Indian Prime Minister. She carried on setting world records for gliding and established the first black African gliding school in Ghana. In 1961, she was invited to meet US President JF Kennedy at the White House. Throughout the 1970s she set glider endurance records and won international helicopter flying competitions.

Joachim von Ribbentrop: 30th April 1893–16th October 1946. A German politician who served as Minister of Foreign Affairs of Nazi Germany from 1938 to 1945 and was a dedicated Nazi. Decorated soldier serving on Eastern and Western Fronts in World War I, earning a commission as an officer. As Foreign Minister, he negotiated a treaty with Fascist Italy and surprised the Allies by negotiating a non-aggression pact with Russia in August 1939 known as the Molotov-Ribbentrop Pact. He was sentenced to death by the Allies at the International Military Tribunal Nuremberg Trials and hanged.

Generalfeldmarschall Irwin Rommel: 15th November 1891–14th October 1944. Respected German general and military theorist. A decorated soldier and officer in World War I, he saw considerable action, gaining a reputation as an effective strategist. Became known as the Desert Fox after commanding the Afrika Korps in North Africa. He organised German defences in France and was given command of Army Group B. He was highly popular with troops. A passive opponent of Hitler but would not participate in the assassination plot with conspirators. On 14th October 1944, after being implicated by others with no proof in the 20th July bomb plot, he took poison in a forced 'suicide' near his home in Herrlingen, Southern Germany, when he was offered choice by Nazis of state funeral, with his family looked after if he committed suicide, or face trial in Berlin with consequences for family.

Franklin Delano Roosevelt: 30th January 1882–12th April 1945. Thirty-second President of the United States, popularly referred to as FDR. President Theodore Roosevelt was his fifth cousin, whom he greatly admired. Became a senator in 1910, then served as Assistant Secretary to the Navy in World War I. He became Governor of New York in 1928 and was elected President in 1932. Instigated social security legislation to protect the poor, the sick, the elderly and unemployed. He was the only president to be elected to serve four presidential terms, although he died during the fourth. President during World War II and at the time of America's decision to join the war after the Japanese attack on Pearl Harbor in December 1941. Formed close working relationship with Winston Churchill.

Harold Sidney Harmsworth, 1st Viscount Rothermere: 26th April 1868–26th November 1940 Leading British newspaper proprietor owning the *Daily Mail* and the *Daily Mirror*. An admirer of National Socialism, he visited Hitler on a number of occasions, promoting peace between Germany and Britain. He supported the British Union of Fascists and described Hitler's achievements as 'great and superhuman'.

Brigadeführer Walter Friedrich Schellenberg: 16th January 1910–31st March 1952. An SS officer who worked closely with Himmler, becoming head of foreign intelligence for Nazi Germany following the abolition of the Abwehr in 1944. Organised genocide in Nazi-held territories. He commanded a group tasked with the plan to kidnap the Duke of Windsor in Spain in 1940. Testified against the SS at the Nuremberg war trials.

Baldur Benedikt von Schirach: 9th May 1907–8th August 1974. A Nazi German politician, becoming head of the Hitler Youth from 1931 to 1940. He later served as Governor of Vienna. He was convicted of crimes against humanity in the Nuremberg trials and sentenced to twenty years in prison. His mother was American and Schirach was a descendant of Thomas Heyward Jr, a signatory of the United States Declaration of Independence. He became disillusioned with Hitler in 1943. He served twenty years in Spandau Prison, Berlin, before being released in 1966.

Dr Paul-Otto Schmidt: 23rd June 1899–21st April 1970. A soldier in World War I, he studied languages and was an interpreter in the German foreign ministry from 1923 to 1945. He joined the Nazi Party in 1943 and became a minister working for von Ribbentrop in 1944. Appointed chief interpreter in 1935 to Adolf Hitler, he served as the translator for Neville Chamberlain's negotiations with Hitler during the Munich Agreement, and during the surrender of France in 1940. In later life taught languages in Munich.

Wallis Simpson (Duchess of Windsor), born Bessie Wallis Warfield: 19th June 1896–24th April 1986. An American socialite who became the wife of the Duke of Windsor, the former British king Edward VIII. Wallis grew up in Baltimore, Maryland. In 1931, during her second marriage to Ernest Simpson she met Edward, then-Prince of Wales. Their intention to marry and her status as a divorcée who was already married caused a constitutional crisis that led to King Edward's abdication in 1936. They married in 1937 and in that year she met Hitler with Edward, then the Duke of Windsor. In later life, the couple lived in France, becoming friends with Diana Mosley (Mitford) but often travelled on ocean liners to the US. After the death of the Duke, she lived in relative seclusion.

Obersturmbannführer Otto Skorzeny: 12th June 1908–5th July 1975. An Austrian-born German SS officer in the Waffen-SS during World War II. He was involved in several daring operations, including the Gran Sasso raid which rescued Benito Mussolini from captivity in September 1943. Skorzeny was imprisoned after the war but escaped in 1948 wearing American army uniform.

Worked for various countries in military intelligence and training until the end of his life. Was considered by some as having possible involvement in assassination of JFK in November 1963.

Alluded to but not by name – **Richard Sorge**: 4th October 1895–7th November 1944. A German journalist and Soviet spy active before and during World War II working as an undercover agent whilst a journalist in both Nazi Germany and Japan. In September 1941 he obtained information that Japan would not attack Russia in the short term, enabling Stalin to transfer huge military resources to face the German attack on Moscow probably saving Russia from defeat. He was tried and hanged by the Japanese in 1944.

Reich Minister Berthold Konrad Hermann Albert Speer: 19th March 1905–1st September 1981. Architect and Nazi politician. Joined Nazi Party in 1931. Became a friend of Adolf Hitler and designed many Nazi buildings and structures. Appointed German Minister of Armaments and War Production in 1942. Imprisoned after the war at Spandau, Berlin, he was released in 1966 and wrote his memoirs, which were highly subjective, attracting much criticism. Died in a London hotel, reportedly of a stroke, whilst visiting England to give press interviews.

Ramón Serrano Suñer: 12th September 1901–1st September 2003. Spanish politician, becoming Interior Minister and Foreign Affairs Minister. Serrano Suñer was an ardent supporter of totalitarianism, adopting a pro-Third Reich stance during World War II, when he supported the sending of the Blue Division to fight along with the Wehrmacht on the Russian front. He was the brother-in-law of General Franco's wife, Carmen Polo. He founded the Spanish blind people's organisation ONCE, the EFE press agency and the Intercontinental radio network in 1950. In later life, he attempted unsuccessfully to persuade Franco to form a transitional government.

Margaret Hilda Thatcher, Baroness Thatcher (née Roberts): 13th October 1925–8th April 2013. British politician and stateswoman who served as Prime Minister of the United Kingdom from 1979 to 1990 and Leader of the Conservative Party from 1975 to 1990. Studied chemistry at Oxford, then became a barrister. Elected MP for Finchley in 1959. Appointed Secretary of State for Education in 1970. She defeated Edward Heath in leadership of Conservatives contest in 1975. She was the longest-serving British prime minister of the twentieth century and the first woman to hold that office. She won an unprecedented three election victories. A Soviet journalist dubbed her the 'Iron Lady', a nickname she enjoyed representative of her uncompromising leadership style. Helped negotiate the end of the Cold War in the 1980s with US President Ronald Reagan and Russian Leader Mikhail Gorbachev. Reformed industrial relations by democratising trade union practices and controversially presided over the dismantling of the British coal industry. In 1990, after facing a leadership challenge, she lost senior Tory support and resigned. In 1992, she was given a life peerage, entering the House of Lords.

Donald John Trump: Born 14th June 1946. Entrepreneur mainly in real estate and media personality serving as the 45th president of the United States from 2017 to 2021. He is a Republican and is viewed as a nationalist and populist figure. He is non-conformist in style and presentation and is critical of establishment politics. He is also highly critical of the media's reporting of politics calling it "fake news" He pursued an America First policy in foreign affairs and withdrew from the Iran nuclear deal and the Paris Climate Change agreement. He also imposed protectionist import tariffs which caused a trade war with China. Domestically, he cut taxes for individuals and business to stimulate the economy but also cut elements of health care established by President Obama. Claimed his electoral defeat in 2020 was fraudulent and, following a riot in the Capitol which he was accused of orchestrating, his social media accounts were closed. Despite controversy surrounding his Presidency, he retained popularity although some label him divisive.

Alexander Wilbourne Weddell: 6th April 1876–1st January 1948. An American diplomat who served as United States ambassador to Argentina from 1933 to 1939 and to Spain from 1939 to 1942. He knew the Duke and Duchess of Windsor and socialised with them.

Fritz Wiedemann: 16th August 1891–17th January 1970. German soldier and Nazi Party activist. Hauptmann Wiedemann was Corporal Hitler's superior in World War I, nominating him for the Iron Cross First Class given in 1918. Joined Nazi Party in 1934 and appointed Hitler's adjutant. Had an affair with Princess Stephanie von Hohenlohe and fell out of favour with Hitler. Sent on various diplomatic missions, including Consul General in the US, where he had a playboy lifestyle, continuing to support Nazism publicly but in private became opponent. Offered to denounce Hitler publicly in 1940 but Roosevelt chose not to. After the war, he was acquitted of any crimes and spent the rest of his life in farming.

Simon Wiesenthal: 31st December 1908–20th September 2005 was a writer and Nazi hunter who was a Holocaust survivor. He studied architecture and was living in Lwów (then in Poland, now Ukraine) at the outbreak of World War II. He was incarcerated in a number of German concentration camps until his release on 5th May 1945. After the war, he set up an organisation dedicated to tracing Nazi war criminals, bringing many to justice. He assisted in tracing Adolf Eichmann, who was later tried and hanged in Israel. His work also assisted in obtaining evidence to convict Hans Stangl, the Commandant of Sobibor and Treblinka death camps. He also helped survivors and refugees of the Holocaust in tracing lost relatives.

Sir Arnold Talbot Wilson: 18th July 1884–31st May 1940. A British soldier and colonial administrator seeing service in India, Iran and across the Middle East, especially in Iraq. He favoured direct British rule of Arab states. Elected Conservative MP for Hitchin in 1933, Wilson had some sympathy with totalitarianism and Spanish Nationalism. He was a writer and also served on a number of Parliamentary committees. He was the third Member of Parliament to die in action in World War II, being killed in action while serving as an aircrew member over Dunkirk in 1940 at the age of fifty-five.

About the Author

Christopher Kerr has enjoyed a varied career as a civil servant, marketing executive, and entrepreneur. He now concentrates on writing, which has become a passion, based upon a keen interest in history, politics, and current affairs.

Christopher's genre is historical/contemporary fiction, set against actual events and real people, to give added authenticity, and perspective to human drama.

His debut novel, 'the Covenant', was published in 2021, followed by 'The Barbarossa Secret' in 2022 (2nd edition 2024), 'Fission' in 2023, and 'Bullion' in 2024.

Christopher lives in a quiet village in North Wales where he is currently planning his next novel, 'Flight of the Eagle', which explores the hidden truth behind the fall of the Third Reich, and how secret organisations were formed in the post-war era affecting present-day global governance.

Thanks

I would like to thank those who have read, listened, commented, and supported me in the writing of this book. That support has been particularly valuable as I have uncovered extraordinary historical information, much of which has been either hidden or suppressed, and explored how to weave this into the lives of the characters. As I progressed on the journey from the 1930's to the present day, involving many real-life people, I recalled much from my own memories and the experiences of the war years recounted to me by teachers, and family which fascinated me. I have tried to capture the spirit of the era in the style of speaking and the mannerisms of the main characters.

I am enormously grateful to those who have been there during the creation of this work for both your input and encouragement – You know who you are.

Printed in Great Britain
by Amazon